Gold Digger

RendezVous Crime

Gold Digger

A Klondike Mystery

Vicki Delany

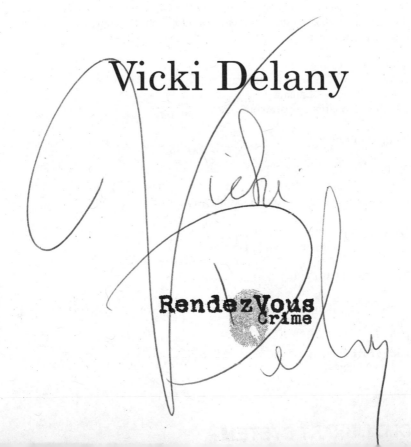

RendezVous Crime

Cover design: Vasiliki Lenis

Le Conseil des Arts du Canada depuis 1957 | The Canada Council for the Arts since 1957

Canada

We acknowledge the support of the Canada Council for the Arts for our publishing program.

We acknowledge the financial support of the Government of Canada through the Book Publishing Industry Development Program for our publishing activities.

RendezVous Crime
an imprint of Napoleon & Company
Toronto, Ontario, Canada
www.napoleonandcompany.com

Printed in Canada

13 12 11 10 09 5 4 3 2 1

Library and Archives Canada Cataloguing in Publication

Delany, Vicki, date-
Gold digger / Vicki Delany.

ISBN 978-1-894917-80-3

1. Klondike River Valley (Yukon)–Gold discoveries–Fiction.
I. Title.
PS8557.E4239 G64 2009 C813'.6
C2009-900680-4

For my children, Caroline, Julia, Alex

Chapter One

"Bloody hell," Angus said.

For the first time in his life, I didn't reprimand my son for swearing.

He had been in his room, sitting up in bed and concentrating on his school book, when I'd knocked and entered. I tried not to notice the penny-dreadful concealed in the folds of the geography tome.

"I have to go to the Savoy," I said as he stuffed the book under his pillow. "I might have made a mistake in the ledger, and I want to check."

"Can't it wait until tomorrow?"

"It can. But I can't. Do you want to come with me?"

"Sure."

In this town, I didn't need a protector to walk the streets after dark (or at least what passed for dark), but I wanted my son's company. He'd been distant of late. Growing up, probably. It had to happen, someday, but I intended to hold the forces of nature back as long as humanly possible.

Angus took my arm as we walked. It was a Sunday in June of 1898, and the town of Dawson, Yukon Territory, was as orderly as an orphanage expecting an imminent visit from Lady Bountiful. The streets were quiet; most people were at home resting after their evening meal. If they were lucky enough to have a home. And a meal.

I opened the front door of my business, and we walked in. The floorboards creaked beneath our feet. The Savoy saloon and dance hall, my pride and joy, the self-proclaimed "Finest establishment West of London, England", was as silent as the grave. It looked rather sad, empty and abandoned. In a moment of excessive fantasy, I imagined the boards of the stage wondering where the dancers with their stomping feet had gone, the rows of whisky bottles complaining to each other that no one was enjoying them, and the roulette wheel twitching under the forced inaction.

I called to the watchman. "Hello. It's only me! Mrs. MacGillivray."

The front windows were small and always dirty, despite Mrs. Saunderson's attempts to keep them clean. Outside it was daylight, but in the saloon the shadows fell long and deep.

"Light the lamp," I said to Angus. "That watchman had better be around here somewhere. Hello?"

An oil lamp flared into life at the same time as the watchman stumbled out of the room off the bar that served as a kitchen and broom closet. He fastened his belt with one hand, wiped sleep out of his eyes with the other, and tried to stifle a yawn. I had recently taken on the man only because he was such a tough looking fellow, complete with broken nose and bulging muscles and tattoos running up his arms. The rest of the week he hired himself out for manual labour.

"Seems to me as if this would be a nice job you have here," I said now. "No customers to please, no heavy lifting. Earn an extra day's pay over a Sunday."

"Yes, m'm," he mumbled, finding the notch in his belt at last.

"My partner, Mr. Walker, or I will be dropping by every Sunday. I expect you to be checking us out before the door is fully opened."

"Yes, m'm."

"Good. I'll be upstairs for a few moments."

"M'm?"

"Yes?"

"Thank you." He shuffled off to the back rooms.

Angus watched him go. "Why didn't you fire him, Mother? You know he was asleep."

"He won't be sleeping on the job again. I've put the fear of God, or at least of myself, which is probably just as good, into him. I'll mention it to Ray tomorrow. Between us we'll drop by a few times over the next couple of Sundays."

Angus lifted the lamp. Shadows danced off his cheekbones. I started for the stairs.

A door crashed open with so much force it almost came off its hinges. A chair fell over, and the loud snap of the breaking of a wooden leg echoed through the room.

I whirled around to see the watchman standing in the doorway to the gambling rooms, bent half-over, holding his stomach and gasping for breath. As Angus and I stared at him, he vomited.

"Bloody hell," Angus said.

"Don't swear, Angus."

The man raised his head and wiped his hand across his mouth. His eyes were wide and frightened. Avoiding the lumpy brown and yellow puddle, swallowing my gag instinct, I grabbed him by the shoulders and tried to straighten him up so he could look at me. "What's the matter with you?"

He pointed behind him and, with a low moan, vomited again. Fortunately, there wasn't much remaining in his stomach, and I was able to dance out of the way.

I ran through the door, aware of Angus following me. Nothing in the gaming room. The roulette wheel stood still, the poker table deserted.

The dance hall was a big room with no windows. The corners were full of shadows cast by the dim remnants of light coming in from the street through the saloon, then the gambling room and into the dance hall.

Angus lifted his lamp higher. I sucked in my breath.

"Bloody hell," Angus said, and I did not reprimand him.

A dark shape lay across the stage. It had form and substance and weight.

We took a step forward. It didn't move.

Angus reached out one arm to stop me. "No, Mother. Don't go any closer."

"This is my property, dear, I have to."

The man lay on his back, leaning slightly to the right side. He was neat and properly dressed with short red and grey hair. A wide streak of dried blood, resembling lip rouge applied by a nearly-blind dowager countess momentarily abandoned by her lady's maid, dripped from the corner of his mouth, across the side of his face, coming to rest in a dark pool on the wooden boards of the stage.

Why does he have a red silk ribbon wrapped around his throat? I thought.

My brain soon cast off the uncomprehending fog thrown up by my protective unconscious. And my gaze travelled down the body, avoiding the empty, staring eyes and the viscous gash across the neck. The front of his suit, the neat waistcoat, the place where the pocket watch used to be, was dark with blood. But the blood was no longer running, and there wasn't a great deal of it, much less than had dripped across his throat and splattered into the boards of the stage.

"Mother. Mother. Look at me, Mother."

I looked. My son's beautiful face stared into mine. He had lowered the lamp, and more dark than light filled the space between us. "Are you all right, Mother?"

"Go for the Mounties. I'll wait in the saloon."

We clutched hands and backed out of the dance hall together, not wanting to turn our backs on the thing lying on the stage.

"Someone murdered Mr. Ireland," Angus said. "That can't have been an accident."

I'd also recognized the face: Jack Ireland, who'd caused me nothing but trouble since the moment he'd arrived in town. The Mounties would have their job cut out for them: once they'd eliminated the handful of people who didn't particularly want Ireland dead, they'd be left with the majority of the population of the Territory.

Chapter Two

The day I first made the acquaintance of the odious Mr. Ireland had started off rather well. I'd been in my office doing the books, my least favourite task, when Ray Walker, bartender, chief bouncer, my business partner, had stuck his head through the door. "Morning, Fiona. Good night?"

I put down my pen. "Of course." I turned the ledger so Ray could read the bottom line.

He whistled softly. "It's Irene, ye ken. She brings the customers in and keeps them here."

"Worth her weight in gold." I tucked the big book into the desk drawer and lifted a hefty sack of gold dust off the floor to illustrate my point. Irene Davidson, Lady Irenee, she called herself—pronouncing the name in the French way with an extra "e" on the end—was, this month at least, the most popular dance hall girl in town. Since she'd started working for us a few weeks ago, our nightly take had gone up considerably.

I didn't care for the way Ray caressed her name, rolling over the "r" in his rough Glasgow burr, the look on his face as he watched her sashay across the room, or how he talked about her at every opportunity that presented itself. It's never a good idea for the boss to get involved with the hired help.

"What brings you here so early?"

"Couldna sleep any longer. Decided I should be doing something more worthwhile than staring at the ceiling. I've got a new lad starting on the faro table today. Needs someone to keep an eye on him."

I put my pen down and rubbed at my fingers, stained blue with ink. "I'm going home after I drop this lot off at the bank."

Ray held the door open for me. He was a particularly unattractive man with a nose that had been broken more often than probably even he could remember and skin ravaged by youthful acne. What little remained of his brown hair fell to his collar in thin, greasy strands. Short and scrawny to the point of emaciation, over the long, harsh winter Ray had looked like everyone else in town. But while the rest of us filled out as soon as supplies began to make it through, Ray didn't gain an ounce. His brown eyes shone with a warm intelligence, and I both liked and trusted him. Maybe not with my life or the life of my son, but enough to accept his much needed help in running the Savoy. I'd never operated a business before, with hired help and premises and stock and all those complications. My work had always been more…personal.

I put on my hat, a plain but charming straw affair with a broad plum ribbon around the band, and left the office, lugging a bag of gold, highly pleased with the weight of it. Gold, dust as well as nuggets, was as much of a currency as money. And often more readily available. Everyone from the dance halls to the banks to the laundries and the Paradise Alley cribs dealt in gold dust.

As I descended the stairs, I could see men behind the bar, serving hard-toiling miners and general layabouts who'd spilled through the door the minute we'd opened for business. Ten in the morning, and clearly some of the customers had merely stumbled the few feet from a neighbouring bar. The door at the back of the saloon leading to the gaming rooms was open, and the roulette wheel clattered cheerfully.

I'd named it The Savoy after the luxury hotel that opened in London during the most productive years I'd spent in that city. I had enjoyed more than a few teas and suppers in that wonderful place with the wealthy and influential men who, not always willingly, had provided my livelihood.

"Mrs. MacGillivray!" One of the drunken sourdoughs caught sight of me and lurched across the room. The scent of rotting teeth and bad liquor (most assuredly not mine) washed over me. "Come 'ave a drink."

"Thank you, sir, but I have errands I must run." I gave him a smile into which I tried to insert a touch of regret.

Once outside, I stood on the step for a moment. The wind had picked up, and the sea of banners strung across Front Street, advertising doctors and dentists, dance halls and ladies' clothing, men's hats and laundry services, flapped and fluttered, making as much noise as ocean waves hitting a rocky shore in a storm. The Union Jack and the American flag with its thirty-eight stars competed for prominence, the latter a sign that the ownership of the Yukon Territory was still a matter of dispute. Occasionally a banner or flag tore loose and blew away, to lie forgotten in the mountains or sink into the river, there to decay and merge into the barren landscape. To the north, Moosehide hill loomed over town, the remains of an ancient rockslide that had long ago taken an enormous chunk out of the side of the mountain.

Summer in the Yukon is delightful. The ground might be a morass of mud and the countryside reminiscent of what a mountainside would look like after a volcanic eruption, but after breathing the coal smoke of London and Toronto, I appreciated the fresh, clean air and the view that stretched for miles. Although the amount of sawdust thrown into the air, as the forest was chopped down and turned into lumber occasionally hindered one's breathing, I often thought that I could simply stand here on my front step all day long, sniffing at the air and watching the clouds passing across the wide sky.

The winter recently finished I'd decided never to think about again. It had been followed by a spring of such heat that it was difficult to believe that one single place on Earth could offer such a range of temperatures.

The hills across the wide Yukon River were touched with mist, and for some reason they reminded me of my home in Scotland. Last seen so long ago.

Enough of sentiment. I walked down the street, heading for the bank, then home for a nap. It was my custom to leave the Savoy when it closed at six in the morning and catch a bit of sleep. At nine, I'd return to work on the books, supervise the opening of the bar at ten, and take the night's earnings to the bank. Back home again for a bit more sleep before going to the Savoy at four to oversee preparations for the evening. If things weren't too hectic, I'd be able to have supper with my son prior to changing into suitable evening wear, returning to the Savoy before things got lively at eight when the dance hall performances began.

It made for a hectic schedule and not a lot of sleep. But gold rushes don't come along all that often, and I'd sleep once I'd made all the money I could out of this town.

It would be nice to be able to spend more time with Angus, but at twelve years of age, the boy didn't particularly want to spend time with his mother anyway.

It had rained during the night, and Front Street was more like a river of mud than a proper city street. Foolishly, the town had been built on a swamp; after a good, hard rain, the muck could reach a tall man's knees. Planks had been laid down to make a rough sort of sidewalk along one side of the street, but sometimes they got so crowded that men would prefer to step off and take their chances with the mud. The result, of course, was that the floors of every boarding house, shop, government office and dance hall were caked with wet and drying mud—which could be expected to consist of more than just good Yukon earth, as horses and half-tamed dogs also filled the streets. Laundries did a lucrative business, and Helen Saunderson, the Savoy's maid-of-all-work, spent a substantial part of her day mopping.

A wagon stuck axle-deep in the sludge held up traffic. The horse struggled against its unyielding burden, neighing in panic, sinking deeper and deeper. His round white eyes stared for a moment into mine.

I looked away.

After attending to the banking, I made my way home. I'd rented a couple of rooms in a boarding house on Fourth Street near York, which was, a year ago, on the outskirts of town. A tiny bedroom for Angus, an even smaller one for me, and a cramped sitting room where my son could do his school work in the evenings and I, on Sundays when the Savoy was closed, could read or simply enjoy a moment of peace.

I shook the sawdust off my pillow, as a light sheen had accumulated since I'd left my bed only three hours before, and I washed my face and hands in the cool, fresh water Mrs. Mann, the landlady, had left in the basin on the dresser. I hung my hat on the hook behind the door, pulled my day dress over my head, unlaced my corset, dropped it to the floor to join dress, stockings, over-corset, drawers and petticoats, and crawled into bed. I fell asleep to the sound of hammering from the property next door. Someone was squeezing an addition onto a house that was already falling over because it had been so badly erected a year before.

Chapter Three

Angus MacGillivray, overflowing with as much enthusiasm as a puppy watching his owner pick up a ball, bounced through the door of the tiny town detachment on Third Avenue.

"Good morning, sir." He stood to attention in front of the desk, his arms stiff at his sides, spine straight, eyes facing directly forward.

Constable Richard Sterling of the North-West Mounted Police looked up. "Morning, Mr. MacGillivray. What brings you here this early?"

Angus's face fell and his shoulders slumped; the puppy's owner had taken the ball and gone inside. "You said I could come on your rounds with you today. Don't you remember? Sir?"

"Oh, right." Sterling could never decide whether he should be encouraging the lad's interest in the Mounties, with the aim of turning the fatherless boy into a productive citizen, or discouraging the somewhat annoying hero-worship. "Give me a couple of minutes to finish this report."

Angus perched on the edge of the only spare chair in the small room as Sterling bent his head to concentrate on the paperwork. "What's your report about, sir?" The boy's blue eyes shone with anticipation. A lock of too-long blond hair fell over his forehead. Angus's huge feet were planted so solidly on the floor that no one else would be able to squeeze into the room. *Must cost his mother a fortune in footwear,* Sterling thought. Not to mention food. The fair, sturdy Angus looked almost nothing like his dark, fine-boned mother: only the generous mouth and strong chin suggested a contribution by the maternal genes.

"My report? A theft. A sourdough befriended a Yankee newcomer who'd passed out from drink, and when the Yankee woke up, he stole the old-timer's mining gear."

"Did you catch him?"

"Oh, yes," Sterling said, with a touch of satisfaction. "Fool went to the nearest supply store to sell the goods. Harold contacted us straight away. He, the Yankee, not Harold, will be contributing to the warming of the constabulary this winter." Police resources were so limited in the Yukon that there were only two punishments meted out for miscreants: a blue ticket expelling one permanently from town or a time in custody chopping wood for the ravenous NWMP stoves.

A steamship whistle blew out on the river.

Sterling stood, picked up the distinctive broad-brimmed, pointed hat, and placed it properly on his head.

"Time to go. Not a lot happening this early in the day. The real action gets going around midnight."

"Yes, sir." Angus leapt to his feet, all awkward arms and gangly legs.

They walked down to the waterfront as the steamship *Queen Victoria* pulled into the makeshift harbour. The port, such as it was, consisted of not much more than rows of boats pulled up onto the mud flats and tied together. In an attempt at some sort of civility, a few planks had been laid to the steamships.

Dawson produced nothing but gold. No food, no clothing, no mining equipment. Everything the town needed arrived by steamship or on rough rafts powered by poles of newly-hewn wood and men's aching backs. A good-sized crowd could always be expected to show up at the docks in anticipation of anything that might prove of interest. Or of profit.

Sterling and Angus stood to one side of the pack, nodding to the townspeople. The river was thick with makeshift boats bringing newcomers from all over North America, from all over the world.

"What we're doing, son," Sterling explained, "is watching. See who gets off the boat and make sure they're not here to cause trouble."

At first Angus stood still, only his eyes moving as he tried to follow the stream of humanity disgorging from the steamship into the milling crowd. But before long, his legs started to get stiff and his right foot fell asleep. He shook his leg to bring some feeling back.

The constable laughed. "A policeman's life isn't always exciting, son. Boring, more often than not." He stopped talking as someone caught his attention. Aged about sixty, the newcomer was a good deal older than most people who came to Dawson, but still not as old as some. He was well-dressed, although his wool suit could do with a good laundering, and his grey-streaked beard and hair needed trimming. He stood solidly beside a pile of nearly-new luggage, negotiating porter's fees with men who'd rushed to the docks to offer their labour.

Sterling wandered over; Angus trotted behind.

"I want the finest hotel in town." The newcomer signalled to two of the workers to pick up his bags. The crowd pushed and shoved around him. Angus took an elbow in the back and lurched forward. He would have fallen had not the press of men on either side propped him up.

The man saw Angus stumble. "You, boy," he said. "I'm here on behalf of the *San Francisco Standard,* and I'm hoping you can tell me the name of the best place in town for a fellow to hear the local news."

"Paper's called the *Klondike Nugget,* sir," Angus said in a low voice, his cheeks turning pink. "You go down…"

"Don't want a newspaper, boy. A reporter doesn't get his stories from the newspaper office. I'm asking where's the best place to hear the news from them that's making it, and I've got a dollar if you can tell me."

Angus held out his hand, apparently forgetting that he was pretending to be a Mountie. "The Savoy, sir. The finest, most modern establishment in London, England, transported all the way to the Yukon."

The reporter pressed a tattered American dollar bill into Angus's hand. "And where is this Savoy?"

"Front Street, sir," Angus said, stuffing the note into his pocket before turning to point. "Just past Queen Street. Right over there. Big sign out front. "

Sterling stepped forward. "Come to write about our town have you, Mr…"

"Ireland, Jack Ireland. Pleased to make your acquaintance, Sergeant." The man held out his hand. Sterling took it. They sized each other up.

"Constable Sterling. North-West Mounted Police. Welcome to Dawson, Mr. Ireland."

"I'd say it's a pleasure to be here, Constable. But I'm not yet sure that's the truth." The reporter looked around, taking in the press of men and boys openly listening to the conversation, the naked hillsides, the mud. Everywhere, the mud. He swatted a mosquito that had settled on his fleshy neck. "But it sure is a relief to come to the end of that miserable trip. This Savoy of yours, boy, is it a hotel?"

"No, sir. It's the finest dance hall, bar and gaming house in Canada. Maybe in the world."

Ireland chuckled. "I'll believe that when I see it. What hotel would you recommend, son?" He held out another dollar.

"The Richmond, sir." Angus took the bill.

The reporter snapped his fingers at the men hovering over his luggage. "You two, take my bags to the Richmond. I'll be along in a minute. What hours does this Savoy keep, son?"

"Huh?"

"He means when does it open," Sterling said.

"Oh. Ten o'clock. Sir."

"Not till ten?"

"Ten in the morning," Sterling explained.

Ireland laughed a deep, hearty laugh. His red beard, liberally streaked with grey, shook, and his open mouth showed a row of small teeth. A single gold tooth caught the sun. His laugh was as contagious as his surname would suggest. It rolled over the watching crowd until everyone was chuckling along. Even Angus smiled. Only Sterling failed to participate in the general merriment.

When he regained control of his breathing, Ireland wiped his eyes. "I must say, my boy, this sounds like my kind of town. Now, I'd better follow those oafs to the hotel, or I'll never see my luggage again. Perhaps I'll run across you later at this dance hall of yours."

"I don't think so," Sterling said. "Children aren't allowed in the dance halls."

Ireland looked shocked. "Would've taken you for much older than that, lad." He winked at Angus. The boy flushed.

The crowd separated to allow the reporter from the *San Francisco Standard* through.

Sterling and Angus watched him go.

Show over, the throng ebbed away. Crates of cargo were being unloaded from the bowels of the steamship, and the townspeople were eager for a glimpse of the contents.

"Two dollars is a lot of money," the policeman said. "More than some men with families to support make in a day."

"Do you want me to give it back, sir?"

"No. A fool and his money are easily parted, and Ireland's come to the right place for that. And there's nothing wrong with directing him to your mother's either. Some people would say that the Savoy *is* the best dance hall in Dawson. But if you want to be a policeman, Angus, think about this: Not many men give away money for nothing, although sometimes they try to make it look that way. But there comes a day when they expect to be paid back. And you don't want to be owing them."

Angus looked at the Mountie. "But how could I pay him back, Constable Sterling? I don't have any money of my own."

Sterling grinned and tousled the boy's blond head. Another few months, and Angus would be too tall for head-rubbing. The way the boy was growing, give him another year and he'd be taller than Sterling. It wouldn't be long before Angus would be encountering men wanting to prove themselves by starting a fight with the boy, not noticing, or caring, that the childish face didn't quite match the man's body.

Up ahead, a drunken prospector stumbled in the mud. He shouted abuse at an elegantly dressed man innocently passing by and took a wild swing. Unfortunately for the drunk, the man had lost over a thousand dollars on the roulette wheel at the Monte Carlo the previous night and was looking for someone, or something, on which to take out his anger. Before he knew what was happening, the drunk was scrambling in the mud and the gambler's boot was back, readying for a kick to the head. Sterling gave a shout of warning and ran.

Chapter Four

Promptly at five o'clock, I walked through the doors of the Savoy, barely avoiding being hit by a drunk that Ray and one of the bartenders were throwing out into the street.

I scarcely glanced at the patron as he flew past. Ray grinned at me. Despite the poor light, his stiff white shirt was so white it practically gleamed, and he'd combed his few strands of greasy hair. He returned to the bar, where men were lined up three deep.

The Savoy Saloon and Dance Hall. How I loved every ugly, hastily constructed, tottering, hideously decorated square foot of it. So cheap and gaudy, my acquaintances in London would have laughed out loud to see it. But it was mine. And there was nothing cheap about the money the place made for Ray and me.

The customers parted respectfully as I sailed into the room. I love a good parade, as long as I'm at the centre of it.

Barney, one of my regular customers, was slumped on a stool, his upper torso lying across the mahogany bar. But he kept talking as he entertained the younger men with tales of George Carmack, and the Indians Jim and Charlie, and of the first strike on Rabbit Creek, soon to be renamed Bonanza. Half of the men in his audience regarded him with eyes full of admiration, eager to hear again the story they'd heard a hundred times before. The other half were disbelieving and turned from the old prospector in disgust or dismissal. But Barney's stories were all true—embellished perhaps, but still true. Barney had found gold. I'd say he wasted it on drink, dance-hall girls, and the sad women who plied their trade in the cribs of Paradise Alley, but I suppose he considered it to be money well spent. He'd had sixteen gold nuggets made into a belt for a birthday present to give to a girl working at the Horseshoe. She'd thanked him with a chaste kiss on the cheek, and the old fellow had just about fainted with the sheer joy of it. These days he passed his nights, and most of his days, in Front Street bars like mine, telling his stories and earning his whisky by the strength of his reputation.

A puddle of spilled liquor was spreading across the floor beneath the centre table, and I was about to signal to one of the bartenders to fetch a mop when the door flew open. A large man stood there, his eyes taking in the room. He was old for this gold-rush town, over sixty probably, and immaculately dressed in pin-striped trousers, a fresh white shirt and black jacket with stiff black waistcoat crossed by a watch chain of thick gold. A heavily-starched collar and perfectly straight bow tie clenched his fleshy neck with such force that it looked as if they were trying to strangle him. His black hat was clean and placed directly in the centre of his head. His face was tinged pink from a recent shave.

Sweeping off his hat in a flowing, liquid movement that reminded me of an actor in a stage show I'd seen in London many years ago, he approached me. It had been a very bad actor in a very bad play, which for some unknown reason had been the hit of the season.

"Indeed, I am at the right place," he said, "for although your establishment is somewhat less than imposing from the outside, one glimpse of your ladyship and I understand that this must be the place of quality in Dawson." His freshly cut red hair was faded and heavily streaked with grey.

I laughed. "Thank you, but I don't think anyone has mistaken me for a ladyship before." That was not exactly true. There had been that embarrassing encounter in Bath in 1889 with Lady Rickards-Sommerfield. Not embarrassing for me, of course, but for my gentleman companion it had marked the beginning of a downward spiral into social disgrace.

"Allow me to introduce myself." He took my hand and touched it lightly to his lips. He wore immaculate white gloves. You didn't see those in Dawson much. "Jack Ireland. *San Francisco Standard.*"

I snatched my hand back. "A newspaper reporter?"

Ireland misinterpreted my reaction. "Don't worry, dear lady. I can see that your fine establishment is one to be celebrated. It will make wonderful background for my stories about Dawson and the Klondike." His eyes passed over me and surveyed the room.

Following Ireland's gaze, I saw my place.

It wasn't much—a long mahogany bar lined one side, a few tables were scattered around the floor. The wallpaper in the saloon was an ostentatious red that clashed horribly with my best dress, but I'd chosen it nevertheless, partially because there was not much else to buy, but also because to uneducated, uncultured miners and labourers heavy red wallpaper spells "class". The centre of the wall behind the bar was occupied by a portrait of Queen Victoria, looking every year of her advanced age. In honour of the two primary nationalities making up the population of the Yukon, we had stuck a Union Jack into the right of the frame and the Stars and Stripes into the left. On either side of the monarch hung a large painting of a voluptuous nude female, one black-haired, one fair.

At the Savoy we cater to all tastes.

I had never met our beloved monarch, but judging from stories I'd heard, some of them directly from the excessively-indulged mouth of her eldest son, she wouldn't have approved of us in the least. By London standards, even by Toronto standards, it was a hovel. But we made more in a night than most gaming house proprietors in Toronto or London could dream of earning in a week. We had so much custom that I sometimes wondered how everyone managed to fit inside. And no matter how much we charged, the customers kept streaming through the doors.

"Madam." Ireland touched the brim of his hat and went to the bar. The men could tell a swell when they saw one, and they shifted to let him through. He shouted for a drink for himself and one for the men on either side.

I caught a glimpse of myself in the ornate, gilt-edged mirror hanging on the back wall. A large crack streaked across the entire width of the glass. The mirror had been dropped when it was hung, but this was Dawson: we were grateful for the slightest touch of opulence, and no one looked at anything very closely, not wanting to see the reality underneath.

I tugged lightly at my waist to pull the bodice lower and display my necklace better. A clean-shaven young man blanched and tossed down his drink in one swallow. He joined the crowd at the bar and shouted for another.

I went into the dance hall to check that Helen had laid out the chairs for the evening's performance. When I returned, Jack Ireland, of the *San Francisco Standard*, was asking Rupert Malloy, one of the men enjoying the free liquor, how long he'd been in the Klondike. I knew the answer—two weeks. But Rupert could play the game, and he began spinning a tale of prospecting in the wilderness, fighting off bloodthirsty Indians, ravenous wolves, and greedy prospectors for a chance at the gleaming yellow metal. He paused and fingered his empty glass with a deep sigh. Ireland snapped his fingers at Sam Collins, the head bartender and our oldest employee.

"Don't waste your time listening to Rup here," said a man standing behind Ireland's shoulder. "You want the real stories of the strike, can't do no worse than speak to ol' Barney over there."

Ireland looked at Barney, almost snoring with his head resting on bar. At the sound of his name, Barney's head jerked up. "So Injun Jim, he says to me…"

"Thanks for the tip, friend." Ireland signalled for Sam to pour a drink for his informant and slid a few feet down the bar. The crowd shifted, like the waters of the Yukon River on a still day when a raft drifts by. Sam Collins's weather- and life-worn face had gone pale, and he stared at the floor as he placed the glasses on the counter.

"Young man there says you know some stories of the strike of '96." Ireland slapped Barney on the back. The old man belched.

"Another drink for my friend here," the newspaperman shouted.

Barney lifted his freshened glass in one worn paw. "Summer of '96," he said before toppling forward, planting his face into a puddle on the shiny mahogany bar.

Ray moved before I had time to snap my fingers. Sam had turned his attention to a newly arrived pack of Yankees, still wet behind the ears from river water, so Ray yelled at the new boy to give him a hand. Together they lifted Barney off his stool. The crowd parted to let them through.

Ireland picked up his drink and walked over to me. "Bet you have some stories to tell." He spoke directly to my cleavage.

"No," I said. "Not a one. If you'll excuse me..."

He grabbed my upper arm. "I'll make it worth your while." Talk in the room stopped as abruptly as if it had been scripted. Everyone stared at us, frozen in place, mouths open, glasses half-raised. They looked as if they were performing in a tableau for the entertainment of the Prince of Wales.

I stared at Ireland's hand, before lifting my eyes to his face. "Release me," I said.

He looked at me, and I tensed, expecting trouble. He backed down and let go. As one, the clientele let out a single breath and returned to their drinks.

Ireland knew he'd lost face. His cheeks were red, his eyes small, dark and cold. His fists were clenched tightly at his sides, and a vein throbbed in his neck.

I smiled my best dance hall hostess smile. "Have you had a look into our gaming rooms, yet, Mr. Ireland? The finest roulette wheel in Dawson. And of course, we have faro and poker as well."

The reporter didn't return my smile. "Quite the piece of work, aren't you, Miss...?" His grammar and accent seemed to shift, depending on to whom he was speaking. He'd been excessively formal with me when first we met, his speech turning coarser and rougher when he talked with the men around the bar.

"Mrs," I said. "Mrs…" I bit my tongue, remembering, just in time, what I was talking to. A newspaper reporter.

"Mrs. what?" He snapped, reading layers of meaning into my hesitation, a skill he would have honed to perfection in order to succeed in his business.

There was no point in not telling him my name. Everyone in town knew it. Besides, it was unlikely that anyone in London read North American newspapers, and in Toronto I'd used another name.

"Mrs. Fiona MacGillivray, at your service, sir. Please allow me to escort you into the gambling room."

"MacGillivray. I'll remember that." He turned on his heels, and the bar hangers-on parted to let him through.

Ireland slapped his money down on the counter. But this time no one rushed to serve Mr. Ireland of the *San Francisco Standard.* The new bartender, so new I didn't know his name, had returned and was busy at the far end. There was no sign of Ray, and Sam was dusting off the whisky bottles behind the bar as if we didn't have a customer in the place. The man wasn't deaf or blind, surely he could see the anxious faces of rows of would-be-drinkers reflected in the glass protecting her Majesty's visage, which hung directly in front of his face.

"Bartender!" Ireland shouted, his face turning redder, the too-ample flesh around his tight collar bulging at the insult of being ignored when he had a full bar watching him. Sam turned and asked a short, fat man with a full glass in front of him if he'd like another. Our head bartender was very pale.

"What the hell does it take to get a drink around here?"

The new bartender heard the shouting, and with a questioning glance at Sam's back, abandoned his end of the bar and rushed to serve the reporter with the deep pockets and the pack of new-found friends. Sam half-turned to check what was going on behind his back.

A man pushed up to the counter and bellowed for a drink. Sam poured him a whisky, his hand shaking so badly that almost as much liquor splashed on the counter as landed in the glass.

"I can tell you some stories, city fellow." A rough hand slapped Ireland's back, and the reporter's attention shifted.

Sam tossed a look at the other bartender and slipped away, avoiding my angry eyes. Going for his break, although it was early, and not a good idea in any event, what with Ray away seeing to Barney. I began to follow Sam to ask if he were feeling sick. He'd have to be on death's door, he'd have to be on the other side of death's door, to be allowed to go home early on a night that was shaping up to be as busy as this one.

"Fee!" A man burst through the door, beaming widely and holding his arms out. "What an honour. Here you are standing at the door, waiting to greet me."

I caught a glimpse of Sam Collins disappearing into the crowded street as I permitted the new arrival to give me a hug. It felt nice to be held in a man's arms, warm and close and safe, but I pulled away after the briefest moment of indulgence. Better not to get men's hopes up. It spoils them. "Graham," I said, "you're back."

"In the flesh. You look wonderful, Fiona."

I smiled. Of course I looked wonderful. I always look wonderful. But I never mind hearing it. "How are things out on the Creeks?"

"It's incredible. Let me tell you, my dear, it's like the inside of a beehive on a sunny day." Graham Donohue had been visiting the goldfields, collecting stories from the miners. He pulled off his hat and scratched at his black hair, normally kept short and neat, now hanging rough at the back of his neck. "Sorry, Fee," he said with a grimace. He plopped his dust-coated hat back on his head. "Think I picked up something that crawls out there."

I stepped back. "Really, Graham, you might have had a bath and a haircut before coming here."

"I couldn't last another minute without seeing your fair face. Why, the memory of you was all that kept me going through the long days and nights out on the Creeks."

I snorted. In a ladylike manner, of course. "Ran out of whisky, did you?"

"Any excitement in town during my absence?" Graham took my elbow and led me away from the crowd spilling off the street into the saloon. A roar from the gambling room announced that someone was a winner. For the moment anyway. A small crowd poured back into the bar, led by the winner, sharing his good fortune with all and sundry. The new bartender sweated profusely and poured drinks as fast as he could move. I was impressed; he'd risen to the pressure of the moment.

"Nothing out of the ordinary," I said to Graham.

He laughed. When he was clean and respectable, Graham Donohue was an extraordinarily handsome man. His nose had been broken a few times, but so good was the bone structure of his face that it scarcely mattered. His cheekbones, high in a thin face, were accented by expressive hazel eyes trimmed by lashes so thick that my dance hall girls swooned over them. He was my height, and so slightly built that he verged on scrawny. Graham's complexion was clear and unlined, and his warm eyes usually sparkled as if they were planning some act of schoolboy mischief such as dipping the pigtails of the girl sitting in front of him into the inkwell. In an attempt to look more his age, he sported a bushy, ferocious moustache that gave him some whimsical charm: so incongruous in his childish face that he looked like a boy who couldn't decide whether or not he wanted to grow up. The slight, boyish exterior concealed a heart as tough as they come. He was a reporter for a major American newspaper, determined to make his name in the Klondike.

Graham Donohue was exactly my type: not too large, apparently unassuming, handsome. And he worshiped the liquor-spotted, spat-upon, sawdust-coated, cheap wooden planks that I walked on.

But I wasn't in Dawson looking for a man.

"There's someone new in town you might like to meet," I said. "A reporter from San Francisco."

The seductive grin disappeared immediately. "Who?"

"Jack Ireland's his name. From the *San Francisco Standard*, I believe."

"Where?"

"At the front of the bar. Older guy, well dressed, big crowd standing around him."

Graham didn't give me a second glance and pushed his way through the crowd. Curious, I rounded the bar.

Ray walked back into the saloon. "Where's Sam?"

"Left in a big hurry. I don't know why."

"No' back in five minutes, and he's gone." Ray turned into a blur of motion, pouring drinks, taking money, weighing gold, listening to men's talk.

He managed the bar and gambling room staff; I kept the books and handled the money, supervised the performers and dancers, and attracted the customers. We made a good team, Ray and I.

Graham elbowed men aside to stand face-to-face with Ireland. My friend had his hands on his hips and his chin thrust forward. Ireland smirked with a sort of sick pleasure that gave me an uncomfortable feeling deep in my stomach.

"Jack Ireland," Graham said. "I'm surprised you're not in hell yet."

"Nice to see you, too, Donohue, my boy. How's your dear sister these days?" Ireland turned to his drinking partners. "This lad and I go back a long way, boys."

"What are you doing here, Ireland?"

"Working on a story, my lad. Same as you, I figure."

"This is my patch, Ireland. I'll thank you to stay the hell out of it. And don't you dare mention my sister again."

Ireland threw back his head and laughed. A gold tooth reflected light from the lamps filled with cheap oil. "A real reporter doesn't put claim to a 'patch', boy. Not like a miner marking his stake. A real reporter knows there's more than enough news to go around."

Graham's face was turning red, which had the unfortunate effect, regardless of the bristling moustache and the layers of mining dirt, of making him look as if he were on the verge of a temper tantrum.

"Ray," I said, "I think..."

Graham took a swing, but his arm was inhibited by the press of men at the bar. The space surrounding the San Francisco reporter had been thick before, but at the first suggestion of a fight, the people standing at the back shuffled forward to get a good look.

With no momentum to back it up, Graham's blow bounced lightly off Ireland's cheek. The drinkers in striking range stepped back, causing a jam as the two groups of onlookers came together. I knew, along with all the regulars, that Graham's next punch would have the older man on the floor. Graham had been a champion boxer in his school days. Slight boys often have to be if they're going to survive a New England boy's school.

Ray leapt across the bar, sending men scattering every which way before him. He was a small man, but in Ray's case his growth had been stunted by the ill-nourishment of a Glaswegian childhood rather than by genes. Ray had never been a boxing champion; he was a street fighter, practically from the moment he vacated the cradle. He grabbed Graham's arm and twisted it behind his back. "That's enough o' that, Mr. Donohue. Time ta be off home."

Ireland made a grand show of straightening his hat and tidying his cuffs, trying to recover from the look of sheer terror that had crossed his face in the long second before Ray sailed across the countertop. But I'd seen it. We'd all seen it.

"Mrs. MacGillivray?" Graham looked at me. He didn't move in Ray's grip. "Am I expelled?"

As if I'd contradict my business partner in front of a room full of customers. "Yes, you are, Mr. Donohue. You may return tomorrow, once you have calmed down. And had a shave and a haircut and changed into clean clothes."

Held firm in Ray's grip, Graham still managed a stiff bow. "For you, the raven-haired beauty of the Klondike, I'll even have a bath."

How could I not smile?

The onlookers cheered lustily at Graham's chivalrous words. They were a long way from home, all these men trying to be so tough. A great many of them had left cherished mothers, wives and children behind in the depression-plagued cities to the south. They were the most sentimental bunch I had ever encountered. Which sometimes made it difficult to wring every last copper or fleck of gold dust out of them.

Difficult, but not impossible.

Graham Donohue looked at Ray. "You can unhand me, sir. Mrs. MacGillivray has asked me to leave. I never refuse a lady."

The crowd cheered. Someone shouted, "Come on, Fee, let the boy stay." They took up the chant. "Let the boy stay!"

Ireland was forgotten, which he didn't appear to be at all happy about. Judging by the way he looked at me, he, the righteous victim of an unprovoked attack, blamed me for the loss of the crowd's attention.

Tough.

I jerked my head towards the door; once an order was given, it had to be upheld, no matter what. Ray and I had both served our time on the bottom of life's ladder, the one with half the rungs kicked out. We knew better than to show a hint of weakness. Graham bowed, and although he was still held in Ray's powerful grip, he managed to be as gracious as the great ship on which I'd left Southampton harbour, heading for the New World. Several men pounded him on the back as he passed.

Ireland swallowed his drink, elbowed the man beside him out of the way and went into the gambling room. His face resembled one of the thunderclouds that would hover over Toronto on a hot summer's day.

"Close one," I said to Ray, once he'd seen Graham out the door.

"What was all that about? Never seen Donohue fly off the handle like that before. Cool as they come, he usually is." At least that's what I think Ray said. His Glaswegian accent is so thick when he's angry or confused or, on a very rare occasion emotional, that even I, born and raised on the Isle of Skye until the age of ten, can't always understand him.

I shook my head: who knows what comes over men at times? The customers, disappointed that the fight had fizzled into nothing, went back to their drink.

All I'd have to do, I'd thought naïvely, was to keep Graham Donohue and Jack Ireland apart, and everything would be well.

Chapter Five

Angus MacGillivray had never enjoyed himself so much in all of his life as he followed Constable Sterling on his rounds. Wherever they went, men nodded at Sterling; the few women smiled and occasionally blushed, and everyone grinned at the sight of the gangly boy tagging along at the constable's side.

It was early evening when they made their way down Front Street. The street was filling with men headed for the bars and the gambling tables. The dance halls didn't open until eight, but the crowd would find ways to entertain themselves in the time remaining.

In front of the Savoy a drunk straightened up from a muddy puddle of his own vomit, clutching his stomach and emitting a low moan, sounding much like a cow in labour. Ray Walker stood in the doorway, disgust filling his battered face. He shook his head, caught Sterling's eye, nodded, called a greeting to Angus and went back inside. The drunk turned and tripped. He waved his arms in the air like an out-of-control windmill, but to no avail, and pitched forward into the street, collapsing face first into the mud.

Several men were lounging outside the bars; they laughed. A plainly dressed, no-nonsense woman with a bosom like the bow of an ocean liner threw the drunk a look that would curdle milk and gave him wide berth. Sterling walked over to the moaning pile of mud. "Get up, man. Horse 'n wagon'll be coming down this road any minute, and then you'll be done for."

The man groaned.

"Get up." Sterling kicked at the fellow's ribs, barely

making contact.

The drunk staggered to his feet as the onlookers cheered. Many wore suits that were once of high quality, but that they no longer had the money—or the energy—to maintain. They were young, with the frightened, vacant look of privileged young men who'd set out seeking thrilling adventure and found only hardship and toil.

"Don't you fellows have any place to be getting to?" Sterling snarled at them. "If you don't, wood needs chopping down at the Fort."

They scattered, looking for another place to drink and to pass the time until they could find passage out of this God-forsaken place.

"Many thanks, Cons'ble," the drunk mumbled, touching the brim of his hat, which miraculously hadn't come off in the fall. He staggered down the street, trying to keep some semblance of dignity whilst coated in reeking, gluttonous muck from head to toe.

Sterling turned to Angus. "Before the dance halls open, I'm going into Paradise Alley. You can't come with me."

Angus's heart sank—he'd been looking forward to the chance to have a good long look around the infamous Paradise Alley, while appearing authoritative and responsible, not like a boy who'd snuck out after his mother'd gone to bed. "I know what sort of things happen there," he said, hoping to sound mature and responsible.

"Do you, now?"

Sterling didn't sound impressed at Angus's maturity, so the boy hurried to add, "My ma told me."

"What did she tell you?"

"To stay well away from there and not to talk to any of the ladies, even if they talk to me first, except to say hello which is only polite, of course."

"Of course."

"But it'll be fine with her as long as you're with me."

The edges of Sterling's mouth turned up. "Let's go then. But if there's any trouble, you get yourself out of there. Understand?"

"Yes, sir."

They left Front Street and walked east on Queen to the section of road below Second Avenue known to everyone as Paradise Alley.

The street was narrow, lined on either side with a wooden boardwalk and the occasional plank, or duckboard, stretched across the road. The cribs, where the women conducted their trade, were tiny, some of them no more than three or four feet across, and packed together, wall touching wall, with pointed roofs and a single tiny window inset beside the door. A name was painted over most of the doorways. Some of the women smiled at Angus and Sterling, a few seductive and inviting, but most merely extending greetings to a friendly face. Some turned their heads away and hurried past.

"My father's a preacher," the constable said, as much to himself as to Angus. "When I was growing up, he talked a lot about heaven and hell. I don't think he'd be able to imagine a place further from paradise than this wretched, mud-streaked patch of humanity."

Angus said nothing.

The women were plain-faced and sturdy, dressed in shapeless, well-worn work dresses. A few had tried to add some cheer to their drab surroundings, and even drabber lives, by threading colourful ribbons through their hair or putting a touch of sequins on their belt or a scrap of fur or lace on the collar. Their hands and faces were red and chapped from hard living in a hostile climate, and many had missing teeth. The road to the Klondike wasn't for delicate women.

A woman stood on the boardwalk on the other side of the street, watching them. "Lovely day, ain't it, Constable?" she called.

"Lovely."

"Nice lad you've got 'ere. Looks like a perfect angel. Your favourite?"

"Watch your mouth, Joey."

She was tiny, the size of an undernourished child; the

bones of her wrists as delicate as a bird's. Angus knew who she was: everyone knew who she was. Madame Josephine LeGrand owned many of the cribs that lined Paradise Alley. And, even though the law didn't approve, she owned the women who worked in those cribs as well. Midwest farm and eastern factory girls looking for adventure, abandoned wives trying to make a living, seasoned prostitutes from Montreal, Chicago, St. Louis or San Francisco, Joey LeGrand had paid their way to the Klondike, where they now worked, day and, mostly, night to pay for their passage.

Angus stared at her open-mouthed; his mother had warned him to have nothing to do with the small woman with the Quebec accent.

Joey stared back. The smile on her thin lips didn't touch her eyes. She placed her child-sized feet on the duckboards and crossed the road. Her dress was of plain homespun, her brown hair streaked with grey and pulled back into a severe bun, her only jewellery a plain gold band on the third finger of her left hand.

"Pleased to meet you, ma'am," Angus stuttered. "I'm..."

"Never mind," Sterling interrupted.

She folded her petite white hands in front of her and smiled up at Angus. "No matter," she shrugged. "I can guess the lad's name." The smile fell away and her attention shifted. "Any reason you're in the neighbour-hood, Constable?"

"Checking that the law is being upheld, Madame LeGrand. Even in Paradise Alley."

"Oh, yes. The Law. Me, I never forget about the importance and the power of The Law."

"See you keep it that way."

"Certainement, monsieur. Bon soir." She grinned at him like a cat at play with a particularly stupid mouse.

Sterling didn't say goodbye. He continued on his rounds, an unusually silent Angus following.

"Anyone ever show you how to box, Angus?" The constable said, apparently out of nowhere.

"No, sir. But I'd like to learn."

"You're growing into a big lad, Angus. Be not much longer before some men in this town try to take you on, not caring how young you are. Sergeant Lancaster was the boxing champion of Manitoba in his youth, I hear."

Angus's initial flush of excitement was quickly replaced by disappointment. He looked at his shuffling feet. "My mother won't allow it, sir. She doesn't want to hear about me fighting."

"You mother doesn't have to know."

Angus lifted his head. "Would he charge for lessons? Ma won't pay."

"He loves to teach boys. He'll probably do it for free."

"When can I start? Tomorrow?"

Sterling laughed. "Let me talk to Lancaster first. We'll work something out, and I'll let you know."

They walked down Front Street. It was almost eight o'clock, but the northern sun was warm on their faces. Outside the Savoy, Helen Saunderson was standing on the boardwalk, her eyes red from weeping, holding a well-laundered and heavily mended handkerchief to her nose. Jack Ireland, the American newspaperman, stood beside her, writing in a small notebook.

"Evening, Mrs. Saunderson," Sterling said. "Everything all right here?"

"Fine, thank you, Constable. Evenin' Angus." Air whistled through the woman's missing teeth. She blew her nose, the sound like a Prairie tornado. "I'm only telling Mr. Ireland here 'bout what happened to my man, Jim."

Ireland patted Mrs. Saunderson's shoulder. "There, there, my dear. You cry all you want. Such a tragic story."

She burst into another round of sobs and buried her face in her handkerchief. Her shoulders shook. Passersby tossed her curious stares and gave them a wide berth.

"Are you sure you want to be talking to a reporter, Helen?" Sterling said.

"I don't see that it's any of your business, Constable. Not unless the telling of a tragic story is against the law up here," Ireland said.

"I was asking the lady."

"I want folks to know what he done to me. My own brother. Took everything I had in the world and left the little uns to starve."

Angus's mother had told him the story: Helen's husband Jim and her brother had a claim out on Bonanza Creek. At first they were among the lucky ones, striking gold their first month on the river. But luck soon abandoned them, as she so often does, when loose gravel on a cliff face crumbled beneath Jim, and he fell to his death on the rocks below. It wasn't much of a tumble either, as the story went, only a few feet, but the back of his head met with the pointed edge of a sharp rock. His partner, Helen's own brother, John, took their gold and headed out of the territory before Helen had time to make her way to the base of the cliff and recover the body. She arrived in town with her husband's remains, his mining equipment, and four children under the age of twelve.

The Savoy's housekeeper had quit just a few days before, walked out in the middle of her shift having accepted a proposal of marriage on the spot from a man she'd never before laid eyes on. Not incidentally, he'd found gold and was celebrating his good fortune. So Helen was offered the job, and with just enough hesitation to assuage her pride, she accepted.

A couple of miners, their hair and clothes still thick with the dust of the dig, stopped at the foot of the step. They looked at the weeping woman, the well-dressed older man taking notes, the boy, the police officer, and hurried down the street in search of a more hospitable drinking place.

"Some privacy, please, Constable." Ireland patted Mrs. Saunderson with one hand and dug in his pockets in search of a cigar with the other.

Mrs. Saunderson gulped, wiped her eyes, and took a deep breath, almost visibly gathering her courage. "If it weren't for Mrs. MacGillivray, I can tell you, sir, there's no telling what woulda become of my youngins. This ain't no town for a woman without a man, and four children. No, sir. You tell your newspaper people that Mrs. Fiona MacGillivray is a fine woman. None better."

"I'll do that," Ireland said, his eyes roaming the street in search of the next story.

"Mrs. MacGillivray once owned a grand hotel in London, England." Helen's eyes widened at the thought of how fine a grand London hotel would be. Deep lines scored her face, and the delicate skin under her eyes, as dark as a grate full of coal, drooped towards her sunken cheeks. The effects of cold, hard work, grief and the scurvy that had stalked the town over the winter past combined to make her look twenty years older than she probably was.

"What the heck's going on out here?" Ray Walker stood in the doorway. "Sorry Angus, Helen. Didn't see you there. What're you doing standing about on the stoop? Ye'r blocking the doorway. Customers can't get themselves through."

Sterling looked at Ireland. "Is it necessary to stand in the entrance?"

Ireland straightened his perfectly aligned tie. "Mrs. Saunderson wanted to tell me her sad story. I'm a newspaper reporter. Hearing people's stories is my job; it's why I've come to the Yukon Territory. Certainly for no other reason." He laughed. No one joined in.

"Then take yourselves down the street. Mr. Walker has a business to run."

"I've all the information I need for now. Thank you," Ireland said. Mrs. Saunderson buried her life-worn face in the rag of the handkerchief. Ireland touched the brim of his fine hat, which was not marked by even the slightest touch of dust, and stepped into the street.

"You'll remember my brother's name, John O'Reilly, won't you?" Helen called. "If it weren't for Mrs. Mac..."

Ireland walked away, his step jaunty. He'd only gone a couple of feet when a pack of half-wild dogs rounded the corner. Angus couldn't see what they were chasing, but they were hot after something. Ireland leapt backwards and would have fallen into the mud had he not stumbled into a huge sourdough.

"Watch where you're goin', damned fool."

At first, Ireland looked as if he were about to give the man an argument. Then he glanced at the bulk looming over him and at the man's biceps—each the size of a side of ham—and thought better of it.

Helen leaned her hefty frame up against the wall and sobbed into her handkerchief.

"Mrs. Saunderson should sit down," Angus said. "And she'd probably like a cup of tea."

She gave Angus a small but grateful smile.

"Get off the stoop, will ye?" Ray said. "Not a customer's come through the doorway since you been standing there. Keep this up, and we'll be outta business. Helen, man's been sick in the gambling hall. You don't clean it up quick, it'll be tracked all over the place, and Fee'll have yer hide."

Helen wiped her eyes and tucked her handkerchief into the sleeve of her dress.

They followed Ray into the gloom of the Savoy. The place had a fine name, and a nice sign hanging outside. But inside it was exactly the same as every other saloon in Dawson: looking as if it had been thrown up in a day—which it had. The floorboards had been slapped together out of green wood; the ceiling was spotted with damp. But the customers stood four or five deep at the bar, and men were pushing their way into the gambling hall, all before the theatre and dance hall opened for the start of the real action.

"It was right good to have someone to talk to," Mrs. Saunderson said. "Someone what might write about what John did to us. Maybe he'll read about it and feel bad and come back with my Jim's gold."

She made her way through the crowd to the small, dark room behind the bar where she kept her rags and pail.

Chapter Six

My office was on the second floor, directly above the bar, overlooking Front Street to the mud-flats, the boat-congested Yukon River, and the tent-dotted hills beyond. If I were the type of woman to pray, I would spend a good bit of every day praying that the floor held. It emitted long, ominous creaks under my steps, and in a few places the wooden planks sagged beneath my weight.

It would do nothing for my dignity, nor my reputation, if one day I fell through the floor of the office, to descend legs first into the saloon, skirt caught on a scrap of rotting wood.

It was morning, and I was doing the accounts. We'd had another good night. Summertime, and the days were long and the nights too bright for southern eyes. All those men who'd struggled up the Golden Staircase to the Chilkoot Pass and rafted down from Lake Bennett or spent the winter in a town on the verge of mass starvation simply had to spend their money.

Jake, our head croupier, told Ray and me that some fool had dropped a thousand dollars in the eight hours he'd spent at the roulette wheel. I've known gamblers in London, Toronto and now Dawson, and it never fails to amaze me how some people just can't give up the game. In London, I'd even seen women standing in the shadows at the side of the clubs, handing money to men to take in and bet for them.

I've gambled myself, and it's a thrill to be winning. But then I've never gambled with my own money; my escorts always allowed me to keep my winnings and kept paying out if I lost. I've worked too hard to get what I have to risk it on a spin of the wheel or toss of the dice. But perhaps I think that way because I know how much I'm taking in as the owner of the gambling hall. And I don't make money when the punters are winning.

Graham Donohue's head popped around the door, interrupting my thoughts. "Is it safe to come in?"

I put down my pen and rubbed my forehead. "I should say no, but I won't. What on earth got into you yesterday, Graham?"

He tossed himself into the spare chair. A floorboard creaked and I winced. "When did that bastard Ireland get here?" he asked.

I gave him a well-practised look of feminine indignation. "Watch your language, Graham, or I'll toss you out myself."

He didn't even apologize. "You don't want that man hanging around, Fiona."

"His money seems as good as anyone else's. And *he* didn't pick a fight, far as I know."

"Jack Ireland and I go back a few years. I could tell you some stories."

"I don't want to hear them. If you'll excuse me, I have work to do." I flashed my pen as evidence.

"Another time then. But here's something you'd better hear, my dear." He pulled a scrap of paper out of his waistcoat pocket.

"Graham, I don't have time to listen to your copy. I haven't yet been to the bank."

He held up one hand. "This isn't my copy, Fiona. Someone else sent it. Listen for a moment while I read you a few select sentences."

I sighed and settled back into my chair. Easier to let him talk and get it over with, then I could get back to work. He was a good man, Graham Donohue, with a kind heart. For a newspaper reporter. And an American. He made no secret of the fact that he wanted, very much, to be more than my friend. But it was best to let things remain as they were. For now.

"Helen Saunderson. House of Ill Repute. Infamous Madam. Fee—spelt F-e-e—MacIntosh. White slavery. Seven starving children."

"Let me see that." I got to my feet, leaned across the desk, and snatched the paper out of his hands. The handwriting was indecipherable. I shoved it back at him and resumed my seat. "Gibberish. Nothing but gibberish."

"Fiona, listen to me." H leaned forward and placed his elbows on my desk. "Jack Ireland sent this story to San Francisco on the first steamboat out this morning. I'll read it to you in its entirety if you want, but the gist is that Helen Saunderson, he mentions her by name, has been forced into prostitution by a whorehouse madam by the name of F-i-e MacIntosh. Who, in the only bit of truth in his whole story, he describes as a black-haired beauty with a voice and complexion fresh off an English country estate."

I was so annoyed I didn't even take time to savour the phrases "black-haired-beauty" and "fresh complexion". "How the hell did you get this? Don't tell me Ireland tossed his rough copy into the gutter, and you happened upon it?"

"Language, Fiona. My delicate ears."

I almost said something stronger, but Graham held up one hand. "I'm telling you this in the strictest of confidence, of course." When Graham flirted with me, his hazel eyes sparkled as if with traces of gold dust; now they were so dark and serious that I settled back into my chair.

"Go ahead."

"I pay some of the men who hang around the docks a generous sum to let me know if they hear of anyone sending newspaper copy out, and still more if they open the envelope and copy the meat of the article."

The regular mail leaves Dawson once every two weeks, most recently only the day before yesterday. Obviously, ambitious newspapermen aren't prepared to wait two weeks to see their stories heading for print. Although if they want secrecy, perhaps they should.

"As I'm sure they're paid to copy your notes, Graham. But I can't see what harm this rubbish can do me. He didn't even get my name right, although the description is good." I picked up my pen once again. If the story spread further than San Francisco, so what? Everyone in Dawson knew that I wasn't a madam, and if anyone from England was still looking for me, Fee MacIntosh isn't even my name.

Graham's expression was indecipherable. "He got Helen's name correct, Fiona. It's quite the slur on her reputation, don't you think?"

I rolled my shoulders back to give them a welcome stretch. Graham must have been concerned indeed: he didn't even glance as the fabric of my day-dress tightened across my bosom. "Really, Graham, I agree that it's nasty of Mr. Ireland to be making up stories about us. And no doubt unethical. His facts are wrong, but this story paints Helen in a sympathetic light. Destitute widow struggling to support her starving children. That's the sort of sentimental rubbish that sells newspapers."

"I don't think she'll see it that way."

"Perhaps you're right." Outside my window, a horse screamed in terror. Men began shouting, and the wanderers gathered round, hoping for a show. "She'll never hear about it. By the time this letter gets to San Francisco and the paper is printed, provided they accept Ireland's rubbish, and a copy makes its way back here, which is also an unlikely prospect, half the town will have moved on, and no one will even know who he's talking about."

"Fiona, for such an intelligent woman, you can be amazingly dense when you're blinded by your own vanity and self-obsession."

I blinked. Men never insult me. At least not the ones who want to impress me. The outbreak of trouble on the street below didn't materialize. A man spoke to the horse in soothing tones, and the crowd drifted away, looking for excitement elsewhere.

"She'll find out all about it any minute now. My acquaintance who copied the letter came over the pass with Helen and Jim. He won't sit on this. He'll tell her."

"Oh, dear. Maybe he, your...whatever, will have told the

messenger to lose the letter when he saw that it's untruthful."

"It's not the messenger's responsibility to check the mail for accuracy. If Ireland wrote that the Czar of Russia had arrived in Dawson to grow potatoes in a wicked plot to make enough vodka to inebriate the entire adult population of the United States, he'd still carry it. As long as Ireland paid. Anyway, it's too late. Boat has sailed. With the letter."

I stood up. "Honest people are sometimes more trouble than they're worth. Helen should be downstairs. I'll go and see to her."

"Yes, Fiona. You'd better."

If one was to judge by the look of the group gathered in the saloon, we might have walked into a funeral. Helen's eyes were open as wide as her mouth, and she looked like a horse panicked by the sound of a gunshot too close to her head. Ray held her arm, his features dark and troubled. My son, Angus, sat at the bar, a piece of toast in one hand and a sheet of paper in the other. He turned at the sound of my footsteps, and his sweet face was filled with a look of such despair, I almost rushed over to gather him into my arms. But I held back, knowing that if I tried to hug him in public, in front of others, he'd push me aside.

A man I didn't know stood beside them. He was dressed in a filthy flannel working man's shirt under a jacket with one pocket hanging by a thread. His trousers were torn at both knees and badly mended. I had smelled him as I came down the stairs. He stared at me for a few seconds before shifting his attention back to the tableau in the saloon, twisting his dusty hat, missing half the brim, in his hands. "Perhaps I shouldn't have come. But I thought you'd want to know what this scoundrel says about you, Helen."

My partner let out a stream of words.

Everyone in the saloon looked at him. Ray's accent was so strong that something very bad must be happening.

I translated. "Ray says that it's better to hear foul news in the open from a friend than to have it whispered into your ears by your enemies. Or words to that effect. Let me see that." I snatched the paper out of Angus's hand. It was written in a strong, educated script.

How many copies of this blasted newspaper story were there? The man must have made yet another copy to show to Helen before handing the rough one over to Graham, perhaps thinking that she'd be more likely to believe him if she saw the words written down on paper.

I looked up. They were all watching me. I crumpled the paper in my hand. "Lies. All lies. Of no consequence. You, sir. Are you Mr. Donohue's friend? Did you copy this from a letter being carried to the Outside?"

The man nodded and twisted his hat. It would be even more of a mess by the end of this. "Yes, ma'am. Mrs. MacGillivray, ma'am. Joe Hamilton is my name."

"Mr. Hamilton. Where is this…missive…directed?"

"Ma'am?" He gaped at me.

"She means the letter, you fool," Donohue said. "What was the address on the envelope?"

"San Francisco, Mrs. MacGillivray, ma'am. The *San Francisco Standard.* I believe that is a newspaper." He stared at me, wide-eyed.

"I know what it is," I snapped. The man's face fell, causing him to look as if he'd missed a word in the final round of a spelling bee. Now I recognized him: he came in the occasional night and hung around the edges of the bar, dragging out a drink for as long as his few cents would stretch. Usually he spent most of his time watching me.

I threw him my best all-business smile. "Please forgive me, Mr. Hamilton. I shouldn't have spoken to you in that manner, but I do find all of this so dreadfully distressing."

Graham Donohue snorted.

Ray poured a generous shot of whisky and handed it to Helen. "Here ye go, lass," he said. "Drink this up. Do you a world o' good."

She lowered her nose to the edge of the glass, and her face crinkled at the smell.

"Swallow it down in one gulp," Ray instructed. "Make you feel better, it will."

It was probably the first free drink ever handed out in my bar, at least to someone who wasn't expected to turn a handsome profit in exchange.

"I'm not feeling too well, Ma," Angus said, his eyes fixed on the bottle in Ray's hand.

I ignored him. "So this pack of insidious lies has been sent to some seditious rag in San Francisco." I thrust the crumpled paper into Helen's hand, the one not holding the now-empty glass. "Burn it and forget about it. If a copy of the paper gets to Dawson, which is highly unlikely, no one will recognize us. He doesn't name the Savoy, he doesn't get my name right, and everyone in town knows that I run a respectable business, so why do we care what this Ireland idiot says?"

Helen reached behind her and slammed the glass on the counter. "Mrs. MacGillivray, he's insulted my good name. An' the name of my Jim, God rest his soul, an' my children. My Mary'll be of marrying age soon enough. No decent man'll want her after reading these lies." Her eyes filled with tears. Ray patted her arm.

I thought that a moot point. Mary was twelve, the same age as Angus, and decent men were sparse on the ground in Dawson.

"Take the remainder of the day off, Helen," I said. "Go home. Try to relax."

The room erupted.

"But, Ma..." Angus shouted.

"Really, Mrs. MacGillivray," Hamilton spluttered.

"Fiona, you can't just brush this off. Poor Helen..." Graham said.

Helen burst into loud sobs.

"Shut up, all o' ye!" Ray bellowed. "Fee's right. Letter's gone, right, Joe?"

Hamilton nodded furiously. "I saw the boat leave myself. Not more than an hour ago."

"Nothin' we can do about that then."

Helen groaned and sagged against the bar. Donohue fetched a stool and eased her into it, and Ray poured another shot. Angus tossed me an imploring look.

My son believes that I can do anything. But flying off in pursuit of a steamship sailing up the Yukon River and catching it is beyond even me. I looked at him and shrugged.

"But," Ray said, "we can watch out for the *San Francisco Standard*, now can't we?" He looked at Graham. Graham opened his mouth, probably to protest that he could hardly confiscate every copy of the paper once it arrived.

Ray threw him a look.

Wisely, Graham took the hint. "Of course we can. Look here, Helen, the moment that paper comes to town, I'll buy up every copy and burn them myself."

She looked up from her sodden handkerchief. Her eyes were red, her nose swollen with crying, and her cheeks had broken out in patches of a hideous colour. "Would you do that, Mr. Donohue? For me?"

I took her arm and helped her out of her chair. "Mr. Donohue has enormous influence in this town, Helen, as do I. We'll ensure that Ireland's lies aren't spread about Dawson. And if you are besmirched in San Francisco, what does it matter? You must admit that Helen Saunderson could well be the name of a hundred, a thousand, other women, couldn't it?"

She noisily blew her nose and smiled at me. Helen rarely smiled a full open-mouthed smile, so conscious was she of her missing teeth. And so little did she have to smile about. It subtracted ten years from her work- and worry-lined face.

"You're right, Mrs. Mac. If you can bear the insult to your good name, then I can too."

Fortunately, no one bothered to remind Helen that my "good" name hadn't even been mentioned.

"What's this then?" A voice sounded from the door. "I thought you were closed at this time of day, Mrs. MacGillivray?" Constable Richard Sterling strode into the saloon.

I stifled a groan. Like all the dance hall owners in Dawson, I didn't know whether to curse the efficiency of the NWMP for keeping us tightly under their law-enforcing thumb, or praise them for keeping the rest of the town, especially our customers, equally in line.

"You know it's my business what hours I keep in my establishment, Constable. Apart from respecting the Lord's Day, of course."

"Of course."

In my less, shall we say, self-controlled past, I would have found Richard Sterling to be an extremely attractive man. He was tall, well over six feet, with a fit to the scarlet tunic of his uniform that hinted at the bulk of the shoulders underneath. His brown eyes were thickly lashed and specked with yellow, along with intelligence and humour. Prominent cheekbones framed his face, and his mouth was so wide and his lips so full that they were almost, but not quite, feminine. I'd never seen him without his broad-brimmed NWMP hat, but once I'd caught the briefest glimpse of dark curls tumbling over themselves at the back of his neck. The next day he'd had a haircut, and all the lovely curls were gone. He spoke well, which indicated some education in his past. A quality that I am constantly trying to drum into my son.

"This is none of your concern, Constable," Ray said.

Sterling lifted one eyebrow. "Mrs. Saunderson, are you in need of assistance?"

"Now see here." Graham Donohue stepped forward. The hair on his head bristled, and I'm sure that if he had hair on his chest (a fact that I am not in the position to know—someday perhaps), it would have been standing up as well. "Mrs. Saunderson has received some bad news. The nature of which is none of your business."

"Everything that happens in the public places, and some of the private ones, of Dawson is the business of Her Majesty's North-West Mounted Police," Sterling said.

His tone was so pompous that I choked back a laugh.

Angus applauded, almost falling off his chair in approval of his hero's brief speech. "Well said, sir."

Ray watched me, waiting for a clue. I nodded and looked towards Helen.

My partner lifted her arm. "Allow me to walk ye home, dear."

"You take the rest of the day off, Helen," I said.

"With full pay, o' course," Ray added.

Graham and Sterling looked at me, waiting for a reaction. Hamilton clutched his hat to his chest and stared at me wide-eyed, looking as if he were ready to recommend me for sainthood. Angus watched Sterling.

"Thank you, Mrs. MacGillivray. That's mighty thoughtful of you." Helen opened her hand, and the scrap of paper fell to the floor. She permitted Ray to help her off her chair, and took his arm. "Haven't I always said the Savoy is the best place to work in all of Dawson?"

I choked back an objection. Feeling generous, I'd been about to offer her half-pay for the day off. Instead, I forced out a smile and wiggled my fingers in farewell.

The door swung shut behind them. Sterling picked the letter off the floor. He made a big show of smoothing it out before reading it. "Nasty."

"All lies."

"Don't you think I'd know, Mrs. MacGillivray, if you were running a whorehouse in this town?"

Angus momentarily forgot that this man was his hero. He stepped off his stool and puffed up his chest. "Please, Constable. Control your language in the presence of my mother."

Sterling and I exchanged a look, both of us stifling an inappropriate burst of laughter. I'd been on the verge of reprimanding the constable for saying "whorehouse" in my son's hearing.

"That was most inappropriate. Please accept my apology, Angus."

My son sat back down. A slice of toast with a thin scraping of butter and a single bite taken out of it lay on the table in front of him. He mumbled something and returned to his cold food, trying to hide his embarrassment.

We don't have a kitchen per se in the Savoy—this most certainly isn't a restaurant. But when punters on a losing streak feel the need to break for food, Helen, or one of the bartenders if she's not here, can whip up something quick enough. Beside the wood stove in the pokey back room that doubles as a broom closet, we keep a kettle and a few cups and plates, a frying pan and toasting fork and supplies of potatoes, bacon, beans, jam, bread, tea and canned milk. Helen pushes food on a not-at-all-resisting Angus whenever he shows up.

"I'd better get back to the docks," Hamilton mumbled. "There might be something important requiring my attention."

"Fiona." Graham glared at me and tossed his head towards Hamilton, heading reluctantly towards the door.

"Mr. Hamilton," I called, in my lightest, friendliest voice. "Thank you so much for bringing that unfortunate letter to my…our…attention."

The man plopped his tortured hat onto his head and turned the full force of his smile onto me. His teeth were badly stained, and several were broken almost to the gum line. "My pleasure, Mrs. MacGillivray. My pleasure." The smell of rotten teeth and the remains of breakfast wafted towards me.

"Offer him something," Graham whispered.

I ignored him. I can be gracious without anyone's help, thank you very much. "If you'll drop by this evening, Mr. Hamilton, perhaps around nine, Mr. Walker and I will be happy to offer you the hospitality of the Savoy."

He almost fainted, the poor man. Barely recovering his equilibrium, he backed out the door, bowing and scraping like a eunuch at the Sultan's court.

Graham laughed and slapped my arm. If an officer of the law hadn't been present, I would have slapped him back, right enough. "Now that I've done my good deed for the day, I'll be off. See you later, Fiona, Constable."

Sterling touched the brim of his hat. His eyes had far too much spark in them to be accounted for by the thin northern sunlight pouring in through the dirt-encrusted, narrow windows of my seedy bar. "Mrs. MacGillivray.

Angus." He followed Graham out.

"That was nice of you, Ma," Angus said. "To invite Mr. Hamilton to stop by."

I turned on him. "How many times do I have to tell you? Don't—call—me—Ma."

Angus tossed back the last piece of toast. "Everyone says that."

"Well, you won't. It's...it's...uncouth. Lower class. Even well-bred Canadians don't talk like that. Do you hear me?"

He shrugged and bounced off his stool.

I grabbed my son by the front of his shirt. "Do you hear me, Angus MacGillivray?"

For a slice of time he loomed over me, dark and threatening. I saw his father in his face, and I released the shirt and stepped back, my heart pounding with emotions spinning out of control. But my son's eyes looked back at me, filled with a deep blue that, until I saw the open sea for the first time, I had only ever seen in my own father's face. They shone without malice, without lust, loving and innocent. As my father's eyes had always looked.

And still did, in my dreams.

I buried my head in my hands.

Angus touched my shoulder, lightly. "I'm sorry, Mother."

I brushed away the tears, pushed aside the curtains of memory, and smiled at my son. "Perhaps you could drop by Mrs. Saunderson's place later. See if she needs any help with the children."

"Certainly, Mother."

He walked out the door, from the back looking exactly like a man, albeit a skinny one.

Out on the street, a wagon driver shouted at his horses to get themselves out of the mud, a woman yelled that she'd been cheated, and a couple of drunks called to my boy asking if this place was open. Most of the houses of entertainment in Dawson operate twenty-four hours a day, but when Ray and I first bought the business (my share coming from the last of the money from the sale of some stolen jewellery), I'd insisted on more civilized arrangements. I like to keep an eye on my property and can't do so all hours of the day and night. At the Savoy, the bar and the gambling rooms shut down when the dance hall closes at six in the morning, and they open again for business at ten. We never seem to have trouble drawing the customers back, although I'd been warned that once out the door, they wouldn't return.

I pulled my watch out of the folds of my dress. Ten o'clock, and no one here to serve bar.

"Mornin', Mrs. MacGillivray." Sam Collins walked through the doors. "Nice day out. Hope it don't keep the customers away, eh?"

"Good morning. It seems that nothing keeps the customers from our door. Ray's running an errand; he'll be back soon. I'll be upstairs if you need me."

Angus chafed at my insistence that he speak properly at all times. Who in Dawson, other than the odd toff and women such as me, trying to keep themselves respectable, bothered with how anyone spoke? Some of the richest men in town could barely string an intelligible sentence together. And some of the educated ones, such as Joe Hamilton, judging by his speech and handwriting, couldn't afford to have a rip in their coat pocket repaired or enough hot water for a bath.

In all of this wild, untamed town, dropped down just a few hundred miles from the Arctic Circle, where the only thing that anyone cared about was the amount of gold in a man's pocket, never mind how it got there, the way my son spoke mattered only to me. But no one knew better than I the importance of education and proper speech.

I climbed the stairs, sat at my desk, settled my skirts around me, picked up my pen, opened the big ledger, and began to do calculations.

I'd told Sam to let me know if Jack Ireland came in. Time, I thought, to have a quiet word with the newspaperman.

Chapter Seven

Men were pouring into the Savoy when I set off for home to have the evening meal with Angus. I stood on the step to catch my breath. It had been a fine day, warm and sunny, but the wind was picking up.

Joey LeBlanc strolled down the centre of the street, not bothering with the boardwalk or duckboards, the hem of her ragged skirt dragging through the mud. She looked me straight in the eye, and her lip turned up in a sneer, which didn't bother me in the least. I've crawled my way up in the world, and more than a few times I've acted outside of the law without caring a fig, but I never deliberately hurt anyone who had even less than I in order to ease my way. Joey might look like a slightly-better-dressed Whitechapel street urchin, but her heart (if she owned such a thing) was as black as a Yukon winter's night. Rumour said that she'd killed her husband in a knife fight in St. Louis after he damaged a piece of the merchandise.

"Nice evening, Mrs. MacGillivray." Sam Collins came out of the Savoy to stand beside me as I watched Joey pick her way through the mud. He was heading home for supper with his wife, Margaret, as he did every evening.

"It's going to be busy tonight."

"Yes, ma'am." He scratched his nose. Like many of the bartenders in Dawson, Sam had grown his fingernails long, so that when he weighed the gold dust in the scales set up on the velvet cloth on the mahogany counter, the residue could collect under his nails. At the end of the night, he might, and often did, scrape a handsome profit out of his own fingernails.

We stood together, enjoying the fresh air of the early evening.

"Strange town, this," Sam said.

I stretched my arms wide and turned my face to the sun. "Can you think of anywhere you'd rather be?" And for sure, I couldn't: this was the most thrilling, intoxicating place I had ever been. The very air breathed adventure and excitement, gold, and the chance to win—or lose—a fortune by nothing but the strength and courage of one's own wits. Along with a goodly portion of luck.

"Yes." His eyes were dark and serious, although I'd meant the question rhetorically. Sam always seemed so serious, but even more than usual in the last day or so.

I opened my mouth to ask him if everything was all right. Perhaps his wife was ill or begging to leave the Yukon. Things were hard for everyone here, but for people of their age?

I never said the words.

The building a couple of doors down, with the walls sagging inwards and the wooden slats on the roof already lifting off, called itself a bakery. Which was pushing the definition of the word, as they sold nothing but waffles at twenty-five cents each, along with coffee. As Sam and I stood in the pleasant evening sun, talking about nothing of consequence, the front door of the bakery blew out in a wall of flame.

Chapter Eight

A screaming woman ran out of the bakery and into the street. Greedy flames fed off the air blowing though the loose fabric of her skirts.

No one moved. Everyone of us stood rooted to the spot with shock. The woman's arms windmilled around and around, as if she were trying to swim through the air. Her mouth formed a dark "O", and her eyes were wide with terror. Flames licked up the back of her dress and, as I watched, ignited her long hair, come loose from its pins in the initial blast.

A blur of movement crossed the corner of my vision, and the burning woman was knocked off her feet. She fell face first into the wet, sticky mud. Richard Sterling struggled to his knees; he'd lost his hat and mud caked his face and uniform.

"Roll, roll!" he yelled.

"Roll, roll!" the crowd screamed.

And she did, twisting and turning in the mud like a monster dragged out of a bedtime story to scare a mischievous child into instant obedience. So wet was the street, the fire was soon extinguished.

The crowd moved forward, all ready to cheer, offer a helping hand, have a drink in celebration. A fire was nothing unusual in Dawson, what with wooden buildings hastily constructed and lit by candles and cheap lamps.

Half of the bakery roof collapsed, and flames spat from the single front window. The woman, her face streaked with mud, her hair and dress half burned away, her eyes white and wild, her face as red as my best dress, shrieked and pointed. "My sister! She's inside! Anna Marie!"

As one, we turned towards the bakery. People were running in all directions, some coming to help or watch the excitement, others running away. Horses screamed with panic, and one pathetically scrawny wretch made a run for it, his owner hanging half out of the cart, sawing at the reins. A shouting Mountie tried to organize men to ferry buckets of water from the river.

I stepped off the duckboard.

Sam Collins knocked me to one side. I kept myself from falling face first into the mud only by reaching out with my left wrist before my knees hit the ground. Pain shot up my arm, my legs buckled, and I screamed. From all sides, men rushed to offer me assistance. Cursing and swearing, I pushed them out of the way and struggled to my feet. Mud clung to my dress, trying to pull me back down.

I couldn't see Sam.

"Richard!" I stumbled through the mud and the press of onlookers to reach Sterling's side. He held the bakery woman around the waist as she fought against him. Her eyes were fixed on her store, collapsing in front of her, and she screamed her sister's name, over and over: Anna Marie, Anna Marie. Sterling told her that the doctor was on his way.

I grabbed at his sleeve, my muddy fingers slipping on the filth caking his uniform. "Richard, you have to do something. Sam's gone in there."

He stared into my face. "Gone where? What are you talking about, Fiona?" The woman took advantage of his distraction and pulled one arm free.

I nodded towards the bakery, now nothing but a wall of flame.

Sterling gripped the struggling woman harder, his face a mask of indecision and so easy to read: If he let go of her and went to help Sam, this desperate woman would run into the flames to save her sister.

It took us a moment to realize that the crowd was cheering. Loud, raucous, happy cheers. I rubbed mud and smoke out of my eyes, using my right hand. My left didn't seem to want to do much of anything.

Flames lit up the building in an extravaganza of red and yellow outlining Sam as he emerged from the waffle and coffee shop, staggering under the weight of the woman in his arms. Sweat ran down his face, carving deep rivers into the soot and dust filling the crevices of his skin. His thick, bushy eyebrows and the edges of his long grey hair were singed. He stumbled onto the street and looked blindly around, eyes weeping from the smoke. The woman's clothing was intact, and her lashes flickered across her soot-stained cheeks. Her lips formed the words "thank you". Men moved forward to take the burden from Sam's arms. Someone slapped him on the back, and he yelped in pain.

At least that's what I later read in the *Nugget*, as written by the only newspaperman on the scene, Jack Ireland. I was too busy concentrating on the pain in my hand and trying to keep my footing as Richard Sterling shoved the burned woman at me and went to help the men fighting the fire.

The doctor pushed his way through the crowd, panting with the effort of running all of a hundred yards. He spent more time seeing to my sprained wrist than even I thought seemly while his young assistant attended to the burn victim, the smoke-stricken sister and the heroic rescuer.

I was dimly aware of men passing buckets of water back and forth. Fortunately, the bakery was one of the few buildings in this row that stood on its own, meaning there were a few inches of space between itself and its neighbours. One wall of the shack to the left, which advertised cigars and liquors, caught fire, but by the time I freed myself from the doctor's attentions, pried Sam Collins away from his crowd of admirers, and we staggered back towards the Savoy, the fire had been brought under control.

I was momentarily blinded by a flash of light in front of my face. I blinked to see the large black box of a camera.

A photographer: how lovely.

For the second time that day, Sam Collins pushed me to one side. He ripped the equipment out of the photographer's hands. I grabbed Sam's arm and stopped him from throwing the camera to the ground.

"Let go, Sam."

Sheepishly he handed the black box back to its owner.

"Wonderful rescue. They'll be eating out of your hands in the U. S. of A., old boy." Jack Ireland barred the way into the Savoy, notebook and pencil in hand. "If you'll say a few words for our readers. What went through your mind as you rushed into that inferno of a building?"

The photographer arranged his equipment in preparation for another shot, and I twisted my head away. There is not much I love in this world more than having my photograph taken, but not when I resemble a camp follower.

Sam looked up; his face was covered with soot, but his eyes blazed with all the strength of the inferno that had so recently devoured the bakery. "You bastard," he mumbled at Ireland, so softly that no one but the San Francisco reporter and I heard him.

Ireland stepped back, at a loss for words. His mouth flapped, the camera belched light and smoke, and Sam went into the Savoy.

I followed. Despite all the excitement out on the street, several men remained at the bar, glasses in hand, and I could hear the roulette wheel spin and the croupier call out, "No more bets." The whole town might burn down around them, but there were men who'd keep drinking and gambling until the whisky bottles exploded and the tables dissolved into ashes.

Ray had kept his place behind the bar. The new bartender, I really should learn his name, strained to see out the door, and I guessed Ray had told him that if he left his post, he needn't bother coming back. My partner took one look at Sam and me and poured two glasses of whisky, from the best bottle, almost to the rim.

My mud-encrusted hand shook as I grabbed the glass. My left hand hurt. I might later regret pushing the overly attentive doctor aside. The liquor burned all the way down my throat. At last my head stopped spinning, my heart began to settle back into its regular rhythm, and I could think reasonably clearly once again.

"Sam," I said, "you need the doctor."

He shook his head and put his empty glass on the counter. Ray filled it. "I'm fine, Mrs. MacGillivray."

"I'll pay," I said, ignoring Ray's stare of disbelief. "Let the doctor have a look at you."

Men were spilling into the bar, roaring with excitement, shouting Sam's name. The story of his heroism was already growing in the telling. His hair and eyebrows were singed, and his eyes were red and full of water, but the skin on his face was still a healthy pink. I turned him around. His shirt was scorched across the shoulders, falling into tatters. "If you won't see the doctor, you should at least get out of the way. You don't want anyone touching that back."

Sam joined Ray behind the bar. Ray grinned. "Good work, Sam."

I jerked my head at a fresh-faced young man sitting in a chair near the bar. He scrambled out of it, and I climbed up, using my hand to keep my skirts tucked flat against my legs. Not a difficult feat: my clothes were so mud-soaked, it would have been an effort to lift the skirts high enough to display anything unseemly. I looked down at the crowd. Every eye watched me, hoping for a miracle. Ray's face was carved into lines of worry, concerned as to what I was about to say.

"Drinks are on the house," I shouted. "For the next five minutes. In honour of Sam Collins, hero of the Klondike."

The men howled.

Ray lifted his hands to his face.

The crowd surged towards the bar, and men ran out of the gambling hall. Eager hands helped me down from the chair.

The men closer to the door fell silent, and a path opened up, like the Red Sea before Moses. Instead of the people of Israel, Margaret Collins, Sam's wife, and Angus MacGillivray walked into the saloon. Margaret was close to being the oldest woman in Dawson. At this moment she looked every one of her years and a good deal more besides. Her thick grey hair tumbled out of its pins, her face was as white as the snow on the mountaintops in

January, and her eyes were full of fear. You could draw a map of Europe in the lines carved through the dry skin of her cheeks. She stumbled and leaned against my son, who was supporting her with one arm around her shoulders.

When she saw Sam behind the counter, the light flooded back into her eyes. "Oh, Sam," she whispered. It was the only sound in the room. A few eager customers took advantage of the lull to push their way forward, but most of the men stood back respectfully. Many doffed their hats.

"I'm all right, old gal," Sam said.

Margaret sagged, and Sam came around the bar to take her from Angus.

"Take him home, Margaret," I said in a low voice. "We'll manage without him tonight. If he needs to see the doctor, which he should, I'll pay."

"Thank you, Mrs. MacGillivray," Margaret Collins said, lifting her head straight. "We can afford the doctor." Her diction was, as always, perfect.

Light flashed in my eyes once again. When I could see properly, Sam had pushed Margaret aside. His fists were clenched and his face red, not from fire, but from anger. Jack Ireland was scribbling in his notebook. Sam grabbed the book out of the reporter's hands. The photographer, a local man (which in Dawson meant he arrived before the-day-before-yesterday), stepped back, using his body to shield the valuable camera.

"What the hell's the matter with you, old man?" Ireland shouted. "Never mind Dawson, I'll make you famous down the entire west coast of the United States. They'll be singing songs about you before I'm finished." He snatched his notebook back. "Is this your lovely wife? Pleased to meet you, ma'am. Can you tell my readers how it feels to have a hero for a husband?"

Margaret dipped her head slightly and smiled, but Sam only got angrier. "Don't you dare speak to my wife, you bastard." He grabbed at the notebook once more, but Ireland stuffed it into his pocket.

"I can make you famous, you fool."

I didn't much care for Jack Ireland, but he did seem only to be doing his job. "Mr. Ireland, Sam and Mrs. Collins need some time to reflect on all that's happened here. If you'll excuse them, I'm sure they'll grant you an interview tomorrow."

Sam started to say something. Judging by the look on his face, it wouldn't have been terribly polite.

I raised my voice. "There's only four minutes remaining of an open bar! Gentlemen, please allow our distinguished reporter from San Francisco and his friend with the camera to go first. There's enough for everyone!"

The men roared and surged forward.

Sam and Margaret headed for the door, clinging to each other. My heart lifted as I watched them go, and for the briefest moment I wondered if I would ever find someone to care for, and who would care for me, in my old age.

I grabbed my son's arm and pulled him out of the crowd to the side of the room. I held him close. He stiffened at first, worried about what a roomful of cheechakos and sourdoughs might think to see a man being hugged by his mother, but then his lanky frame relaxed and he settled into my arms like the twelve-year-old boy he was.

"Gee, Ma, Mother I mean, when I heard about the fire, I was worried. They said all Front Street was in flames."

"They say a lot of things, Angus. But it *was* terrifying for a while."

"They said Mr. Collins saved the life of the woman who works at the bakery." He looked at me, taking in the untamed hair, the muddy dress, the way I protected my left arm. "Did you help him, Mother?"

"Me? I didn't do anything, I'm afraid. Save fall in the mud and make a dreadful mess." I tucked a length of dangling hair behind my ear and realized that I'd lost my hat. "But what they say about Sam, that part is true. It was the most amazing thing, Angus. While every one of us, except for Constable Sterling, stood around in shock, Sam rushed right into the burning shop and carried that woman out."

"Constable Sterling?" My son's lovely blue eyes were wide. "What did he do?"

"Angus, I have to go home and wash and get out of this dress. I do hope it isn't ruined. And my hand hurts something awful. You didn't see my hat anywhere, did you, dear?"

"Nope. Do you need to see the doctor, Mother?"

"Not unless it gets worse. When we get home, I'll rip up one of my old petticoats to make a sling. That should help." It would also look quite fetching; I might recover most of what we lost in free drinks, if not more, should I look suitably heroic and ever-so-slightly-incapacitated. I'd avoid rouge and put on an extra bit of white face powder, take the colour out of my cheeks, before coming back.

"Time's up," Ray shouted. "Free bar's closed."

The men groaned good-naturedly; everyone had received at least one free drink. Definitely a record in my place. I'd better get some control over my generosity: it seemed to be spreading.

It was getting late. I'd be hard-pressed to get home, clean up, tend to my wrist, eat supper, change, and be back in time to supervise the opening of the dance hall at eight. Ray was busy behind the bar with one man short. Too bad Angus couldn't help out. But if he were caught working in the Savoy, we'd be closed down in a heartbeat.

Cursed NWMP.

I watched Angus heading for the door. Before he could get there, he was stopped by Jack Ireland, reporter's notebook back in hand. I considered intervening, telling my son to be on his way, but what harm could it do? Ireland was just doing his job, and Angus would love to be quoted in the newspaper.

Chapter Nine

"You're a right mess, Mrs. MacGillivray."

"Thank you for pointing that out, Chloe. I hadn't noticed."

She flushed. She was a cheap piece of flotsam, Chloe, washed up on the shores of the Klondike like so much garbage. I didn't like her one bit, and she certainly didn't like me. So scrawny that she resembled one of the wretched nags pulling overloaded wagons down Front Street, with protruding front teeth and a complexion the colour of snow after a pack of dogs had passed over it, she didn't even make me much money. At the end of the night, you could be sure Chloe would have collected the fewest discs of all the girls. But for some reason unknown to me, the most-popular dance-hall girl in Dawson, my own Irene, the Lady Irenee, was fond of her. So Chloe stayed on because Irene liked having her around.

"We heard all about the fire." Irene's voice was low and husky. "Was it real bad?" She clutched one fist to her heart. Irene, now, was pretty. In London and Toronto, they would have called her fat, but in the Klondike, where even the dance hall girls had clawed their way over the Chilkoot Pass, Irene was lushly perfect. Her cheeks were deeply scratched with the memory of ice-cold winds, but her chubby frame reminded men of well-fed wives and mothers and hearty farmhouse suppers by a blazing fire. She was well into her thirties but possessed so much flirtatious, wild energy that all the men in Dawson loved her. I'd snapped her up the moment she'd arrived in town which turned out to be the best business move I'd made since arriving in Dawson and purchasing the shack that became the Savoy. The miners loved her. Almost as much as they loved me.

But they couldn't dance with me.

"It was bad," I said in answer to the girls' questions about the fire. "Fortunately, they put it out before it could spread any further."

"Folks are saying Sam saved her." Cheerful, simple-minded Ruby whispered from her usual place behind Irene. Ruby was as shy as a convent schoolgirl during the day, but when she put a foot on the stage, she turned as bold and teasing as the east-end whores I'd known in my early days in London. But for Ruby, teasing was as far as it went. Otherwise she'd be on the street with her posterior in the mud as quickly as I'd found myself this afternoon. Any girl earning outside income, wouldn't be allowed back. Not that I cared one whit what they did in their own time, but my business had a reputation to maintain.

"And so Sam did. It was most exciting." I was still in awe of what had happened this afternoon and how Sam had acted while the rest of us stood and stared like befuddled fools. I've heard it said that still waters run deep. Made me wonder what sort of man Sam had been in his younger days. "Hadn't you ladies best be getting ready?"

They moved off in a bustle of giggles and cheap fabric and heavy scent. Only Irene remained behind.

"Is Sam gonna be all right?" she asked, her eyes wide with worry. The eyes were Irene's best feature. When she fastened them on her dance partner, the poor chap thought he was the only man in the world.

"He's gone home with Margaret. She'll look after him."

Irene smiled. "I like Sam."

"So do I. We've got a full house tonight. News of the fire seems to have brought every layabout and nancy boy in town to the Savoy."

The girls had come in as my son was leaving. They'd tossed their curls, fluttered their painted eyelashes, swished their skirts, and good-naturedly called out his name.

Angus's ears had burned red.

I'd decided that I didn't have time to go home and change, so once Angus had finished talking to Ireland, I'd sent him to ask Mrs. Mann for the remnants of an old white petticoat that I could rip up to hold my wrist tight.

He stared at me, shocked, but not at the thought of sorting through my undergarments. We'd spent weeks on the Chilkoot trail together: at his young age, Angus knew more about women than his schoolmates back in Toronto would in their lifetimes. "Mother, you can't continue to wear that dress. It's filthy."

"Dear heart," I said with a smile, "it will help to remind everyone of the near-tragic events that transpired today. Sam's not here to fuel their admiration. I'll have to do."

His face twisted up like a prune.

I hugged him once again. "Now give me a smile and do as you're told." I held my son at arm's length. The twisted prune of his mouth slackened ever so slightly. "And I'm hungry, so please ask Mrs. Mann to wrap up my food or make a sandwich out of it or something, will you?"

A small crowd gathered around Irene and me. The men's tongues were almost lolling to one side, as if they were lead dogs heading out into the winter wilderness on a NWMP patrol.

"I couldn't help overhearing your kind words, my dear lady." Jack Ireland bowed in front of Irene, so deeply he might have been at court. "We can all only hope that the Hero of Dawson finds the comfort he so deserves this night."

"And you, sir, are?" Irene asked.

"Permit me to introduce myself. Jack Ireland. *San Francisco Standard.* At your service."

"A newspaperman." Irene raised her expressive eyebrows.

I dipped my head towards the back, telling Irene to cut it short. She ignored me and fluttered her lashes at her prey. "Are you newly arrived in Dawson, Mr. Ireland?"

"I am, dear lady. Fortunately, I was here in time to capture in picture and word the exceptional heroics of your friend, Mr. Collins."

"In picture?" Now she didn't have to force her eyes to open wide: they managed that feat all by themselves.

"I've been fortunate enough to obtain the services of a photographer."

"A photographer." Her bosom heaved, and the froth of many-times-repaired lace at the neck of her blue gown quivered.

"I'm anxious to obtain some background information about Dawson and its people." Ireland took Irene's arm. "Perhaps you can help with my research."

Ray pushed the onlookers aside. "Can I walk ye to the dressing room, Irene?" he asked.

She looked at Jack Ireland. Well dressed, well-spoken, sophisticated. A newspaperman. She looked at Ray Walker. A Dawson barman. Scraggy, skinny, with an accent so sharp she sometimes couldn't understand a word he said.

"Thanks, Mr. Walker. But Mr. Ireland here's offered. Haven't you, Mr. Ireland?"

"It would be my pleasure." The American tossed my partner a look of such superiority that I wanted to slap him. Ray's face closed as tightly as the shutters on the windows of Mr. Eaton's Toronto store on a Sunday afternoon.

Ray and I watched Ireland guide Irene through the crowd. She clung to his arm as if she couldn't possibly navigate the route without his help.

"Don't worry about it," I said to Ray. "She'll empty his pockets, and then he'll be gone."

My partner glared at me. "For God's sake, Fiona, change that dress. Ye look like me uncle Cameron after a night sleeping the drink off in the gutter 'cause he's afraid to face me granny."

He went back to the bar, elbowing a drunk aside who dared to step into his path. Someone shouted in the gambling hall, whether because he was winning or losing, impossible to say. It was almost eight o'clock, time for the dance hall to open. My wrist hurt, and I stamped my foot in frustration. Where was my son with my supper and my ripped up petticoat?

As if mentally summoned, Angus arrived, clutching a bundle to his chest. Close on his heels came Constable Richard Sterling.

Angus handed me the package, and I accepted it with one hand. It was still warm.

"Good evening, Constable," I said.

"Mrs. MacGillivray." He'd changed into a fresh uniform, shiny buttons done up to the neck, a clean hat straight on his head, every wild curl forced into submission. "If your arm's bothering you, perhaps you should see the doctor."

"No need, Constable. I'll be fine. If you'll excuse me, my son's brought my dinner."

Graham Donohue was next though the doors. He laughed heartily as he walked through the room, slapping men on the back in greeting.

"Nice dress, Fiona." He looked me up and down. "Is that the latest fashion in Europe?"

"Oh, shut up," I said.

"I hear there was some excitement out on Front Street earlier."

"Sam Collins saved the Vanderhaege sisters," Angus told him, delighting in being the spreader of good news. "Mother helped him."

Graham looked at me, his head cocked to one side in disbelief.

"I didn't help matters in the slightest. You missed a great story."

"Luck of the job. I've been hearing about it all over town, came in to see if Sam's here. All of Dawson's talking about him."

"Constable Sterling was a hero, too," Angus said. "He saved Miss Vanderhaege. The older one."

"A hero also," I corrected.

"That's what I said."

"Never mind."

Graham looked at Sterling. "So I've heard. Well done, Constable. I suppose they'll give you a medal. Or something."

"All in the line of duty, Donohue. Not something you'd

know much about. Angus, if you've given your mother her things, get out of here. If you'll excuse me, Mrs. MacGillivray." He turned and was swallowed up by the crowd. Men clutching drinks in hands filled the space he'd vacated.

"I gave Sam the rest of the day off," I said as one skinny young fellow trod on my foot. I threw him my most ferocious glare, and he retreated into the safety of the pack.

"That was kind of you," Graham said. "Must be a first. No, I'm wrong—that was Helen. You'll be applying for sainthood soon enough, Fee."

"If you'll excuse me…"

"How are the Misses Vanderhaege doing, Mr. Donohue?" Angus asked. "Have you heard?"

"I've just come from the infirmary. The doctor says they'll both be fine. Anna Marie is suffering from smoke in her lungs, and Anike has burns on her back and legs, but they'll heal. We're lucky the whole street didn't go up in flames and take the town with it."

I shrugged. "Too darn wet." The package was cooling in my hands. Bread by the smell of it, and fresh. "I want to eat and tidy up. Angus, tell Ray I'll be down shortly and then go home."

"Yes, Ma."

I spun on my heels. "What did you say?"

"Yes, Mother."

"That's better."

Chapter Ten

Angus made his way towards the bar. Richard Sterling was standing with his back to the wall, underneath a painting of a lady wearing nothing but stockings and a bonnet, watching the men. Ray was behind the bar; his hands never stopped moving, but his eyes remained focused on the door leading to the gambling room, and the dance hall beyond. Something was bothering the little Scotsman: not hard to guess what. Everyone in town knew that Ray carried a torch taller than himself for Irene. The Savoy was busy tonight, and with Sam Collins off and Ray distracted, the two newer bartenders were having trouble keeping up.

Angus looked back to see his mother carrying her parcel to the stairs leading to the second floor, moving slowly under the weight of her mud-encrusted skirts. Only once, as she reached out to grab the banister without thinking about it, did her composure slip and her face twist in pain.

Graham Donohue slapped Angus on the back, and they walked towards the bar together. A man sporting a tangled grey beard so long that it almost touched his belt offered to buy the boy a drink. Angus's ears flushed, but the miner winked at the watching policeman.

"I'll take you up on that offer, George," Donohue said with a laugh.

"Be a frosty day in hell before I buy you a drink, Graham Donohue. Which reminds me, I hear you got beat out by the newcomer."

Donohue stopped smiling. "What newcomer might that be?"

"American fellow. Name of England or France, some foreign country."

"Ireland?"

"Yeah, that's the one," the miner said, enjoying himself enormously. He ran one dirty finger over the rim of his glass. "He was here when it all happened, weren't he, Angus? With a fellow taking pictures and all. Interviewed old Sam Collins right on the spot. Ain't that so, Angus?"

Angus nodded. "He took a picture of Ma, too. She wasn't at all pleased, not with mud on her face and her hair in a mess."

"Your ma'd be the most beautiful woman in Dawson even if she'd been swimmin' in mud, son." The miner sighed.

Donohue's face was turning red, and the veins in his neck had suddenly doubled in size. "Are you telling me that bastard, Ireland, had a photographer out in the street when the bakery was burning?" The words came out as an angry hiss, spoken through clenched teeth.

"Watch your language, Donohue," Sterling warned. "Boy here."

The miner tugged at his beard. He grinned, showing a mouth empty of teeth. "Guess that's what I'm sayin', all right."

Donohue shoved the man aside and pushed his way to the bar. Angus steadied the miner, who was now chuckling heartily. "That got under his skin right enough." The old man downed his drink. A few drops spilled out of the corner of his mouth and disappeared into the bushy beard.

"I don't think you should've told Mr. Donohue that, sir," Angus said. "He looks real mad."

The miner wiped the back of his hand across his mouth. "Stir the pot and see what rises to the top, lad. Best fun to be had in this miserable town." He went to the bar, still chuckling.

"Great fun for some," Sterling muttered so that only Angus could hear. "But it makes work for the Mounties. Have you got some reason to be hanging around?"

"My ma gave me a message for Mr. Walker, sir."

"Deliver your message and get out of here. Or I'll have to take you in."

Angus grinned, the prospect of a night in jail speaking more of adventure than hardship.

Sterling smiled back. "Hurry up, son."

Generally, the men who'd come through so much and travelled so far from home looked fondly on the few children in town. They slapped Angus's back and tried to talk to him about their own family. He was too polite to push them aside. When he stopped for a second time to look at the photographs that a young cheechako had pulled out of his jacket pocket, Sterling yelled, "Angus, deliver your message and go home!"

Angus bolted, and the would-be prospector stuffed the photographs back into his pocket as if they were about to be confiscated and used as evidence.

"Ma's gone upstairs, Mr. Walker, to clean up. She'll be back real soon." Angus shouted across the last few yards to the bar as he dashed for the door.

"Hold up, just a minute, Angus," Sterling said. He caught up with the boy out on the boardwalk. The traffic streaming up and down Front Street was heavy. Horses and carts struggled through the mud; women crossed the street on the duckboards, lifting their skirts in an attempt to keep them clean. A few doors down, the building that had once been a bakery was a blackened shell. "I spoke to Sergeant Lancaster this afternoon."

"The boxing champion?"

"The very one."

"What did he say? Will he teach me?"

"He'd like to meet you. Then he'll decide."

"Can we go now?"

"No, I'm on duty. Tomorrow's Saturday. How would that do? Saturday morning."

"That would do fine, sir."

"Good. Come to Fort Herchmer at eight. You can meet Lancaster then."

"We have to keep this a secret from Ma, right?"

"I won't lie to her, Angus. If she asks me what's going on, I'll tell her."

"I guess."

"But if she doesn't ask, then there's no need to bother her, now is there?"

"No, sir!"

"See you tomorrow at eight."

Angus walked down the boardwalk, almost skipping. He passed a young woman, dressed in a well-worn and heavily stained calico dress, topped by a limp hat, which looked as if a dog had enjoyed an afternoon romp with it. Angus touched his cloth cap politely and skipped happily on his way.

Boxing lessons. Time to become a man.

The door to the Savoy burst open, and the house musicians spilled out into the street. There were four of them to provide the music in the dance hall for the rest of the night and long into the early hours of the morning. One man tucked a violin under his chin, another picked up his clarinet, and the trombonist put his instrument to his mouth. The caller, who normally played the piano, took up his bullhorn and announced to all that the Savoy, "the finest establishment west of London, England", was open for their entertainment. As the caller shouted out the wonders to be found inside, the orchestra played "Hot Time in the Old Town Tonight" loudly, and none too well. All along the street, musicians and callers were setting themselves up to advertise the pleasures to be found inside their own dancehalls. It made quite a racket, not at all what Richard Sterling's mother would have called a "joyful noise", although it was joy, to be bought and paid for, that they were advertising.

Eight o'clock on a Friday evening in Dawson, Yukon Territory. The dance halls were open for business.

Chapter Eleven

"He lose much?" Sterling asked.

"'Bout five thousand," Jake said, his face showing not a glimmer of emotion as he gathered up chips. "Fellow's been in here since opening. That last bet musta wiped him out." Jake was nattily dressed in a stiff white wing-tip collar, a colourful silk neck piece and sharp bowler hat. His enormous black moustache curled up at the edges. Turning his attention back to the job, he spun the big wheel. "No more bets."

"What a fool," Sterling mumbled. But he wasn't surprised. He'd seen as much, more, lost and won in one hand of poker or one throw of the dice.

The dim space of the gambling room always reminded Sterling of the shack of a church his father had preached in all the years of his childhood. The walls were cheap wood, the floorboards no better, the kerosene lamps much too dim. Men crowded into the room as eager to make their fortune at the tables as Reverend Sterling had been to save the souls of his flock. The results would be the same—disappointment and despair.

The smoke in the poorly ventilated room was so thick, it was difficult to see the far side of the room, where a serious poker game was underway. Mouse O'Brien sat at the table: the game would be nothing but serious. O'Brien was a giant of a man, not much off seven feet tall, with a chest the size of that of an ox, and shoulders and thighs to match. He kept his hair cut short and his moustache neatly trimmed and wore custom-made suits, starched white shirts, and a diamond stick pin in his perfectly folded cravat. He always carried a bag containing a pair of spare shoes to put on in place of his muddy boots whenever he walked through any door. He was called "Mouse", a nickname he accepted with good grace—recognizing that he had no choice in the matter—ever since he'd been heard to squeal, as loudly as a pigtailed schoolgirl, when a tiny brown field mouse had crossed his path on the trail to Bonanza Creek.

Stacked in neat rows on the green-baize table in front of Mouse was a pile of chips. His big hands dwarfed the cards he held, and the only man left in the game, of the table of four, sweated heavily. Johnny Jones, who had more money than skill. Or nerve. Sterling stood behind Jones. The dealer's eyes flickered, but he said nothing.

Jones had a good hand—three tens. Good but not great. He pulled a handkerchief out of his pocket and wiped his brow. Mouse looked up from his cards and spoke to one of the men watching. "Get me a drink, will you, friend. I can't leave the table right now. I'll make it worth your while."

Jones folded. The edges of Mouse's lips turned up as he raked in the pot. Sterling would have bet a month's wages that the big man's hand had been garbage.

"I'm finished." Jones got up from the table, moving heavily. "Holy Christ, I'm wiped out."

"Language, Johnny," Sterling cautioned.

Jones threw him an ugly look. Sterling braced for a confrontation. It wouldn't be the first time a heavy loser had looked for someone on whom to take out his anger.

"Good game, Mr. Jones," Mouse said, as he checked his gold pocket watch. "Thank you for the sport, and let me offer you this." Mouse held a small gold nugget between his fingers. "Get yourself in another game." Jones considered the offer, pride struggling with greed. He snatched the gold and headed for the faro table.

"That wasn't necessary, Mouse," Sterling said. "He wouldn't have taken me on."

Mouse shrugged his shoulders, like glacier ice shifting on

the mountains. "Boy can't play worth a damn…doggone… but he can't give it up either. A man's gotta feel sorry for him. Game's over, boys. Time for my favourite lady to give me a song." The giant gathered up his winnings and lumbered into the dance hall.

Sterling followed as Ruby's thin, quaking voice struggled to the end of its song.

Like all the dance halls in Dawson, the one in the Savoy was considerably less than advertised. The tiny stage had been roughly carved out of green wood by workers who didn't know or care what they were doing, and in a big hurry to get it done and move on to the next job. There were no windows, and the kerosene lamps smoked badly, but no one ever complained. Complaining in Dawson never got a man any further than out the door.

Flags—crossed Union Jacks and Stars and Stripes—had been draped above the stage and used to decorate the private boxes on the second story. Below the boxes, rows of uncomfortable benches, filled with cheering, stomping miners, surrounded the stage in a horseshoe pattern. The room was tightly packed with sweating bodies and clothes gone too long without a wash; cheap lamp oil and dancers' cologne mingled with the generously applied scent of the toffs and the stink of the labourers. Over it all lay the smell of male anticipation and scarcely restrained excitement.

Ruby's voice was nothing short of terrible, and the song she sang sickeningly sentimental, but some of the older men wiped away a tear or two as she dragged out the last, painful note.

The audience applauded wildly as Ruby curtsied, allowing the front of her low cut gown to hang temptingly open, and departed the stage. The men shifted in their chairs, sat just a bit straighter and whispered to their neighbours. Fiona MacGillivray stood at the back of the room, close to the wall. She had wiped most of the mud off her dress and her arm was bound in a sling of purest white cotton. Her thick black hair was pinned into a storm cloud behind her head, but stray tendrils caressed her temple and the back of her neck. Her dark eyes never stopped moving across the room.

Ray Walker stood beside Fiona, but unlike hers, his eyes were still, fixed directly on the stage. He could afford to take a break: at the climax of the stage show, the bar would be quiet for a few minutes.

A hush fell over the shabby room, lasting only as long as it took for a heart to give one beat. The orchestra held their instruments still, and the audience—grizzled old miners, tender-footed gold-seekers, hard-hearted gamblers, ruthless businessmen, Indian fighters with nowhere left to go, and one Scottish bartender—held their collective breath.

Irene stepped out from behind the curtain. Her gown, trimmed with fake jewels and sequins and tattered feathers, wouldn't stand a close look, but no one was close enough, or concerned enough, to give it a thorough inspection. She held her arms out in front of her and began to sing. Her voice sounded rich and pure, and she sang the song from the depths of her heart while the orchestra struggled to keep up. Light from the kerosene lamps flickered across her face and cast her sharp cheekbones into high relief. Grizzled old miners listened to her with their hands held to their hearts and tears falling down their faces into their beards. Mouse O'Brien held a snowy white handkerchief to his eyes.

Irene's song finished, and she curtsied to the audience as softy as an ostrich feather drifting to the floor. The men went wild, cheering and stomping their feet. Gold nuggets flew through the air. Irene gathered them up with a gracious smile, her eyes judging the worth of every one as she did so.

"Gentleman." The caller crossed the stage once Irene had gathered her loot and departed. "Time to take your partners for a long, dreamy, juicy waltz."

The benches were pushed to the sides of the room and men rushed forward, clutching the tickets that they'd bought for one dollar each. They thrust their ticket at a girl, the orchestra struck up, and the lucky men took their partner through a few hurried dance steps. Exactly one minute later, the music stopped, mid-note, as the one-dollar dance came to an end. The girls dragged their man off to the bar so he could have the opportunity to buy a drink, whether he wanted one or not. The bartender then handed the girl a disk that she'd trade at the end of the night for her twenty-five cent share of the profits. The girls stuck their disks into the top of their stockings. This would carry on until six o'clock in the morning. By then, the more popular girls could scarcely walk for the weight encumbering their legs.

When Irene stepped onto the dance floor, her smile bright and her arms held out to her sides in invitation, a rush of men threatened to sweep her away.

"Gentlemen, gentlemen, please." Fiona moved graciously through the crowd. "Behave yourselves. The night has only just begun. There's plenty of time for everyone to enjoy a dance."

Respectfully, the men stood back. Too bad, Sterling thought, women couldn't join the NWMP: with Fiona MacGillivray on the force, no one would dare to put a foot out of place. He pushed aside the picture of thick black hair tucked into the pointed hat and lush curves straining the seams of the red coat.

Irene favoured Jack Ireland with a gracious nod and a flirtatious smile. The reporter slipped his arms around his prize's ample form. She touched the back of his shoulders, and they moved into the dance.

Ray Walker growled low in his throat.

"Hadn't you better be getting back to the bar, Ray?" Fiona glared at him.

Graham Donohue planted himself directly in front of the dancing couple.

Ireland shifted Irene to guide her around the obstacle. Donohue stepped with them. They might have been a dancing trio. Ireland stopped. Irene twisted her head to see what was going on behind her. Fiona crossed the floor, pushing men and dance hall girls out of her way. One by one the couples on the floor drifted to a halt. The orchestra, knowing that no one was paying them any attention, stopped playing.

"If you'll excuse us, partner," Ireland said, his common man accent back in place. "Lady Irenee and me are havin' ourselves a dance."

"You're in my territory, Ireland." Donohue's words were slurred. He leaned forward, trying to loom over the fractionally shorter older man. Ireland laughed without mirth and turned to Irene. "Fellow needs to learn that a newspaperman ain't got a territory. In our business, it's winner take all." His eyes dropped to the scooped neck of Irene's dress, leaving the onlookers in no doubt as to what the winner of this contest intended to claim.

Irene giggled, wiggled her hips, and attempted to flutter her stubby eyelashes.

An old-timer guffawed. "Ain't that the truth, boy. And not just in the newspaper business, either."

Ireland extended his arms to his dance partner.

Donohue took a swing at him.

He was an experienced fighter, had at least twenty years advantage, maybe more, on the reporter from San Francisco, and Ireland's attention was distracted for the moment by the simpering Irene. But drink slowed Donohue down. Ireland saw the blow coming and, given a chance to play for the audience, pushed Irene out of the way, although she was in absolutely no danger, before pulling his head to one side so that the punch glanced off his cheek.

Irene staggered into the arms of a gambler who always dressed as if he were about to do immediate battle against the Plains Indians. Graham swung to deliver another, more accurate punch.

The room erupted.

"Twenty dollars on the old fellow," someone yelled from deep inside the crowd of observers.

Coins, bills, nuggets and bags of gold dust flashed in answer. Men rushed in from the bar and the gambling hall to join the fun. They jostled for position, both to watch the fight and to lay bets.

Fiona MacGillivray pushed men out of the way and screamed directly into Donohue's face in a most unladylike manner, spittle flying everywhere. "You're banned, Graham. Out of here. Now!"

Ray Walker tried to force his way through the press of men and women to reach Irene. She smiled up at the man who'd caught her, realized that all eyes were on her and, with a light moan, sank into a swoon. Holding the fainting beauty in his arms, the lucky man called for brandy, room to breathe, and a doctor. He attempted to drag Irene out of the crush to safety, but not ready to leave the centre of attention quite yet, she smiled up at him, and with another moan and a shudder, which had all the men leaning forward, she courageously attempted to gather her strength.

"Ray," Fiona said sharply, her eyes cold and dark. "Forget Irene and get Graham out of here." Walker looked at Irene, and he looked at his business partner. Indecision tore at his life-battered face.

Sterling grabbed Graham's wrist. "You're under arrest, Mr. Donohue."

"What?" Graham spat, twisting in the constable's professional grip. "That goddamned bastard comes into my town, and you arrest me. What the hell for?"

"For the use of vile language, for one thing," Sterling said. "But mainly for attacking a man thirty years older than you with no provocation in the full sight of a hundred men and several ladies."

"Well, not quite thirty," Ireland said, straightening his tie and smiling at the people around him. "There, there, fellow. Allow me to help the lady." He eased Irene away from Ray, who had taken her from her rescuer. "My dear, shall we finish our dance?"

Donohue spluttered; Walker looked as if he were about to take a swing at Ireland himself.

"Ray," Fiona snapped. "There'll be a rush on the bar any minute now. You'd best get in there. And if you lot don't start playing," she shouted to the orchestra, "I'll dock your pay. Dances begin again. One minute, starting now." For a woman of such delicate, gently-brought-up appearance, Fiona MacGillivray could put on a voice like a sailor in the British Navy when she had a mind to. The orchestra launched directly into the middle of their tune, and the men grabbed their partners. At least forty seconds of dancing before the trouble started, then a minute or two spent standing with their girl, arm about waist if lucky, and another minute of dancing. For some of these men, who'd abandoned all in pursuit of gold, this was the only bit of good fortune they'd had in months. Ray Walker returned to his bar with a grumble, a nasty glance at Fiona, a longing look at Irene, and an angry grimace at Ireland. Sterling escorted Donohue out the door.

The man might have been drunk, and his protests were loud and effusive, but he knew better than to resist arrest.

"Fiona, Light of the Land of the Midnight Sun, you can't do this to me. Tell this fine, upstanding Man-of-the-Law to let me go."

Fiona walked with them to the door. "The next time you set foot in my place, Graham Donohue, be on your knees." Her black eyes burned like chips of coal consumed by a single red spark, deep inside. "You've cost me ten minutes of prime dancing time." She looked at Sterling. "Throw away the key." And with a toss of her head, which had the soft black tendrils that caressed her cheeks jumping, she plunged back into the crowd, encouraging men to go to the bar, to buy another dance ticket, maybe return to the tables for one more round of poker or spin of the roulette wheel.

Sterling relaxed his grip on his prisoner. "You've really messed this one up, Donohue. What came over you? Ireland's a fool and a popinjay, but you don't go picking a fight with every idiot in town. Didn't know you had a fancy for Irene."

"Irene." Donohue shrugged, straightening his rumpled coat. "Plenty like her around. But that Ireland, don't mistake him for a fool. Man's trouble no matter where he goes."

"You've met before?"

Donohue laughed, the sound cold and bitter. "You could say so. Lead the way to your finest cell, Constable." The ugly laugh died, and his voice broke. "They won't give me a blue ticket will they, Sterling? I'm counting on my stint in Dawson to make my reputation. Can't we just forget about it? Pal."

"Don't insult me with a question like that again, Donohue, or I *will* recommend you get a card." Sterling walked out into the strange half-night, confident that his prisoner would follow in his footsteps. A blue ticket was a serious matter, and the NWMP enforced the ban without mercy. They had no facilities, and no food, to care for a jail full of criminals, particularly through a long, desperate winter. Better all round to simply exile miscreants.

A girl who worked at one of the less reputable dance halls dashed by, giggling wildly, her red skirt and frothy white petticoats held almost up to her knees. A fat man in late middle age, well dressed in a severe dark suit topped by a stiff black hat, followed, trying to keep his footing in the mud and his eyes on his quarry at the same time. The girl tossed Sterling a cheerful wink, peered over her shoulder, squealed at the sight of her pursuer without the slightest alarm and lifted her petticoats higher. She was not wearing stockings, and her legs were thick and white. The man stumbled after her, struggling for breath.

The Vanderhaege sisters' bakery was a reproachful dark patch in this street of the midnight sun, of painted, colourful women laughing too loud, and men drunk, if not on liquor at least on possibilities. Overhead, the tattered advertising banners and competing national flags cracked in the night's stiff breeze.

"Tonight you'll spend in jail," Sterling said. "If you run into that Ireland fellow again, take my advice and keep well clear. This is your second offence, Donohue. Another one, and you will find yourself holding a blue ticket."

Chapter Twelve

The fight on the dance floor served to get the men in the mood: for the rest of the night they were like moose caught up in the rut. Fights kept breaking out all over. Ray stood behind the bar sulking until I wanted to give him a good punch myself. Most of the fights that threaten to break out in the Savoy I can disperse with a smile, a toss of the hair, flutter of the eyelashes, and the occasional firm, no-nonsense tone that reminds them of their mothers. But I am aware of the limits of my charm; I needed Ray behind me, and on this night he wasn't always there. He was too busy watching and scowling while Irene danced one dance after another with Ireland, plied him with drink, laughed at his jokes and gasped at his stories, while her stockings filled with his drink chips.

Hindsight is a wonderful thing—I should have banned Jack Ireland, not Graham Donohue. And I certainly should have advised Irene not to cozy up to Ireland.

But that was all in the future. On this Friday night, the girls were staggering with fatigue after a night spent dancing like wild jungle women with sweaty, unwashed, drunken miners, fancy boys and the odd true gentleman. Of course, I have no personal experience of jungle women, but I did once see an illustrated book when I was a child, sneaked out of the library of the big house, written by a famous African explorer. Mighty terrifying it was too, almost as terrifying as what would have happened to me if I'd been caught with it.

The bartenders drooped as they washed up their glasses. The orchestra played as if their instruments were filled with rocks and the strings made of cow intestines.

Almost time to close the dance hall then the bar and gambling tables.

Ray called last round, and men began to make their way to the door. A few of the newcomers complained, but once they were told that other places were still open, they didn't mind leaving quite so much. I wasn't completely scrupulous about shutting the place at six o'clock. If there was a good game going—meaning a big spender on a losing streak—Jake, my head croupier, had the option to keep the tables open as long as necessary to clean the sucker—I mean the customer—out.

But the dance hall closed at the drop of six, at which time the exhausted dancers lined up to cash in their chips. Then they were ready for nothing but their beds, with maybe a bite of breakfast first. The odd punter waited outside for his favourite to appear, but my girls generally didn't go in for after-hours entertaining. They left that for the cribs on Paradise Alley, which kept the demand for the dollar-a-minute dances nice and high.

Irene turned in her chips and joined Jack Ireland who was waiting for her, leaning against the wall under the cracked mirror. She slipped her hand through his arm with an expression I could only describe as greedy, and they walked towards the door in unison. Ray stepped out from behind the bar, where they were still busy finishing last call. Ray's face reminded me of a thundercloud Angus and I had seen from the comfort of our train as it passed across the vast, open Saskatchewan prairie.

There wasn't much Ray could do. Irene was obviously under no pressure to leave with Mr. San Francisco Standard. The Scotsman glared at them with an expression that turned his normally unattractive face into that of a gargoyle adorning the heights of a government building.

I linked Ray's arm through mine, still trying to protect my throbbing left wrist wrapped in its makeshift sling. "Rough night." He shrugged me off.

"Lovely evening." Jack Ireland grinned like the proverbial cat with the proverbial cream. Said cream, Irene, patted her hair and avoided my eyes. Ray growled, and I sensed another fight coming. If Ray hit one of the customers, the Mounties might close us down, or even give Ray a blue ticket. Fortunately, I was standing on his left, where my one working hand could reach. I took his little finger and folded it back towards the wrist. I smiled at Ireland. "Hard to believe it's morning already."

Ray tried to pull his hand away. My grip held. They'd taught us wild children a thing or two, and taught it well, in the grimy, hopeless alleys of the East End, where the stench of the Thames had found its way into my very dreams.

Ireland tightened his grip on Irene's waist, almost jerking her off her feet. "Goodnight, Mrs. MacGillivray."

"Goodnight, Mr. Ireland. Irene."

Ray's body stiffened even further. I maintained my hold on his finger. He could have broken my grip in a second, if he wanted to make a scene for the enjoyment of half the drinkers in Dawson.

The couple walked out into the dusky light of early morning. A horse and cart clattered by, the horse letting loose his day's supply of bodily waste, the back hooves tossing the filth in all directions. Irene whimpered as the muck splattered the skirt of her best coat. As if she hadn't been splattered with a good deal worse since arriving in Dawson. Ireland pretended to block her from the spray, long after all danger had passed. As far as I was concerned, they deserved each other.

I released my partner's little finger.

"Don't you ever do that to me again, Fee," Ray growled, genuinely angry.

One of the bigger gamblers staggered past. If I remembered properly, he'd lost a good deal of money at faro, one night after the other. "I hope to see you again tomorrow, sir," I said with my best smile.

He bowed deeply, and said, in a Boston Brahmin accent, "Always a pleasure, Mrs. MacGillivray. You have the best table in the Yukon, if not the entire of Western North America." Give me a willing loser any day. So much easier than the fools who expected to win at poker or find true love with a dance hall girl.

That thought, of course, brought me back to Irene and why Ray and I were standing on the step glaring at each other.

We watched as my best girl picked her way delicately across the boardwalk, hanging onto Jack Ireland's arm.

"Ray," I said, patting his hand. "She isn't worth the sweat on your brow." I never did have a talent for metaphor.

He looked at me. "Christ, Fiona. Will you just mind your own business for once? No one appointed you Queen of Dawson, last I heard."

Ray Walker was a good partner. His rough, communal Glasgow habits balanced my every-woman-for-herself East End and Belgravia Square instincts. I kept the punters and drinkers lining up for more, and Ray kept them in line. Together we'd turned the Savoy into the most profitable dance hall in Dawson, Yukon Territory.

I looked at my scrawny, rat-faced, angry partner, and I folded my pride into my petticoats. "Ray, sometimes I can't understand a word you're saying. And my family true Scots from long before the time of the Bonnie Prince himself. Sometime I'll tell you the story of how the MacGillivray clan stood shoulder to shoulder with the Prince at Culloden. Every last one of them. And how we lost everything in the Greatest of All Battles. Oh, it was a hard time, I'm tellin' ye. Why if the fight had gone t'other way, I might not be standin' here. I might be sitting warm and snug, a grand lady in me own castle in the heart of the Highlands. And wouldn't that be a sight?"

Ray cracked a smile. "I love you dearly, Fee. Time to close up."

As I watched him go, I thought about what I'd said. I hadn't even tried to put on the bad grammar and the accent. All I had to do was to think about my family: about the groundskeeper's cottage where we had lived, my father's fierce pride in our family's legacy, and the memories were back again.

Such a sweet little thing I had been.

Long ago.

Chapter Thirteen

I poured canned milk onto my porridge and eyed my son. Angus was being unusually vague about his plans for the day. Mrs. Mann, our landlady, fussed over him, as she always did. She was a wisp of a woman, with a mass of steel-grey hair scraped into a severe bun that weighed about as much as all the rest of her. Her accent was full of the memory of Germany, but she was justifiably proud of her English.

"I hear talk that a fellow's arrived in Dawson with a real cow, Mrs. MacGillivray," she said, ladling more porridge into Angus's bowl. "Imagine. Milk." Her tongue fondled the word as if she were dreaming of finding diamonds under her pillow. But she was thinking of something even greater than the Hope Diamond. For if she and I had learned one thing in the starvation winter of '97—'98, it was that nothing, not gold nor diamonds nor banknotes, nor even one's good name, mattered a damn when there was nothing to buy to eat.

"Wouldn't milk be nice, Angus?" I said.

He grinned around a mouthful of grey porridge. "It sure would. I don't even remember what fresh milk tastes like."

"Like sunshine falling on the farms of Bavaria," Mrs. Mann said, passing the sugar bowl.

"It would make a nice change. Buy some if you can. Never mind what it costs. I'll have real milk in my coffee tomorrow, and Angus can have a glass to drink, and we'll pour it over the porridge on Monday. Buy enough for yourselves as well. We had a profitable night last night."

Angus pushed aside his scraped-empty bowl and rose to

his feet. "Thanks for the breakfast, Mrs. Mann." The kitchen was so cramped, he had to squeeze by her to get to the back door. "Please excuse me, Mother." Something was up: his grammar was too perfect.

"Anything special happening today, Angus?" I asked.

"No, Mother. I thought I might go to the infirmary to check on Miss Vanderhaege." He twisted his shirtfront in his hands.

"Who?"

"Miss Vanderhaege? From the bakery?"

"Oh, right."

That the boy was lying, or at least not revealing the truth, was about as obvious as the fact that I wanted milk straight from a cow with no interference by factory nor can if I was ever to enjoy a cup of coffee again.

"Make sure you spend some time with that book of geography."

"Yes, Mother." He kissed me on the top of my head and said goodbye to Mrs. Mann. He took his coat from the peg and closed the door gently on the way out. Mrs. Mann's husband had built the tiny wooden house himself. The walls were thin, and the floorboards loose, so that one always knew exactly what everyone else in the house was doing at any time of the day or night. One morning I couldn't get to sleep and had lain awake listening to the Manns enjoying an intimate moment—a very long intimate moment—before they rose to begin the day.

At their age!

"Such a nice boy," my landlady said, gathering Angus's empty dishes. "But he doesn't tell the whole truth. Perhaps he visits a young lady in town?"

I finished my coffee with a grimace. There were no signs of any young lady—he wasn't mooning about, sighing heavily at inappropriate moments or searching for faint stars in the sun-touched night, all the while whispering words of poetry. Besides, Angus was only twelve. No, this was something worse. He was shutting me out, trying to become a man.

So concerned was I by Angus's strange behaviour that I forgot to worry about Jack Ireland and what further trouble he might cause.

Chapter Fourteen

"How's the take?"

"Great. Our best night yet. Nothing like being next door to the most exciting event to happen in town all week, and to be the employers of 'the Hero of the Yukon' to boot, to have the crowds begging to be allowed through the door."

On the morning of the eventful Saturday, when I was naïvely hoping I'd seen the last of Jack Ireland, Ray came into my office looking as if he hadn't slept a wink. And he still wore the same shirt, rumpled and soiled, that he'd had on the previous night.

I put down my pen and tested my left wrist. Mrs. Mann had made up a poultice, which looked only slightly less disgusting than it smelled, and she'd wrapped the whole thing up in a soft, clean cloth. My wrist felt almost normal.

"I'll go down and open up," said Ray.

"Not dressed like that, you won't. Go home and wash up and put on a clean shirt."

He looked at me, his eyes unreadable. "You're not my boss, Fiona. Last I looked, we owned the Savoy together."

"I'm not your mother either," I snapped. "But if I were, I'd tell you to stop mooning over a common or garden, no-account dance hall girl and pay attention to business. Because if you don't, we won't be partners for much longer."

"Do you want to buy me out? I dunna think ye can afford it. But I might consider an offer."

My head swam. How had this escalated so fast? Oh, right, I had insulted his ladylove and questioned his business sense.

"Look," I said, shifting my sling and wincing slightly for effect. "Last night was a bad night for us all, except for the size of this bag of gold." I nudged the loot with my foot. "You go and get a few hours sleep, and I'll fetch one of the new fellows to watch the saloon. The blond one seems the brightest. Where's he staying?"

"McKellen's on Harper Street."

"I'll drag him out of bed and tell him to get to work."

"I don't need any sleep. Let Murray alone. I'll change and be back in time." He struggled out of the chair. "And, Fee, that perfume you're wearing? Throw it out."

* * *

By seven o'clock that evening, we were packed to the rafters. Sam Collins held court behind the bar, pouring drinks, taking money and weighing gold dust, trying to avoid repeating over and over the story of the rescue of the bakery sisters. Being Sam, he downplayed his heroism, but the customers were happy to build it back up again.

I'd put on my best dress, a dangerously low-cut, crimson silk delight, which cascaded off ruffled shoulders, leaving my arms bare. The skirt panel was made of the finest Belgian lace trimmed by red ostrich plumes. It had the merest suggestion of a train, enough to swish gracefully as I walked, offering a teasing hint of what lay under the hem. The dress was a genuine Worth—by far the best thing I still owned. It had been given to me by Lord Alveron in London in 1893, in a suite at the original Savoy, shortly before my abrupt departure from England. The dress had been reworked many times: rips and stains patched, the train diminished a piece at a time to cut away the marks of wear, the bustle shrunken and then rebuilt attempting to keep pace with the ruthless dictates of fashion.

The string of pearls that had accompanied the dress—passed down to Lord Alveron from his great-grandmother, who, whispers said, had been a mistress of some minor European king—had been sold long ago in order to obtain

Angus a place in a good boys' school. Instead of the pearls, I always wore a thin gold chain with an inexpensive glass bauble nestling in the depths of my abundant cleavage. I had spent long hours searching the pawnshops of Toronto for a piece so cheap that looked so good. With this dress I always wore my hair pinned into a loose chignon into which was tucked a single red ostrich feather.

I'd discarded the sling. For although it had the men fussing over me even more than usual, it was a darned nuisance, and my wrist felt so much better. If Mrs. Mann were to sell that poultice, she could put the town's doctors out of business.

The musicians were gathered by the door, getting ready to do their nightly routine, and down the street we could hear the noise from another dance hall that had sent their caller out early, when Irene stumbled in, looking not at all her usual cheerful self. Ray had disappeared into the gambling hall, attracted by the sound of a sore loser screaming that he'd been taken.

I hurried towards Irene. She walked awkwardly, as if protecting bruised ribs or tender muscles. "For goodness's sake, what's the matter with you?" I grabbed her by the arm. She gasped, and her face crunched in pain.

"Excuse us, gentlemen, please," I raised my voice to the crowd of admirers that had instantly gathered around Irene. "Lady Irenee needs to prepare for her performance. Let us pass, please."

I pulled Irene towards the stairs. She pulled back. "Come with me," I whispered. "You're hurt. Can't let them see that. What happened?"

"Nothing happened. Let go of me. Norm! Nice to see you," she called to one of her admirers. "Let's have a dance after the show, and you can tell me all about Bonanza Creek."

"Are you insane?" I smiled through gritted teeth. "Come upstairs and let me have a look at you."

She pushed me aside. Her shawl fell open to reveal the top of her breasts—milky white skin and a cluster of purple and blue bruises.

Chapter Fifteen

I stepped back in shock, and Irene took the opportunity to scurry away, her hand protecting her side.

The orchestra went to the street for their eight o'clock call. Ray came out of the gambling hall, a warning arm tossed not-very-casually around a young dandy's slight shoulders. Ray released the boy and pushed him away with a growled threat that had him heading for the door. Ray smiled at Irene and reached out to touch her arm. I pushed through the crowd to reach them, sensing trouble.

A glass shattered on the floor, and a young miner, still coated by the dust of the digs, took a swing at another man. The few dancers who'd lingered in the bar to chat up their prospective customers screamed in delighted terror.

With a longing glance at Irene, Ray headed to break up the fight and she slipped away.

Richard Sterling and a sergeant, short and stocky, came though the doors. At the sight of the police, all the fight drained out of the two men, and they left with no more trouble.

Sterling's companion crossed over the invisible line into my private space. His nose lay almost flat against his right cheek, and he was missing a couple of teeth. I held out my hand to stop him from coming any closer. He took it. I've known ninety-year-old women to have a stronger handshake. "Mrs. MacGillivray. A pleasure to meet you, at last. I've heard so much about you. Your son is a…"

"Sergeant Lancaster," Sterling shouted, "I suggest we follow those fellows and make sure they don't get up to any more trouble."

"Who?"

"The men who were fighting."

I ignored the constable and smiled at the Sergeant. "You've met my son, Sergeant?"

"A fine boy, a fine boy. He'll make an excellent..."

"If you'll excuse us, Mrs. MacGillivray, Walker." Sterling almost shoved Lancaster towards the door.

"How odd," I said to Ray as we watched them leave.

"Fee, if I had a shillin' for every odd thing that happened in Dawson in a day..."

I remembered Irene. If Ray saw the state she was in, he'd be on the warpath for sure, no questions asked. Not that I needed to ask many myself. She'd left the Savoy last night with Jack Ireland and arrived at work today much the worse for wear.

"Can I have a break, Mr. Walker?" Murray, the new blond bartender, asked. The other young bartender was busy ferrying bottles of Champagne to the private boxes in the dance hall. Probably time I learned his name.

"No."

"Please, Mr. Walker. I really need to...you know," the boy whinged. He glanced at me out of the corner of his eyes and blushed.

"Five minutes," Ray snapped, taking the boy's place behind the bar with a considerable degree of ill grace.

Helen came out of the back room with mop and bucket to clear up the broken glass and shooed drinkers out of her way.

I took a good long look around the bar. For once everything was quiet. The drinkers stood in polite groups, speculating as to which of the fellows in their circle would be next to strike it rich. Funny how they all still thought that big money was waiting to be made out on the claims. Such fortune had finished long ago, by Yukon standards. The only people making money any more were the dig owners like Big Alex Macdonald, the business types like Belinda Mulroney and Mr. Mann, and the dance hall owners. Like me. All the poor fellows still streaming into town by raft or steamboat or foot? Nothing left for them but to scratch out work labouring for someone else.

The door swung open, and Graham Donohue walked in, as bold as a fat tick feasting on the back of a short-haired dog. He puffed on a freshly lit cigar, looked around the room, saw me watching, waved cheerfully, and stood apart from the crowd, confident that I would join him.

I did. "Thought you were in jail, Graham."

"Fortunately, my reputation in this town preceded me, and they released me on my own good name."

I snorted.

"That's a most unladylike sound, Fiona. You should take care to control it."

"Graham..."

"I saw something interesting from my cell this morning," he said. "I've heard that there's an old sergeant who's set up a boxing ring behind the jail. Let me order a drink, and I'll tell you all about it."

"Graham, I have absolutely no interest in the comings and goings at the Fort Herchmer jail."

"Fiona..."

"Don't Fiona me. If you cause one single scrap of trouble, I'll have you outside in the mud in seconds flat. I've had a week of nothing but men strutting around like peacocks with their best tail feather missing, fights and brawls, injured dancers."

He smiled softly. "You're protecting your arm. Have you been to see the doctor about it?"

"I'll go when I have the time. Which will probably be sometime late January. Now, if you'll excuse me."

"One drink, my fair lady. And I'll tell you the story of my night in the foul dungeons of Fort Herchmer."

"Graham," I said, "I have a job to do."

"Very well. We'll talk later." Graham left me, presumably to entertain all and sundry with the tragic story of his incarceration. They'd be invading the fort ready to rescue French counts locked into iron masks in the ancient cellars by the time Graham had finished.

I'd begun to hope that the night would be relatively uneventful, when Jack Ireland strolled into the dancehall.

He surveyed the room, his gaze smooth, cool, arrogant. His shirt was white, his heavy gold pocket watch ostentatious, a diamond stickpin in his paisley silk cravat.

Irene's dance finished and, rather than taking her partner to buy a drink, as was part of her job, she pushed him away. Sam stopped at the bottom of the stairs leading to the private boxes, clutching a fistful of empty champagne bottles. Ray forgot that he was about to evict someone and loosened his grip on the man enough that the reprobate ducked back into the press of patrons. Helen Saunderson stood in the shadows wringing her rough hands on a tattered dishrag and watching Ireland.

He walked toward me, exchanging greetings with men as he passed. "Front page coverage in the *San Francisco Standard* this week, Mrs. MacGillivray. Collins, come over here!" He waved an arm. "You'll be a hero, like I promised you."

Sam scuttled out of the room. He touched Helen's arm as he passed and drew her away.

"What did I say? All I want to do is make those two famous, and they act like I've poisoned their tea."

"I think, Mr. Ireland, that they're entitled to their privacy. We're a strange bunch up here in the Yukon. If a man or woman wants to be left alone, we believe one should respect that."

He genuinely looked confused. "Privacy? You can't eat privacy. Soon as my story runs, people will be pouring money into the *Standard* offices. To buy Mrs. Saunderson and her children out of bondage."

"If you…"

He held up a hand. "Now hear me out, Fiona."

"Mrs. MacGillivray."

"Fiona. Those nice people in San Francisco don't know or care that this isn't some cheap whorehouse you're running here. They want to help an unfortunate family out of their troubles. And if it makes people feel good to help, I'm not going to criticize them."

"Oh, stop your nonsense," I said. "A lie is a lie."

Ireland had lost interest in the debate and turned away.

Irene watched him from the far side of the room, and he studied her lazily. "Whatever you say, Fiona." He cocked his index finger, and Irene brushed aside the man holding his ticket up to her and walked towards us. You could have shattered her smile with an ice pick.

"Mr. Ireland, good evening."

"Irene, my dear. Can I have the honour of this dance?"

She nodded, and they swept into the music. Irene moved with as much enthusiasm as the wooden planks beneath her feet, but my girls know they can reject the offers of any man who they fear might mean them harm. I blended back into the crowd, encouraging men to dance.

Irene danced almost every dance with Ireland. They made a nice looking couple, although I didn't care for the way he tossed her about the floor as if she were his own private property, nor for the flashes of pain that crossed her face.

I planted myself in the dance hall to keep an eye on them, although I normally spent the night passing between the hall, the saloon and the gambling rooms, the latter being where the most serious fights were likely to start. Graham Donohue stayed in the bar, and Ray Walker came in now and again, scowling.

"Everything all right here, Mrs. MacGillivray?" Richard Sterling stood beside me, all looming bulk, crisp red tunic, neat brown pants, high, shiny boots and broad-brimmed hat. I took a step back.

"Sorry," he said, colouring slightly.

"Everything's perfectly fine, Constable. Thank you."

He touched the brim of his hat. "I'll be on my rounds, if you need me."

I watched the dancing for a while longer. Irene didn't smile. Her countenance was dark and troubled, but she still danced with Ireland. Maybe I'd been wrong and she'd fallen down the stairs at her rooming house. It had been known to happen, just not as often as stiff-minded matrons and pompous priests liked to believe.

It was Saturday, so we didn't have much time left until

midnight closing. I was looking forward to going home and crawling into my narrow bed for the only full night's sleep I enjoyed all week. Hopefully Mrs. Mann would have left some of that magical poultice out.

I was standing at the far side of the room, up against the back wall, trying to stifle a yawn, when the orchestra called out, "Take your partners for the next dance," and for a brief moment everyone shifted so that a space opened up before me, leading all the way to the door.

In which I saw Jack Ireland dragging a reluctant Irene behind him.

I practically sprinted to catch up with them, almost tripping over the train of my dress, which was just long enough to wrap itself around my feet. I wrenched the train out of my way with a muffled curse. Surprised faces watched me fly past.

"...out of this dump," Ireland was growling as I arrived within hearing range.

"I'd just as soon not leave right now." Irene's voice was as low as a whisper made to a lover, but not nearly as welcoming. "Mrs. MacGillivray won't like it."

"Never mind Mrs. MacGillivray. Stick with me, and you won't have to kow-tow to the likes of her again."

"Did I hear my name?" I stumbled to a stop in front of them, yanking at my skirts to pull the tumble of fabric out from under my feet. "Had enough dancing, Mr. Ireland? It's almost closing time, anyway. Irene, please go up to my office, I have to talk to you about last week's hours. There seems to be a slight problem."

"Yes, Mrs. MacGillivray," she said with such a gush of gratitude that it was clear I hadn't been mistaken as to what had happened after she'd left with Ireland the previous night. There had been no tumble down the backstairs.

"Irene," he said, "I'm leaving. And you're coming with me."

"Not if she doesn't want to," I said.

Ireland turned his black eyes on me.

I didn't look away: I've been stared down by harder men

than he. "But it is most definitely time for you to leave, Mr. Ireland."

"You just wait until you see what my paper has to print about you."

"What? That I serve nothing but toasted crumpets and tea and hold secret revival meetings behind locked doors every evening? That's the only thing you could write that would hurt my business. You haven't been in Dawson long, Mr. Ireland, and I suggest that you don't make your visit last any longer."

"Come on, Irene, let's get out of here." His hand closed around her arm.

"Irene," I said, "you don't have to go if you don't want to."

"It's all right, Mrs. MacGillivray. I'm staying. I'm sorry, Jack, but I've changed my mind. I've decided not to go to San Francisco with you."

Ireland's eyes bulged, and a purple vein throbbed in the side of his neck. He tightened his grip on Irene's arm, and she grimaced. "You're making a mistake, Irene. I can make you a star."

"I don't want to be a star." Her voice broke as she tried pry his hand off her. "I want you to leave me alone."

"I suggest you release her, Mr. Ireland," I said, conscious of the press of men gathering around, attracted by our angry words.

He released Irene, turned to me, and shoved me in the chest with such force that I lost my footing and fell backwards. Eager hands caught me, and I struggled to pull myself free.

Ireland turned his attentions back to Irene. He grabbed her by the shoulders and shook. A section of her hair flew out of its pins. "I've paid you good money. You're bought now, like a whore. You're coming with me."

"I don't want to."

He slapped her across the face, hard.

Men's boasting voices and women's false laughter died away; musicians stopped playing mid-note; dancers froze mid-step. One man snickered, the laugh cut short.

Ireland pulled back his fist and punched my best dancer full in the stomach. The blood drained from her face, and Irene folded over and vomited.

Chapter Sixteen

Irene would have fallen to the floor if Jack Ireland hadn't been holding her arm. He slapped her again, hard. The ugly sound echoed throughout the room. Silence spread out from the centre of violence like a tidal wave sweeping all before it.

"You whore. You'll do what I tell you."

I freed myself from my rescuers' hands, lunged forward and raked my nails across Ireland's face.

He released Irene's arm and fell back with a cry. "What the hell?" He touched one hand to his cheek and looked at the blood on the pads of his fingers.

I danced back and brought my foot up with a straight-legged jab, placing the heel of my high-heeled boot directly into his crotch. He screamed—the sound high-pitched, unworldly—and doubled over.

Blood swam before my eyes. I clenched the back of one hand with the fist of the other and prepared to bring them down across the back of his unprotected neck.

My target disappeared before I got into position. Ray Walker had run through the door, slammed his not-too-considerable weight into Ireland and knocked the reporter off his feet. Then, like the scrawny streetfighter from the back alleys of Glasgow that he was, Ray proceeded to kick with a vengeance at every exposed bit of Ireland's body.

Women screamed, men shouted, as many trying to drag Ray off as were encouraging him to kick harder. I waded through the throng, shouting Ray's name. I wrapped my arms around his skinny, sunken chest and tried to drag him away, with as much effect as a horsefly attacking a bull moose in rut. I hoisted my skirt past my knees and jumped up to wrap my legs around Ray's non-existent hips, hoping to drag him down by my weight if nothing else. I heard fabric tear. Ireland had curled into a ball, trying to protect his tender parts. Blood streamed from his nose, blending with the stuff coming from the scratches and the effluent from his eyes into a gory mess of blood, tears and mucus.

If Ray killed Ireland, we'd be shut down for sure, with jail time for Ray, maybe me as well. I prayed for the sound of the booming voice of Constable Sterling arriving to break up the fight, but all I could hear were Ray's grunts, Ireland's moans, the distant roar of men yelling and women screaming. And the sound of my own voice, shouting Ray's name, over and over. Eventually some semblance of common sense fell over the bystanders, and a group of men dragged Ray away, although they were considerably hampered by my weight hanging off him.

I clambered down. Two men held Ray by the arms, and others helped Ireland to his feet. A dark stain spread over the front of the trousers of the *San Francisco Standard*'s prize reporter. The smell of fear and blood and bloodlust filled the crowded room. The men were murmuring in a dangerous tone.

Ireland pushed away the men holding him. He lunged towards Ray, but Murray grabbed his arm.

"You bastard," Ireland spat. A mouthful of blood and a shiny white tooth fell onto the floor. "You'll pay for that."

"Perhaps, but not in Dawson." Mouse O'Brien pushed his way through the crowd. Mouse was so big that he could push his way through a brick wall if he ever took a mind to. "Every man here saw you hit that sweet little lady, Miss Irene. We reckon you got what you deserved. Ain't that right, boys?"

The onlookers shouted their agreement. Now that someone was expressing their feelings, in a calm, rational voice, the muttering and the threat of further violence began to die down.

"We also reckon that if you show your ugly face in this bar again, we'll finish what Walker didn't."

The men cheered. One of the dancers took Irene's arm, and they slipped into the crowd.

Mouse held up one hand. The crowd hushed, the silence broken only by Ray's heavy breathing and the wheezing of Ireland's lungs.

"'Course, maybe we won't have to. Looks like Mrs. MacGillivray here coulda managed you all by her pretty self." The men howled with laughter. It was hard to tell through the mess of blood and snot, but Ireland appeared to redden at the insult. His breathing was ragged, and I suspected he'd suffered a broken rib or two.

"Your time in Dawson is done," Mouse said. "Now get outta here and go clean yourself up. You stink. You've interrupted my dancing." He walked back into the crowd.

Sam Collins stood in the shadows watching as Murray and a couple of onlookers dragged an unresisting Ireland out of the dance hall. The men holding Ray gripped him tighter as they passed, but the fight had gone out of the Scot. He glared at Ireland but made no move to break free. I followed to make sure the newspaperman did indeed leave the Savoy.

Helen Saunderson watched from the doorway of her kitchen slash broom closet, wringing her dishcloth in her hands. The other new bartender, whose name I still didn't know, stood behind the bar with nothing at all to do. Not a single person waited for a drink. Everyone stood still, watching us pass.

Murray made a move to shove Ireland into the street. I held up a hand and walked around to face the newspaperman. "Surely I don't have to tell you that you are not to step foot in these premises again, Mr. Ireland."

He glared at me with such venom that I took a step backwards. In all my life, I don't think I've ever seen so much hatred in a man's eyes—the emotion amplified a thousand times by the angry bruises, the right eye swelling shut, the rivers of blood drying across his face. And the rank smell of humiliation and urine-soaked trousers.

"You toffee-nosed English whore," he hissed. "You're hiding something beneath your fancy dresses and proper manners. I'll find it, then I'll ruin you. Don't think I can't. Or I won't."

"Please don't insult me again, Mr. Ireland," I said. "I am most certainly not an Englishwoman. Goodbye."

I nodded, and Murray propelled Ireland out the door, not giving a care for the reporter's bruised and battered body.

Margaret Collins, Sam's wife, leapt back to avoid colliding with the man being so unceremoniously expelled. Her eyes widened with surprise.

"Margaret," I said. "What're you doing here at this time of night?"

"Worrying about Sam," she replied, watching the battered man struggling in the mud. "It's almost closing, and I thought I'd walk home with him. Who is that?"

"American newspaperman," I said. "Nothing but trouble."

"Mountie coming," Murray said.

Constable Richard Sterling was making his way down the street, attracted by the not-at-all-unusual commotion of someone being thrown out of a bar. With a final blood-speckled spit, Ireland staggered off in the opposite direction. Sterling watched him go. The reporter looked like any other Saturday night drunk trying to remain upright.

Sam came out of the back and saw his wife in the doorway.

She raised one eyebrow.

"Come inside. Help Helen clean up. Quickly."

By the time Constable Sterling walked into the Savoy, Murray and the other new bartender, who I was beginning to think of as Not-Murray, were serving one last round, men were leaning against the bar, laughing uproariously at each other's jokes, Ray Walker was keeping a steely eye on the roulette wheel, Helen Saunderson and Margaret Collins were putting away pails and wringing out rags, the orchestra was playing its heart out, and the girls were dancing as if it were the last dance of their lives. A fight with the severity of the one that had so recently gone on here was no joke to the North-West Mounted Police. Bars and dance halls had been closed down for less.

A couple of the girls, led by Ellie, the eldest, had helped Irene upstairs. I hurried to follow them and made the first two steps before Richard Sterling reached me.

"Mrs. MacGillivray, one moment, please."

I turned and tried to appear as a woman with absolutely nothing in the world to hide. "Good evening, Constable."

His eyes passed over the front of my best dress, caressing my body from throat to knees and back up again. That was a first from the oh-so-proper constable.

"I'm feeling somewhat unwell and need to go upstairs and lie down for a moment." I cranked out a smile that had all the warmth of the last inch of a cheap tallow candle.

"Is everything all right here, Mrs. MacGillivray? We, the NWMP I mean, are always ready to help, you know."

"And greatly appreciated you loyal servants of Her Majesty are, let me assure you," I babbled inanely, reminding myself of my son talking too formally when trying to hide something. I took a deep breath. "Of course, everything's perfectly fine. Doesn't it look normal?" I waved a hand over the crowd. The customers, who had been listening to every word, smiled at us like the back row of a music hall chorus that was about to be booed off the stage.

"If you say so, Mrs. MacGillivray." Sterling touched the edge of his broad-brimmed hat. "Almost closing time."

"I'll be down by then." I climbed regally up the stairs, praying that he wouldn't follow me. Sterling had never behaved at all improperly, and tonight of all nights I didn't need the handsome officer of the law asking for favours in return for…what?

Irene lay on the lumpy couch in my office, her eyes closed, her breathing ragged. Ellie crouched on the floor beside her, holding a cool, damp cloth to her forehead.

"She don't look at all well, Mrs. Fiona," Ellie said. Being the oldest of the dancers, she was the only one permitted to call me by my first name. "Look at this." She loosened Irene's gown and pulled it away from the half-conscious woman's shoulders. A mass of purple and yellow bruises streaked across her breasts. The remains of angry fingerprints ran across her upper arms.

I sat on the edge of my desk. "Closing time in…" I checked my watch "…ten minutes. Get one of the other girls, Ruby I think, tell her to come up here. Never mind what she's doing. She can sit with Irene. Then go for the doctor. Tell him I'll pay. When Ruby gets here, I'll go down for closing."

Ellie handed me the cloth. "Is she gonna be all right, Mrs. Fiona?"

"Of course," I said, with more optimism than I felt. "Those marks will heal." No need to tell Ellie that I wanted the doctor to check for internal injuries. The other marks weren't terribly serious, but the blow to the stomach that I witnessed might have done some real damage. When I was a child working the London slum of Seven Dials; a prostitute who rented rooms from my protector had been beaten up by a customer. Nothing but bruises, her pimp said, no lasting harm, as he pushed her back out on the street. She worked for one more night, then she died. Died right where she sat, they said, in a dark corner of the Bishop and Belfry Pub cradling a glass of gin and an eel pie before going outside again. Her life left her with a rush of blood that still stained the Bishop's floor the day I left Seven Dials.

If I caught sight of Jack Ireland again, I would tear him apart.

Irene's eyes opened. She tried to sit up, and I pressed her back down.

"You rest," I said.

"I'm fine, Mrs. MacGillivray. I don't know what came over me." A cloud passed behind her eyes. "Jack?"

"Escorted to the street. He won't be back. Not if Ray Walker and Mouse O'Brien and every dancing man in Dawson has anything to say about it."

She half-smiled and tried to sit up again. “Back to work then. We don’t dance, we don’t get paid. Isn’t that so, Mrs. MacGillivray?”

Again, I pressed her back into the couch. “My mother taught me another saying: You die, you most certainly don’t ever get paid again. I’ve called for the doctor. You wait right there until he arrives.”

“I can’t afford the doctor!” Her legs beat a steady rhythm in the air as she struggled to get up. The couch was deep: broken springs and my firm hand kept her down.

“I’m paying, Irene. The way things have been around here lately, I might hire him permanently.”

Ruby slipped into the room.

“She gonna be all right, Mrs. MacGillivray?”

“Don’t talk about me as if I’m not here,” Irene said.

“I’d say she’s going to be fine. I have to go downstairs for closing. I’ll make up the money you’re losing by not being on the floor.”

Ruby cocked her head. “I don’t care about the money, Mrs. MacGillivray.”

“Nevertheless, I’ll make it up.” Ruby didn’t care about the money. Tonight. But when it was time to pay her bills or count her savings, she would be cursing me for keeping her from closing-time tips.

I stood in front of the mirror to give myself a quick appraisal before venturing back downstairs. For a moment, I didn’t recognize my reflection and wondered what that wild woman was doing in my office. Then I knew why Richard Sterling had been studying me: not in admiration of my beauty or appreciation of my feminine charms, but because I looked like a particularly dangerous escapee from a lunatic asylum.

Chapter Seventeen

Blood, drying to an ugly brown, splattered the front of my Worth gown, particularly noticeable against the excellent Belgian lace, which I had struggled so hard to keep a virginal white all these years. The dress hung by a thread at one shoulder, and the rip in the bodice was borderline illegal. My hair had been pulled out of its pins and stood up like stalks of corn in an Ontario field in August. The broken red feather stuck out sideways from my hair. A streak of blood bisected my left cheek like a bolt of devil's lightning. I almost screamed at the sight of it and grabbed the damp cloth out of Ruby's hands. I scrubbed frantically.

"What am I going to do? I can't go back down looking like this. But if I'm not there for closing, Sterling will know something's wrong!"

"You put that shawl around your shoulders," Irene said. "And you wash your face and tuck your hair into its pins as best you can manage, and you wear that dress like battle armour."

I looked at her reflection in the mirror. Her colour was recovering, and her face was set into lines of fierce pride. I cleaned my face, and Ruby helped me arrange my hair into some semblance of order. I draped my heavy shawl over my shoulders, the orange, handmade woollen one that I kept behind my desk chair for protection from the cool northern nights. I could do nothing about the bloodstains. Tomorrow my best dress, a genuine Worth, presented to me by Lord Alveron in a suite of the Savoy Hotel, London, would be torn up for rags, but tonight I would wear it with pride. We'd been through a lot, this dress and I.

"How do I look?" I stepped away from the mirror to face the two women. They smiled. "Like a winner," Irene said with a chuckle. But she stifled a gasp, and her hand touched her stomach as she laughed.

Footsteps, one pair light, cautious, one heavy, full of authority, sounded on the stairs. "That's the doctor now," Ruby said. "You go, Mrs. MacGillivray. I'll stay with Irene."

"Good evening, Doctor. I have to close up now. I'll settle your bill tomorrow." I swept past him and out of the room.

On a Saturday night in Dawson, Yukon Territory, everything shut down at two minutes to midnight for the Lord's Day. Up and down Front Street, the gambling wheels slowed to a halt, hands of cards (no matter how good they were) landed face down on the green table, bottles of whisky were fastened shut, and dancing girls pulled off dancing shoes to release cramped toes with a contented sigh. Men left the dance hall, passed through the gaming rooms, and walked out of the saloon like an army of ghosts, picking up silent recruits as they went. No one argued, no one begged for one more spin of the wheel or one more round of drinks. There was no point in offering a bribe to the orchestra to keep playing or to the dealer to keep dealing or to the bartender to keep pouring.

As was my custom, I walked behind the exiting crowds, starting at the back of the dance hall, making sure that no dead-to-the-world-drunk got left behind, or that no Englishman or American unfamiliar with the laws of the Territory would try to stay one minute past midnight.

On this night, the men were particularly polite. "Lovely evening, Mrs. Fiona," they said, doffing their caps. "Such a pleasant night. See you Monday." Or, "You look particularly beautiful tonight, Mrs. MacGillivray. That shawl certainly becomes you." Barney, the old drunk, winked so broadly that I wondered if his face might collapse under the effort.

It didn't, but I turned to see Constable Richard Sterling standing behind me.

"Peaceful night, Mrs. MacGillivray," he said. "Everyone filing out like they did leaving my father's church after a sermon about the Hell that he says so eagerly awaits most of them."

"Didn't know you had a father, Constable. Don't they churn you fellows out of Mountie school like sausages, all in a neat row?"

"A bar in the Prairie town where I had my first posting had a lot of trouble one night," he said. "They tried to hide it from us, but it was hard to keep the secret after the troublemakers torched the place."

"Nice quiet night, eh, Constable?" The fellow who dressed like an Indian fighter shouted at us as he made his way to the door, barely held up by his friends. "Pretty boring, ain't it?" He and his mates all sort of collapsed into the middle together, thus supporting each other and keeping themselves upright at the same time.

"Don't talk ta the coppers," one of the friends muttered as he tripped over a loose floorboard.

Sterling raised one dark eyebrow and looked down at me. "It was quite the mess, burned lumber and scorched furniture everywhere. Fortunately no one was hurt, but the smell of shattered whisky bottles and the end of someone's dreams lingered over the town for weeks."

"Fascinating story. You must tell me more. When I have time. If you'll excuse me, Constable?"

The yellow patches gleamed in his brown eyes, but he said nothing further.

That wasn't the first time trouble had accompanied Jack Ireland into my place. But tonight I was sure I'd seen the last of him—he'd hit the most popular dance hall girl in the Yukon in full sight of a packed hall. He was finished as a newspaperman here; once word spread of what had happened, no one in town would talk to him.

He'd be on the next steamboat out of town.

Guaranteed.

Chapter Eighteen

The rare smell of frying bacon, sausages and fresh eggs wafted through the house, and Angus climbed eagerly out of bed. They were getting heartily sick of bacon, one of the staples of both the trail and the winter of near-starvation, but eggs were a rare, expensive treat. Anyone arriving late at the Sunday breakfast table would find himself eating the scraps, if he were lucky enough to have been left some.

Angus scooped a handful of cold water from the basin that rested on the table beside his bed, splashed it on his face, hastily pulled on trousers and a shirt and made his way to the outhouse.

When he returned, Mr. Mann was sitting at the table watching Mrs. Mann crack eggs into the huge, battered frying pan. A glass of pure white milk waited at his place.

"Only three places set? Where's Ma?"

"Your mother left a note," Mrs. Mann replied. "She wasn't feeling well and asked me to leave her sleep this morning."

"But she'll miss her eggs!"

Mr. Mann slurped his coffee and leaned back to allow his wife to place a brimming plate in front of him. Bacon fried to a crisp, the plump sausages she called wurst, eggs with cheerful yellow centres and pure white edges. Plus two thick slices of fried bread.

"And the milk. She was looking forward to having real milk in her coffee today. She won't mind if I wake her."

"You shush and eat." Mrs. Mann began preparing another plate, one containing almost as much food as Mr. Mann had been given. She tossed a generous hunk of bread into the pan. It sizzled and spat and drank up the grease.

Angus downed his entire glass of milk without pausing for breath.

"I'll make your mother's breakfast later," Mrs. Mann said.

"If I'm late, I don't get no breakfast."

"Yous don't pay for your breakfast, boy," Mr. Mann said.

"You don't get *any* breakfast, Angus." Fiona stood in the doorway. The hair on her head poked into the air, and dark circles emphasized the tired droop to her eyes. She wore her red dressing gown, the one with a bold gold Chinese dragon streaking across the back, and she hugged it closely to her thin frame.

"You go back to bed, Mrs. MacGillivray," Mrs. Mann ordered. "You don't look at all well."

"I'm fine, thank you. It's hard to sleep when your cooking smells so wonderful." She planted a kiss on the top of Angus's head and took her seat.

Mrs. Mann handed him his plate, and Angus dove in head first.

The landlady poured a cup of coffee. "Milk's on the table."

"Milk," Fiona repeated. "Real milk?"

"Inside the udders of a cow only yesterday."

Fiona lifted the blue pitcher and held it under her nose. She closed her eyes and breathed deeply.

Angus laughed. "You don't smell milk, Mother. You pour it into your coffee and drink it."

"Sometimes you have to stop and appreciate the moment." Her tired eyes crinkled up at the edges, and the dark circles faded.

Mrs. Mann placed another sausage in the pan and sat at the table with her own coffee while it cooked.

"My red silk dress, the best one, with the lace skirt panel, was ruined last night," Fiona said. "I'll give it to you after breakfast. Perhaps you can cut it up and salvage some of the lace or the plumes."

"I can repair," Mrs. Mann said.

"Not this time, I'm afraid. It's beyond saving."

"What happened?" Angus's fork chased down a liquid patch of egg yolk with a hunk of fried bread.

"A man fell down, far too enthusiastic on the dance floor. I tried to help him stand up, and he was bleeding from a bad crack on his forehead. Blood stains, you can't wash them out, not once they've dried. And then he grabbed at me to steady himself and ripped the dress right down the front. It's fit for nothing but rags."

"Gee, that's too bad." Angus scraped the tines of his fork across his empty plate, trying to gather up every last bit of egg and grease. "That was great, Mrs. M. Any more?"

"No." The landlady went back to the stove and tossed bacon into the pan.

"I'm sure Mrs. Mann and I won't be able to manage to eat all of that bread." Fiona nodded towards a tower beside the stove, awaiting its bath in bacon and sausage fat. The landlady always prepared extra for Angus, although she never admitted it.

"Thank you, Mrs. Mann, that smells like heaven." Fiona picked up her fork. Mrs. Mann served them both and sat down. The frying pan popped and sizzled with grease and a new batch of bread.

"Hurry, woman," Mr. Mann said. "Church time."

She popped a slice of sausage into her mouth. "Plenty of time, dear. Plenty of time. But as you've finished already, perhaps you'll fetch some water from the well."

Mr. Mann grunted, but he picked up the bucket and went out.

Angus's mother hid a smile behind a piece of toast and scraped her bacon onto his plate.

Chapter Nineteen

Mr. Mann doesn't like me much, and he clearly doesn't approve of me. But then I've run into a great many men in my life who don't like or approve of me. As well as those who like me very much but absolutely don't approve of me: they're the worst sort. But the Manns like the money I bring in, and they appreciate the extras, like this morning's milk, which I provide for us all. Mrs. Mann seems begrudgingly fond of me, as if she'd rather not be but can't quite help herself, and they both care for Angus a great deal. Angus simply likes everyone. So we all live together in some degree of contentment.

No matter how long I tried to make it last, I finally reached the end of the pot of coffee. I could make more, of course. I'm not incompetent, although I have pretended to be so at times. But the remainder of the valuable milk, now resting in the cool, dark place under the floorboards Mrs. Mann used as her larder, would have to serve us tomorrow as well.

It looked as if it might turn out to be a lovely day. The sky was a brilliant blue, with the depth of colour of an enormous sapphire that once passed through my hands. (Very quickly, I might add, the stone being far too distinctive to hang onto for long.) You rarely see that colour in England, and since arriving in Canada I have become extremely fond of it. Today, there were no clouds, not even a wisp hovering behind the hills that hid the jagged rim of the distant mountains to the east.

"How would you like to go for a walk?" I asked my son.

He smiled at me. My heart stopped beating for the

briefest of moments as I considered what a handsome young man I had produced.

"That would be fun, Mother. We could head down the river. There'll be plenty of ducks and geese around at this time of year. We might even be able to find some eggs, if it's not too late. Ron says that the moose come out of the mountains to drink, and you can get real close to them. John O'Leary saw a bear, just the other day, not far from town. The mosquitoes are bad, though, so you should wear gloves and cover the back of your neck with a shawl or something. Mother?"

My admiration of my son turned to horror at the very thought of stepping foot into the bush. The moment we arrived in Dawson, and I shakily disembarked from the boat that had dumped us here onto, if not firm ground, at least mushy swamp, I swore I'd never leave civilization again. "I meant shall we go for a walk into town. See who's about and listen to the gossip."

"I'd rather not," he said, "if you don't mind."

"Perhaps you can find one of your friends to go down to the river with you."

He kissed me on the cheek. "Enjoy your walk, Mother."

If I didn't love my son so much, I would curse the fates for not giving me a daughter. A dainty girl to dress in pretty, frothy gowns and tie her fair hair in ringlets and ribbons and to parade through town to the admiration of all. I smiled at the thought, realizing that the daughter I dreamed of was the complete opposite of the girl I myself had been. When my parents were alive, and we lived on Bestford, the great Scottish estate, I'd run almost as wild as Angus did today. Until they corralled me for daily lessons in the big house, at any rate. I suppose what I would like most would be to have a daughter who didn't have to fight her way through the world. Who didn't have to live by her wits and the variety of skills she learned in the fen and the schoolroom and the streets. And in the bedroom.

Angus tripped over something in the hall. "Damn."

"Angus!"

"Sorry, Mother."

I laughed, full of love of my son and rinsed my tin mug in the cold, slimy water in the bucket on the wooden plank that served as a sink.

I dressed carefully in my best walking dress. It had a sage green skirt of practical cotton teamed with a white blouse with leg-of-mutton sleeves and green ribbons. I pulled a wide black belt firmly around my waist, took a deep breath, tugged at the belt one more time, and put on my hat. An ostrich feather in a green somewhere between that of the skirt and that of the ribbon bobbed high above the whole contraption.

A bright sunny day, following upon a day or two without rain, had gone a long way towards drying up the streets. Ladies kept to the boardwalk and duckboards, but gentlemen dared to walk down the centre of the road, and horses and wagons managed to get through without too much of a struggle.

I made my way south on York Street towards the river, enjoying the warm caress of the sun on my face and the sound of the soft wind rustling through my ostrich feather. Many of the serious gamblers and dance hall girls leave town on a Sunday morning, taking boats downriver to the United States, where anything goes and there are no stern-faced, broad-brimmed-hatted Mounties to enforce the Lord's Day Act. Thus for one day a week the town takes on a façade of boring respectability.

On Front Street, the 25-cent waffle-bakery was struggling back to life. The elder sister stood in the street, eyeing the newly hung sign, her scorched hair shorn off almost to the scalp. I waved to her and crossed the street, carefully minding the hem of my skirts. The only bit of my ensemble, other than the mismatching green of every piece, that wouldn't have withstood the scrutiny of a Sunday stroll in Hyde Park were my boots. No one ventured out-of-doors in Dawson without thoroughly practical footwear.

"Mrs. MacGillivray, how nice to see you," Miss Vanderhaege said in her strong Dutch accent.

"I'm very sorry about your misfortune. I do hope your sister's recovering nicely."

"She's well, well." She smiled broadly, revealing a set of teeth that reminded me of a prized stallion. "We rebuild. Open for business tomorrow."

"I'm glad to hear it, Miss Vanderhaege. You've been lucky."

The smile died, and the horse's teeth disappeared behind her chapped lips. "Lucky? More lucky if the fire hadn't happened."

I couldn't argue with that, so I took my leave.

I walked past the Savoy to check things out. From the point of view of an observer on the street, it really was nothing to get excited about, in a street of matching nothing-to-get-excited-about establishments. Our casually-employed watchman, who paid about as much attention to his duties as I did to his rate of pay, had deserted his post to watch the passing parade. He almost swallowed his thin cigar at the sight of me. I nodded and continued on my way. If there is a more boring job on Earth than watching over the houses of entertainment in Dawson, Yukon Territory, on a Sunday morning, I don't want to know about it.

I walked to the end of Front Street, down to where it curved to meet the Klondike River. That was far enough: I'd seen and, more importantly, been seen, quite enough. A book waited for me at home, *Wuthering Heights* by Miss Emily Bronte, which Angus had traded one of his boy's adventures for as a gift to mark my birthday.

Margaret Collins came scurrying down the boardwalk towards me. I nodded and stopped to pass the time of day.

"Lovely morning, Margaret."

"That it is, Mrs. MacGillivray."

"Are you enjoying your walk?"

"Yes, Mrs. MacGillivray." She wore an inexpensive, unadorned straw hat and a long, full cloak fastened all the way up the front, which I thought a bit too heavy for such a warm day.

"Since living in the Yukon, I've found that it's best to

appreciate every beautiful day one is granted. Wouldn't you agree?"

"I would, Mrs. MacGillivray."

"When I lived in London, all of society would rush to the park to enjoy a sunny day. But I found that in Toronto, instead of enjoying what they'd been given, people complained constantly, about the heat in the summer and the cold in the winter."

"Really?" Margaret said with not the slightest bit of interest.

What on earth was the point of trying to make polite, mindless conversation with an American anyway? They were all of them blunt to the point of being rude.

A bustle of giggling dance hall girls swept around us. Mrs. Collins picked up her skirts and pushed past me to continue down the boardwalk, her grey head held high.

I was crossing the street on a duckboard when I almost collided with Joey LeGrand, who was coming the other way. The duckboards were narrow, and we were thus forced to acknowledge each other's presence. We both knew that we had absolutely no need to pretend to be polite, which I found to be much more satisfactory than the salons of London, where a lady was expected to greet her most hated enemy with joy and pleasure. Joey grunted and stood firm in the centre of the board. She was so small that I could have pushed her aside with one stiff arm. But I believe in saving my fights for the important things. I stepped into the road without batting an eyelash and sailed across the street as if such had been my intention all along.

A minute later, Dawson's most famous citizens, Alex Macdonald and Belinda Mulroney, approached me, deep in conversation, clearly talking about business. Those two were not keeping the Lord's Day.

Big Alex tipped his hat. "Quite the night last night, Mrs. MacGillivray. The Savoy is once again the talk of the town."

Belinda tossed me a smile. "That's a lovely hat, Fiona."

I thanked her with genuine warmth, exchanged a bit of empty conversation, and continued on my way.

And so the boring stroll continued.

At one point I was sure I saw Graham Donohue coming towards me, but when I lifted my hand in greeting, the man spun on his heels and took off down Queen Street. I must have been mistaken. It couldn't have been anyone I knew.

Men never avoid my company.

Unless they owe me money.

Or are accompanied by their wives.

I went home, had a nap, and read a bit of *Wuthering Heights,* before joining my small household for a meal of stringy grey beef, over-boiled cabbage and tinned peas. As usual, Mrs. Mann served the Sunday supper at a most uncivilized time; in London it would be scarcely past tea time.

I was settling into the comfortable chair in my sitting room prior to resuming the book when, out of nowhere, the idea popped into my head that I'd made an error in the accounts. If it had been an error in my favour, it would have waited until the next day. But as it was an error that was not in my favour, I wanted to check on it immediately.

"I have to go to the Savoy," I said to Angus. "I might have made a mistake in the ledger, and I want to check."

"Can't it wait until tomorrow?"

"It can, but I can't. Do you want to come with me?"

And so we came across the remains of the loathsome Mr. Jack Ireland, late of the *San Francisco Standard.*

Chapter Twenty

Angus ran to fetch the Mounties, and I cracked open a bottle of whisky and poured myself a good shot. Then I helped our watchman out of his disgustingly filthy flannel overshirt and handed him a glass of whisky. He was highly embarrassed at vomiting in my presence, but I'd come close to losing the contents of my stomach myself—those tinned peas! The very thought of it was enough to have me choking it all back. At least I'd been forewarned that I was about to encounter something unpleasant.

I sat on the floor beside my employee with my legs stretched out in front of me, and we drank our whisky in companionable silence.

"Mrs. Saunderson will not be at all happy tomorrow morning," I said at last.

"M'm?"

"To find such a mess. In here as well as…in there. She may even threaten to quit. Upon which I'll offer her an extra twenty cents. And she'll say that isn't enough for all she has to put up with, so I'll up my offer to twenty-five cents—and not a penny more—and with a great sigh, she'll fetch her cloth and mop and bucket."

"M'm?"

"Never mind."

Angus burst through the doors, followed by Richard Sterling—is that man never off duty?—and Sergeant Lancaster. I struggled to my feet, using my Sunday watchman's head as point of leverage.

"You wait here, Mrs. MacGillivray," Lancaster said. He

had the sour expression of one whose ambitions have not quite panned out and who never allowed himself to forget it. "Your son can show us."

I ignored him. "Angus, go and get Ray."

"But, Ma."

"Now."

He ran out the door.

The watchman gripped his empty glass and looked around for the bottle, which I'd closed and slipped under the counter before collapsing to the floor in a shocked stupor.

"Gentlemen, follow me." I led the way through to the back room and its macabre still life.

"Jack Ireland," Sterling said as the two Mounties approached the body. Despite my early outburst of bravado, I hung behind, back pressed against the wall.

"You know him, Constable?" Sergeant Lancaster asked.

"Yes, sir. American. Reporter. Only arrived in town day before yesterday. Saw him get off the boat myself."

"Pretty quick to make enemies, even for Dawson." The sergeant chuckled. "Don't suppose this was an accident, do you? Or a suicide?" His tone turned wistful.

"'Fraid not."

"Someone had best fetch the inspector, then."

"Right."

"Won't be happy to be roused out from his after-supper pipe."

"No, but he'll be even less happy if we don't call him."

This was starting to sound like a comedy act so dreadful, I wouldn't allow it anywhere near my stage. I abandoned my refuge against the wall and stepped forward. I opened my mouth, while the words took shape behind my tongue. *Don't stand here blabbing, you fool. Find the killer! Arrest him!* And I would have said something, had not Sterling looked at me. His face was wooden and more impassive than I'd ever seen it, but his eyes were full of compassion.

"Someone has to go for the inspector," Lancaster repeated.

"I'll fetch him," Sterling said. "You guard the body."

The sergeant shivered at the thought. "No. I'll go."

He touched his hat as he passed me.

"What a fool," I mumbled, once Lancaster was out of earshot.

Sterling read my mind. Either that, or he has exceptionally good hearing. "He's not a bad man, Sergeant Lancaster. They say he was headed for high rank, until he lost a company of new men, raw recruits, in a snowstorm."

"The boys died?"

"No. Just fingers and toes lost to frostbite. But Lancaster blamed himself." Sterling shrugged. "Killed his career all by himself, with regret and guilt. Or so they say. What do you make of this, Mrs. MacGillivray?"

"What? Oh, Ireland. He's dead."

"Thank you for that considered opinion." Sterling knelt by the body. He didn't touch anything, only looked.

Reluctantly, I walked over to stand at the foot of the stage. "He was not a nice man, Mr. Ireland."

"You're right about that. First, we'll have to eliminate the handful of people who didn't particularly want Ireland dead. Then we'll be left with the majority of the population of Dawson."

Sterling stood up at the moment I leaned over to take a closer look, my churning stomach having settled down and my pesky curiosity taking control. Sterling was on the stage, and I stood on the first step. He loomed over me. All the inquisitiveness of a police officer fled from his perfectly structured face, his expressive eyes softened, and the edges of his mouth turned down. He lifted one hand as if he were about to touch the top of my head, to run his fingers through my hair.

I had sworn that no one would ever again look down on me. My heart pounded, and I took a step backwards down the stairs.

Heavy boots sounded on the floorboards in the gambling room. Sterling and I were facing the door when the men arrived. Angus and Ray came first, with Lancaster and his inspector close on their heels. The watchman followed.

"Oh, for the love of God," Ray said. "Jack Ireland, of all people."

"You know this man, Mr. Walker?" the inspector asked.

"Jack Ireland, it is. He came in here for the first time only yesterday, maybe the day before. Spreading money around like he'd printed it himself." Ray shook his head. "Fee, my dear, are you all right?"

The inspector's attention shifted. He nodded to me, the greased edges of an enormous handlebar moustache curling heavenward. I hate a moustache that requires artificial embellishment. "Perhaps the lady would be more comfortable sitting outside?"

I peeked out from under my lashes. "I *am* feeling faint, sir."

"Constable!" he barked. "Escort Mrs. MacGillivray and her son home."

"If you don't mind, Inspector," I said, patting my chest to gather breath. "Perhaps Sergeant Lancaster would do me the courtesy. He has been so terribly gracious." I smiled at them all.

Ray raised his eyes to the roof.

Lancaster tried not to look thrilled at being singled out and failed utterly.

Richard Sterling and Angus MacGillivray looked at the body, both of them avoiding my face.

"Very well." The inspector was new in town, and I didn't know his name—a substantial oversight on my part.

"I'm sorry, sir, but I do not believe we've met?" I offered a slightly strained smile, which contained a hint of distress beneath a lady's natural desire to be polite.

"Inspector McKnight," he said, with a smile almost as condescending as mine. And I knew that I'd best not play this man for a fool. "At your service, madam." He was a scrawny fellow, about my height, with a pair of glasses so thick, he must be half-blind. But his eyes, enormous behind the lenses, were sharp and intelligent. "Who's the fellow who found the body?"

The watchman stepped forward, wearing nothing above the waist but his dirty undershirt. "This were how I found him, sir. I didn't touch nothin'. Then I went and fetched Mrs. MacGillivray right away, Mr. Walker not bein' available like."

"Mrs. MacGillivray?" Lancaster said, "shall we go?"

"Angus?"

"Please, can I stay, Ma? Mother, I mean. Ray might need me." Angus looked around the room, seeking support.

It came from an unexpected quarter. "Let the boy stay, Mrs. MacGillivray," Richard Sterling said. "If Walker wants to get a message to you, Angus'll be needed."

Angus beamed, looking more like an angel than the hard-hearted criminal investigator he probably thought himself to be.

I sighed heavily. "If you insist. Gentlemen, good night." I picked up the skirts of my plain, but nonetheless flattering, green skirt and swept out of the room. Sergeant Lancaster tripped over his right boot, leapt into the air in an attempt to recover, blushed to the roots of his non-existent hair, and stumbled after me. I stood by the door, patiently waiting for my escort, and favoured him with a grateful smile.

"Sergeant," McKnight called after us, "fetch the doctor once you've seen Mrs. MacGillivray home."

It wasn't that I was uninterested in the remains of Jack Ireland, late of the *San Francisco Standard*. On the contrary, the demise of the unlamented Mr. Ireland might turn out to be of considerable importance to my business as well as my life. But it was necessary to leave the men to their work. I could count on Ray and Angus to report exactly what transpired. Ray would tell me the facts, and Angus would reveal every nuance that lay under the surface.

Sergeant Lancaster said not a word on the walk back to Mrs. Mann's boarding house. The streets were deserted. A few rats scuttled about, seeking refuge in the gaping boards that were the feet of the hastily constructed dance halls, shops and homes. A wolf howled in the hills, sounding very close indeed. Dawson might try to pretend it was a cosmopolitan city, but I'd never heard the call of a wolf on the streets of London. Not even in Toronto.

"Here we are. This is my home. Thank you, Sergeant." I smiled at my escort. My feet ached, my head throbbed, my ribs hurt from the pressure of my corset. I had no desire to linger in discomfort making polite conversation.

Lancaster touched his hat and shifted his feet. I hoped Mrs. Mann had the stove stoked and the kettle full.

"You're a fine lady, Mrs. MacGillivray. You've raised a fine boy." The words burst out of Lancaster like I hoped steam would shortly rise from Mrs. Mann's kettle. "Good night." He touched his hat and stumbled into the dusk.

How odd.

Chapter Twenty-One

"Can't say as I'm sorry to see the end of that bastard," Ray Walker said, once the men had all finished watching Fiona depart.

"Why is that, Mr. Walker?" Inspector McKnight asked.

"'Cause he was a filthy woman-beating piece of human garbage."

"Did you kill him?"

Ray snorted. "No. And don't you go trying to pin this on me. If I'd killed him, I wouldn't ha' left the body anywhere near the Savoy."

"Ray didn't kill anyone," Angus shouted.

"Thank you, laddie."

McKnight turned to Sterling. "What do we have here, Constable?"

Sterling looked up from where he knelt by the body. "A slash to the belly, sir. Looks bad, but not life-threatening, at a guess. Probably distracted him enough for the killer to move in and deliver the cut to the throat."

McKnight knelt on Ireland's other side.

Angus didn't know how close he dared get. He was amazed he hadn't been asked to leave. He edged forward until he stood at the bottom of the steps. Sterling and the inspector talked in serious voices, paying him no mind.

Ray pulled up two benches, one to sit on and one to prop his feet on and looked like he was about to settle in for a well-deserved nap. He scratched at his scalp, causing a big clump of thin, greasy hair to stick out at the back of his head.

Angus adored the tough little Scot, although not as

much as he admired Richard Sterling. But now he was unsure if Ray Walker was worthy of his respect.

He'd arrived at Ray's room, in a building called a boarding house, although it wasn't anywhere near as nice as the boarding house in which he and his mother lived with the Manns, where they had home-cooked, plentiful meals, a nice warm kitchen, clean sheets and towels, and a proper outhouse. Ray rented one room in a house full of men. The place was dirty, and it smelled bad.

Angus had knocked at the door, loudly.

"Who the hell is it?" Ray had bellowed.

"Angus MacGillivray, sir. You have to come quick."

The door opened a crack. Ray's head popped out. His hair was tossed as if he'd been sleeping. But it was only early evening.

"Angus? What on earth? Your mother?"

"Ma's fine, sir. But she sent me to get you. She said you have to come quick."

"The Savoy? Not a fire?"

"No, sir. The Savoy's fine too."

"What then? Speak up, lad. I'm not running out into the night to accommodate some flight of fancy of your mother's."

Ray Walker, of all people, should know that Angus's mother had never had a moment of fancy in her life. "Someone's..."

"Come back to bed, Ray. I'm getting cold." Inside the room, a woman giggled.

Ray looked behind him. "Hush, you."

Back to Angus. "Someone's what?"

"Dead."

"Dead?"

"On the stage. In the Savoy. Dead. Murdered, looks like."

"Wait right there."

The door closed in Angus's face. But it was a very thin door. He could hear Ray cross the room, a woman's soft question, the light slap of hand on ample flesh, and another giggle, followed by a whispered "quiet" from Ray.

Finally the door opened, and Ray came out, stuffing his shirttails into his trousers. The laces of his boots dragged along the floor.

"Let's go." Ray pushed past Angus and shut the door. But not before Angus had a good look at Betsy from the dance hall. She was sitting up in the narrow bed, the crumpled sheets bunched around her plump legs. Angus stared at her heavy breasts, pale pink with dark brown centres and large, hard nipples. She wiggled her fingers at him and ran her tongue across her lips.

"Not a word to your mother, you hear me, Angus. Not a word."

"But, sir, I thought..."

"You thought nothing. Now tell me what happened, for heaven's sake. A body—that's all we need."

Angus mumbled something about the Savoy—the stage, blood, death—but his mind couldn't get rid of the image of Betsy licking her plump pink lips. He knew perfectly well what Ray must have been doing with her in his room. But he was having trouble understanding why. Betsy was one of the dance hall girls. The girls who danced at the Savoy weren't whores—women who had intimate relations with men in exchange for money. And besides, wasn't Ray in love with Irene? That's what his mother had told him, and she knew everything there was to know about things involving love and men and women. So if Ray was in love with Irene, why was he...doing stuff with Betsy? And they weren't even married!

"Ray?"

"Not a word, boy. Not a word."

* * *

Angus edged closer to the stage, afraid to attract attention, attention that might get him sent off to the care of his mother, but equally afraid of missing something important. He mounted the steps, trying not to make a sound.

Difficult, if not impossible, on the Savoy stage, constructed of cheap wood and insufficient nails. He stood behind Richard Sterling and peered over the constable's shoulder, swallowing the bile that rose into his throat, threatening to choke him, or worse.

Sterling and McKnight were talking in low voices, as if they were mindful of showing respect to the dead. Sterling had pointed out that the wound in Ireland's stomach wasn't deep enough to kill. At least not right away. He would have died from it, eventually, if it had been left unattended. But not here, on the stage of the Savoy. With that wound, a healthy man could have staggered into the street looking for help. But the slice across the throat would have sent his lifeblood splashing across the stage in all directions. He wouldn't have been able to stand up after suffering that.

"You can look, Angus," Sterling said, acknowledging the boy's presence. "But mind you don't touch anything."

Angus leaned closer to get a better look, trying to take it all in. His stomach was beginning to settle.

"Had to have gotten a good amount of blood on his clothes," Sterling said.

"Agreed," McKnight said.

The doctor arrived in the company of Sergeant Lancaster. Breathing heavily from his exertions, Lancaster took a seat on the bench beside Ray. The doctor walked to the foot of the stage. "Dead, I'd say."

"Really, doctor," McKnight said. "Is that your professional opinion?"

"Don't know why you dragged me away from my pipe," the doctor grumbled. "The fellow's obviously dead from a knife wound to the abdomen."

"If you could take a closer look?" Sterling asked.

"No need." The doctor snapped his fingers at the men who'd come in behind him. "He's dead. I took the liberty of calling in at the funeral parlour on my way past. When you're finished looking for clues, these men will take care of him. Drop by my office tomorrow during hours, and I'll have the death certificate ready." The doctor slapped his hat back on his head and started to leave, but he hesitated at the door. He walked over to Ray's bench.

"Perhaps I should call on Mrs. MacGillivray? I understand she found the body. She might be in need of sedation. Exposure to the brutal reality of life and death can be most upsetting to the delicate female constitution."

Ray yawned. "Right. I remember my mum. Gave birth to twelve children, buried nine o' them, nursed my gran for months as her guts rotted inside o' her, and then cared for my own dad when he died. Her delicate wee constitution almost cracked under the strain."

The doctor's chest rose, and he puffed up all over, reminding Angus of a frog the boys had watched for what seemed like hours on a summer's day at the creek behind his school in Toronto. "I was of course referring to the fact that Mrs. MacGillivray is a lady."

Angus held his breath, expecting that Ray would take offence at the blatant insult to his own mother. Instead, the Scotsman chuckled. "We know exactly what you were suggesting, Doc. Don't we, lads?"

The doctor's eyes narrowed. He struggled to think of something appropriately cutting to say.

"Thank you for your time, Doctor," Sterling said. "An officer will be around tomorrow to get that certificate."

"Someone should check that man's credentials," Sterling said as the door swung closed behind the doctor. "He wouldn't be the first fellow to arrive in Dawson pretending to be something he isn't."

"I don't think his intentions towards Mrs. MacGillivray are entirely honourable." Sergeant Lancaster wagged a finger at Angus. "You watch out for him, young fellow. Until she marries again, it's up to you to protect your mother's reputation."

"I'm fully aware of that, Sergeant," Angus said. And he was. At school, they'd lectured the boys extensively about a man's responsibility to his mother, a God-given responsibility, particularly important in the case of a widowed mother such as Angus's. But it was a hard job, in a place like Dawson, with the sort of company that came into the Savoy and the fact that, as a child, he wasn't allowed to spend much time in the dance hall.

McKnight rolled the body over, checking to see if there was anything underneath. There wasn't and he let it fall back. The limbs were stiff, as if Jack Ireland were exerting all his control to keep them from moving.

"What's the matter with him, Constable Sterling?" Angus whispered, forgetting in his curiosity that he should be keeping quiet.

"He's dead, Angus," Sterling said, not laughing.

"I mean other than that, sir. Why are his arms so stiff? It looks like he's frozen solid."

"Rigor mortis, son," Inspector McKnight said, standing up with a soft grunt. "Happens in the hours after death. It wears off after a few days."

"Rigor helps us determine how long a man's been dead," Sterling explained. "It starts in the head and moves down. Now, Ireland here is pretty stiff most of the way down, but his feet still have a ways to go yet."

"So at a guess, I'd say he's been dead anywhere from six to nine hours. No more than twelve. Constable?"

"Probably, sir. But it would have been cold in here last night. Cold delays rigor. Might be more."

"Good point," the inspector said.

"Pardon me, sir, but that doesn't seem quite so clever. It's close to six o'clock now. Me and my ma found him around five. The Savoy was full of customers at midnight, and Ma and Mr. Walker and the staff would have been here for a while after that, say until about one. Anyone would've noticed a dead body lying in the middle of the stage. So he couldn't have been killed more than sixteen hours ago. Common sense tells me that."

"That's true, Angus," Sterling said. "But suppose he wasn't killed here, in the Savoy? Maybe he was killed a couple of days ago. I know everyone saw him here last night, but I'm saying suppose. And then the body was carried in here after closing?"

"I see," Angus said.

"I'm guessing you want to be a Mountie, young man, and good for you," McKnight said. "We could stand here all night talking about police methods and medical clues. But that'll have to wait for another time."

Angus beamed. He had been included in the men's talk, not sent home under his mother's skirts.

"His pocket watch is missing, Inspector," Sterling said.

"It was a good one?"

"Looked good, but I didn't see it close up. I think he had a diamond stickpin as well."

"Theft?"

"On the stage of the Savoy, on a Sunday night? Unlikely Ireland would have wandered in here all on his own, to be waylaid by a pickpocket."

"Maybe someone wanted it to look like a theft gone wrong," Angus suggested. "I read a story where that happened. Is there any money missing?"

"No wallet," McKnight said.

"Ireland liked to flash his money around," Sterling muttered. "He would have been carrying some."

"Something to think about. You fellows can take him away now," McKnight said to the undertaker's assistants, standing silently in the shadows.

Angus turned his head as they hoisted the stiff body onto their makeshift stretcher. The scent of death hung heavy in the air. Angus had smelt death in the piled carcasses of the abandoned horses they trudged past on their way from Dyea to the Chilkoot Pass. But this was different. Surprisingly sweet. Whether because the body was that of a man, not a horse, or because it was fresh, or because it was being moved, he didn't know. He held his breath and avoided looking at the dark patch and the pattern of splashes left behind.

"A half-competent doctor might have been able to find out more," McKnight said, once the men had left with their burden. "But in this case, I doubt it. There isn't much of a mystery around what happened here. Only about who. Sterling, you know these people. Did this Ireland fellow have any enemies?"

Ray Walker laughed.

"Pretty much everyone he met," Sterling said, giving Walker a hard look. "I know there was trouble here last night. Trouble bad enough that if the Mounties knew about it, it might have had the Savoy closed down for a few days. You want to tell me what happened, Ray?"

"No."

"All I have to do tomorrow morning is ask around. Mention a few words: Ireland, Walker, Irene. And everyone'll assume I know all about it and be happy to talk till the cows come home."

Ray examined his fingernails. Lancaster got up and found another bench on which to place his ample posterior.

"And once they start talking, who knows what people'll say. Give some folks a listening ear, and they'll make up all sorts of wild embellishments, just to keep you paying attention to them. Have you found that happens, Inspector?"

"All the time. And the longer a story grows, the more incredible it becomes in the telling."

Ray wiped one hand across his brow and down the side of his face.

"You want to tell the Inspector and me what happened last night, Ray? Or do you want to make us work at getting a story that might be more than the truth?"

"Ireland." Ray spat on the floor. "Hit Irene. In front of everyone. Attacked Fee too. Don't worry Angus, your mum fought back. Your mum protects herself. And what's hers. But Irene, she don't know how to fight a man. I'm the bouncer here. Can't have the customers beating on the dancers, can I?"

"And that was it? Nothing personal, no excessive force?"

"I did my job, Sterling. Now you go and do yours and find out who did the world a favour and rid us all of Jack frigging Ireland. But it weren't me."

Ray stood up. His accent had gotten so thick that even Angus was having trouble understanding what he was saying. The Scotsman's face was as red as Angus's mother's best dress. The one that had been her best dress until yesterday. *Blood,* she had said to Mrs. Mann, *can't wash it out. Rip the dress into rags.* His heart almost stopped. Where had his mother gotten enough bloodstains to ruin the dress she cherished so much? She'd said they came from a man with a crack on the head. But she had never before allowed herself to be soiled by the customers.

Coincidence? Of course. Coincidence.

Ray said, "He was shown the door and tossed out into the street. Where, hopefully, he fell into a pile of warm dog shit."

"You didn't see Mr. Ireland being evicted?" Sterling raised one eyebrow. "Why was that?"

"My supper's waiting," Ray said. He was a good half foot or more shorter and fifty pounds lighter than the constable, but he gave off an aura of impressive strength as he pulled himself up to his full height. "You're keepin' me from it. If you've got something more than wild accusations, say it. Otherwise I'm going for my supper."

"You're free to go, Mr. Walker," McKnight said. "But don't leave town until you hear from us."

"I've a business to run, laddies. I'm not leaving." He kicked the bench over as he walked towards the door. It crashed to the floor, and a crack split the wood right down the middle.

"I think he intended that to be your head, Constable," McKnight said. "I'm going back to the fort to fill out a report. Tell me what else you know about this Walker fellow on the way. It's interesting that he wasn't the one to throw Ireland into the street."

"You can't accuse Mr. Walker of this," Angus shouted. "Ray wouldn't kill nobody."

"Friend of his, are you?" McKnight asked.

"Yes, I am," Angus said.

"Your mother relies on him, does she?"

"Huh?"

"It's much the other way around, sir," Sterling said. "Ray Walker could exert control over any bar or whorehouse in any port in the world, but only Mrs. MacGillivray can keep this place respectable. And profitable."

"Like her, do you, Constable?"

Sterling looked into the Inspector's face. "I admire her, sir. Very much. A woman on her own, she's accomplished a great deal."

"You want to be a detective, son," McKnight looked at Angus. "The first rule is that you don't let your feelings get in the way of the job. Remember that. If your duty calls upon you to do so, you will find yourself arresting your grandmother. That's a rule you also might need to remember, Constable. I suggest we start by looking for that pocket watch and stickpin."

"Angus, put out the lamp," Sterling said, "and go home."

Chapter Twenty-Two

"They think Ray did it."

I was in the kitchen when Angus came in. A strange, sour odour lingered about him, reminding me of a Billingsgate fishmonger at the end of an unnaturally hot day.

The Manns were still up, although they usually went to bed early on Sunday to prepare for a long week ahead. One look at my face as I'd stumbled through the door earlier, and Mrs. Mann had the kettle on, and Mr. Mann had pulled up a chair to hear the whole story. They were relaxed and dressed in their nightwear (Mr. Mann with hastily-pulled on trousers beneath his long flannel nightshirt), enjoying a mug of warm tinned milk before bed. Mrs. Mann had taken her hair down. I'd never before seen it unbound. It fell almost to her waist in a shimmering river of slate grey, looking much like the Klondike River on a cold, damp day before freeze-up. They had sat with me, waiting for Angus.

Angus changed his clothes quickly, and when he returned to the kitchen, Mrs. Mann had a mug of warm milk, the real stuff, and thick slices of yesterday's currant cake ready for him.

"They think Ray did it," Angus repeated around a mouthful of milk and cake.

"Nonsense," I said. "You imagined it." No matter what his age, I had never assumed that Angus imagined anything. His eye for detail and his interest in everything surrounding him were phenomenal. On the rare occasions that I'd engaged in conversation with other mothers, I had been surprised at how they dismissed their sons' words as fantasy or imagination. I prided myself on being able to tell when my child was playing and when he was being serious.

But tonight, I didn't want to hear it. I would not accept that Ray might be a suspect. "At the beginning of an investigation, the police suspect everyone in the vicinity," I said. "And they narrow their suspects down from there. That's all, Angus."

"No, Ma. Mother. Really. They almost accused Ray right there. That Inspector McKnight is sharp. But not as sharp as Constable Sterling. He noticed that Ireland's feet weren't fully into what they call rigor mortis yet."

Mr. Mann gasped. "Young man, ladies is here."

"Sorry, sir. Sorry, Mrs. Mann. But they can tell how long a man's been dead by how stiff the body is. It's really interesting. Like if…"

I scarcely heard him. I remembered the red rage on Ray's face as he put the boot into Ireland's undefended body, Irene's sobs, and Ireland's bruised and ugly face as we tossed him into the street.

Was it hard to believe that Ireland had come back to the Savoy looking for Ray or maybe Irene? He was new in town; he might not have realized just how completely Dawson shuts down on a Sunday.

Even if Ireland had returned to the Savoy, not knowing that no one would be there, well, no one would be there. Ray had no reason to stop by on a Sunday. Of course, neither did I.

But if anything had happened between Ireland and Ray after we'd closed and everyone had headed off into what passes as night in the Yukon in June, I would swear on my son's golden head that Ray Walker wouldn't leave Jack Ireland's dead body displayed on the stage of the Savoy for the next person passing to discover then go off home to enjoy his Sunday lunch.

"Time for bed." Mr. Mann downed the last of his milk. "Come, Helga. This is not for decent woman." He glared at me as if the murder were all my fault. "Very bad business. Fancy women, drink, gambling. Nothing but more bad."

His righteous indignation was somewhat spoiled by the eagerness with which he'd wanted to hear every detail.

He turned to Angus. "Work tomorrow. Seven."

"Huh?" Angus said.

The day before, Mr. Mann and I had decided it was time Angus started work. We'd both noticed my son slip in to the house, keeping his face in the shadows, hoping we wouldn't see that the soft, pale skin under his left eye was turning purple and the eye was swelling shut.

"Boy is with fight," Mr. Mann had said to me after Angus left the kitchen with a handful of biscuits. "He too soft, needs vork. Vork keep him away from trouble. On Monday he start vorks in store, I give normal pays." Mr. Mann owned a hardware shop down by the river, where he conducted a roaring trade, buying up nails and hammers, screwdrivers, and just about anything else from men who'd taken one look at the town and we33re now desperate to sell everything they had and flee back to civilization. Whereupon he sold the goods to others, equally desperate to get to the gold fields or to set themselves up in town, but who'd neglected to bring the necessary hardware.

"Tomorrow you start in store." Mr. Mann pushed his chair back from the table.

"Start what?" Angus said.

"Vork."

"Work?"

"Vork."

"Mr. Mann and I have agreed that it would be good for you to spend some time over the summer helping him at the store."

"Working?"

"Yes, working."

"At the hardware store?"

"Don't repeat everything I say, Angus."

"But, Mother."

"No buts. It's been an exceedingly long day."

"Good night, Mrs. MacGillivray, Angus." The Manns went off to bed.

"Ah, Ma. Mother. Do I have to?"

I poured more water into the teapot, mindful of getting the last bit of flavour out of the black leaves. "Yes, you do." The mixture looked weak, so I swirled the tea ball around in the hot water. "How did Ray seem, when you called on him to come to the Savoy?" Despite myself, I wanted to know if Ray had been surprised at the discovery of Ireland's body.

Angus shifted in his chair. His face flushed and he looked into the bottom of his mug.

"Angus? I asked you how Ray reacted." I put the teapot down.

"Fine, Mother. He reacted fine." Angus's face was as red as my late, lamented, best dress.

"Fine. What do you mean, fine? Fine can mean anything. Over the winter we all said the weather was fine if it hadn't reached minus fifty yet. Mrs. Jones is fine, considering that an earthquake swallowed her house whole. Mr. Smith is fine..."

"What earthquake?" Angus asked.

I took a deep breath. "This murder is a bad thing, Angus. It can hurt all of us at the Savoy. If the Savoy closes down, for any reason, I'll have trouble making ends meet. I spent everything we owned getting to the Yukon. Do you understand?"

"Ray didn't kill Mr. Ireland. He was so surprised when I told him that he...uh, he..."

"He what?"

"Left without tying his shoelaces."

Suddenly, I was simply dreadfully tired. "Let's go to bed. You have your first day of work tomorrow, and I can only imagine what the Savoy will be like once word gets around about the murder. Every curiosity seeker between here and Seattle, if not San Francisco, will be wanting to take a look at the scene of the crime."

"Goodnight, Mother." Angus touched his lips to my cheek.

"Goodnight, dear."

My son's wild enthusiasm about the wonders of the police investigation and all the scientific mysteries involving a dead human body had dried up the moment I'd asked about Ray's behaviour. A dull feeling in the pit of my stomach told me I wasn't the only one worrying about Ray Walker. If I trusted my son's sharp perception about people up until now, could I disregard it when his conclusions made me uncomfortable?

I looked into the tin cup holding the dregs of my tea. Once, during the exceedingly short time in which I'd been a member of the Prince of Wales' inner circle, I'd attended a reading of a gypsy fortune teller who was momentarily the passion of fashionable London. She had, with much clanging of gold bangles, rustling of taffeta and heavy sighs, read my past and foretold the mysteries of my future through the arrangement of Earl Grey leaves in the bottom of a Royal Doulton teacup. If she had divined that I had been abandoned as a newborn in the wilds of Equatorial Africa and raised by a pack of particularly intelligent and loving gorillas, she wouldn't have been much further off the mark than she was. Perhaps the Earl Grey had put her off. Most of the other ladies, I'd noticed, were read through English Breakfast.

Now, as then, the tea leaves revealed no secrets. I trusted battered tin no more than Royal Doulton. But I trusted my son.

I went to bed with a heavy heart.

Chapter Twenty-Three

I scarcely slept a wink, what with dreams of soggy tea leaves, the portly Prince of Wales, Ray Walker in the grip of blood lust, a crying, battered Irene, and the blank, empty eyes on the dead face of Jack Ireland.

When I judged that it was time to get up, I dragged an unhappy Angus out of bed.

Mrs. Mann, knowing that facing the first day of a real job was hard on a young man, had prepared him a special breakfast of eggs and fried bread.

I was served porridge as usual for a Monday morning. But as it arrived in a deep bowl full to the brim with fresh cow's milk, I was more than happy to dig in. Besides, don't they say that bacon is not good for a lady's figure? I was past thirty years of age; time to start taking care.

Thirty! Heaven help me!

My own mother was married, mother of me—her only living child—with death breathing heavily down the back of her neck when she was but the age I am now.

* * *

I carried my big ledger down to a table in the saloon, in order to keep an eye on the door while I worked and to catch Mrs. Saunderson as soon as she arrived. I didn't bother to check on the state of the stage, feeling strangely reluctant to venture into the back by myself. Angus had told me the doctor had come and the body had been taken away. The men who'd gathered to investigate wouldn't have troubled themselves to clean up the mess.

"Good morning." Mrs Saunderson burst through the door, catching me wool-gathering. "It's looking to be a lovely day." She took off her plain straw hat. "Strange to see you sitting down here, Mrs. Mac. Something the matter with your office, or are you just waiting for a cup of coffee? Won't be but a minute. My Luke said the funniest thing last night, let me tell you about it, he said..."

"Mrs. Saunderson, Helen, I have something to talk to you about. Even before we have our coffee. Please have a seat."

The blood drained from her face, and she clutched both hands to her chest. Her eyes filled with water. "Oh, Mrs. MacGillivray. Please, no. The little 'uns are only just now getting some colour back into their sweet faces, what with good food and all." The tears started to fall. She collapsed into the chair and buried her head in her hands.

"What on earth are you talking about, Helen? I'm pleased to hear your children are eating well. I've noticed the same with Angus, that as soon as fresh food started getting through, he perked right up. He's probably grown another couple of inches in the last month. Why, we had milk from a cow for our breakfast this morning. It was wonderful."

"Fresh milk," she said, through her tears. "Even now I can't afford no fresh milk. And without this position, I won't even be able to afford tinned milk. Please, Mrs. MacGillivray, give me another chance."

At last I understood. I pulled a handkerchief out of my skirt pocket and handed it to her. "Do stop crying, Helen. I'm not about to sack you, if that's what you're thinking."

A glimmer of hope flashed behind her red eyes. "You're not?"

"Certainly not. I simply have an unpleasant task to tell you about."

"Oh, thank you, Mrs. Mac. Thank you." She blew her nose heartily and handed back the handkerchief.

"You can return it once it's been laundered," I said. "Now, as to the matter at hand. There is a... considerable... mess...in the dance hall."

"Mrs. Mac, I've seen me share of men's messes in this life. I'll make your coffee, then I'll go clean it."

I stood up. "This isn't a normal mess, Helen. You'd best come with me."

She looked at me.

"Someone died yesterday. In the dance hall. On the stage."

"Died? Here in the Savoy? Oh, my goodness. But how? We was closed yesterday."

"I don't know how, or why."

"Will you be wanting me to lay him out, then, Mrs. Mac? That's no job for a stranger. Don't he have no kin, no friends?"

I wasn't explaining this very well at all. "No. That's not it. The body is gone. Taken away."

She heaved a sigh of relief. "That's good then."

"He didn't just die. He was murdered. Stabbed."

"My goodness." She crossed herself.

"I haven't dared go back there this morning, and I'd feel more comfortable if you would accompany me, Helen."

"Surely I will. But murdered! Mother of God."

"There's some blood and…such like to be cleaned up."

"Why didn't you just say so? Blood's a right problem to get rid of."

Mrs. Saunderson, now that she was faced with a simple task of cleaning, as normal a part of a lower class woman's life as breathing or cooking, ignored my miserable attempts to soften the bad news and charged on ahead.

Not wanting to appear any more muddleheaded than I already had, I attempted to keep up.

The gaming room was dark and empty. Difficult to even imagine how full of colour and movement, smoke and the smell of unwashed bodies, the unabashed joy of the winners and quiet despair of the losers, it would soon be. Men would be pouring through the door in less than two hours, all of them ready to throw their money, very hard-earned money at that, into my bank account.

"Do you know who the dead gentleman was?"

"Jack Ireland."

She stopped walking so abruptly I bumped into her. "Ireland? The newspaper feller?"

"Yes."

She crossed herself again and turned to face me. The look of polite sorrow had been replaced by a smile. She placed her hands on her hips. "Is that so? Jack Ireland. I'm a good Catholic woman, Mrs. Mac, and it's a sin to be happy at another's misfortune. I'll take it to confession and ask forgiveness, but I don't mind tellin' you that I'm right glad to hear it."

"Helen, you can't mean that. Ireland treated you badly, to be sure. But to be happy at his death?" Of course, I myself was quite pleased that the detestable Mr. Ireland had been prevented from causing us any more trouble, but I wasn't about to express in public my quiet satisfaction at his untimely demise.

Helen, on the other hand, virtually rubbed her hands together in glee. Chuckling, she led the way into the dance hall.

Jack Ireland's lifeblood had splattered across the boards, and there it had dried, staining the wood dark. No one would be able to notice it from the audience. And it wasn't as if the stage wasn't stained already, with everything from tobacco juice to vomit and urine. The vomiters we couldn't do much about, save toss them into the street, but the man who'd unbuttoned his trousers and urinated on the stage when his favourite girl accepted a dance with his rival? He was still spending his days chopping wood in Fort Herchmer.

Vomit and urine and tobacco juice were one thing, but my girls would balk at dancing on the stage if they saw bloodstains beneath their feet.

Helen Saunderson and I stared at the dark patches. I'd thought it would be much worse. In my imagination I'd seen the stain covering the entire stage, perhaps even dripping down the stairs and spreading across the dance floor.

Helen might have read my thoughts. "This ain't nothin', Mrs. Mac. A few drops. You had me thinking there was a flood or something."

"Can you get the stains out?"

"Probably not entirely. But enough so's it won't show worse than any other mark."

"Good. Thank you."

As I turned to leave, Mrs. Saunderson reared back her head and let loose with a mouthful of spittle, aimed directly at the heart of the stains.

I tried to say something, but my mouth simply hung open, a most unladylike position. I snapped my jaws shut.

She saw me watching her. "Fellow ruined my good name. Mighta ruined my daughters' chances for a good marriage. I'll fetch your coffee. Then I'll clean up in here."

She marched out, her back straight and her head held high.

I fell onto a bench. That was quite a display. I'd remember not to get on Helen Saunderson's bad side.

But how much of a display was it? She hated Ireland, that was plain to see. How far would she go to get revenge on the man who had supposedly slandered her? She'd appeared to be genuinely surprised at my news of the body and then its identity. Could that have been an act? Did she arrive at work this morning knowing exactly what had been found in the back room of the Savoy? She'd been distressed at the thought that I was about to sack her. Was it because she feared I was going to cast her adrift in order to avoid implication in any scandal that would arise from the murder?

I still didn't understand why Helen was making such a fuss over it all. But then the upkeep of my "good name" has never worried me over much. Although, when I stopped to think about it, if my lack of reputation ever endangered Angus, denied him a position at school perhaps or shut him out of the homes of his friends, I might have been ready to do some serious damage.

Which is why it is always better, I had learned, to move in the very highest of circles, where men scarcely care about their reputation or anyone else's as long as their wife or, most important of all, her mother, doesn't find out. I do have one addendum that I will add to my life's lessons: It is even better to swim in the waters of a town so wild, so full of naked ambition, so free of inhibition, that no one cares who you are or where you come from. As long as you have coin in your pocket.

My head hurt. There would be time later to sort out who amongst my acquaintances might be a murderer.

Chapter Twenty-Four

I sat on the hard, uncomfortable bench and looked around the empty dancehall. The benches were pushed up against the walls, except for two that had been placed in the middle of the room, for some reason. A mouse scurried across the floor and jumped up the stairs onto the stage. Its whiskers twitched cautiously and, catching sight of me out of the corner of its black button eyes, it disappeared into a crack that at a casual glance appeared to be far too small to accommodate its chubby frame. My stomach rolled over at the thought of what the creature might discover in the dark, empty space underneath the stage.

I fled.

Ray Walker was sitting at the big table in the centre of the room, reading my ledger. He looked up when I came in. "Not a good idea, Fee me dear, to leave the accounts spread open on the table with the door unlocked and not a soul in sight. Ye don't look well. Rough night?"

"Oh, shut up." I slammed the ledger shut.

"Rough night," he said.

I placed my hands on the table and leaned forward. "What do you know about Jack Ireland's body being found in the Savoy? If you know anything, you'd better tell me." Helen came out of the back with a tray. "Coffee!" I said. "How lovely!"

I threw my body into a chair with so much force, my tailbone groaned in protest. "I told Helen about the unfortunate events of yesterday. She'll have the stage as clean as a whistle by opening. And biscuits too, isn't that nice."

Ray accepted his coffee with a tight smile. He might

think I looked awful, but I hope that as far as my appearance is concerned, awful is a relative term. Ray himself looked like he'd been dragged out of a snowdrift and left to thaw in front of a one-twig fire.

Coffee served, Helen retreated to her back room.

"These biscuits are as tough as hard tack," Ray mumbled. "They could be used to stake out a man's claim."

"Will you shut up about biscuits and how the hell I look. I want to know what you know about the murder of Jack Ireland, and I want to know it now."

Ray's eyes narrowed. "Why are you asking me this, Fee?"

Helen's bucket clattered as she dragged it out of her storage closet. Ray and I smiled at her. She disappeared into the back rooms.

"I'm asking you," I whispered, "because if you're involved, I'm going to be dragged through the muck with you, and I'd prefer to avoid that."

"Now, I wasn't there, but folks told me the last words anyone heard from Jack Ireland was that he was going to get you, Fee. So I'm thinking you may have had more reason to want the man dead than I did."

"Me! You can't turn this back on me!"

"Come on, Fee. There are parts of your life you don't want exposed to the world."

"Now see here, Ray Walker! Constable Sterling, what brings you out so early this fine morning?"

Sterling stood in the doorway, blocking the morning sun. "If you two are having a business meeting, I can wait here. Pay me no mind."

"Please join us. Would you care for coffee? It's fresh. Let me pour you a cup."

"That would be nice, Mrs. MacGillivray. Thank you." The Mountie pulled up a chair. "Morning, Walker."

"Morning."

I sprinted into the broom closet and grabbed a cup from the cupboard. I couldn't find a saucer, too bad. My heart was pounding in my chest, and not from that minuscule bit of exercise.

"Have you made an arrest yet, Constable?" I put the cup down on the table and poured the coffee. "Please, have a biscuit. Made fresh this morning."

"I've come to talk to Mr. Walker," Sterling said. "About the events of Saturday night." He selected a biscuit, which is what the Canadians call a "cookie". Horrible word. Belongs in the nursery, not as a part of polite, adult conversation.

Ray leaned back in his chair. "Busy night, Saturday. Always is."

"Everyone's trying to soak up enough drink and dances and spins of the wheel to see them all the way through to Monday," I added.

Ray eyed me. "Really, Fiona? Is that what they're doing?"

Sterling cleared his throat. "Tasty cookie this," he said, trying to stifle a grimace of distaste and avoiding my eyes as he put the remaining half back onto the table. Goodness, he thought I had made them.

I once boiled an egg. Forgot about it and left the pot over the fire until all the water had evaporated. The egg exploded as I reached into the burnt pot to take it out. I never dared to try cooking again. I wouldn't call the horrid food I managed to scrape together on the Chilkoot trail cooking. Angus had to intervene out of sheer desperation,

"Can you tell me any more about what happened on Saturday, Walker, Mrs. MacGillivray?" Sterling pulled a small note pad and a stub of pencil out of his tunic pocket.

"Where's Inspector McKnight today?" I asked, dipping my biscuit into the coffee to soften it. "I expected he would be the one looking into Ireland's death."

"Who said anything about Jack Ireland? I only asked you about the events of Saturday night."

"Oh, don't play clever with me, Constable Sterling. You don't come in every morning to join us for coffee and chat about our business."

He grinned, and I remembered last night and that brief moment standing on the steps of the stage, with a dead body lying at our feet, when I had thought he was going to touch me.

"McKnight is pursuing other lines of inquiry. He'll be around later to talk to you. This isn't Alaska; we don't have many murders in the Yukon. Ireland is the first this year, and the boss is determined it'll be the last. Now, about Saturday?"

Ray shrugged. "Told you all about it last night."

"So you did. But I'd like you to tell me again."

"Ireland wanted to keep dancing after his minute was up. He wouldn't let go of the girl and objected when I told him to leave. So he got thrown out. That's about it."

Sterling lifted one eyebrow. "Was Jack Ireland here for long?"

"I seem to think he might have been. Did you see him, Fee?"

"Oh, for pity's sake, Ray. It probably took the Constable less than a minute to find out precisely when Ireland was here and what transpired. People will have been talking about nothing else, and no doubt the story is growing bigger and more extravagant every minute."

Helen clattered back through the bar carrying her pail and a dripping mop. Liquid sloshed in the bucket, and the contents of my stomach rose into my throat. I averted my eyes. "Jack Ireland made quite the nuisance of himself. He insulted one of my girls and tried to start a fight when Ray stepped in, which is, as you are no doubt aware, part of his responsibilities here. Mr. Ireland was escorted to the door and politely told never to return."

"As you said, Mrs. MacGillivray, the men are talking about little else. I dropped in to a couple of the dance halls on my way over here. I'll admit that the story gets more interesting in the telling. They're saying that Walker would have kicked Ireland to death if you hadn't intervened. Isn't that taking things beyond your job, Walker?"

Ray growled.

"Exaggeration, of course, Constable. Ray was, naturally, extremely angry at the insult to the dancer. An insult that was accompanied by an act of physical violence. Ray takes the girls' welfare to heart. Don't you, Ray?"

"I'm inclined to believe you, Mrs. MacGillivray," Sterling

said. "Bar gossip is about the most unreliable evidence the police can get. The men are saying you put Ireland onto the floor yourself before Walker intervened, and that you single-handedly dragged Walker off of Ireland."

I laughed lightly and waved my hand in the air. "You see the things you might start to believe if you listen to gossip."

"Which lady was it, Mr. Walker, who Ireland offended?"

Ray said nothing.

"Irene," I said.

"Irene?"

"Irene."

"Irene what, Mrs. MacGillivray? What's her last name?"

"Davidson."

Sterling wrote in his notebook.

I was about to make my excuses and take my leave when he spoke again. "People are also saying that you're very fond of Irene Davidson, Walker. A fondness that she doesn't appear to return. They say you weren't happy about the attentions Ireland paid her. He promised to take her to San Francisco and make her a famous actress, or so they say."

Ray said nothing. I wanted to shake some sense into him. He was a suspect in this killing, and his sullen refusal to speak up didn't show him in a good light.

"Did Ireland have reason to believe that Irene Davidson might give him more dances than he paid for?"

"Unfortunately, he may have," I said. Obviously the man knew everything, no point in pretending otherwise. "I believe they spent some time together the previous evening, after closing. Perhaps he thought that gave him the right to certain liberties."

"Gossip, Fee." Ray was not doing a very good job of hiding his anger at the direction in which these questions were heading. "Now you're the one spreading gossip."

"Sorry, I didn't quite get that, Mr. Walker."

"He accused me of listening to gossip. Which I never do. Much too common." I glared at Ray. He threw daggers back. We must have presented an interesting sight to the observant constable.

I waited for Sterling to ask me what else I knew about Irene's involvement with Ireland. A meaningless phrase like "spent some time together" covered a lot of sins. But his focus shifted.

"At what time did this trouble take place?"

"At about, ahem, the time you arrived to watch us closing down."

"I didn't see you, Walker. In fact, a couple of your bartenders were showing Mr. Ireland the door. Under Mrs. MacGillivray's supervision, if I remember correctly. Where were you at the time?"

"Supervising the closing of the gambling rooms, of course," I answered for my taciturn partner. "Precisely where he would be expected to be at that time of the night." I opened the inexpensive watch I keep pinned at the waist of my dress when I'm working. "Goodness me, look at the time. Almost opening. If you have no more questions, Constable?" I got to my feet and gathered up my ledger and pen.

Clearly, Sterling had plenty more questions, but he was too well brought up to remain seated when a lady got to her feet. Unlike Ray, who remained slumped over the table.

I tossed the constable a demure smile and dared to flutter my eyelashes. But only once. "I can't tell you how pleased I am that you're investigating this horrid business so seriously, Constable Sterling. That such a thing could happen in our establishment is simply beyond belief. Isn't it, Ray? Ray!" If my partner had been any closer, I would have kicked him.

"You can count on me to do my duty, Mrs. MacGillivray." Sterling tucked his notebook and pencil back into the pocket of his scarlet tunic. "Inspector McKnight will want to speak to you later. And you too, Walker."

"I can be found in my office every morning from nine o'clock until shortly before noon, unless I'm running errands. He's welcome to call on me then."

Sterling nodded politely, put his hat on his head and made for the door.

I tossed the ledger on the table, collapsed back into my chair, and took a deep breath. "What the bloody hell's the matter with you, Ray?"

"Lucky the constable isn't here, Fee. He'd have you up on charges for language like that."

"Damn the constable."

The corners of my partner's mouth turned up.

"Don't you understand what's at stake here?" I said. "There hasn't been a single murder in Dawson this year. And this one happens right in the middle of our place. The police will be dead keen to solve it. Fast. I wouldn't trust that McKnight not to pick the first available suspect and drag him off to a hanging."

"Or her?"

"What?"

"Or drag her off to the hanging, Fee."

"Are you saying they're going to investigate me?"

"No, I'm not. Sterling wouldn't arrest you if he came upon you up to your elbows in blood dissecting the corpse with a paring knife."

"What the hell does that mean?"

"I didn't kill Ireland, Fee."

"But..."

"But I don't want the police investigating Irene, that's all."

I couldn't see why they would think Irene had murdered anyone. We'd thrown Ireland out, hadn't we? Irene would scarcely have come back to the deserted Savoy the next day to meet up with him once again.

Would she?

Why was Ray so worried about her? Or was he? Maybe he was trying to be clever: throw suspicion on Irene so that everyone would think he was protecting her. What nonsense. My imagination was galloping away with me.

"If there is anyone in this town who didn't want Jack Ireland dead, I'll stand him to a month of drinks," I said. "I have to get over to the bank. Constable Sterling is much too polite to make any sort of a detective. He could have pushed us a lot harder."

The edges of Ray's mouth lifted a fraction higher. "Only with you, Fee. Only with you."

"What does that mean?"

"Nothing. Where's Angus this morning?"

"Working. He has a job helping Mr. Mann at the store."

Helen came into the room, her steps hesitant, wondering if it was safe. As the police had gone and Ray and I didn't appear to be about to rip each other's throats out, she started to pile the abandoned coffee things onto her tray. She eyed the plate of largely untouched biscuits. "No one hungry this morning? Not to worry. Murder does that to a person's appetite. They'll keep nicely for your afternoon tea, Mrs. Mac."

Ray stifled a laugh.

Chapter Twenty-Five

The bank clerk winked at me. He was a good-looking young man, French Canadian, who had always greeted me with scrupulous politeness and a no-nonsense attitude as befits two educated persons of business conducting important financial matters.

"I beg your pardon," I said, my chin up. "Are my books not in order?"

"Everything is in perfect order, Madame MacGillivray, as always." He leaned closer to the iron grill separating us. "I 'eard you fought a few rounds with a drunk the other night."

The line behind me curled out of the ramshackle building and snaked a long way down the street. The people closest to me shifted. Sensing that some confidence was being exchanged, they edged closer.

"Broke 'is nose with an uppercut, eh?" The clerk practically drooled.

The things that excite men.

"Most certainly not." I tossed my head. "I merely explained to the gentleman in question that his behaviour was not at all proper, whereupon he left."

"Fellows who were there say after you put 'im on the floor, 'e returned after closing to get vengeance, and Walker killed 'im. *Non?*"

"Non! Absolument, non! Give me my account book. Don't you dare be repeating that sort of malicious gossip. I didn't break any noses, and Ray Walker didn't kill anyone. You tell people we did and I'll…I'll…be cross. That's it, I'll be cross."

I snatched up my banking book and whirled around.

Every person in the bank, and a few who stood outside peering in through the windows, watched me.

"What nonsense. Foolish nonsense, like a pack of ill-raised children calling each other names in the park while their nannies' attention wanders," I muttered, passing through the crowd. As I hoped, a great many of the onlookers, particularly the handful of women present, took up the words. "Nonsense," they whispered to each other. "Childish."

I walked away from the centre of town, heading back to my lodgings on Fourth Street, for no other reason than it was my custom to do so. I didn't feel much like a nap. Angus would be at work. I contemplated making a detour and dropping in to the store. Would he be pleased to see me or embarrassed that his mother was keeping an eye on him?

I hesitated at the cross street in front of a small shop advertising its purpose as "Sewing done here. For Ladies and Gentlemen", wondering which way to go.

Irene and Chloe came out of the shop, Irene turning a hat in her hands. It was a nice hat, with a few feathers stuck in the band and a broad brim offering protection for a lady's face from the effects of the sun. Badly-made stitches tried, and failed miserably, to disguise a wide rip across the crown. But Irene placed the hat on her head with satisfaction. I would have tossed it into the garbage before even leaving the shop, but in Dawson one makes do.

"Mrs. MacGillivray," Irene said with a bright smile. Chloe showed her teeth. "Don't you love what she did with my hat? Why, you can scarcely see the stitches. Right as rain, ain't it?" She touched the hat brim and gave me a pleased-with-herself smile.

"Lovely."

"I'm glad I ran into you." She grabbed my arm in a gesture that came perilously close to familiarity. Wasn't that like an American! I shook her hand off, but she didn't take offence, scarcely seeming to notice.

"We're on our way to the Savoy," she breathed. "The seamstress said Jack Ireland was found dead in the dance hall last night. Is it true?" Irene wore a practical day costume of soft pink blouse with generous sleeves above a cream skirt. A wide black belt wrapped itself tightly around her waist. The hat, unfortunately, had a purple ribbon drooping down the back that didn't go at all with the pink blouse. Her cheeks were a too-bright red, and her eyes flashed with enjoyment at the news. She patted her generous chest, the dream of many a man working out on the creeks.

Plain Chloe wore a cotton dress of an unattractive plum, which clashed with her complexion, and an unadorned straw hat.

"Unfortunately, it is true," I said.

Irene leaned closer, out of the hearing range of the small crowd of men surrounding us. The moment we stopped walking, they had gathered around, as eager to soak up the presence of the most-popular dance hall girl in the Yukon Territory and (if I may say so) the most beautiful woman. They were like a litter of new-born puppies pushing and shoving each other aside to get at their mother's teats. "Isn't it wonderful?" she said. "Do you think Ray did it? For me?"

I stepped back. "I most certainly do not. And there was nothing wonderful about it in the least." I looked her up and down. "You seem to be much improved this morning. Aches and pains gone away, have they?"

Chloe tugged at her friend's arm. "Come on, Irene."

Irene shook her off.

"I tell you, Mrs. MacGillivray, as soon as I heard the news, my bruises seemed to heal themselves. Ain't that right, Chloe?"

One old fellow, braver than the rest, had edged forward. He shivered at the mention of Irene's bruises. I turned to our crowd of admirers. "If you gentlemen are looking for somewhere to pass the time this morning, the Savoy is open for business. Please tell the bartender that Mrs. MacGillivray sent you." They scattered, a few of the men who were newer to town naïvely thinking that mention of my name would give them a discount.

I lowered my voice. "If you know anything about Ireland's

death, Irene, you had best speak to the police."

She adjusted her hat ever so slightly and pouted. "Me? Heavens, Mrs. MacGillivray, I don't know nothing. I'm just glad he's dead. The bastard. See you tonight." She waved her fingers cheerfully and walked past me.

I watched her go. Another person not too sad at thc demise of Jack Ireland. A young dandy, dressed like a proper English country gentlemen in a tweed suit with gold-topped walking stick, stepped up to offer Irene his arm. She accepted it, and they strolled down the street, the feather on her hat bobbing with enthusiasm as she chattered away. Chloe, forgotten, tagged along behind.

Chapter Twenty-Six

He had only been working at the hardware store for ten minutes before Angus MacGillivray knew beyond the shadow of a doubt that the life of a shopkeeper wasn't for him. He stuck it out through the morning, dragging stock from boxes stacked at the back of the tent as the stuff up front was sold off, and waiting on customers, although Mr. Mann wouldn't let him handle any money or gold dust. Mr. Mann's shop was down by the waterfront. It fact, it sat smack dab on the waterfront, on a marshy patch of land that had been underwater during the spring floods. But it was close to where the steamboats and rafts tied up after their trip up the Yukon River.

More than a few men staggered off the boats, took one look at the town they'd tried so hard to reach, and offered to sell the nearest merchant all they had. For pennies on the dollar. And merchants such as Mr. Mann were more than happy to help them out. There were as many men eager to buy as to sell, and at the highest prices in all of North America. Mr. Mann specialised in hardware—construction supplies such as nails, hammers and saws—although he was agreeable to handling anything and everything that he could buy for one price and sell for a higher amount. His canvas tent was one of the largest of the multitude that stood storage-box-to-storage-box, guy-rope-to-guy-rope, and tent-peg-to-tent-peg all along the sandbar. The tent on one side of them sold tinned goods, on the other, men's clothes, most of which were heavily worn and many-times repaired.

When Angus and Mr. Mann left for work that morning, Mrs. Mann had handed Angus a large package, wrapped in brown paper, and Mr. Mann had told him that he would have half an hour for his lunch.

He'd never so much as thought about where food came from and how it was prepared before he and his mother had headed for the Chilkoot trail and the Yukon Territory, but he'd soon learned enough to help feed the porters and themselves. Angus had begun to think that he might like to be a chef in a fancy restaurant some day. That was, of course, if for some reason he didn't become a Mountie. Or a cowboy, riding the range, herding cattle.

But working in the hardware store, along side the taciturn Mr. Mann? He couldn't imagine anything worse.

At noon, delighted to escape from the narrow world of the canvas tent and Mr. Mann's watchful, hooded eyes, Angus carried his meal down to the docks to watch the boats coming in and the crowds gathering.

It was a pleasant day, the sun warm in a white and blue sky. The docks didn't offer any place to sit as every tree or patch of green grass had been chopped down or pounded underfoot long ago. Angus placed his lunch on a tall wooden box and unwrapped it. Mrs. Mann didn't disappoint, and he dug enthusiastically into a thick sandwich. This working stuff made a man hungry.

A poster had been nailed to the box advertising a prize fight between Slim Jim, "The Pride of New York City" and "Canada's Own" Big Boris Bovery. Angus wished he could go to the match. But they'd never let a boy like him across the threshold.

The sandwich was dry, could do with a lot more butter, and the bread wasn't fresh. But the beef filling was thick, and there were two more sandwiches in the packet, along with a pile of cookies.

"What are you doing down here, my lad?" Sergeant Lancaster bellowed into Angus's ear. "Sterling gave me your message. Said you can't make the lesson 'cause you have to work. In a store. That's no excuse for a man missing his boxing lesson. Take me to meet this boss of yours."

"That's probably not a good idea, sir. He wouldn't understand."

"Nonsense, boy. Soon as the fellow knows what's what, he'll let you off work. Nice lunch you have there. Your mother make it for you?"

"No, sir. Mrs. Mann, our landlady."

Lancaster eyed the remaining sandwiches.

"Would you like one, sir?"

"No. No. Can't take your food, eh? You're a growing boy."

"There's more here than I can eat." Angus said. Reluctantly, he pushed the package over.

Lancaster snatched a sandwich and bit off a generous mouthful. "Let's go talk to this boss of yours."

"I don't think..."

"Lead the way, boy."

Before Angus could fold up his lunch wrappings, Lancaster snatched a couple of cookies. Angus's boxing instructor was big, burly—owing more to fat than muscle these days—nose broken multiple times, almost bald, with a bullet-shaped head, ears like cauliflowers, and as ugly as sin. All that good stuff, Angus thought, that came with being a genuine boxing champion.

Mr. Mann agreed that Angus could take the occasional afternoon off work in order to have his boxing lesson. Mrs. MacGillivray had no need, he said with a heavy wink, to know that her boy wasn't working in the store in the afternoons. He also told Angus that his pay on lesson days would be cut in half. Oh well, if his mother asked what happened to half his pay, Angus would explain that Mr. Mann decided he didn't need help some afternoons. But he didn't expect her to have much interest in counting the few cents that would amount to his day's wages.

Lancaster led Angus through town to the fort. "Shopkeeping's no job for a man," he said at one point, stepping around the carcass of a horse that had moments before simply decided to stop working and to lie down to die in the middle of the street.

"Mr. Mann does well at it," Angus ventured to say, feeling some need to be loyal to his employer. "He makes good money."

"Shop work's for immigrants and women," Lancaster explained. "You can stay there for awhile. It's important you begin to earn some money to support your mother, but not for long."

Angus was happy to be given the chance to take lessons. And from a former champ at that. After all, there was no one else who could be relied upon to protect his mother. But his face still hurt from the "accidental" blow Lancaster had landed on it at the first lesson.

"Tell you what," Lancaster said, as they crossed the Fort Herchmer central square. The wind was low, and the Union Jack hung limply on the flag pole. "There's a match Thursday at the Horseshoe between Slim Jim and Big Boris Bovery. How'd you like to come with me,?"

"Would I? Yes, sir! That would be wonderful, sir!"

"Good lad."

Reality intruded, and Angus's heart sank. "But they won't let me in, sir. I'm only twelve."

"Don't worry about it, son. I'll vouch for you." Lancaster slapped him so hard on the back, Angus almost tumbled across the square. But he scarcely minded. A real prizefight. He couldn't wait.

Now all he had to do was make sure his ma didn't catch wind of it.

Chapter Twenty-Seven

My screams brought Ray double quick, followed by most of the staff and a good many of the barflies and gamblers.

News of the murder and the dead body found on our stage had brought out everyone from the mildly curious to the seriously ghoulish. When I'd checked the dance hall shortly after my dinner break, I'd found a man down on the stage on his knees, rocking back and forth and moaning. He was, he informed me, attempting to get the boards to "give up their secrets". He had no sooner been escorted to the door—the last thing I needed was someone suggesting to the dancers that the stage might be haunted—than another man slipped in. He fell to his knees for a different purpose. I found him rubbing his fingers across the stained boards and licking them. I screamed and the finger-licker wasn't escorted out quite as politely as had been the moaner.

I escaped to the privacy of Helen's kitchen slash storage room. Ray followed me.

"Less than a month since these people began flooding into town. I'm beginning to wonder if my nerves can last for the remainder of the summer," I said.

"Fee, ye've got the strongest nerves of any woman—any man, at that—I've known. We could close down and open a restaurant, if it's getting a wee bit too much for you. Serve breakfast and light lunches. How much money did you take to the bank this morning?"

I smiled, embarrassed at my outburst. "Probably more than my father, bless him, earned in his lifetime."

"There's always that restaurant."

"If I were doing the cooking, then we'd have the Mounties investigating us for sure. Go along, Ray. I'll be out in a minute."

"Light lunches. What d'you suppose that means? Never had a light lunch in me life." He opened the door and disappeared into the noise and smoke of the saloon.

I pinched my cheeks to put a touch of colour into them and patted my hair. I was wearing my second best dress, promoted to best. It was a pale green satin, the colour of distant ice floes reflecting the weak North Atlantic sunshine. Its clean folds fell, largely unadorned, in a perfect, curving line from high neckline to hem. It went exceptionally well with my dark hair, adorned with nothing but a single ribbon, cut from excess cloth, salvaged when (thank goodness) the over-sized bustle faded from fashion. Because the dress was so simple and the front cut so high, covering my throat, I'd added interest by wrapping strands of fake pearls around and around my neck. But I never felt quite as lovely wearing the green dress as I had in the crimson Worth. Still, I smoothed the fabric over my hips, took a deep breath, and marched into the packed bar.

"You're looking even more stunning tonight than you normally do, Fiona." Graham Donohue appeared at my elbow. "That shade of green does your hair perfect justice." He bowed deeply and held his whisky glass up in a toast.

I recovered, just a bit, from mourning the red dress and gave him a smile. "Quite the crowd tonight."

"The Savoy's the talk of the town, as usual. They're saying Jack Ireland expired in the centre of the stage. Tsk, tsk. Such a loss to American journalism." He tossed back his whisky.

"Really, Graham! The man's dead. Have some respect."

"I hated him in life, Fiona. I won't pretend I'm sorry about his death."

We walked through the crowd. Men touched their hats and stepped aside to let us pass. The bartenders were busy.

I eyed Graham. "You knew Ireland before Dawson. Whatever did he do to you?"

"No need to worry about that now, is there, Fee?"

"I'm not worried in the least. But the Mounties might want to know."

Graham peered into the depths of his glass. "I need another drink."

Giggling and swaying their hips, a group of women spilled into the room. They walked through the space the admiring men created for them, heading straight for me.

"Ooh, Mrs. MacGillivray. We don't know if we can perform tonight," Chloe said with a shiver. The others nodded their agreement. "Killed. Right there on our stage. Suppose there's blood, or something awful, on the stage, and one of us slips in it?"

"Really, Chloe. Ladies. I can assure you that Mrs. Saunderson has cleaned the entire dance hall thoroughly. You know what a conscientious worker she is."

They nodded. One girl leaned over to ask another what conscientious meant. A few of the dancers turned to head for the back.

But Chloe couldn't drop it. "Suppose he's left his spirit behind? My gran always said..."

The departing girls gasped and stopped in their tracks.

"Stuff and nonsense," I snapped. Time to stop this foolishness before I had a roomful of petulant dancers on my hands. "This is the Yukon Territory, Canada, in the year 1898. Don't tell me you believe that Old World peasant nonsense, Chloe? I would have thought you too sophisticated for that."

The girls glanced at each other out of the corner of their eyes. They weren't Old World peasants.

"Follow me, and we'll have a look at the stage, and you can see for yourself how clean it is." I marched out of the saloon. The girls followed in a neat, obedient row like a flock of strangely dressed nuns behind Mother Superior.

If the finger-licker had managed to get back in, I would strangle him with my own hands.

But there was only the orchestra, unpacking their instruments and warming up, and Ellie and Irene, relaxing on benches before it was time to start the night's work.

"Some of the *less experienced* ladies are worried about the state of the stage," I announced to the room. Two of the girls at the back slipped away from the group to edge towards Ellie and Irene, not wanting to be included among the less experienced.

Ellie laughed. "You should've seen some of the places what I've danced in. They pushed the corpses up against the wall so we wouldn't trip over 'em. Sometimes we used 'em as props. I remember the night Big Gertrude…"

Ellie loved to talk about "some of the places I've danced in".

"My gran says…" Chloe murmured, standing alone as the other women gathered around Ellie to hear the story of Big Gertrude before getting ready for their night's work. But no one was listening to her.

The orchestra struggled to their feet and gathered up their instruments. The dancers scurried off behind the stage in a flurry of lace and ribbons, pearl buttons, white cotton and colourful silk.

I wandered into the gambling room. Graham beckoned to me from his place at a table, where a high-stakes game of poker was underway. Chips were piled in the centre of the table and in front of every man. A cloud of dense, pungent smoke rose from their cigars.

"Fiona, give me a kiss for good luck."

I tossed a wave towards Graham and carried on around the table. As if I would ever appear to prefer one customer to another. Might as well shut the business down on the spot and put myself out to pasture. Or open Ray's restaurant: breakfast and light lunches.

I continued through to the bar, arriving precisely as Inspector McKnight and Constable Sterling walked through the front door, following the orchestra as it returned from its eight o'clock performance on the street.

We met in the centre of the saloon. The crowd gathered around to eavesdrop.

"Good evening, gentlemen."

"Evening, Mrs. MacGillivray," McKnight said. "We're looking for a fellow named Donohue." He certainly didn't worry about observing the social graces, our Inspector McKnight.

I looked at Sterling. He avoided my eyes.

"Your man at the door says Donohue is in the next room. Is that correct?"

"Uh, I'm not sure. Why do you want him?"

"To assist with our investigation, of course. Now, if you could point this Donohue out to me, it would make things much simpler."

"Certainly." There was no point in pretending not to know Graham. Anyone in the Savoy, including Richard Sterling, could identify him. But I was not happy about taking McKnight into the gambling hall. I didn't know what he wanted with Graham, and I didn't want to find out. I hesitated.

"Mrs. MacGillivray? If you're not feeling well, I'm sure one of your employees can assist us."

"This way." I led the two policemen into the gambling room. The air was so thick with smoke from the men's cigars that it was difficult to see the far side of the room. The roulette wheel clattered to the end of its spin, and Mouse O'Brien cheered lustily as he gathered up a pile of chips in his big hands. "Place your bets, gentlemen," the croupier droned. No one looked up from the faro table, and the men at the poker games stared single-mindedly into their cards.

McKnight looked at Sterling. Sterling gestured with his head to where Graham Donohue was pushing a sizeable stack of chips into the middle of the table. McKnight crossed the room and placed his hand on Graham's shoulder. "Mr. Donohue, will you come with us, please. We'd like to ask you a few questions."

Chapter Twenty-Eight

Graham Donohue instinctively pulled his hands back from his chips and clutched his cards to his chest. "I'm busy at the moment."

"Too bad," Inspector McKnight said. "I intend to talk to you. We can conduct our business here, if you like."

The dealer's eyes opened wide, and he looked at me for instruction.

I gave him a shrug. I had no better idea than he as to what we should do.

"We're having a serious game here," a poker player growled. It was the Indian fighter I'd noticed before. Probably not the sort of man who had a healthy respect for Her Majesty's Officers of the Law.

"Graham," I said, sensing trouble brewing, "I'm sure it won't take long to answer Inspector McKnight's questions. And then your game can continue."

"You leave this table, pal, game's over," the Indian fighter said. He fingered his belt, looking disappointed not to find a six-shooter, or whatever they called it, resting there. Guns were banned from town. The two other players appeared relieved at having their game interrupted. I surmised that they didn't have promising hands.

"If you don't come willingly, Donohue," McKnight said in a low voice, "then I will be forced to place you under arrest."

Graham tossed his cards at the dealer and gathered up his chips. The Indian fighter growled, deep in his chest.

"If you interfere in this matter," Sterling said to him, "you'll find yourself under arrest. Dealer, portion out the remaining chips. This game is over."

Graham got to his feet with a heavy sigh. The Indian fighter threw his cards on the table. "Don't know what sort of town you're running here. I'll be on the next boat out." He stuffed his chips into various pockets.

But he didn't mean "next" in the literal sense: he joined the game at the faro table.

I hurried out the door in pursuit of Graham and the Mounties. The police stood on either side of my friend. Richard Sterling rested a hand on one of Graham's elbows. The life of the bar swirled all around us. In the dance hall, Betsy's voice reached a high note, reminding me that I should be in there, watching. Ray was occupied peeling a man up off the floor.

"Do you have a place where we can talk to Mr. Donohue?" McKnight asked. "In private."

"No," I said.

"For heaven's sake, Fiona," Graham pleaded, "say yes. I want to get this charade over."

"Very well. You can use my office. Follow me." I led the way up the stairs. All conversation stopped as every man in the room watched us. And not just those who were hoping to get a peek at my ankles.

I threw the door to the office open, and the three men marched through. I debated leaving, but decided on principle—it was my office—to hang around until they told me to go. I closed the door.

"Sit," McKnight told Graham. Graham walked around my desk to sit in my chair, facing into the room. A thin sheen of sweat covered his brow, and his hands shook as he pushed a lock of dark hair out of his eyes. He avoided looking at me.

McKnight took the visitor's chair. A match flashed as Sterling lit the lamp on the bookcase before leaning up against the wall.

"It has come to our attention, Mr. Donohue," Inspector McKnight began, "that you were in a fight with the late Mr. Ireland the day he arrived in town."

"So?"

"You want to tell me what you had against the fellow?"

"Am I under arrest?"

"If you were under arrest, Mr. Donohue, we wouldn't be having this conversation on the second floor of a dance hall. I can arrest you if you'd prefer."

"I met Ireland years ago. I was working at the *New York World* when they hired him on."

"Year?"

"Late '85, early '86. Around then."

"Go on."

"Ireland arrived at the *World* as if he were cock-of-the-walk, big man around town, instead of the washed-up has-been he was even then. He was a right bastard."

I expected Sterling to reprimand Graham for his language. That he didn't made me truly understand the seriousness of the situation. What was vile language from someone facing possible murder charges?

"Lots of unpleasant men around," McKnight said, quite sensibly. "Why'd you dislike this one so much?"

Graham shrugged, trying to appear casual and unconcerned. Which only made matters worse; he looked like a man with something to hide.

Worry touched at the front of my mind. Could he be hiding something?

"Constable," McKnight said, "take Mr. Donohue to Fort Herchmer. Perhaps he'll talk to us in the morning."

"He besmirched the reputation of a gentleman of my acquaintance," Graham snapped.

"And you've carried a grudge for what, almost fifteen years? Seems a bit much. We've been told that you had several run-ins with this Ireland since he arrived in town only a couple of days ago. People said you attacked him the moment you first laid eyes on him. Must have been some besmirching, wouldn't you agree, Constable?"

Sterling grunted. He wasn't looking any too happy either. He and Donohue weren't exactly friends, but I'd always believed that they respected each other, perhaps even trusted each other, as much as a police officer and a newspaperman can. The constable glanced at me, then his eyes slid away.

"It was my sister's husband, my brother-in-law," Graham said, "who Ireland accused, in print, of knowingly selling faulty rifles in the war."

"What war would that be?"

"The War Between the States, you fool. What war do you think?"

McKnight didn't respond to the insult. I suspected he'd deliberately provoked it. "Plenty of wars to choose from. Did he?"

"Did who what?"

"Did your brother-in-law sell faulty rifles? Knowingly?"

"No, he did not."

Sterling spoke for the first time. "Your sister's husband must be a good deal older than you. That war ended more than thirty years ago."

"He was. My sister, named Garnet after our mother, was eighteen years my senior and more of a mother to me than a sister. She raised me after our parents died when I was a baby. She didn't marry, spent her youth caring for me. She was forty when she met Jeremiah MacIsaac. He was widowed, had grown sons he didn't care much for, loved her enough not to mind her age. She was happy. They were happy. Until that bastard Ireland ruined it all."

"Did the newspaper publish the story?" McKnight asked.

"Yes. Jeremiah sued. And won. Ireland had forged some of his documents. The *World* fired him."

"So it ended happily."

Graham leapt up from his seat, knocking the chair to the ground. His dark eyes blazed. "No, it didn't end happily, Inspector. Some people believe everything they read in the papers. And a good many more don't care whether it's true or not. The scandal put an enormous strain on Garnet. Acquaintances cut her dead in the street; friends closed their doors in her face. Naturally, she was delighted when Jeremiah was vindicated, but she was never the same again. The affair broke her heart. She died about a year later."

I believed him. I'd seen Ireland at work; his story about Helen Saunderson, lies interwoven amongst the truth, would have killed the woman's reputation if anyone in Dawson were inclined to care about such things.

"Please, Mr. Donohue," McKnight said, "sit down." He hadn't batted an eyelid at Graham's explosion, just sat in my visitor's chair as if he were ordering cucumber sandwiches for tea.

Richard Sterling expressed my thoughts. "Sounds like Ireland to me, sir. Fellow hadn't been here a day before he was stirring up trouble and threatening a lady's reputation."

For the first time since we'd entered the room, McKnight glanced behind him.

"Not me," I said, answering the question in his eyes. "I don't have a reputation worth threatening. My charwoman, Helen Saunderson."

McKnight turned back to Donohue. I guessed he'd be talking to Helen next.

"Now that we've established that you had a motive for the murder of Jack Ireland..."

"What the hell? Are you trying to frame me?"

"Sit down, Mr. Donohue. I'm not attempting to frame anyone. Her Majesty's North-West Mounted Police don't operate in that fashion." He didn't bother to mention what police forces he thought did operate in that fashion. "Where were you yesterday in the early afternoon?"

"When?" Graham's eyes shifted at the question. The colour rose in his neck, and beads of sweat dotted his forehead. His moustache drooped. He looked down at his hands, folded neatly across my desk. The knuckles were white.

"Sunday between, say, noon and three in the afternoon? Where were you?"

"I, uh, don't remember."

"You don't remember? That's odd. It was only yesterday. I remember perfectly well what I was doing yesterday afternoon, although I might not remember a month from now. What were you doing yesterday at noon, Constable?"

"Me? I was in my bunk writing a letter to my sister."

"Mrs. MacGillivray? Can you tell us what you were doing yesterday in the early afternoon?"

I didn't want to. It was none of their business; let McKnight prove his point without involving me. I hesitated. McKnight didn't bother to turn around to look at me. Graham studied his hands, his expression unreadable. If I said I didn't remember, then I would be the one looking as if I had something to hide. "I took a stroll through town. I spoke to Mr. Alex McDonald and Miss Belinda Mulroney. Among others. I then..."

"Thank you, Mrs. MacGillivray. That will suffice."

"Do you want to tell me what you were doing yesterday, Sunday, between noon and three o'clock, Mr. Donohue?"

Graham looked up. His eyes darted around the room. He looked at Richard; he looked at McKnight. But he didn't look at me. One of the people I'd seen on my Sunday stroll had been Graham Donohue, slipping down a side street as if he wanted to avoid me. I gripped my hands behind my back and said nothing, willing Graham to speak up. He had been out for a walk on a pleasant afternoon. Like half the town, including me. Why wouldn't he say so?

It was very close to the Savoy that I'd seen him.

"Writing." He shouted out the word. "I remained at my boarding house, writing my regular dispatches to the paper. All day Sunday. Until about six, when I put down my pen and went in search of my dinner. There. Now I remember." He looked at me at last. His smile was sickening.

Not one of us believed him.

"Can anyone confirm that? Your landlady, or a fellow border?"

"Nope. No one. When I'm writing, I keep to myself. Don't want to be disturbed."

"Did you send a boy to get you food, perhaps?"

"Didn't see a soul, not all the day long. Not till dinnertime. That's how I always spend the Lord's Day." He looked pleased with himself. If I couldn't tell by the expression on his face that he was lying, the story was proof enough. He'd told me he got ravenous when writing his newspaper stories and kept a messenger boy occupied most of the day running back and forth to his favourite restaurant, ensuring he was constantly supplied with a stream of hot meals and sandwiches, snacks and coffee.

"Very well, Mr. Donohue. That's all for now. You can leave."

They weren't arresting him?

"I would hope so." Graham got to his feet and tugged at the bottom of his waistcoat. He stroked his moustache and pulled his watch out of his pocket to check the time. "Won't say I'm sorry the son-of-a-bitch is dead. But if I'd killed him, I'd be bragging about it all over town."

I opened the door and stepped aside, searching Graham's handsome face to see if the truth were carved there. He avoided looking at me, which was enough to convince me of his guilt. Graham loved looking at me.

"One more thing, Mr. Donohue."

Graham stopped but didn't turn around. The tension running across his shoulders and in the hand that rested on the doorknob was almost painful to observe.

"Don't leave town."

Graham didn't shut the door behind him. Downstairs, a man called for a round for everyone. In the dance hall the lively music ended abruptly, and the orchestra picked up a sad, melodious tune. Time for Irene's big number, the one that always left the men sobbing into their dust-covered shirtsleeves and unwashed handkerchiefs.

"He's lying," McKnight said.

"Yes, sir. I'm afraid he is."

"But men have lots of reasons to lie, Constable. And not all are to do with murder. Find out where he was yesterday."

"Yes, sir."

"But while we're here, let's talk to Walker."

"Sir?"

"Walker, the bouncer. Go and get him."

"Yes, sir."

We listened to the heavy tread of Sterling's boots on the loose floorboards, followed by the creak of the steps.

"What do you think happened here yesterday, Mrs. MacGillivray?"

"You're asking me? Why?"

"Because I sense you're a woman who notices everything that happens around you. You may pretend to be the empty-headed, self-obsessed beauty, but you wouldn't be here, in Dawson, owner of this establishment, if such were true, now would you?"

I smiled at him. "You never know, Inspector. You seem to think everyone is the possible killer. Why not me?"

"Because you're much too intelligent to leave a body on your own doorstep, Mrs. MacGillivray. I have not the slightest doubt that had you decided Ireland needed to die, he would be so. This town hangs on the edge of the wilderness. Plenty of ground in which to hide a body, plenty of wildlife to make sure it stays hidden."

"You flatter me, Inspector."

"That is not my intention."

I smiled again and dipped my head, disguising, I hoped, the shiver of fear that passed through me. I hadn't met many men who didn't try to flatter me, and few of them meant me any good. If the Inspector decided to investigate my past, I might have to vacate town without delay. I hoped it wouldn't come to that. I liked it here. And Angus loved it.

Leaving town in a hurry was almost a habit of mine. When I was ten years old, frightened and confused, I'd left Bestford, the great estate on Skye where I'd been born, in the company of a group of travellers, with nothing to call my own except the clothes my mother had laid out for me that morning, the last morning of her life. At twenty-seven I had departed London ahead of a particularly vengeful Lord of the Realm and his team of hired inquiry agents. But that time I was not alone: I had a diamond and emerald necklace concealed in my petticoats to smooth the way and a seven-year-old child to complicate matters. I sailed to Canada and settled in Toronto under a new name, but four years later I was on the first available train out of Union Station, which happened to be going all the way to Vancouver, with a scented cedar box crammed with jewellery and a son of eleven.

Every time I'm driven out of town, I do at least manage to leave in a better situation than the last time.

We heard Ray complaining all the way up the stairs. "Busiest night of the year so far, got to keep an eye on the lads every minute." He burst through the door in a whirlwind of tiny Scottish fury. "I'm a busy man, Inspector. Make it fast. Fee. Wondering where you'd gotten to."

"We can make it as fast as you want, Walker. Please sit down." McKnight gestured to the chair behind the desk.

Ray sat. His small eyes moved from one of us to the other, wet with suspicion. Sterling took his post against the wall, and I settled back into the door. Interesting that McKnight again took the visitor's chair, the one facing away from the room, looking out over the street, instead of the much better one behind the desk.

Interesting also that he allowed me to remain in the room.

"As soon as you tell us where you were yesterday in the early afternoon, you can get back to your business."

Ray's face almost collapsed in relief. "That's it? That's all you want to know?"

"We talked last night. So for now, yes, that's all I want to know."

"I got outta bed around ten. Had breakfast at the Regina Café, good food there, and lots of it. Met a man from my hometown, can ye believe it? an' we spent most of the day walking around town, talking about Glasgow and the old days. Turns out we know a lot o' the same people. His granny was great friends with me aunt. Small world, isn't it?"

"This fellow's name?"

"Johnny Stewart. Nice lad."

"What time did you and Mr. Stewart part company?"

Ray shrugged. His face was unlined, untroubled; his eyes were clear. He was telling the truth: I would bet my life's savings on it. Come to think of it, Ray and I were so intertwined in the business, I already had.

"Sometime after five, probably. We went back to the Regina for a wee bit o' supper around four, 'cause Johnny had to be in bed early. Wanted to have a good night's kip."

"We'll need to speak to Mr. Stewart."

"He's gone up to the Creeks. Prospecting. That's why he needed to get himself to bed early. He was leaving with a bunch of cheechakos this morning, first light. Told him the next time he's in town, we'd treat him real special at the Savoy, Fee. Maybe even give him a room. That all right with you?"

"Any friend of your grandmother, Ray, is welcome here."

"My aunt Lenora," he corrected me.

"Are you saying that this man has gone to Bonanza Creek?" McKnight interrupted.

"Yup," Ray said, getting to his feet. "Told him he was wasting his time prospecting. More money to be made here in town, I said. But he has his heart set on finding gold and going back to Glasgow a rich man."

"And once you and Mr. Stewart parted company, where did you go?"

"Back to me room. Where I was when Angus came and fetched me." The slightest of clouds passed over Ray's face, and his eyes darted around the room. Once again someone was looking everywhere but at me. "If that's all, Inspector? It's a busy night downstairs."

"We'll want to talk to Mr. Stewart. Can you describe him?"

Ray shrugged, not particularly concerned. "Bit shorter than me. Skinny. Clean shaven. Lost most of his hair on top."

"Age?"

"Thirty, thirty-five." Ray shrugged again.

"That's all for now, Mr. Walker. Thank you."

Ray left, still avoiding my eyes.

"I hope you got most of that, Constable. Was the man

speaking English? Mrs. MacGillivray, did Walker confess to murder?"

My attention snapped back. "What? Of course not! Oh, you're making a joke."

McKnight may have smiled. Beneath that overgrown moustache, it was hard to tell. "My mother came from Paisley. That's near Glasgow." He took off his glasses, pulled a clean handkerchief out of his pocket and wiped at the lenses.

"I know where Paisley is."

"Now, your late husband, Mrs. MacGillivray, he must have been a true Scottish lad. Although you've got a hint of the Highlands yourself when you get overly emotional."

I was about to say something—a nice chat about the old country, keep the tone friendly—but at his last comment, I snapped my mouth shut. I have never been overly emotional in my life. And if McKnight could hear Scotland in my voice, he had a very good ear indeed. Next, he'd be reading my mind.

Sterling extinguished the lamp, and we left my office. McKnight placed his glasses back on his nose and chatted merrily about the variety of accents he'd heard in his travels.

I wanted to tell him to shut up: I had things to think about. Instead I slapped on my most gracious dance-hall-owner smile and ran my pearls through my fingers.

We stopped at the bottom of the stairs. "Find out what Donohue was up to, Constable. No good, I'm thinking," McKnight said, pulling a cigar out of his coat pocket. "Tomorrow you can head for the Creeks. Locate this Scottish fellow, Stewart. Make sure he backs up what Walker said. Probably not necessary. I'm pretty sure Walker's story was accurate. That part of it at any rate, the part that covers the time we're interested in. But something happened once he and Stewart separated that Walker didn't want to talk about, and I don't like not having all the answers.

"Mrs. MacGillivray." He nodded politely, bit down on the end of his cigar, and made his way through the crowd.

Constable Sterling raised one expressive eyebrow.

"And after you've finished that," I said, "you can find out who really killed President Lincoln and in your spare time identify the leaders of the Fenians."

"All in a day's work," he said with a gentle smile.

"You don't really think…"

"I don't think anything, Fiona. Mrs. MacGillivray. I'll dig up the facts and let them think for themselves. Good night." He touched the brim of his hat.

"Good night, Constable."

Chapter Twenty-Nine

"What are you doing here at this time of night, son?"

Angus almost leapt out of his skin as the deep voice sounded in his ear. The other boys scurried off into the shadows behind the buildings.

It was after midnight, but in Dawson in June, still bright enough to read by.

"Nothing, Constable Sterling, sir. Nothing. Hunting rats, that's all."

In the shadows, one of the boys swore as his shin made contact with a piece of rough lumber. His friends whispered hushes were almost as loud as a steamship whistle when it caught its first sight of town.

"Rats, eh? Mighty big rats around tonight. Your mother know you're out?"

"She doesn't mind, sir. She says it's fine."

"Angus."

"Sorry, sir. No, she thinks I'm at home. You won't tell her, will you?"

"Come on, I'll walk you home. Those rats had better be off home too." More scurries in the dark. "And no, I won't tell your mother. She has enough on her mind what with worrying about the Savoy and the trouble there yesterday."

"That death, Mr. Ireland, it won't hurt my ma, will it?"

"It might, Angus, it might. Murder has a nasty way of touching everyone it comes into contact with. Makes men mistrust each other. Everyone wants to cast blame, to throw suspicion away from himself. Even the innocent try to hide. It's a nasty business."

"But my ma didn't have nothing to do with it. She didn't even know this Ireland fellow."

"Sometimes that scarcely seems to matter. Watch it!" Sterling grabbed Angus by the arm and pulled him out of the way as a man, stinking of weeks on the creeks and cheap drink, flew around the corner. A screaming whore and her red-faced pimp followed him. At the sight of the uniformed Mountie, all three settled into a somnolent stroll.

"Evening, Constable. Nice night, ain't it?" The pimp, a sallow-faced fellow, spoke through a mouthful of rotten teeth.

"Hold up there, you," Sterling called. "Do you owe this lady something?"

"No," the drunk mumbled.

The woman winked at Angus. She wore a lot of paint on her face, and her skirt was hitched into her belt, making it too short to be decent. Once-white bloomers peeked out from under the skirt. Suddenly Angus felt as if he had a raging fever. Sweat dripped down the back of his shirt and an uncomfortable, but not entirely unpleasant, feeling stirred between his legs.

"Then we'll have to take it to the Fort," Sterling said. "Come on, all of you."

"All right." The man fumbled in his pockets. "Ain't worth two bits, that lump of lard." He tossed a tiny nugget into the mud.

The woman spat. "Couldn't get it up with block and tackle, he couldn't. I ain't got all night to watch him play with it."

"Watch your mouth, Iris."

The pimp scrambled through the mud in pursuit of the gold. "Don't you come around here again," he said to the drunk, who sprinted away.

"Get back to work." The pimp raised his fist to the woman, but Sterling warned him off with a growl. She ducked her head and disappeared into the shadows.

"Why do they do it, Constable?" Angus asked when they were alone again.

"Do what, son?"

"Those women. Why do they do what men like that tell them? Why don't they say no?"

"Lots of women aren't like your mother, Angus. They don't know how to get by on their own. Other than that, I can't say."

"There are some things I don't want to ask my ma about any more."

"I can understand. Remember this, when you're older and you start thinking about women, you don't want to do anything that'd make your mother ashamed of you, if she hears about it. Not that you have to tell her everything, mind."

"Yes, sir." Angus didn't really know what Sterling was talking about. But the constable's cheeks were turning red, and Angus decided it would be best not to ask any more questions.

No doubt everything would be perfectly clear as soon as he was a man.

They walked in companionable silence, enjoying the warm air of the strange northern half-night. Past midnight, yet the streets were a jostling mass of men. Most were heading towards the dance halls or staggering away, but there were a good number of men with not enough money left in their pockets for either another drink or a place to spend the night. They wandered through town, waiting for morning to catch the first boat out of town or join the next group of workers heading to the gold fields. A few women dotted the crowd, the majority not at all respectable. Several NWMP officers exchanged greetings with Sterling and Angus.

"How was the day's work?" Sterling asked.

"Awful. Just awful. I'd sooner die than spend my life working in a store like Mr. Mann does."

Sterling laughed. "Man's gotta do what he can to get by."

"Well, I won't!"

"If you're lucky, son, you may not have to. But don't look down on men who..."

"Sterling. I need to talk to you." Graham Donohue stepped out from the doorway of a tiny cigar store. A lamp burned inside, and a pretty young woman in a dress cut daringly low came to the door to see what was going on.

"What are you doing, Donohue, hiding in the shadows?"

"Keep your voice down. Come over here." Donohue beckoned.

Sterling walked over. Angus tagged along behind. "Isn't this a bit melodramatic, Donohue, even for you?" the Mountie said.

"I have to talk to you. Is that Angus MacGillivray behind you?"

"Yes, sir. It's me."

"If you have something to say about Ireland, we'd better find Inspector McKnight," Sterling said.

"No! You have to listen to me. Angus, go home. This is men's business."

Angus looked at Sterling. The constable nodded. "Get off home, son. Sounds like this is a police matter."

"Yes, sir."

The men moved around the side of the building. The woman standing at the entrance to the store shrugged and went inside. Angus had never had reason to go into a cigar store. But now that he was making some money working for Mr. Mann, it would be nice to get a present for Ray or Constable Sterling if he could find out when their birthdays were. He followed the woman.

She raised one eyebrow. "You're a young one. Looking for something special?" She ran her tongue across her lips, and Angus felt himself flushing.

He walked to the side of the store, very uncomfortable but trying to look as if he were cool and casual and looking for something to buy.

Men's voices came through the window.

"What are you up to, Donohue? You put yourself right in the picture. I was surprised the inspector didn't arrest you on the spot. Can't remember what you were doing yesterday afternoon!"

"You have to believe me. She was standing there listening to every word. What could I say?"

"Who was standing where?"

Angus started to move away from the window. He didn't like the way the woman's cat-like eyes watched him. And from what he could see of her merchandise, there wasn't anything he'd be interested in buying. Unless the good stuff was kept behind the curtain that blocked off half of the room. But one word caught his attention.

"Fiona. Why the hell did McKnight let her stay?"

"It was her office."

"Do you let women listen in on all your interrogations? Not much of a police force, if you ask me."

"That was hardly an interrogation. More like a friendly chat. If you have something to say, Donohue, say it. Otherwise you're wasting my time."

"I couldn't tell you where I was yesterday afternoon, not in front of her."

"Donohue," Sterling said in a low, warning voice.

"I spent Sunday afternoon with Cracking Kate."

"What!"

"You heard me. Cracking Kate. In her place. I got there about eleven. I…uh…fell asleep. Woke up around three. Then I…uh…left around four."

Angus didn't know anyone named Kate. Seemed strange that Mr. Donohue would spend the afternoon sleeping in a woman's rooms. In Toronto or Vancouver, her reputation would have been ruined permanently. But things were different in Dawson. He leaned closer to the window.

"You idiot. You're telling me you frequented Cracking Kate's crib. She's one of Joey LeGrand's whores. Are you a fool?"

"It's none of your business what I do, Sterling. I'm telling you now 'cause I could hardly say that in front of Fiona, could I?"

The cigar-store woman also edged closer to the window. If her ears could have perked up, like a dog's, they would have. She saw Angus watching her and touched her index finger to her painted lips.

Sterling's laugh was mean, ugly, the like of which Angus had never heard from the Mountie before. "You're right about that. Fiona finds out you're putting money into Joey LeGrand's pockets, you'll be lucky to leave town with your scalp, never mind other more private body parts. You fool. I've half a mind to tell Fiona myself: Joey's women have got to be the worst-treated whores in Dawson. If you don't have the pox, you will soon."

"I don't need your approval, Sterling," Donohue growled. "I'm telling you where I was on Sunday between the hours of noon and three. Like your inspector asked."

"Someone has to talk to Kate."

"She'll remember me. Isn't every man pays for three hours of sleep time. You won't tell Fiona? This is police business only?"

"I won't tell Fiona. But I have to tell Inspector McKnight. What he does with the information is out of my hands."

"Look, Sterling, it was the first time I'd visited her. I had a rough couple of days. Seeing Ireland..."

"Save it for your priest."

The woman had wiggled her slender body beside Angus, so that both of them were pressed up against the wall. She snorted.

"Shush," Angus whispered.

"Angus, where are you?" Sterling yelled. He ran into the cigar store as Angus and the woman stumbled all over themselves to reach the centre of the room. Angus admired the merchandise. The woman wiped a speck of dust off the counter top.

"What are you doing here?" Sterling shouted.

"Looking for a gift, sir. For Mr. Walker."

Sterling grabbed Angus by the arm and almost jerked him off his feet. "I catch you in a place like this again, I'll have your hide, boy."

He looked at the woman. She placed the countertop between them. Behind the rouged cheeks, her face had faded to a pasty white.

"You allow this boy, or any other underage lad, across the step again, I'll have you on charges for corrupting the morals of a minor. Do you hear me, Greta!"

"Yes, sir, Constable Sterling, sir. I weren't doin' nothing. He wandered in all on his own.. Me and the boy, we was lookin' at the cigars. Tha's all."

"So help me, Greta..."

"I wanted to buy something for Ray, really," Angus wailed. He had no idea why Sterling was mad at poor Greta. She was just trying to make a living selling cigars. "Get outside, Angus," Sterling shouted.

Angus ran.

Clearly there was more happening in Greta's store than the selling of cigars, but right now Angus had more important things to think about: Graham Donohue. His mother's admirer had visited a Paradise Alley whore?

Sterling caught up with him halfway down the street. "My conversation with Donohue is absolutely none of your business, Angus."

"Yes, sir."

"I don't know how much you overheard, but you won't repeat a single word to anyone, do you hear me?"

"Yes, sir."

"That was an official police conversation, Angus. Not to be repeated to anyone else. Not even your mother. Particularly not your mother."

"I'm sorry, sir. I understand."

"I doubt that you do. But, please, don't go into that store again. You want to get a present for Walker, I'll take you shopping, how's that?"

"Fine, sir."

"Go home, Angus. You have to work at the store tomorrow, and I'll be on my way to the Creeks. Waste of bloody time."

"The Creeks? What are you going there for, sir?"

"Police business, Angus. I'll be away for a couple of days. I'll tell you about it when I get back. Now get off home."

"Good night, sir."

"Good night, son."

Angus walked to Mrs. Mann's boarding house deep in thought. Graham Donohue, his mother's friend, paid money to a whore. And to make matters worse, if that were possible, to one of Joey LeGrand's whores. Angus's mother hated Joey, although he didn't really understand why. There were plenty of whores in Dawson; you couldn't be a boy running through the streets without knowing that. One of his friends, Billy Rodgers, bragged to all the boys that he'd had a whore. For free, Billy said, "'cause she'd wanted young meat for a change." Billy'd puffed up his chest and strutted about like a peacock in the London zoo, and Angus hadn't believed a word of it.

But what was going on in the cigar store, anyway, that had made Constable Sterling so mad? There hadn't been many cigars for sale, and the few there looked to be of poor quality. The woman minding the store had been wearing a lot of rouge, and when she'd looked at Angus she had made him very, very uncomfortable.

But then again, lately, a great many women made Angus MacGillivray uncomfortable.

He'd always liked the company of women; women were nicer to be around than men and boys. Some men didn't like women much. They called them bad names, and laughed at them, and sometimes even hurt them. But not men like Constable Sterling and Ray Walker and, he had thought, Graham Donohue.

Sometimes, Angus wondered if Mr. Donohue would ask his mother to marry him. Maybe he'd take them to live in America. Angus didn't know what he thought about that. He loved Dawson, untamed, unpredictable; there probably wasn't another town in the world where boys his age were as free to run as wild as they pleased. All of his life it had been Angus and his mother, only them, together. He hadn't been entirely sure how he felt about the idea of having Graham Donohue as his father. But now he knew he didn't want that to happen.

It was late, and he was tired from working in the store, and sore from his boxing lesson, and his head hurt from thinking too much.

He decided to forget about it for now—he'd figure everything out someday.

Chapter Thirty

"Will you marry me, Mrs. MacGillivray? I offer you a respectable name and a father for your son." Sergeant Lancaster fell to his knees and grabbed my hands between his. The path leading to my front door was comparatively firm, and not as mud-soaked as most of Dawson. Lancaster wouldn't find it too difficult to get the muck out of his trousers.

He looked up at me, his eyes rimmed by years of failure and disappointment, and I didn't know what to say.

"I don't know what to say."

He struggled to stand, breathing heavily from the exertion. "You are the fairest, most beautiful, kindest woman I have ever met," he stammered, too embarrassed to look into my eyes. He struggled to say my first name. "F...F...Fiona. I can't bear to see you labouring in that dance hall for a moment longer. Why it's only slightly more respectable than a house of ill-repute! You deserve so much better. Mrs. MacGillivray, Fiona, I ask you again: Will you do me the enormous honour of agreeing to be my wife?"

"I...I...I don't know what to say," I repeated.

"You need time to think it over. And to speak to your son. I understand." Sergeant Lancaster stood back. At last he looked at my face. "Take all the time you need. Fiona, my dearest. Remember that children's opinions can be tainted; they don't always know what's in their best interest. I'll be back on Wednesday for your answer."

He turned and disappeared into the semi-darkness. Two drunks passed by, their arms about each other's shoulders, roaring an Irish drinking song into the night, something about someone named Johnny who they hardly knew.

I had until Wednesday to think of a polite way of crushing the old man's dreams. He had courageously offered to bed (with full church and societal approval) the most desirable woman in the North in order to save her from earning herself a fortune. He sincerely thought he was doing me a favour.

It's a strange world we live in.

Earlier, after McKnight and Sterling had left the Savoy, leaving a residue of tension and suspicion lingering behind them, Ray had spent the rest of the night bellowing at the bartenders and croupiers as if he were an overseer at the building of the pyramids, and Pharaoh had died prematurely.

The entertainment had come to the usual rousing end; the percentage girls, who didn't perform on the stage and wore their street clothes for dancing, moved into the crowd seeking out partners, and the performers scurried backstage to change out of their costumes.

Irene descended into the crowd with a huge smile, nodding to her throng of admirers like the Queen on the Horseguards parade.

No crocodile tears for the late Jack Ireland here.

Shortly before closing, Irene walked her dance partner up to the bar. He was properly dressed for a day of pheasant hunting in the Scottish highlands in a suit of fine Harris tweed, pants cut off at the knees, patterned socks, perfectly knotted tie.

It is exceedingly unlikely there is anywhere else in the world where one can in a single day encounter such an assortment of dress as in Dawson, Yukon Territory.

The pheasant hunter ordered a drink for himself and one for Irene. Ray stood to one side of the bar, watching, his eyes and expression dark. Irene tossed him a huge smile and, while her partner dug coins out of his pockets to pay for the drinks, she leaned over to whisper into Ray's ear. A grin nearly split his face in two. The pheasant hunter reclaimed Irene, and quite properly (she wasn't the most popular dance-hall girl in Dawson for nothing) she took his arm, eyes wide and moist mouth smiling. They walked through the doors to the back, leaving Ray with a stupid, happy, love-struck smile on his face.

At least someone was happy. My right shoe was digging into my little toe, and I'd laced my corset too tightly.

Finally, closing time arrived. Ray kicked out the stragglers; the bartenders tidied up their bottles; the croupiers closed the tables and stacked chips, and I saw the giggling girls out the door. Most of them had made almost as much money in drink chits in this one night as they normally did in a week.

Murder was good for business. Although not for me. I was exhausted.

"I'm leaving," I told Ray. "I can't stay on my feet a moment longer." One dancer remained behind, sitting at a table in the middle of the saloon. "Do you want something, Betsy?"

"No, Mrs. MacGillivray."

"Then why are you still here?"

She flushed and glanced at Ray, who immediately turned to Sam and told him what to do to close up. As if Sam had started on the job this morning.

Oh, for heaven's sake!

"Good night, Ray. Try to get some sleep," I said, with more than a touch of malice. Nothing worse for business than relationships between the staff—and triangles were the worst of all. "You're looking quite worn out, Betsy. I'd be happy to walk you back to your lodgings."

She stopped rubbing at a spot on the table. "Eh?"

"I said that I'll walk you back to your lodgings. We wouldn't want anyone to get the idea that an employee of the Savoy was anything less than a respectable lady, now would we?"

"No, Mrs. MacGillivray." She got to her feet as if her boots were dragging her to the bottom of the ocean.

I turned my best full-wattage smile on Ray, the very one that had once had the Prince of Wales' knickers in a knot. A great deal smarter than the Prince, Ray snarled in return.

Betsy and I walked through the dark streets. Night had

finally fallen on Dawson, although it would not remain for long. High above, the stars were dim, as the sun had not completely gone away. It had simply dipped its face behind the southern mountains. Although the day had been warm, the night air was sharply cool, reminding us of just how far north we were.

The streets were crowded, and almost every man we passed nodded or touched his hat. I acknowledged every one of them. Sometimes on the streets of Dawson I felt like a toy Angus had had as a small child—a cheap thing that he was inordinately fond of with a head at the end of a tightly-wound spring, constantly bobbing up and down.

"Do you like working at the Savoy, Betsy?"

"Why, yes, Mrs. MacGillivray. I do. I like it very much."

"Do you like Mr. Walker, Betsy?"

"Yes, Mr. MacGillivray, he's a fine man. Fair like. To all us girls."

"Glad to hear it."

"Here we are, Mrs. MacGillivray. This here's my lodgings. Thank you for walking me home." We'd arrived at a tiny wooden house, painted white. With a cheerful red door and matching shutters, it was a good bit nicer than many.

"My pleasure," I said.

Betsy started up the walk.

"Just one thing."

She turned around. Her pale, podgy face reflected weak moonlight. "I alone hire and fire the women at the Savoy. If you want to be good friends with Mr. Walker, then you may find alternate employment."

She blinked. "Mrs. MacGillivray, I don't know what…"

"Mr. Walker would never dream of interfering with how I run the dance hall. Do you understand me, Betsy?"

She swallowed. "Yes, Mrs. MacGillivray."

"Good. I'll see you tomorrow." I turned and walked away, feeling Betsy's eyes boring into my back. Doubtless she was wishing they were daggers. Stupid cow. Everyone in town knew Ray was besotted with Irene. They could sort that out themselves—and might even be on the way to doing so—as much as I might disapprove. But if Betsy were allowed to continue thinking she had a future with Ray, there would be nothing but trouble. For all of us.

She'll thank me one day, I chuckled to myself, as I exchanged greetings with the Indian Fighter. *No she won't, she'll hate me for the rest of her days.* I nodded to Mouse O'Brien, stuffing his night's winnings into his pocket. I really didn't care what Betsy thought of me, now or in the future; I only wanted peace in my establishment. Irene was my best dancer. If Betsy caused trouble with Irene over Ray, she'd be on the street in a flash.

"Evening, Mrs. MacGillivray." A man stepped out of the shadows. In London or Toronto, I would have been on my guard, but Dawson was so law-abiding that I habitually wandered through the night streets with my mind half-occupied. But not totally.

I stepped backwards, clenched my fists, raised them slightly, and settled into a modified fighting stance—legs apart, knees bent, balancing on the balls of my feet.

"Pardon me, ma'am. I don't wish to startle you." He moved into the outline of yellow light spilling from the lamp in the window of a cigar store. Some of these stores were in the business of selling cigars—but for most of them it was a front for an independent prostitute.

I relaxed only slightly and dropped my arms to my sides. I would never trust a man who waits in the shadows. "Sergeant Lancaster. What can I do for you?"

He moved closer, and the full strength of the lamplight illuminated his open, friendly features. I wiped my palms on my green satin skirt.

"I noticed you pass by, Mrs. MacGillivray." He stumbled over the words. "Accompanying that… lady…to her rooms. But there appears to be no one to see *you* safely home. That don't seem proper. I'd be proud to offer myself as your escort."

It's never a bad move to play friendly with the local constabulary. I smiled, pulling demure from the depths of my repertoire. "That is most courteous of you, Sergeant. Of course you may see me home." I linked my arm though his. His hefty frame shivered under my touch.

We walked through the streets of Dawson in silence. On Front Street, most of the saloons and dance halls were still open, and light and laughter spilled through the doors. On the hillsides looking over the town and across the river, the occasional lamp illuminated a rough canvas tent. Beyond there was nothing but the dark, impenetrable wilderness, waiting patiently for the day when we would all of us pack up our liquor and mining implements and tents and shops and just leave.

We arrived at Mrs. Mann's boarding house, and I said my thank-yous and attempted to pull my arm from Sergeant Lancaster's unyielding grip. I tugged harder. And harder. I am familiar with the softer parts of the male anatomy—beginning with the instep—but before I was forced to resort to violence, he realized that his grip on my arm was most unseemly, and he released me with a murmured apology and a shuffle of big-booted feet.

"This seems like a respectable home."

"Did you think I would live someplace that wasn't?" I said, too tired to want to continue playing. "Good night, Sergeant."

"One moment, please, Mrs. MacGillivray." He grabbed my arm. He was very big, but mostly soft and flabby—muscle gone to fat. I stared at his hand, and he withdrew it immediately. He blushed, took a deep breath and forced himself to continue. I tried not to sigh too loudly. "There's something I'd like to talk to you about, Mrs. MacGillivray. But not here, on the street. That don't seem proper. May I come in for a moment?"

"Most certainly not! Whatever are you thinking, Sergeant." I love using propriety on the rare occasion that it suits me to do so. "I'd have to wake up my landlady to serve as a chaperone, and the dear woman deserves her rest."

Embarrassed apologies tripped over Lancaster's tongue. Sweat dripped off his bald head, and he wiped it away with a shaking hand.

"Good night, Sergeant."

"Mrs. MacGillivray," he shouted so loudly that I was sure the wolves on the mountainsides could hear. "I can't bear to see a lady as fine and as lovely as yourself cast adrift, alone in this harsh, godless world. And your son, such a fine young man, he's in desperate need of the firm guidance of a father's strict hand."

"What?"

And then he dropped to his knees and proposed to make an honest woman of me.

I opened the front door and crept into the house, kicking my shoes off as I walked down the hall to the back. Tomorrow I'd go in search of new ones: bugger the cost. I'd also wait until tomorrow to worry about Sergeant Lancaster's unwelcome proposal.

Angus was at the kitchen table, fully dressed, sound asleep with his head resting across his right arm. I leaned over and kissed his soft cheek. Not a trace of whiskers yet. Good.

"My dear boy," I whispered. I checked my watch. No point in putting him to bed: Mrs. Mann would be rattling pans, stoking the stove, and gathering up breakfast things in less than an hour. And then it would be time for Angus to head off to his job at the store. "Good night, my dearest." I touched the tousled blond curls. He looked more like his father every day.

I went to my room, trying not to make a sound and without lighting a lamp.

Chapter Thirty-One

Angus listened to his mother's door closing, and the soft swish of fabric as her clothes dropped to the floor. Water splashed and bedsprings creaked and she sighed once, heavily. Then all fell quiet. Angus's mother was a very sound sleeper. Bit of bad luck, her coming in on him like that. But tonight she'd got home later than usual, and Angus dared wait no longer. He'd been stuffing the last bit of food into his pack when he'd heard her footsteps on the path and her gentle voice talking to some man.

He'd shoved the pack under the kitchen table before falling into a chair and pretending to be asleep. Only when he'd heard the door opening did he remember the note he'd left on the table for her to find in the morning. Fortunately, the house lights were all off, and in the gloom she hadn't seen the paper.

He gathered his pack and settled it over his shoulders. He tried to open the kitchen door quietly and winced as the hinges creaked. He slipped into the weak light of dawn. They'd be furious, for sure, his mother and Mr. Mann. But Angus couldn't face another day in that store.

The town that scarcely slept was stirring back to life as he walked through the streets. Shopkeepers, cooks and housewives were already going about their chores. Drunks staggered back to their lodgings and eager men marched through town heading for the gold fields.

Angus arrived at the Fort Herchmer gates close to seven thirty and sat on a boulder to wait, not wanting to think about what would happen if he were too late or if plans had changed at the last minute. He mentally reviewed the contents of his pack—one change of clothes, a blanket, extra socks, bread and cheese, some cold meat and dried apples. He'd been careful to take no more food than he would have eaten had he stayed behind, although he couldn't resist grabbing the tin of yesterday's scones.

Traffic to and from the fort was light at this time of day, and no one paid undue attention to the boy sitting off to one side.

Angus didn't have a watch, and he was beginning to fear that he'd missed his quarry, when at last he saw Constable Sterling approaching, leading a big white dog with a two-sided pack draped across its back. The Mountie's step was strong and determined: a man setting out on a long journey.

Angus stood up and waited, his heart pounding and his hands sweating.

Sterling's eyes widened in surprise. "Morning, Angus. What brings you here, son?"

"I'm ready to go with you, sir," Angus shouted. He cleared his throat and tried to lower his voice. "To Bonanza Creek."

"What are you talking about? You can't come with me. I'm on NWMP business."

"I know that, sir. I'll keep you company."

"I don't need company, Angus."

"I want to be in the Mounties, sir, just like you. You said you'd show me what policing's like."

Sterling touched the big dog on the head, and it dropped to its haunches. "In a few more years, Angus. You're still a boy. Give it time."

"What other chance will I have to go to the gold fields, sir? And to watch a real police investigation? I won't get in the way. Really I won't. I can help you." Angus eyed the dog. "With your pack and things."

"Does your mother know you're here?"

"Yes, sir. She says it's all right. She knows I want to be a Mountie some day." He dug into his pocket. "Here's a letter." He handed the scrap of paper over.

Sterling took it with a frown, smoothed out the wrinkles and read.

Angus forced himself to keep breathing. The letter said that Angus was welcome to accompany Constable Sterling on his journey to Bonanza and Eldorado Creeks in the performance of his police duties. She, Mrs. MacGillivray, believed that the experience would be good for a city-raised, fatherless boy with ambitions of joining the NWMP.

Sterling tucked the letter into his jacket pocket.

"I came over the Pass, sir," Angus said. "I know how to travel in the wilderness."

"This is Mrs. Miller." Sterling nodded to the dog, now sniffing at a tuff of grass. "Named for the prune-faced wife of the meanest son-of-a-gun ever to grace Her Majesty's Service. We call her Millie. Millie won't carry your things."

"No, sir."

"I can't feed you; I didn't bring enough for two. Three, counting Millie."

"That's all right, sir. I have my own." Angus patted his pack.

"How much?"

"Enough for five days, sir."

"Any money?"

"Yes, sir."

"What else do you have in there?"

"Two pairs of socks. Change of clothes. Blanket. Some bandages."

"That should be enough. You understand that you do what I tell you, when I tell you, without a word of disagreement?"

"Yes, sir."

"This is probably a wasted trip. We'll spend a couple of days nosing around the Creeks looking for this fellow Stewart then come back. I've little doubt the man we're looking for will confirm Walker's story. If we manage to find him, which may not be easy. So I'll let you come. But don't assume it'll happen again, Angus. Police work isn't done for a lark."

"Yes, sir. I mean, no sir."

"Let's go. It's a long trail, and it'll be nice to have someone to talk to other than Millie." Sterling pulled at the lead and murmured to the dog. Millie set off at a trot, her bushy tail wagging cheerfully.

Angus shifted his pack and fell into step. It had worked! He'd counted on the fact that it was unlikely his mother had ever written a letter to Constable Sterling. He'd tried to give the handwriting a feminine slant, with a light touch of the pen and a flourish here and there, but he feared that he'd overdone it.

If his mother and Constable Sterling ever got together to discuss this letter, he'd be in real trouble. But he'd worry about that when the time came.

Chapter Thirty-Two

I was dreaming that I was in the Savoy, the *real* Savoy, the luxurious hotel in London, and the Prince of Wales was on his knees, serving me champagne in the tall black boot of an officer of the Horseguards, when a knock on the door of my bedroom had me struggling to consciousness.

"What, what!" I shouted.

"Pardon me, Mrs. MacGillivray, but Mr. Mann wants to have a word with you before leaving for work."

I leaned out of bed and fumbled for the dress I'd worn last night, lying in a heap on the floor. My sleepy fingers found the watch still fastened to the waist band. I flipped it open and squinted at the delicate face. Eight o'clock. I'd been asleep for barely an hour.

"Mrs. Mann, this matter will have to wait. I am still asleep. I got in late last night—this morning that is."

"Mr. Mann insists he must speak with you, Mrs. MacGillivray."

"Tell him I'll stop by the shop on my way to work later this morning." I dropped the dress and the watch and snuggled back under the covers.

"Angus is gone," she said.

Mrs. Mann certainly knew how to get my attention.

"I'll be there in a minute." I scrambled for robe and slippers and ran into the kitchen, not at all concerned that my unbound hair tumbled to the small of my back and my brilliant red dressing gown might not suit the Mann sense of propriety at the breakfast table.

They sat at the scrubbed kitchen table. The kettle hissed on the stove, but otherwise there was no sign of breakfast preparations.

Mrs. Mann handed me a scrap of paper. The handwriting I knew as well as my own:

I have gone to the Creeks with Constable Sterling on a NWMP investigation. We will be back in a few days. I want to be a Mountie, not a shopkeeper. Sorry, Mr. Mann. Don't worry, Mother. Your friend and loving son, Angus MacGillivray.

I crumpled the paper in my hand and without a word returned to my room. In a blind fury, I washed my face and hands in the cold water in the bowl on the table. I put on drawers, petticoats and stockings and laced up my corset. I pulled a plain day dress over my head, not bothering to check for dust and stains. I stuffed my hair into pins without so much as a glance in the mirror and put on a hat I rarely wore because it was too large, with an ostentatious blue feather hanging off to one side and something resembling a pear plopped into the centre of the whole mess.

The Manns tried not to stare as I walked back into the kitchen, my head held high, the blue feather bobbing. She was slicing bread for toast and had set a pot of oatmeal on the stove. He held spoon in hand, waiting for his breakfast.

"I will sort this matter out, Mr. Mann," I said, expressing a good deal more confidence than I felt. Holding my head high, I sailed through the door. Unfortunately, the blue feather caught on a splinter in the doorframe, and I had to spend a precious moment of righteous indignation freeing it.

Wasn't this the God-forsaken patch of earth! In London a lady would never find herself restrained by the woodwork.

I set off across town, heading for Fort Herchmer. The ground fairly shook under the force of my footsteps. A few passing shopkeepers and dance hall customers of my acquaintance opened their mouths as if to extend me a good morning. They took one look at my face and spun on their heels.

But gradually my steps began to falter. By the time I reached Fort Herchmer, I had slowed to an indecisive crawl. My original intention had been to march directly to the commander's office and demand that a force be sent out to retrieve my son. And throw Constable Sterling in the brig, if that was what they called it here. Put him on bread and water and hard labour for a decade or two.

But a sliver of common sense forced itself through my motherly indignation. It was highly unlikely any of this was Richard Sterling's fault. No doubt Angus was, at this very moment, creeping along in the wake of the Mountie, hiding behind trees and boulders. Once they were too far from town to turn back easily, Angus would leap out and exclaim, "Imagine finding you here! May I join you?"

The object of my rage shifted. What was that boy thinking? He'd be the one on bread and water. For the rest of his natural life.

They couldn't be far ahead of me. Angus had sat, pretending to be asleep, at the kitchen table not much over an hour ago. Now that I'd decided I would not send the full force of the law in pursuit of the constable, I considered going after them myself. I looked down at my boots. I was wearing the ones that I'd decided to throw out because they pinched. My chances of catching up with the long-legged Richard Sterling and the energetic twelve-year-old Angus were precisely nil.

"Mrs. MacGillivray, are you in need of assistance?" A handsome young constable stood in front of me. He didn't look old enough to shave.

"I...I've just remembered that I have forgotten something. Something important. I'm perfectly fine, thank you, Constable."

"Can I escort you back to your lodgings, Mrs. MacGillivray?" His innocent brown eyes overflowed with concern. I looked at the fort. In the centre of the large square, the Union Jack fluttered proudly in the stiff breeze.

Groups of men passed us, coming and going. Every one of them looked at me.

"Mrs. MacGillivray?" the boy said. "Can I fetch someone to assist you?"

Sergeant Lancaster was crossing the parade ground. He hadn't seen me.

I ducked behind a patch of thin, ill-nourished shrub.

"Thank you, Constable. If it's not out of your way, you may walk me home." I peeked out from the shrubbery. Lancaster had taken a right turn and was walking away from me. I straightened up and slipped my arm through the young man's. He blushed to the very roots of his hair.

"What is your name?" I asked.

"Reginald McAllen, Mrs. MacGillivray, ma'am."

"Do you know my son Angus, Constable McAllen?"

"Yes, ma'am. He hangs around the fort sometimes, usually tagging after Constable Sterling. If I may be so bold as to say so, Mrs. MacGillivray, that's a mighty fine hat you're wearing. Don't see hats of that quality in Dawson much."

I tossed him my warmest smile and opened my mouth to invite him to drop into the Savoy and enjoy a drink on the house.

"My ma used to have a hat like that. Goat ate the feather. She wasn't half mad."

I withdrew the unspoken invitation.

"Well, here we are. This is my residence. Thank you, Constable McAllen." I freed my hand from his arm.

He touched his hat. Two of his fellow Mounties strolled by. They stared at McAllen, and one of them pursed his lips in a silent whistle of astonishment.

I started up the path. "Constable McAllen?"

"Yes, ma'am."

"You're a credit to your mother. You may tell her I said so."

This time even the edges of his ears turned pink. I couldn't begin to imagine him confronting any member of the criminal classes.

Mrs. Mann stood at the sink, washing up the dishes. Mr. Mann had left for work, for which I was most grateful. No doubt he would blame me for everything, and I wasn't in the mood to find myself under the force of his wrath.

I hung my hat on the hook by the door and sank into a chair.

Mrs. Mann wiped her hands on her apron. "Gone?"

"Gone. When I get my hands around his scrawny neck..."

She poured a cup of coffee and placed it in front of me.

"This policeman? He's a good man?"

"Yes, I think so."

"Then Angus will be back in a day or so, and very pleased with his adventures and very proud of himself. And very surprised that he has caused you pain. And then very sorry."

I looked at her. "How can you be so sure?"

"I have a brother. We were five good girls and one wild boy in my family. He drove my mother to dis… dis… worrying, that boy did."

I filled in the word she was searching for, "To distraction," and sipped my coffee.

"Distraction. Ready for breakfast?"

"Might as well. I'll never get back to sleep. Is Mr. Mann terribly angry at Angus?"

She busied herself with the bag of oatmeal, a pail of water and a pot.

"Yes," she said. "But he was boy also. He'll forgive."

Of course Angus would be forgiven. A tongue lashing, followed by a hearty pat on the back, and the incident would never be mentioned again. But if he were a girl, things would be different. As a child, I'd received some education beside the Earl's daughter. Euila's governess drove it into our heads every single day that one tiny slip, one scarcely considered indiscretion, was enough to ruin a lady's reputation for life. And then we would die—poor, abandoned, lonely, dependent on the charity of distant relations. Unmarriageable. When she said so, she always looked at me out of the corner of her eye with a smirk, silently telling me that my reputation, unlike Euila's, was worth nothing. And wasn't that the truth: if I had guarded my reputation, I might very well be washing some man's underwear or birthing my twelfth child this very minute.

"I don't think Angus likes working at the store."

"No." Mrs. Mann handed me a steaming bowl of oatmeal.

The fresh milk was finished. I poured a generous serving of canned.

"Angus wants to be a mounted policeman," she said, passing the sugar bowl. "Boys have their dreams."

"That they do." I stirred sugar into my oatmeal.

"He took food. A tin of biscuits, some bread, cheese."

"I'm sorry. I'll pay you for it."

"He took no more than he'd eat if he was here. Less."

"Mrs. Mann, do you think that hat makes me look old? Like someone's mother? A man's mother, I mean, not a boy's?"

She sat opposite me with her own mug of coffee and addressed me by my Christian name for the first time. "Fiona, God chose not to bless me with children. But if I had a fine son like Angus, I'd be so proud, I'd not worry about my hat."

Chapter Thirty-Three

"Take a good look, Angus," Constable Richard Sterling said. "In all the rest of your long life, you'll never see the likes of this again."

Millie whimpered. Man, boy and dog walked down into the valley.

Only fifteen miles lay between Dawson and the start of the gold fields. But it was slow going; the trail was scarcely a trail at all, just a path hacked out of the wilderness, scarred by the footsteps of hundreds, thousands, of men and women, animals and equipment. Underfoot, every patch of vegetation had long ago been crushed into mud. But on the hillsides rising sharply above the trail, white and yellow and purple flowers covered the ground in a gentle mist. Higher up, the tips of the mountains and the bottoms of ravines that the sun never reached were covered with dirty grey snow.

Millie's tail was beginning to droop, and the straps of Angus's pack dug into his shoulders like the fingers of an angry housemaster when at last they reached sight of the town at the joining of the Bonanza and Eldorado creeks, the place the miners called Grand Forks.

The hillsides were bare of trees, except for a few lonely growths high up. There was scarcely a blade of grass to be seen. Every tree had been cut down, and every inch of ground dug up. The hills were white with piles of gravel pulled from the mines and discarded, the riverbeds black with mud. Steam belched from beneath the earth and, instead of trees, the hillsides were crossed with ditches carrying water to the claims where men worked the sluice boxes, washing away gravel and clay, hoping to find a lump of shining gold left behind. White canvas tents and rough log cabins dotted the hillside, a few with lines of laundry stretched out on the ropes and cooking fires in front.

Miners, their faces streaked with dirt, their clothes ripped and ill-repaired, their beards full, their hair uncut, and their eyes blank, watched them pass.

"Everyone looks so..." For once, Angus found himself at a loss for words.

"Tired," Sterling said. "They're tired. Men and nature both. Can't imagine what it must be like to work underground most of the day, or bent over pile after endless pile of muddy gravel."

"But isn't the gold running in the water? You only have to scoop it up and wash away the dirt, right?"

"Some of it was like that. But not much, and no longer. Most of the streaks of gold run through rock. And the rock is buried deep, under the permafrost. These men spent all winter melting the permafrost and digging into solid rock. And now that it's summer, they have to wash the tons of gravel in the sluice boxes before they can pan for gold."

"But soon they'll be rich, right? That'll make it all worthwhile."

"The good claims were taken, Angus, long before most of these poor fellows even got news of the strike. Most of these men've been hired to work someone else's claim. They'll break their backs and nothing they find'll come to them. And those who do own the ground they're working and strike it rich? They'll hand their gold over to your mother or one of the other dance hall owners for a chance to play the tables or dance with Irene or Ellie, or to sit in a private box wearing an ironed white shirt and buy champagne at forty dollars a bottle."

Angus said nothing more for a long time. Millie, who up till now had seemed to enjoy the walk from Dawson, kept her head to the ground and her ears flat.

"What do we do now, Constable Sterling? How do we find this man, Mr. Walker's friend?"

"We ask around. But first let's have a rest." Sterling sat down on a rock at the side of the trail and rummaged around in the saddlebags draped over Millie's broad back. He found a chunk of dried meat and tossed it at the dog's feet. She swallowed the food, licked her lips in appreciation and looked over at Angus wondering what he had to share.

Seeing that Sterling was unwrapping a sandwich for himself, Angus pulled out a hunk of bread and a slice of apple. He broke a corner off the bread.

"Don't feed Millie," Sterling said. "She's a working dog, not a pet."

Angus munched on his bread and apple, trying to ignore Millie's expressive, pleading brown eyes.

A steady stream of men walked by, paying the newcomers no mind. One fellow had a dog tied to a sled piled high with his belongings. Millie pricked up her ears as they drew close, but the dog gave her no more attention than the men did Sterling and Angus. Angus could see the outline of ribs beneath mangy fur, and the dog's eyes were red and weeping, too over-worked and underfed to sniff at a strange dog.

"I've been told Ruth's Hotel is the best place to start," Sterling said, stuffing his sandwich wrappings back into his bags.

Refreshed by the snack, Angus got to his feet and hoisted his pack onto his aching shoulders. He could see no sign of any hotel. A few canvas tents and rough wooden shacks climbed the lower slopes of the naked hill or cluttered the barren valley where, presumably, the creek had once run. The waterway still tried to keep to its ancient course, but it was stuffed with silt, packed with mountains of gravel, and overrun with mile after mile of sluice boxes.

A woman, dress streaked with dirt, filthy hair falling out of its pins, hands red and raw, eyes rimmed with fatigue, stood in the doorway of a grimy tent watching with scant interest as they passed. Rows of men's underwear, trousers, and shirts fluttered in the wind coming from behind her.

She glanced at Sterling's uniform, still neat and tidy, and Angus's clean coat, and went back to her work.

"There it is," Sterling said, as they passed the laundry.

"What? Where?" It took Angus more than a few moments to understand that they'd arrived at the hotel. It was a hut, backed up against the hillside, made of green wood held together, and not very well, with packed mud. A single rusty stovepipe poked through the ceiling. A few wildflowers grew directly out of the roof, adding a nice touch of colour to the endless brown and grey of mud and gravel surrounding them. A single bench, made out of a rough plank wobbling on top of a boulder, sat at the doorway. Even in Dawson Angus had never seen anything quite as bad as this. But Sterling hadn't made a mistake: a crudely drawn sign stuck into the mud beside the front door boasted Ruth's Hotel.

Sterling led Millie to the side of the hotel, where he unloaded her packs and ordered her to stay. She stretched luxuriously before turning three times and rolling herself into a furry white ball.

"You can leave your bag, Angus. Millie won't let anyone take it."

Angus placed his pack on the ground beside Sterling's. One brown eye stared at him from under the dog's bushy tail.

The door to the hotel stood open. Sterling had to duck as he stepped through the doorway. Angus stretched to his full height and was pleased that he grazed the top of the doorframe.

The building had no windows; the only natural light came in through the door. It was just one cramped room, with benches around the walls and a stove in the centre. Lamps, clothes, boots and bags hung from the roof posts. Sterling didn't have enough headroom to stand up straight.

The air was rank with the smell of unwashed clothes and the damp mud of the building itself.

They were greeted by the broad behind of a plainly

dressed woman. The rest of her was bent over a basket sorting through a pile of clothes. She straightened up and turned, one hand supporting the small of her back. “Afternoon, Constable. Looking for a bed?”

“Just information, thanks. Are you Ruth?”

“I am.”

“Constable Black says hello.”

She might have grinned, but Angus couldn’t be sure, so poor was the light.

“Well, if it’s talk you’re wanting, let’s go outside where I can see better.”

Sterling and Angus backed out of the hotel. Ruth sat on the bench, placed her basket beside her and pulled out a sock. She found a sewing needle in the collar of her dress and pushed one finger through the toe of the sock. “How is the old fellow?”

“Not missing Grand Forks.”

“Don’t imagine so. What do ya wanna know?” She began darning the sock. Her eyes squinted, and she pulled her head far back from her task. Angus wondered why she wasn’t wearing glasses. There was no place to sit, and he felt most uncomfortable looming over the woman. But she didn’t seem to mind.

“Looking for a fellow name of Johnny Stewart. Scottish, cheechako, passed by here yesterday.”

“What’s he look like?”

“Small, about five feet five or six, clean shaven, although that won’t last for long, hundred and twenty to hundred and thirty pounds. Mid to late thirties, not much hair left. Probably has a strong accent. He hasn’t done anything wrong. I only want to ask him a few questions about a friend of his.”

Ruth broke the thread with her teeth and put the mended sock to one side of the basket. “You want coffee? Only thirty cents.”

Thirty cents for a cup of coffee! Angus couldn’t believe it.

“That would be nice, thank you, Ruth,” Sterling said.

The woman struggled to her feet with a groan.

Sterling gave Angus a wink. “If I don’t buy a coffee,” he

whispered, "she won't answer my questions."

Ruth returned with the hot drink in a battered tin mug. She handed the coffee to Sterling, resumed her seat with an uncomfortable grunt, rooted through her basket, and came up with another sock. The heel was worn so thin, there was almost no wool left. Sterling took a sip of his coffee and tried not to grimace.

"How come you got your son with you?" she asked, squinting at Angus through one eye. "Ain't seen the Mounties do that before."

Angus flushed, thinking that he should correct her, but proud of her misunderstanding. He rarely thought of his father, who'd died in a riding accident before Angus was born. His mother never talked about him, and she didn't have a picture.

Sterling ignored the question. "Did you see Stewart?"

"Might have. Yesterday, round suppertime, bunch of cheechakos comes down the trail. They was speakin' English, but you wouldn't know it by me. Musta got all the way to Dawson by boat, 'cause they thought that trail were a tough one." She chucked. "They was lookin' for accommodation, but my place weren't quite up to their likin'. Hard to believe, ain't it boy?"

"What? Oh, yes, ma'am. It seems perfectly acceptable to me. Ma'am."

She chuckled again. "Don't be so polite, boy."

"Yes, ma'am. I mean no, ma'am."

"They won't be so fussy comin' back."

Sterling laughed. "No, they won't. Did you see where they went from here?"

Ruth nodded down the creek. "That way, but I can't say much more. One fellow asked where they could get somethin' to eat. I told him ta try Mary's. She does good food, Mary. Expensive though."

"Where can we find Mary's?"

"Just keep walking that way. Couple hundred yards or so. If'n you don't see it, ask anyone."

"Thank you for your time." Sterling drained the

contents of his mug and handed it to the woman, along with thirty cents. "If you should see these men again, tell Stewart I'm looking for him. But only because I want to help a friend of his."

Ruth took the money and returned to her mending without giving them another glance. Sterling woke Millie and loaded her up.

Chapter Thirty-Four

As I was up, dressed and mad as a rattlesnake, I might as well go to work. Today was Tuesday. Tomorrow I'd have to face Sergeant Lancaster and try not to laugh as I told him I wouldn't marry him. I'd worry about that tomorrow. Today, all I could think about was my son and what he might get up to in the gold fields. Although, once I calmed down, I realized that the worst that was likely to happen was that he got gold fever and decided to become a miner. That would last about a week at the absolute outside. Richard Sterling would be as angry at Angus's antics as I, but he'd keep my boy safe.

Until I could kill him!

I arrived at the Savoy to find that Helen had all the chairs in the saloon piled on the tables in order to wash the floor. Sam Collins's wife, Margaret, nursed a cup of tea on the single chair remaining upright, her feet resting on the table to let Helen mop around her. Her skirts were bunched up to her knees and I caught a glimpse of well-mended but spotlessly clean stockings and shoes with the soles almost worn through.

Seeing me, she dropped her feet to the floor.

"Put your feet back up, Margaret," I said. "Can't interfere with Helen's mopping."

"Keep to the wall," Helen said.

"Can I go upstairs?"

"No, floor's wet."

"I want to get to my office. I won't leave a mark."

"You stay right there, Mrs. Mac," Helen ordered. I wondered if she'd ever been housekeeper in a girl's school.

"I've done washing these floors, and just 'cause you comes in early, don't mean I want to do 'em again."

"Sorry," I said meekly.

"You wipe your shoes at the door, and you can come sit here."

I did as instructed then crept, suitably chastized, into my own establishment. I flipped a chair off the table and sat across from Margaret Collins.

"How's Sam doing?"

"Very well, thank you for asking, Mrs. MacGillivray."

"He's recovered from his brush with fame?"

I'd meant the comment as a joke, but Margaret's eyes darkened. "Sam doesn't want fame. He did what was right, what any decent man would have done. That's all."

I held up one hand. "I know, Margaret, and I'm sorry trouble came of it. But, well, Mr. Ireland isn't around to cause any more of a disturbance, now is he?"

"And praise God for that," Helen said in a firm voice.

She placed a cup of coffee in front of me and pulled up a chair to join in the conversation. "Ain't right to speak ill of the dead, but that Mr. Ireland..."

"The Lord works in His own way. But I can't pretend to be sorry Jack Ireland has gone to meet the devil," Margaret said primly.

I stumbled around, searching for something to say. "You have a lovely accent, Margaret. Quite distinctive. Where are you from?"

She smiled. "Pennsylvania. God's own country." Her teeth were good for a woman of her age and class, and her smile took years off her work-lined face.

"Second only to Missouri," Helen said.

An old argument between friends.

"Why did you leave God's Country to come to the Yukon?" I asked. Not that I was particularly interested. But I had to pass the time somehow until the floor dried.

"I left Pennsylvania a very long time ago indeed," Margaret said. "I haven't been back since." Something had always seemed out of place with Margaret, and now that I paid some attention to her, I understood what it was. She spoke much, much better than one would expect from a bartender's wife.

I sipped my coffee. I would ask no further questions. Even in the Yukon we were capable of some degree of good manners.

"Tell Mrs. MacGillivray," Helen said. She looked at me. "Margaret's had ever such an interesting life."

Mrs. Collins sighed, reluctant to repeat the story.

"Come on," Helen urged.

"My family didn't approve of Sam," Margaret said. "We had a big farm, by far the largest in the county. My younger brother studied to become a doctor. Sam's family were homesteaders. They dug themselves a hardscrabble farm out of rocks and dirt and had a mess of boys to split the land between one day. My father forbade me from having anything to do with the Collins family."

"You disobeyed him." Everyone of us in the Yukon has a story to tell; we wouldn't be here otherwise.

The corners of Margaret's stern mouth twitched as she savoured the memory. "Sam and I ran away. He had a cousin homesteading in North Carolina, who offered us a home if Sam would help around the farm. We arrived in March of '61." The smile faded.

"Wasn't North Carolina nice?" I asked, wondering at the sense of doom with which Margaret had filled the last sentence.

"Spring of '61. North Carolina," she repeated.

"Yes," I said, smiling. What was I missing? Was North Carolina, wherever that might be, not a pleasant place in the spring? It couldn't possibly have more mosquitoes than the Yukon, could it?

"War broke out just weeks after we got there. Lots of farming people in North Carolina quite sensibly, in my opinion, didn't want to take sides or have anything to do with the war. But not Sam's cousins. They were so dreadfully eager to go and fight for secession, and they got Sam all caught up in the excitement with their talk about freedom."

"War," I repeated. "Nasty business." Was there a war in

1861? I hadn't even been born yet, what did I know or care? There was always a war going on somewhere. Seems to me that it never did anyone any good. So why do men keep having them? Because it must be doing someone some good, of course. Although not the poor men who have to fight or the poor women who stand to lose everything they hold dear.

Margaret fell silent, but Helen picked up her story. "Sam left for the war in May '61, and he didn't come back home till it was all over. Ain't that right, Margaret?"

"I thought he was dead. Didn't hear a word for months. Then we got a letter from Sam's cousin Jake saying that Sam had been captured by the Yankees. Yankees. My own brothers were Yankees."

I settled back into my chair. "Then it turned out all right then. Sam was safe, out of the war."

Margaret looked at me.

"The Yankees weren't nice to their prisoners, Mrs. Mac," Helen Saunderson said.

"Oh," I said.

"Sam came home in '65," Margaret said. "We'd been married for four years, and we hadn't been together more than a couple of weeks in all that time."

"That must have been difficult." I knew I sounded about as shallow as the dregs of coffee left in the bottom of my cup. But what else could I say: *You'll get over it one day?*

"Sam healed and fattened himself back up. He was a hero. He'd been captured because he refused to leave a wounded man behind. He tried to carry the soldier back to Confederate lines. He would have escaped, if he'd left the man to die. A man he'd never set eyes on before. But Sam couldn't leave him. The fellow died in the prison camp because the Yankee soldiers wouldn't send for a doctor to tend to him. When the war ended, the Confederacy was broken, and its heroes weren't recognized. Not like the Union soldiers. They got medals for waking up in the morning.

"But despite all that happened to Sam, we were luckier than many. Sam's cousin Jake never did make it home.

Then the carpetbaggers came."

It didn't take a genius to assume that the carpetbaggers were not nice people. I shook my head in disapproval at their actions. Whatever those actions might have been.

"They took the farm, so we left for California. But luck didn't come with us, Mrs. MacGillivray. We've had a hard life. But I'm not sorry for a moment of it, except for what those Union bastards—excuse me, Mrs. MacGillivray, Helen—did to my Sam."

"Did you ever hear from your family?"

"Only once. I wrote to my mother, two years after Sam was taken prisoner. I told her all that had happened. I said I missed her. She never received the letter. My father sent it back, with 'Confederate Traitor' written in big black letters across the envelope."

"And you never wrote to your mother again?"

"There didn't seem to be much point."

I thought for a moment of Margaret's mother, waiting anxiously for a letter, day after day, year after year, as more than thirty years passed. And her husband defacing and returning the one letter that did arrive.

"Floor's dry, if'n you want to go upstairs, Mrs. Mac," Helen announced.

"It's been nice talking to you, Margaret," I said as I stood up. Now there was a trite comment. In neither the overflowing streets of Seven Dials nor the drawing rooms of Belgravia—not even in the comfortable homes of Toronto—did one encounter such human emotion nakedly displayed. This really was the New World, and I didn't quite know what to make of it. I'm much more comfortable hiding behind a civilized façade of good manners and polite indifference than being confronted by this strange American habit of revealing one's innermost feelings to almost-perfect strangers.

As a nation, they won't get anywhere as long as they continue to display such tolerance to the relaxation of common decency. Not compared to the fortitude of the peoples of the British Empire, for which I had not the slightest bit of affinity, but felt a certain not-quite-understood pride nevertheless.

As I trudged up the stairs to my office, it occurred to me that I had gone a whole half an hour without giving a thought to the whereabouts of my wayward son.

I worked on the books, making several mistakes when my mind wandered, and I found myself thinking more about Angus than the columns of figures I should be concentrating on.

It couldn't be easy for Angus, being my son. We'd had a nice life, in Toronto. I'd rented a beautiful home in the best part of town. Angus had gone to a good Episcopal school, in the company of boys from the best families. The sons of bankers, lawyers, men of business and blue-blooded aristocrats who'd come to Canada when their bloodlines outlasted their family fortunes. His schoolmates invited Angus to skating and tennis parties; he spent weekends at near-palatial summer homes on Stony Lake. Then one day, I arrived at his school in the middle of the night, forced the night porter to rouse my son from his bed, informed the headmaster, still rubbing sleep out of his eyes and wearing a hastily tied dressing gown, that Angus was leaving, and ordered my driver to toss his trunk into the cab. We caught the next train out of Union Station heading west. The boy looked out the window and didn't even complain that he hadn't had a chance to bid his friends goodbye.

Finally, I decided the ledger was accurate enough and took our earnings to the bank. But despite the fact that I had enjoyed all of a half-an-hour's sleep the previous night, I didn't want to go back to Mrs. Mann's boarding house for my usual nap. Not that Angus normally hung around during the day when I rested, but the place would be so lonely without him.

Mrs. Mann had promised to send word the minute he got home.

"Still here, Fee?" Ray stuck his head around the door.

"How long does it take to get to the Creeks, Ray?"

"I don't know. Less than a day, maybe. Why?"

Less than a day. No doubt by the time they found this…whatever his name was…it would be too late to head straight back to Dawson. So I could expect Angus home tomorrow. Probably shortly after lunch. He'd have eaten all the food he took with him and would be ravenous. Angus could eat a prodigious amount.

"Everything all right, Fee?" Ray asked.

"Angus has run off. Gone with Richard Sterling to the Creeks on some stupid police investigation. He didn't even tell me was he was going." At last I started to cry.

I never cry. Some women can cry with grace, so they still manage to look dewy-fresh and perfectly lovely. Not me. Crying makes my nose red and my eyes all puffy, and the skin on my face turns white and lumpy like a batch of bad dough.

Ray stared at me in horror, whether at the news of Angus or my tears, I didn't know. "Is the man mad? Ta take a twelve-year-old lad on police business?"

"I'd guess Sterling didn't have much to say about it." Through my tears I told Ray the story. Dawson and the New World were having an effect on me: now I was the one pouring out my heart.

"They've gone looking for Johnny Stewart, my pal from Glasgow."

I fumbled in the depths of my sleeve and brought out a handkerchief. It was well laundered and many times mended. Someone had embroidered JPD in perfect, tiny blue stitches in one corner. I didn't remember knowing anyone with the initials JPD.

Ray came around the desk and patted me on the shoulder with as much awkwardness as if he were trying to soothe a rattlesnake. "There, there, Fee. If Angus is with Sterling, he'll be okay."

"But I don't know if he found Sterling," I blubbered shamelessly. "Maybe he went after Sterling but didn't go in the right direction. Maybe he's lost in the wilderness, set upon by Indian barbarians."

"Now you're letting your imagination run away, Fee. No one can get lost in the wilderness round here. The trail leading from Dawson to the Creeks is better marked than the road from Glasgow to Edinburgh, although a mite rougher in places, I hear. And as for Indians, they take one look at Angus, and they'll be more than happy to bring him home, expecting a fat reward."

I got to my feet and turned to look out the window. As usual, a horse was floundering in the mud: the mud too thick, the horse too ill fed, the cart too heavily loaded. And, as usual, the driver screamed until the veins in his neck were about to pop and flailed at the emaciated beast's flanks as if that would do any good. Better if he got behind the cart and pushed, or better still, unloaded the cart. The Vanderhaege sisters' bakery was back in full operation, the burnt-out shell torn down and a new one replaced in a day. Graham Donohue walked by, keeping to the far side of the street. He glanced at the Savoy but scurried away. Something was bothering him. If I'd been less worried about my son, I might have found time to worry about what had spooked our intrepid American newspaperman so much since the murder of Jack Ireland. But right now, Graham's guilt, or innocence, was nothing more than a niggling thought in the back of my mind, sort of like thinking about a pesky mosquito when one is confronted by a hungry grizzly bear.

"You're right, Ray," I said. "But how can I not worry?"

"Did you speak to anyone?"

"No."

"I'll go 'round to the fort. Say I'm looking for Sterling. That he owes me money or some such. Ask when he's due back."

I turned and gave Ray a weak smile. "Thank you. I'd appreciate that." I blew my nose in a completely unladylike manner into JPD's handkerchief.

"Angus is a smart wee lad, Fiona. He won't go far if he's by himself. And if he's caught up with Sterling, then the Constable'll look after him. You know that, don't you?"

"Yes, Ray. I do know all that."

"I'll see that the boys are ready for the day, then I'll be off to the fort. Nose around a bit. Maybe someone saw

Angus. Now you, Fee, you should go home and have your nap and tidy up. Won't do yourself any good, not sleeping."

"Yes, Ray."

We both looked up at the sound of footsteps in the hallway, followed by a discreet cough.

Sergeant Lancaster stood in the doorway, clutching his hat to his chest. I'd only left Lancaster a couple of hours ago. I could imagine him wandering through the darkened streets gazing at the moon like a love-struck fool.

I was not in any mood to pretend to be polite. "Yes, Sergeant. Can I help you with something?"

Of course, like a love-struck fool, he didn't pick up anything in my voice or manner that he didn't want to. "Is this man bothering you, Mrs. MacGillivray?"

Ray swallowed a laugh.

"Certainly not. I am…distraught…and Mr. Walker is reminding me of my responsibilities." I hated being caught in a naked display of emotion. Like an American. I glared at Lancaster.

Lancaster glared at Ray, and Ray could hardly hide his smirk. "Guess I'll be off then, Fee," my partner said. "Unless you need me to hang around. A chaperone, like."

"Go away."

He left, still chuckling. Ray loved Angus. His belief in my son's safety gave me a good deal of comfort. I turned to Lancaster. "Now that you're here, Sergeant…"

"I don't care for that man," Lancaster said. "I don't think his intentions towards you are entirely honourable, Mrs. MacGillivray."

More honourable than yours. I sat down with a thud. Most unladylike, to make a sound when seating oneself.

"Mrs. MacGillivray." Lancaster rounded the desk and stood looking down at me. His eyes were on fire, his breath rough and uneven. "Fiona. My dear. Surely you must understand that in this place your precious, God-given reputation is open to any man's evil thoughts. Think of your late husband. He must be looking down from Heaven, so dreadfully worried about you."

That did it. Time to get rid of the overbearing Sergeant Lancaster, even if I did myself and my business an injury. I opened my mouth.

"Think of your dear son."

I closed it again. What if something did happen to Angus? Since Ray's lecture, my fears were receding, but suppose Angus never caught up with Sterling. Or perhaps they were set upon by bandits. Although no one had reported bandits operating in the Yukon. If something terrible came to pass, I would need all possible assistance, and the good will, of every member of the NWMP. And, according to Sterling, Lancaster, useless as he might be, had the respect of his fellow officers. I cocked my head to one side.

"Please, Sergeant Lancaster. I appreciate your courtesy, but I need some time alone." Taking a chance at appearing too theatrical, I touched my forehead with the back of my hand. "I am feeling quite unwell."

Lancaster blushed, with considerably less charm than young McAllen had earlier. I had touched upon a feminine matter—a matter of some delicacy. Enough to have most men running for the hills (or the bars) in terror. I wondered if Lancaster had ever been married. If he had, he'd probably bored Mrs. Lancaster to death. I didn't even know, nor did I care to find out, his first name.

"Pardon me, my dear. I apologize." He stumbled backwards, bumping his fleshy hip on the corner of my desk. "When I saw you standing at the window, looking so lovely, I thought you might be in need of assistance." He backed his way out of the room. I fluttered my fingers to say goodbye.

Once I heard the heavy tread of his boots on the stairs, I jumped up, slammed the office door shut, and burst into another round of tears.

I could take almost anything life could threaten me with—I'd proved I could. But I needed my son. If anything happened to Angus, it would be more than I could bear.

Chapter Thirty-Five

If it were possible, Mary's restaurant was even more unappealing than Ruth's Hotel. Mary claimed that she hadn't seen the men Sterling was looking for, which came as no surprise to Angus: if Stewart and his companions hadn't liked the look of Ruth's, they wouldn't eat food served up at Mary's.

They spent the rest of the day wandering through Grand Forks, asking after anyone matching Stewart's description. Most of the men they stopped looked at them with a shake of the head and continued on their way. One miner told them he'd seen a man matching Stewart's description working a sluice box close by. They followed his directions to find a Scotsman who had arrived at the Creeks only recently. But he stood a good six foot six, with the weight to match and a head overflowing with curly red hair.

"This is hopeless," Angus said. His feet hurt and his pack was rubbing the skin off his shoulder blades. By the time he crawled into his bedroll, if ever that marvellous occasion happened, he fully expected he'd be able to see bare bone. "There must be ten thousand men here. Stewart could be anywhere."

"This is police work," Sterling said, "and we've only just gotten here. But it's time to call it a day. It's looking to be a nice night, so we can take our chance out in the open 'cause there's no trees to string a covering from, or we can try back at Ruth's hotel."

Angus shivered. "My ma catches sight of that hotel, she'd have a thing or two to say about it."

"If you ever become a Mountie, Angus, you won't want to tell your mother about some of the places you have to visit. Or the people you meet. There's level ground over there. It should do."

They unpacked their bedrolls. Sterling fed and watered Millie before starting up the tiny travelling stove he'd pulled out of his pack.

"That's nice," Angus said.

"The men told me there'd not be much firewood up here. Do you have anything to cook?"

Angus shook his head. "I brought bread and cheese and cold meat and stuff."

"You can have some of my bacon and beans, and tomorrow I'll have some of your bread and cheese. How's that?"

"Good, thanks."

"Hot food's important, for the spirits as well as the belly."

Angus lay down almost as soon as they finished eating. He thought he'd never be able to get to sleep, what with the rough patch of ground he lay on and the noises all around him, but the next thing he knew, Sterling was shaking him awake, Millie was pawing at his chest, and the sun was over the hills to the east.

"Why don't we have some of that bread and cheese for breakfast?" Sterling said. "No need to start up the stove. We can buy coffee someplace."

They trudged through the gold fields all day, making their way up Eldorado Creek. They didn't find a trace of Stewart. Tomorrow they'd backtrack and travel down Bonanza Creek.

That night, as Angus's weary eyes began to close, he watched Sterling sitting wrapped in his blanket, looking out over the mines to the purple hills in the distance, puffing on his pipe, scratching behind Millie's ear. He fell asleep wondering if his father had ever owned a dog.

A man came to their rough camp on the morning of the third day, while Sterling was starting the stove to make breakfast, and Angus was eyeing dark clouds gathering overhead. A day of rain and this hillside, stripped of all vegetation, would turn into a river of mud. He wondered if he was prepared to spend a night in a hotel like Ruth's and decided that he preferred to endure the mud and the rain.

"Heard you're looking for Johnny Stewart," the man said. He was a Scotsman, his accent deep but with a touch of education smoothing out the rougher edges. His face was battered, and his nose flattened as if he'd been a prizefighter, many years before. "What've you got to offer for information about him?"

"Nothing," Sterling said, opening the can of beans. "The NWMP doesn't deal in bribes. It's your duty to give me what information you have."

The man spat.

"But I can promise you that I'm not interested in Stewart. He's in no trouble. It's about a friend of his. I only want to talk to him."

"Care for a biscuit, mister?" Angus said, holding out Mrs. Mann's tin. The scones were getting stale, but he didn't think this hard man would object to that.

"Why thank you, lad, that's mighty kind of you." The man took the scone and bit into it. A look of sheer pleasure crossed his fight-ravaged face, and he devoured the rest in one bite. "Just like my mum used to make, back home in Inverness." Angus would have sworn that the corner of the man's eye was suddenly wet. "Johnny Stewart. Working the Number 44." The man walked away, licking crumbs off his fingers.

"Her Majesty's North-West Mounted Police do not offer bribes, Angus," Sterling said, trying to sound stern. A grin touched the edges of his mouth.

"Sorry, sir. I thought he looked sad. Did I do wrong?"

"No. He was sad. A long way from home and wondering what on earth he's doing in this miserable place. Like all the rest of them." He stirred the beans. "When my mother makes beans, she puts in a huge lump of pork fat and plenty of molasses. She cooks them all day long, then she puts a pan of corn bread in the oven. She always served me up the biggest bit of pork and a slab of cornbread cut from the edges of the pan. Does your mother make beans, Angus?"

"My mother? She doesn't cook. Even on the trail, one of the packers or me got the meals."

Sterling shook his head. "Sorry. Forgot who I'm talking to for a moment. Well, these seem to be ready. For what it's worth. Eat up, and we'll find out what your biscuit bought us."

There were no signposts pointing to this claim or that, so they had to ask all the way. After three days on the Creeks, all the men they spoke to were starting to look the same to Angus. Worn out, dirty, tired, interested in nothing. They came across a group of men taking a break, smoking their pipes, on the top of a slag heap. They were slightly less dirty than most of the others, and the hope hadn't completely faded from their eyes. The men looked up as Sterling, Angus and Millie approached.

"I'm looking for a man name of Johnny Stewart," Sterling said, raising his voice to be heard at the top of the makeshift hill. "Any of you know him?"

The men said nothing, but their eyes shifted to a small fellow sitting at the edge of their group.

He drew on his pipe. "I'm Stewart."

"Constable Sterling, NWMP. Can I talk to you for a moment, sir? Won't take much of your time."

Stewart looked at his friends. They looked back without interest or emotion. He stood up, like a man whose every joint protested at the movement. "If ye keep it short. Break's almost over."

The man's accent was identical to Ray Walker's.

Sterling led Stewart away from the listening group of men. Angus and Millie followed, simply because they had nothing better to do.

"You're not in any trouble, Stewart, I only want to ask you a couple of questions."

Stewart puffed on his pipe. His hands were covered in angry white blisters, and he winced with every step he took. Less than a week on the job, and Stewart looked like he'd been underground for twenty years. Men arrived from the south all the time, Angus had heard amidst much laughter in the Savoy, thinking they would dig for gold like they dug for carrots and potatoes on the farm or in their mother's back garden.

"Sunday last you were in Dawson. Can you tell me what you did there?"

Stewart's eyes barely flickered. "D' ye have any food in that saddlebag, laddie?" he said. "Working underground's mighty hard work."

Angus dove into his bag. There were a few of Mrs. Mann's scones left, most of them broken into crumbs, but one remained almost whole, scattered with raisins, plump and inviting. He held out the tin, and a satisfied Stewart alternately smoked, ate and talked.

"Drifted around town in the morning, then ran into a lad from the old country who knew my gran."

"This man's name?"

"Ray Walker."

"About what time did you meet Mr. Walker?"

"Late morning. Eleven or so. We talked mostly, about Glasgow and the old days, and walked through town? He showed me the sights. Ha! Not much o' them. Walker told me not ta waste my time prospecting. Said the real money's to be made in town. Guess I should have listened to him, right, boy?"

Angus opened his mouth to agree then, catching sight of Sterling's stern face, snapped it shut. He wasn't supposed to be offering his opinions.

Millie paid the men no attention and licked her private parts with gusto.

"What time did you last see Walker?"

"Hey, Johnny. Time to get back at it." The men on the slag heap yelled as they reluctantly got to their feet.

Stewart blew a sigh, full of cheap pipe smoke and expensive regrets. "We had supper round five o'clock, maybe a wee bit later. I had ta get off to bed; we was leaving first thing the next morning. Prob'ly left Walker five thirty, six."

"You were with Walker the whole day?"

"Yea."

"He couldn't have been in your sight the whole time."

"The fellow had to go to the loo now an' again, didn't he? So did I. But no more than that."

"Nothing appeared to be out of the ordinary when he got back from the privy? His clothes look the same?"

Steward shrugged. "Clothes are clothes. Didn't notice anything funny. Sorry, Constable, but I gotta get back to work. First days on the job, can't seem to be slacking off. Me and Ray, we spent Sunday talking 'bout Glasgow and our aunties and grandmas. I've nothing else ta tell ye."

"Thank you, Mr. Stewart," Sterling said. "I appreciate your giving me your time."

"Couple more days, and we'll strike it rich, what d' ye think, laddie?" Stewart snuffed out his pipe and stuffed it back into his coat pocket. He winced as the blisters on his hands rubbed against the dirt-encrusted wool.

"I think that's great, sir." Angus said, trying to sound as if he believed it. "My ma owns the best dance hall in all of Dawson, it's called the Savoy. On Front Street. When you and your friends are in town, you should come and visit."

Stewart was a couple of inches shorter than Angus, but he reached up and ruffled the boy's hair. "My wee lad's about your age," he said. "Him and his sister and their mum's waiting in Halifax. Waiting for me to strike it rich and come and fetch them."

"Stewart," one of the men called. "For Christ's sake, you wanna be fired? Get up here."

The Scot climbed up the pile of gravel and slag, his back bowed and his shoulders bent. He turned around and looked at Angus. His eyes were blue and very bright. "You think they'll be waiting long, son?" And he disappeared into the unforgiving earth.

Angus blew out a lungful of air. Sterling scribbled in his notebook with a stub of pencil. Millie continued to wash herself, making happy doggy noises all the while.

Sterling put his notebook and pencil back into his jacket pocket. He read the expression on Angus's face. "No one forced these men to come here, son," he said. "They're free men. Not slaves. Let's head home."

Angus pulled himself back to the moment. "Did he tell you what you wanted to hear, sir?"

"I didn't *want* to hear anything, Angus. I simply wrote down what Stewart said." They started down the slope. "He confirmed what Walker had to say about the events of Sunday afternoon." His voice dropped as if he were talking to himself. "So maybe it was what I wanted to hear at that."

Chapter Thirty-Six

Five long days passed. Ray went to the fort where he found out that Sterling had, indeed, gone to the Creeks. No one would, or could, tell him why, but he guessed it had something to do with his friend, Stewart. Mr. Mann stopped ranting about the ungrateful boy and assumed a worried frown. I was usually up when he came in for his breakfast because I didn't sleep much.

The bartenders, the croupiers and the dance hall girls, most of whom had gotten to know Angus, and to care for him, looked at me with questioning eyes and glanced away when they saw the negative reply in mine. Helen almost wore her apron to bits, wringing it between her tough old fingers. Some of the prominent citizens in town—Mouse O'Brien, Big Alex Macdonald, Belinda Mulroney among them—had started to put together a party to go to the Creeks in search of Sterling and Angus. That people cared so much, in this cold, hard town, where no one ventured except in search of fortune, touched me again to the point of tears. Hearing of my plight, Sergeant Lancaster refrained, wisely, from pressing his suit.

Of course, nothing could dampen business at the Savoy. Everything that happened to us seemed only to increase our custom. I was so run off my feet those long nights that I scarcely had a moment to think about my missing child.

Then on Friday afternoon, Richard Sterling and Angus MacGillivray walked into the Savoy. Sterling looked like Zeus, the avenging Greek god I'd learned about in the schoolroom, and Angus... Angus looked as if he wanted the earth to swallow him whole. News of the depth of our concern, not only mine but also half of Dawson, had reached them.

I was making my way into the gambling hall when all conversation in the saloon died. Convinced that some unimaginable terror had struck, I whirled around. Every man in the place was looking at me. My knees buckled. Sterling pushed Angus in the small of his back, propelling my boy a few reluctant feet through the narrow passage that had opened between us.

Ray stood behind the bar, a glass of whisky half poured. The look of relief on his face was so great that I understood, only at that moment, that he had been far more worried about my son than he'd let on.

I marched past Angus hissing, "Upstairs," underneath my breath. Sterling followed. Not a man spoke as we climbed the stairs. But as I walked down the corridor, exclamations, questions, and shouts erupted beneath my feet like the spring flood spilling through a broken dam.

I didn't know whether to take my son, as tall as I, over my knee or to kiss every inch of his beloved face.

"Mother, I can't begin to tell you how sorry I am," he said, his head downcast. "I left you a note. I told you not to worry."

Still undecided, I turned on the nearest available target. "How could you?" I growled at Constable Richard Sterling. "How could you take a twelve-year-old child into the wilderness without his mother's permission? I ought to have you up on charges."

"That might well happen, Mrs. MacGillivray," Sterling said. He didn't look at Angus, scuffing the floorboards with one mud-encrusted toe. "We walked into Fort Herchmer less than half an hour ago, to find that the whole town is in an uproar of unprecedented proportions, and some prominent citizens were in the process of putting together a group of men to go in search of a member of the NWMP. Inspector Starnes is not pleased, I can assure you." Inspector Cortlandt Starnes was the officer in charge of the Mounties in Dawson.

"It's all my fault, Mother," Angus said to the floor. His voice broke, and for a moment I thought he might burst into tears, but he swallowed hard and fought to regain some of his composure. "I didn't mean to get Constable Sterling in any trouble. I thought it would be a good opportunity to learn to be a Mountie."

"We'll deal with that shortly, Angus." I glanced at Sterling. He struggled to hold his thoughts inside his big frame.

"Do you have anything to say about this, Constable? Surely you realize that as the adult, and the authority figure, you bear more responsibility than my child."

"Angus?" Sterling said.

"I lied, Mother. I told Constable Sterling you'd given me permission to accompany him to Grand Forks."

"And you believed him?" I shouted at Sterling. Fortunately, the patrons downstairs had resumed their normal pitch of conversation, or they would have heard me.

"Show my mother the letter, Constable," Angus said.

"Let's just say that Angus can be most convincing, Mrs. MacGillivray. I'm truly sorry we caused you such distress. I take full responsibility. I have to get back to the Fort. I've been ordered to give the Inspector a report once Angus has been safely returned to you. I'm sorry."

He turned and walked out the door.

"Don't you move a muscle," I ordered my son. "Constable. A moment, please." I walked down the hall and stood in front of Sterling. There was only one small window at the end of the corridor, and the single lamp at the top of the stairs flickered, almost out of fuel. "I have no doubt my son tricked you into taking him on this expedition. He can be quite charming when he chooses to be. I can guess the contents of this letter, even if you don't want to show it to me. If you need any help with your superiors, please let me know."

"That's kind of you, Mrs. MacGillivray. I won't pretend that I'm not worried about what the Inspector has to say. You have some powerful friends."

"I'm sorry."

He held up one massive paw. "Don't apologize. If it were someone dear to me who'd gone missing, I'd have called on the devil himself to intervene. You did the right thing. You have a good boy there, don't be too hard on him. He was a help, and good company on the trail. I'd better be going."

"Perhaps you could join us for dinner tonight," I blurted out, without thinking. "With Angus and me, I mean. At our boarding house. I'd like to hear of your adventures."

He looked at me, his brown eyes unreadable.

"If you're not in jail or something," I stammered.

The corners of his mouth lifted once again. "I'd like that, Mrs. MacGillivray."

"Nine o'clock?"

"Nine o'clock. If I'm…indisposed, I'll send a message." The stairs clattered beneath his boots. I stood still for a moment, just thinking. I could follow Sterling's progress across the room and out into the street as the drinkers' conversation fell silent in his wake.

I walked back to my office.

"So," I said to my ashen-faced son, "tell me about this letter."

Chapter Thirty-Seven

I sent Angus home with his pockets full of money. I told him to give the money to Mrs. Mann and tell her we were having company for dinner and to do the best she could. After that, he was to go to Mr. Mann's store down by the waterfront and work for the rest of the afternoon. Provided he was still wanted.

Make no mistake, I was absolutely furious. He'd forged my signature, lied to an officer of the law, failed to show up at his place of employment, disappeared for five days and worried his mother half to death, not to mention a good portion of the citizenry.

But he had come back. Safe and sound.

When I ventured downstairs, some of the men watched me, but most of the excitement had passed with the departure of Sterling, and shortly after, Angus, both of them still in one piece.

"Everything all right, Fee?" Ray asked.

"I hope so." I walked around the back of the bar, and Ray bent forward so that I could whisper into his ear. Only he, and Her Majesty, glowering disapprovingly at us from her portrait, could hear. "It would appear that Angus strung Sterling quite a line, and Inspector Starnes is furious about it all. What a mess."

"Speaking of the police." Ray pointed his chin towards the door.

I turned to see Inspector McKnight enter the saloon. The customers gave him a wide berth. "Evening, Mrs. MacGillivray. Do you have a minute, Walker?"

"No. Ye might not have noticed, but we're busy at the moment."

"I think you'll be interested in what I have to say. In private." The Inspector looked at the group of drinkers lingering nearby, unashamedly hanging on his every word.

Barney belched in his face.

Grumbling, Ray led the way to Helen's kitchen, and I followed, as did a pack of miners. I shut the door firmly in their dirty, bearded faces.

There was scarcely enough space in the room for three people to stand, and only one chair. McKnight seated himself. As I hadn't been invited to follow them, I could scarcely complain about this shocking breach of manners.

"I thought you'd want to know that Sterling located your friend, Mr. Johnny Stewart."

"I figured that was why he went to the Creeks."

"Mr. Stewart confirms your alibi."

"Could of told you that," Ray said. But some of the tension he'd been carrying all week slipped from his shoulders and he almost, but not quite, cracked a smile.

"That's wonderful," I said. "It's kind of you to take the time to come here and inform us in person, Inspector."

He made no effort to stand but twisted his hands in his lap and coughed. "Well, uh, Mrs. MacGillivray, there is one small thing you could do for me."

Ray and I exchanged knowing glances. So that was the way it was to be played, was it?

"I'd be pleased to offer you the hospitality of our house, Inspector," I said, the words choking in my throat. Bribery of the local constabulary might be common business practice for bars and gambling houses in every other corner of the world. But not in Dawson. For the first time, I was about to bribe an officer of the law. Perhaps we'd find out that Stewart hadn't given Ray an alibi after all.

McKnight flushed. "You misunderstand me, Mrs. MacGillivray. I was sort of hoping that once all this is settled, you might introduce me to Miss Ellie." The words out, he leapt to his feet. "Nothing improper, you understand. She's so admired that it's quite difficult, impossible really, to get a moment to speak to her. Privately. And I would like to." He studied the wall behind my head. "Speak with her, I mean. For just a moment. Nothing improper, of course. But if you think it improper…I'd best be leaving." He bolted for the door.

I smiled and touched his sleeve. "It would be my pleasure, Inspector. Why don't you come by this evening, say around quarter to eight? I'll be happy to introduce you. Ellie doesn't go on stage until well after eight, perhaps you could escort her to the bar and enjoy a drink or two. My treat, of course."

"Mrs. MacGillivray! That would be perilously close to a bribe." He looked at me through his thick eyeglasses. "A brief introduction to the lady is all I ask. I'll see you this evening."

The door stuck momentarily on badly-installed hinges. McKnight wrestled it open and ran, his ears scarlet.

I laughed, after ensuring that the Inspector had been swallowed up by the noisy crowd.

"You shouldn't o' promised to introduce them," Ray said. "It's not right."

"Don't be ridiculous. The fellow wants to meet the object of his affections for a minute or two in a packed bar." I walked out, still chuckling.

Chapter Thirty-Eight

By seven o'clock, I was regretting my impulsive invitation to Constable Sterling to join us for dinner. I was exhausted. All week, I'd been living on worry—no sleep, and even less food than I'd consumed over the winter—and now that Angus was safely home, I wanted only to collapse like a rag doll.

McKnight arrived, thoroughly scrubbed, hair greased and combed flat, moustache stiffly groomed, promptly at 7:45 p.m. As promised I introduced him to Ellie. She performed like the professional she was: absolutely *thrilled* to make his acquaintance, she had heard *so very much* about the *famous* Inspector McNichol. He was too infatuated to correct her mistake over his name—probably didn't even notice. I left them as she was promising to save him a *special* dance after the show.

I waited until the orchestra did their bit on the street, and the stage show got underway before slipping out.

"Fiona, my dearest. You look perfectly lovely this evening." Graham Donohue fell into step beside me on the boardwalk. He hadn't been around the Savoy much lately, and when he did drop in to hear if there had been any news about Angus, his demeanour towards me had changed. He was acting wary, skittish almost, like a half-trained dog afraid he'd misunderstood his master's command and had made the wrong move. "I hear Angus is back from his misadventure. They're saying Sterling's going to be drummed out of the Mounties for it." He seemed almost pleased at the scrap of news.

"Who's saying, Graham?" I stopped and turned to face

him, hands planted firmly on hips.

"Everyone." He shrugged. "You know, people."

"I don't listen to idle gossip."

"Since when? Admit it, Fiona. You live for idle gossip." He laughed but stopped fast enough when he saw the look on my face. "Everyone is also saying that Angus is hale and hearty, although a bit sheepish."

"In that respect, everyone is correct. What's the matter with you, Graham? I thought you and Constable Sterling were friends."

"Sure we are."

"You don't sound like a friend. You sound pleased to hear he might be coming into some misfortune."

"Now why would you think that, Fiona, my darling? I'm simply repeating the news of the day. Like the good newspaperman I am."

"In that case you'll be glad to hear that I intend to ensure Constable Sterling is not reprimanded in any way over this incident. The whole thing was clearly Angus's fault."

Graham's face fell. Too late, he tried to hide it by pasting on a smile.

We stepped aside to allow a pair of neatly dressed gentlemen to pass. They tipped their hats to me.

"We can't stand here discussing this on the street." I linked my arm through Graham's, tossed him a flirtatious smile, and poked him lightly in the chest with my free hand. Time to drag Graham out of this strange mood that had descended upon him. "Constable Sterling is joining Angus and me for dinner. Come along. I'm sure Mrs. Mann has prepared more than enough to accommodate another hungry lad."

"You're having dinner with Sterling? And Angus?" He wretched free of my arm.

"Good heavens, Graham. What is the matter with you?"

"I've remembered an important appointment. Most critical. Pardon me, Fiona, another time perhaps. For dinner, I mean." He almost ran, scarcely avoiding knocking the gentlemen off the boards.

I was quite fond of Graham. If I were looking to settle down with someone, which is indeed a substantial if, it had occurred to me that I could do a great deal worse than Graham Donohue. He was good-looking, not overbearingly large, intelligent, interested in everyone and everything. He had a good job and got on well, but not excessively well, with my son. And, most important of all, he simply adored me. Of course, most men do. But either they slobber all over me, like the customers at the bar, or want to rescue me from myself, like Sergeant Lancaster. Graham was happy to just be my friend.

I could think of only one reason he had turned against Richard Sterling, the policeman, and was behaving so very oddly.

Graham Donohue had killed Jack Ireland.

Chapter Thirty-Nine

As I walked home to get ready for my dinner guest, I carried on an angry inner debate. Had it been an outer debate, I might have come to blows with myself.

I have to tell Richard what I know about Graham.

Graham's my friend. I can't betray my friend.

It's my duty to inform the police.

Let the police figure it out for themselves. That's what they're paid for.

But they don't know Graham as I do. They might not see the signs of guilt written all over his face.

Justice isn't achieved through facial expressions. But through evidence. Facts.

My duty.

My friend.

Jack Ireland. Does anyone really care who killed him? Do I?

No.

In the end I decided to keep quiet and see how things panned out. If the police accused someone else, I would report (betray?) Graham. Otherwise, I would stay well enough out of it.

By the time I'd made my decision, I was in no mood to entertain. But habit took over, and I slipped on a gown that was too modest for the Savoy and too delicate for walking on the duckboards through town. So unsuitable was it for any occasion in Dawson, I hadn't worn it since leaving Vancouver. It was muslin, tiny white flowers dotting fabric of the palest blue, the colour of a Scottish sky on an early spring day, which is probably what attracted me to such an impractical garment in the first place. I brushed my hair, gathered it loosely back with a thick white ribbon and added the slightest touch of rouge to my cheeks. I chewed my lips to bring up the colour and looked at myself in the cracked mirror above the bed. I winked at my reflection as someone knocked on the door to my bedroom. "Come in."

Angus stared at me.

"Yes?"

"You look beautiful, Mother. Like a picture in a book."

I touched his cheek. "I'm glad you're back, Angus. Don't ever frighten me again, do you hear?"

"I'm sorry. I didn't think."

"No, you didn't."

"Will Constable Sterling get into trouble?" My son's face crunched up in concern, and he looked not a day more than his twelve years. He'd dressed in a clean shirt, washed his face and hands and plastered his hair to his scalp with water. As it dried, the hair was already springing up into wild tufts.

"I'll make sure he doesn't. Now, what do you suppose Mrs. Mann has prepared for us? It smells wonderful."

Sterling arrived precisely on the dot of nine o'clock. Mr. Mann offered him a glass of whisky (lemonade for Angus and me). While Mrs. Mann bustled over the stove, we sat around the kitchen table, there not being anything in the way of a front room, and my private sitting room much too small to accommodate us all. The German immigrant and the Saskatchewan farm boy exchanged general chatter about how fast the town was growing, and Mr. Mann asked what the government was doing to keep the Territory in Canadian hands. Mrs. Mann laid only three places at the table, and although I insisted they join us for the meal, she pushed and prodded her husband out of the kitchen as if she were forcing a suspicious pig to market.

She served the soup, in mismatched bowls, instructed me as to how to present the roast and potatoes, pointed proudly to the freshly baked fruit pie cooling on the counter and scurried off to join her husband in their room.

The knowing look she gave me as she disappeared, full of old-world wisdom and new-world bravado, had me blushing like a schoolgirl. She'd gone to so much trouble, not because I paid her to do so, but because she thought Richard and I were courting.

"Are you all right, Mother?" Angus asked. "Your cheeks are all red." I would have to have a serious talk with the boy about the inadvisability of drawing attention to another's awkward moments.

"Wonderful soup," Sterling said, digging in with enthusiasm.

"What happened, sir?" Angus asked. At least he'd waited until the Manns left the room. "You're still in uniform."

"And not locked up either." Sterling tore a generous hunk off the loaf of dense brown bread and spread on liberal quantities of butter. "Haven't had butter in a while. I told the Inspector it was all a misunderstanding, and no harm was done."

"He accepted that?" I asked. The soup was potato and cabbage. Common enough, but with a dab of butter and a splash of milk—fresh milk—added to raise it above the ordinary.

"He said he'd been a lad once, dreaming of joining the NWMP." Sterling looked at Angus, soup spoon hanging in the air, halfway to his mouth. "He also said he'll allow a boy one indiscretion. But not more than one."

I collected the empty soup bowls and served the roast, potatoes and vegetables, feeling quite domesticated as I did so. A proper wee Canadian housewife. But, like Marie Antoinette playing milkmaid at Le Petit Trianon, it was only a game.

Sterling and Angus told me about their expedition to the Creeks, and I was glad that I'd never have to go there—Dawson was dirty enough for me, thank you very much. But I was pleased to hear once again that Ray's friend from Scotland had confirmed his account of their activities on Sunday. Angus asked about the murder investigation, and Richard said it didn't seem to be going anywhere, but Angus was not to repeat that to anyone.

To my horror, there weren't enough clean dishes on which to serve the pie. We'd used the small plates for the bread. I surreptitiously wiped smeared butter and scattered breadcrumbs off the plates, attempting to hide my sloppy housekeeping behind my body. I need not have bothered. They wouldn't have noticed if I'd brought in a bucket of sand and scoured the crockery in the middle of the table.

Conversation turned, as it usually did, to people we all knew. Sterling told us that the man who dressed as if in his dreams he wanted to be an Indian fighter, really had been an Indian fighter. But not what most of us thought of in those terms. He had been captured by Indians as a child, raised by them, and remained fiercely loyal to his adoptive family to the point of fighting alongside them against the American Army.

"Wow!" Angus said. His eyes lit up, and I suspected that the Indian Fighter would be facing a long day of storytelling some time soon.

"The excitement over Sam and the saving of the Vanderhaege sister soon died down," I said, slicing thick slabs of apple pie. The scent of cinnamon rose into the air with every movement of my knife, and I breathed it in, content in my peaceful domestic setting. Apples in the Yukon in June! Truly a miracle. There wouldn't be much, if anything, left from the money I'd given Mrs. Mann to shop for the dinner.

"Usually does," Sterling said. "Soon as it's replaced by something else. Good pie, this."

"Mr. and Mrs. Collins have been all over the United States," Angus said. "Did you know that Mr. Collins worked on a cattle ranch in Montana?"

Sterling turned to accept a dented tin mug from my hand. Our fingers met, and he jerked his hand back as if it had touched the hot stove instead. I placed the cup in front of him, feeling the heat rise into my face. The Mountie looked up at me through long, thick black lashes.

Angus chattered away. "I'd like to be a real cowboy. Don't you think that'd be exciting? They've lived all over the United States. They're from Virginia, but they travelled to Louisiana after they got married. Sam couldn't get work there. He told me that black men took all the work, 'cause they didn't get paid as much as a white man. Doesn't seem fair, to anyone, does it, sir? He fell off a horse and hurt his back so he couldn't ride any more, then they went to California."

"Thank you for the lovely dinner, Mrs. MacGillivray."

"Fiona, please."

"Fiona."

"I asked him why they didn't go back to Virginia, where they had family, and Mr. Collins said that the war was on, and he didn't want to have to take sides."

"You must thank Mrs. Mann for the meal. Not me."

"I will."

"That would be hard, wouldn't it? To be forced to take sides."

"More tea?"

"No, thank you, Fiona. I'd better be going."

"If you have to."

"I do."

He got to his feet, and I took his hat and coat down from the hook. We walked to the front door, where he stood clutching his hat in his big hands. "Thank you for a lovely evening. May I say you look particularly beautiful tonight. That's a delightful dress."

"Thank you."

"Good night. Fiona."

"Good night, Constable."

"Richard, please."

"Richard. Good night."

I stood in the doorway and watched him walk up the path. He reached the road and turned to smile back at me, a shy embarrassed little smile. Then he continued down the street.

"Do you know Constable Sterling lived in Saskatchewan when he was a child?" Angus said when I returned to the kitchen. He helped himself to another generous serving of apple pie. "Saskatchewan has got to be the most boring place there is. Remember when we crossed the prairie on the train? Nothing but mile after mile of grass. I bet he was glad to get away and join the Mounties."

"Good night, Angus. If you finish that pie, pour water into the dish so it'll be easier for Mrs. Mann to clean tomorrow." I'd told Ray I was going to take the entire night off, so I drifted off to my room, where I slept the whole night through without even a dream.

Chapter Forty

The next morning, as I left the Savoy to do the morning banking, I saw a familiar, and unwelcome, figure marching determinedly down the street in my direction. I fled back into the saloon, waving at Not-Murray standing behind the bar and mouthing, "I'm not here". Skirts in one hand, bag of money in the other, I galloped up the stairs and stood on the landing, listening, trying not to breathe too loudly.

"Is Mrs. MacGillivray in her office?" Sergeant Lancaster.

"Nope." Not-Murray.

"Sure she is," Helen said cheerfully, walking into the saloon from the gambling hall with her mop and bucket. "I caught a glimpse of her running up the stairs. Must have forgotten something."

I'd hoped that if I was able to avoid my suitor for long enough, he would give up the pursuit. Clearly, I wasn't to be so lucky.

I lifted my head high and drifted elegantly back down the stairs, lugging the moneybag.

"Sergeant Lancaster, what a pleasure to see you. Unfortunately I can't stay to talk, I must get to the bank immediately."

"I just passed the Commerce, Mrs. MacGillivray, and folk are lined up down the street a good way. No point in you hurrying. I was hoping," he coughed lightly and looked at Helen and Not-Murray and the handful of early drinkers, all of them watching us, "you could spare me a few moments. For a private conversation about the matter that we...ah...discussed the other day. I'm right pleased to hear your son's back, by the way. Although if you want my opinion, Inspector Starnes should have drummed Sterling out of the force for causing you such distress."

"Thank you for the warning, but I never wait in line at the bank. If you'll excuse me."

"I'll escort you. We can talk on the way." His brass buttons and high boots were polished to a shine the like of which I hadn't seen since leaving Vancouver.

"Very well." I looked over my shoulder as the sergeant hastened to hold the door. Helen grinned so broadly, I wondered if she'd deliberately set Lancaster on me. Not-Murray and the customers returned to more important matters.

"Allow me, Mrs. MacGillivray." Lancaster reached out and tried to grab the moneybag.

I tightened my grip. "Certainly not, Sergeant. The contents of this bag are my responsibility."

We wrestled over the bag for a few seconds until Lancaster finally realized I wasn't about to surrender it, and if he intended to take it, he would have to flatten me. At that moment I think he also understood I wasn't going to accept his proposal either. Colour rose into his face, his shoulders slumped, and some of the shine seemed to disappear from the buttons marching neatly down the front of his red uniform jacket.

"I'll be on my way, Mrs. MacGillivray. My proposal stands. I hope you'll be able to consider it one day. I…uh…I admire you very much. Good morning."

"I'm sorry, Sergeant," I said to his retreating back. His disappointment had been written so boldly across his face that I felt quite guilty. It was a most unusual feeling, and one I didn't care for. I've always avoided guilt.

I went to the bank.

Naturally, I didn't join the lineup outside, and I concluded my business quickly.

Inspector McKnight was leaning against a cart pulled up to the side of the street, smoking a cigar. A dog, so thin that if I were so inclined I could count every rib, sniffed without much interest at the Inspector's boots.

"A moment of your time, Mrs. MacGillivray."

I looked carefully at my watch, more to hide my confusion and to look important than to check the hour. I had slept so long and so well last night I wasn't planning on going home for my usual after-bank nap.

"I won't keep you for too long."

"My pleasure." I smiled prettily.

He fell into step beside me. The dog followed.

"The killing of Mr. Ireland remains the primary concern of the NWMP."

I said nothing. I hadn't thought Inspector McKnight was accompanying me in order to pass the time of day.

"I don't seem to be making a great deal of headway. Most murders, you may not know this, are committed by a member of the family."

"You don't say!" I put on my shocked-and-dismayed face.

"As Mr. Ireland had no family in Dawson, that line of investigation takes us nowhere. The next thing we do is to try and find out if the murdered man had any enemies."

I laughed and almost tripped over the miserable dog.

"However," McKnight said, "it would appear Mr. Ireland had nothing but enemies."

"He wasn't a very nice man."

"So I understand."

"If you have a point to make, Inspector, please make it. I'm a busy woman." What would I do, what would I say, if he asked me about Graham? Would I have to go to jail if I lied? I couldn't imagine myself in jail. The clothes must be simply hideous, and the food doesn't bear thinking about. Not to mention the constant company of other women.

Ray would look after Angus, I could count on that, but who would look after Ray? I took a deep breath.

"Tell me about Irene Davidson?"

"What?"

"Irene Davidson. The dancer. She's your most popular entertainer, I understand."

I stopped walking. The dog also stopped. "Why are you asking about Irene?"

"I've been told she was involved with Ireland."

"Well, yes. But that was nothing. One night. Heavens, this is Dawson."

"There are marriages in Dawson that don't last much longer."

I chuckled, assuming he had made a joke.

He hadn't.

"Miss Davidson left Friday night with Jack Ireland. She came to work on Saturday bruised and sore. I've been told that on the Saturday night before his death, Ireland was physically abusive to her in the dance hall of the Savoy, and that you intervened and banned Ireland from your place. Is all of that correct?"

"Well, yes. He'd roughed Irene up. But I can assure you that women don't murder a man for hitting them. Although we'd be safer if they did."

"I will ignore that comment, Mrs. MacGillivray."

"Ignore it if you want. I don't know why you're telling me what I already know."

"I'm hoping you can remember something you mightn't have mentioned. Something about the behaviour of Miss Davidson or Mr. Ireland Saturday night."

"I noticed that Mr. Ireland behaved like the common boor he was. And I noticed that Irene was frightened and upset and happy to see the back of him."

"Did you see Miss Davidson leave the Savoy after closing on Saturday?"

The traffic of the streets swirled around us. Most passers-by were paying a good deal more attention to us than they should. Black clouds, pregnant with rain, hung over the hills on the far side of the Yukon River. A mosquito buzzed around my ear and I swiped at it. Of all the hardships in the Yukon, the bugs have got to be the worst. They made one almost long for winter.

I hadn't seen Irene leave. I thought Ruby had taken care of her; I hadn't asked. "Well, no. I'm sure Ruby saw her back to her lodgings."

"That would be Ruby Weller, a dancer at the Savoy?"

"Yes."

"Miss Weller claims that Miss Davidson insisted she was able to manage by herself, so Miss Weller left her in your office."

"Miss Davidson had gone when I locked up. I always check my office last."

"Are you sure she wasn't there? Perhaps you just didn't see her."

"What are you getting at, Inspector? I've told you what I saw that night. And it isn't a night I will easily forget."

"No one seems to be able to confirm Miss Davidson's movements after the doctor and Miss Weller left her."

"It was late. It was a Sunday morning. She went home."

"Her landlady had a toothache. She couldn't sleep, so she sat up all night in the kitchen, which I can verify has an excellent view of the front door. Apparently Miss Davidson didn't return to her lodgings at least before the landlady left in the morning to seek relief."

"Unfortunately, Inspector, as we have both pointed out, this is Dawson. Unmarried women sometimes have admirers, and they might behave inappropriately, as much as you or I might be shocked by such goings on."

He took a sharp breath. "Don't play me for a fool, Mrs. MacGillivray." The dog whined at the change in tone.

"I am doing nothing of the sort, Inspector. I am telling you that nothing you've told me this morning has any influence on my interpretation of the events of last Saturday night." The dog cocked one half-missing ear at me. "But I will tell you that I have, unfortunately, seen too many women beaten and abused by men they thought were their protectors. And not one of them has taken the law into her own hands." Well, not after the first occurrence anyway. "And that's all I'm prepared to say to you on the matter." I lifted my skirts and swept past him.

"You'll talk to me when the law demands it of you, Mrs. MacGillivray."

I turned around and faced him, so angry I was almost shaking. "I suggest you feed that dog. For some reason he seems fond of you."

I meant what I'd said, and not about the dog, either. Women didn't kill their abusers after one attack. I would swear that Irene had nothing to do with Ireland's death. But what if she were accused? Would I turn Graham over to the police to save Irene?

I would have to.

What a mess.

At least McKnight hadn't accused me of having anything to do with it. From his point of view, I might be considered to have a motive. Ireland had been heard by the entire bar to threaten me. But McKnight earlier acknowledged that I wouldn't endanger my business by killing someone on the premises and leaving the dead body there to be found. Hadn't he?

Indeed he had.

My head hurt, and here I'd started the day in such good humour. I decided I would simply not think about it again. Everything would settle down. The Mounties would never find out who killed Jack Ireland—they were certainly not under any pressure from the townspeople to solve the case—I could ignore my moral dilemma, and life would soon return to normal.

Whatever passed as normal in Dawson, Yukon Territory.

A filthy old drunk leered in my face, groping for my breast. "Let's have a squeeze, sweetie." He smelled of cheap whisky, cheaper cigars, rotten teeth and unwashed clothes.

I stiff-armed him off the boardwalk without breaking my stride.

Chapter Forty-One

I walked into Helen's scullery to find Ray with his hands firmly planted on either side of Betsy's ample rear end. Her dress was gathered up around her hips, giving me a much better view of her drawers, now sliding to the floor, and the wide expanse of her white bottom, than I wanted.

"Oh, for heaven's sake!"

Betsy shrieked and fell over trying to free her nether regions from Ray's grip, pull down her dress, and pull up her drawers. She hit the floor with a loud thud and lay there, looking up at me. I was comforted by the sheer terror in her eyes.

Ray fumbled to do up the buttons of his trousers. "This isn't what you think, Fee."

"Betsy, wait for me outside my office. I will determine what wages you are owed."

"Please, Mrs. MacGillivray."

"Tidy your hair and return your clothes to some semblance of decency. I don't want the clientele wondering what sort of establishment I run here."

She struggled to her feet, pushed hair back into its pins, straightened her dress, burst into tears and fled.

I looked at my business partner, stuffing his shirttails back into his pants. "What you do with my girls in your own time is your business. But on the premises! How could you? Suppose I had been Inspector McKnight! Do you want to see us closed down?"

"Don't blame Betsy."

"If I don't, then I have to blame you. And I can't fire you, can I?"

He did have the good grace to look ashamed. Not at the act, I was sure, but only at being caught in it.

I turned to leave.

"Give her a break, Fee." He fastened his belt. "Betsy doesn't deserve to be fired. I called her in here. Said I had something to tell her."

"I warned her, Ray. I warned her what would happen if she continued fooling around with you. I can't have problems between the girls. Trouble between her and Irene will come out on the stage and ruin their performance, and before you know it the men will be going to the Monte Carlo or the Horseshoe in search of a better show."

Ray rubbed his face. "D'ye think Irene would care one bit, Fee? Is that it? I doubt Irene would mind if I lined up the whole chorus in here. One after the other."

"Don't be vulgar. By tomorrow it might not much matter to anyone what Irene thinks. I came to tell you that McKnight is focusing his investigation on her. I thought you would be concerned. Apparently I was wrong."

I swept out of the room. The only thing better than a dramatic entrance is a dramatic exit.

If Irene were arrested for murder! Heavens, it didn't bear thinking about. The most popular dance hall girl in Dawson, dragged off the stage in chains! I'd thought that nothing could dampen custom at the Savoy, but that might well do it. The men would be furious at me for letting such a thing happen, regardless of anyone's guilt or innocence.

Betsy was sitting on the floor outside my office, sobbing her heart out. Her nose was a bulbous red, and she was wiping snot onto the sleeve of her dress. She struggled to her feet when she saw me approaching.

"We business people walk an exceedingly fine line, Betsy," I said, opening the office door. "The police tolerate the dance halls because the men insist on it. Give them a hint of impropriety outside the boundaries they've set, and they'll close us down in a minute."

"I'm not a whore, Mrs. MacGillivray. I quite fancy Mr. Walker." She wiped her sleeve across her face.

"If you want to pursue Mr. Walker, you're welcome to do so." I raised one hand. "But not as long as you're an employee of the Savoy. If you wish to remain here, you'll ignore him from now on. I'm the boss of the dance hall girls. You have no reason to deal with Mr. Walker. Ever. Shall I prepare your wages?"

She blew heartily onto her sleeve. "No."

"Be back at eight o'clock for the show. But until I decide otherwise, you're to dance in the back row. With commensurate wages."

"Mrs. MacGillivray..."

"I'll assign one of the others to sing your songs. Of course, if that's not a suitable arrangement, you can seek employment elsewhere."

"No."

"No, what?"

Betsy bowed her head and mumbled, "Please, Mrs. MacGillivray. I don't want to work nowhere else."

"Be back by eight. And be prepared to dance in the back row."

I went into my office fully aware that I should've thrown the useless cow into the street. I'd made the same mistake as she once: failed to understand who was the real boss. But I'd learned, fast, and not repeated that error again. Betsy had been warned twice now, and still I kept her on.

I was getting soft.

Chapter Forty-Two

Angus had loved every minute spent on the Creeks. Questioning the woman outside the miserable hovel scratched out of mud she called a hotel, sleeping on the naked hillside, eating five-day-old supplies. It had been wonderful and confirmed that all he wanted in life was to be an officer in the North-West Mounted Police. But here he was, once again, standing behind the box that served as a counter in the canvas tent that served as a hardware store.

If he weren't twelve years old, he'd cry.

The only thing Angus regretted about the expedition to the Creeks was that he'd missed the boxing match. By all accounts it had been a good one. Most of the men down at the waterfront were talking about it—even Mr. Mann had been there. Sergeant Lancaster had come into the store yesterday and entertained Angus, accompanied by Mr. Mann's robust actions, with details of every punch, every feint, every duck. Big Boris Bovery had won, and maintained the honour of the Empire, but only after a hard fought battle.

Sergeant Lancaster suggested that Angus return for his lessons, starting the next day, and Mr. Mann approved.

Angus agreed, eagerly. They hadn't had to forcibly arrest anyone up at the Creeks, or pressure a reluctant witness into submission. But if he was going to live his dream and become a member of the NWMP, Angus knew he had to learn how to defend himself.

At last, seven o'clock arrived. Time to pull the flap down over the front of the canvas tent.

"Go, Angus," Mann said in his gruff, broken English. "I vill close."

Angus knew he should offer to stay and help, because it was the right thing to do. But because he hated the store so much, he simply said, "See you later, sir," and slipped into the maelstrom of Dawson on a Saturday night.

It was early still. His mother would be at the Savoy, and Mrs. Mann wouldn't have dinner ready yet. He had things to think about, important things, confusing things, so he decided to walk through town before going home.

An unusually high number of people smiled at him or tossed him a wicked grin or stopped for a moment to talk. It seemed as if every person in Dawson, from children scarcely out of nappies to the oldest sourdough, had heard all about Angus's disappearance.

Angus walked through the streets with his head down and his shoulders hunched. He wondered if, until the end of his days, people would be talking about him as the boy who ran off to the Creeks in a silly attempt to be a Mountie. Perhaps they would carve it on his tombstone:

Angus MacGillivray
Wanted to be a Mountie
Ha ha.

He walked across the mudflats and looked towards Front Street and the Savoy. His mother would be there, all fancy silk and lace, but warm hugs also. And Helen, with a mug of hot tinned milk and maybe a cookie or two. He looked up at the sun, still high in the sky, and sat behind a giant boulder overlooking what passed as the docks in Dawson: a soft indentation in the Yukon River, where vessels constructed of nothing more than hope tied up.

From behind his veil of gloom, Angus MacGillivray saw Ray Walker coming towards him. He started to stand. Ray was a great guy. Angus never gave up hope that his mother would some day marry Ray. Or, if not Ray, then Graham Donohue—but after what he'd overheard the other night in the cigar store, maybe Mr. Donohue should come off the list—or, best of all, Richard Sterling. Even Sergeant Lancaster seemed fond of Angus's mother. Although Angus did have his doubts as to whether Sergeant Lancaster would be the type of father Angus had long dreamed of.

Before he could get to his feet and shout out a greeting, Ray passed the boulder and Angus heard the soft murmur of voices. Someone had joined Ray.

"They suspect ye," Ray's voice said.

"Rubbish. I ain't done nothin'. I haven't killed no one."

"It doesn't matter what you did or didn't do. What matters is what the police think."

"Where did you hear this nonsense?"

"Never you mind."

The woman's voice collapsed upon itself. Fading, softening. "I didn't kill him. Do you understand, Ray? Do you care?"

The man struggled for breath. "You know I care."

The woman almost purred. "Then we can forget all about it." She sounded like a huge Persian cat Angus faintly remembered his mother owning when they lived in London. That cat was always washing her fur and licking her paws and stretching luxuriously—and hunting rats in the alley at night.

"The Mounties won't leave it."

"You're worried about this McKnight. Don't be. He's a fool."

"He's not a fool. But even more dangerous than McKnight, there's Sterling."

The woman laughed, a deep, hearty laugh so convinced of its own merits Angus was willing to agree with every word she said. "Sterling's so besotted, he's useless."

"Don't underestimate Sterling. He might appear blind where she's concerned, but nothing'll distract him from his duty. I'm telling you, they think you did it."

"But I didn't!" The woman moaned. "I didn't kill him. Sure, I was thrilled to hear he was dead, but I'd nothing to do with it. They'll always find a woman to blame, won't they? The bastards. Curse every last one of them. Can't find the killer, so to save themselves, they'll blame it on a woman."

A mosquito landed on Angus's arm. He swiped at it, but was too late. Blood oozed from the pinprick of a bite.

"What should I do?" the woman said with a deep sigh.

Angus peeked out from behind his rock. He should stand up and say hello, but he'd been listening for too long. Ray and Miss Irene would think he'd been eavesdropping, spying maybe.

"It might be best if you left town."

"Leave town! I didn't kill no one. Why should I run away? I can't leave Dawson. I'll never make this kind of money anywhere else."

"This is about more than money, Irene. How much'll you be making in the Fort Herchmer jail? Or on the gallows?"

"You wouldn't let that happen, would you, Ray? You'd make sure they knew I didn't have nothing to do with it?"

"Who's going to listen to me?"

The woman's voice dropped. "All you have to do is tell them I was with you that night. All night long."

"But, Irene..."

"I can make it happen, Ray. A bit late, but it can still happen."

Angus dared to lift his head above the protection of his boulder. Irene's chubby white hands stroked the front of Ray's shirt. She undid the top button; her fingers moved down to the next.

Ray grabbed her moving hands in one of his. "Not here." His voice sounded exceptionally deep; he seemed to be having trouble catching his breath.

Irene laughed, low in her throat. "All the night long, Ray."

"Christ woman, I canna..."

They broke apart as two men appeared on the deck of the nearest steamboat. The men were arguing, their heads close together, their voices raised. They paid no attention to the private drama going on under their noses: the small, fierce man and intense, frightened woman in conversation, the hidden boy listening.

"We can't talk here," Irene said. "But understand what I'm saying, Ray Walker. I worked too hard to get here, and I ain't leaving Dawson, running from something I didn't do. And as I didn't do it, it wouldn't hurt you none to tell them we was together." She stretched the last word on her tongue. "Now would it?"

"But I've already told 'em I was with me pal till about six..."

"They're men. They'll understand."

The voices faded away. Angus pressed his back into the shelter of the rock. The men on the steamboat had stopped arguing and were looking at him.

Angus waved.

They waved back.

He got to his feet and ran to the street. Miss Irene, his mother's best dancer, had asked Ray Walker to lie for her. To give her an alibi for the time Mr. Ireland had been murdered.

He had to tell Constable Sterling. Right away.

But she said she hadn't done it. She only wanted to avoid trouble.

The police would never convict an innocent woman. So by pretending to be somewhere she wasn't, Irene would only confuse the investigation. Make things harder for the Mounties.

And what did Miss Irene mean that Sterling couldn't solve the murder because he was besotted? Besotted with what? Sterling was a good officer. The best the NWMP had in the Yukon. Maybe in all of Canada.

Angus knew where his duty lay. He had to tell Constable Sterling what he'd heard. If he moved quickly, Ray wouldn't have time to tell a lie and get himself into real trouble.

Chapter Forty-Three

Ray disappeared for the rest of the afternoon, and I was glad of it. God spare me from having to deal with men, their precocious pride and overactive libidos. When he got back, I'd have a serious talk with him about the dangers involved in messing with the staff.

The dangers arising from my anger, that is.

Without me, Ray would long ago have lost every penny he'd sunk into the business and be working as a bouncer at the grimmest crib in town, if not panning through mountains of dirt up on the Creeks.

It was past time I reminded him of his obligations.

Of what would have become of me without Ray, it was best not to contemplate at this time.

Another Saturday night: the eager clientele was desperate to get in every last drink, every spin of the wheel and deal of the cards, or the last possible dance with the most beautiful and popular of the performers, and failing that, the cheapest of the percentage girls. Perhaps because they remembered what happened here last Saturday night, everyone was particularly well-behaved.

Big Alex McDonald sat in his box and ordered bottle after bottle of champagne. Mouse O'Brien dominated the poker table and pulled in his winnings in handfuls. The usual drunks lined up at the bar, and the usual hangers-on filled the dance hall, tongues hanging out, counting the change in their pocket to see if they could come up with the dollar for a dance. And my girls didn't disappoint. Everyone of them managed to free the easy-spending men from their hard-earned cash. Betsy was in good form. Flirtatious, saucy, appealing. No one would suspect how much she resented being demoted to the back row. If her take were good enough, I'd consider forgiving her sins and returning her to centre stage.

Only Irene was distant, preoccupied. She'd run in a few minutes after eight, dishevelled and noticeably distracted. Her performance had been poor; she'd stumbled during one elaborate dance that she'd flawlessly executed every night since I'd hired her. During the play, she forgot her lines several times and Ruby, who played her husband complete with britches (suitably loose, of course) and overlarge, fake moustache, had to step in and make up words on the spot to accommodate. Not that anyone in the audience would care. Very few of them paid much attention to the words of the play anyway. But once we were open for dancing, I noticed a couple of men leave Irene at the bar with a disappointed shake of their heads.

That would never do.

Inspector McKnight spent the entire evening standing at the back of the dance hall. His attention was making me very nervous indeed.

When Ray at last decided to put in an appearance, towards the end of the disastrous play, I glared at him and dragged him behind the bar. "What's the matter with Irene?"

"Christ, Fee, I don't know. Why are you asking me? First you're on at me about Betsy, and now it's Irene. It isn't my fault if you can't manage your staff."

Beside the bar, a man threw the contents of his glass into another's face. The other wiped his eyes and swore. The crowd gathered for a fight.

Ray crossed the floor in a few steps, grabbed the whisky tossing-fellow by the back of his collar, escorted him to the door and threw him into the street.

I returned to the dance hall, and the unblinking, near-eyed stare of Inspector McKnight.

Shortly before midnight, when I was checking with Sam

about the night's take, and the girls were graciously declining one more dance, and the croupiers were announcing that the games were about to end, and Ray was bellowing "No more drinks!", Richard Sterling walked into the Savoy.

I tossed him my best smile, still feeling a few shivers of pleasure from last night's pleasant dinner. He had to have seen me, but he pretended not to, and marched into the dance hall with a straight, officious back. I abandoned Sam in mid-sentence and followed. I am not accustomed to being ignored, and I intended to find out the cause of it.

Sterling and McKnight were speaking in whispers. I leaned up against the opposite wall and openly watched them, while all about us my business went into the routine of shutting down for the Lord's Day.

Finally, the police approached me. "Mrs. MacGillivray." McKnight touched his hat. Sterling said nothing but managed to look highly uncomfortable.

"We'd like to talk to one of your employees, Miss Irene Davidson, at Fort Herchmer," McKnight said.

They wanted to arrest Irene in the middle of the Savoy? With half the men in town standing around watching? They'd have a full-scale riot on their hands.

"We don't want to make a public display of this," Sterling said. "Could you approach Miss Davidson on our behalf, Mrs. MacGillivray? Discreetly."

My mind raced, but could find neither a flippant remark nor a way out of this mess.

"Please, Fiona. Mrs. MacGillivray. We need your help." Richard Sterling's brown eyes pleaded with me.

"Oh, very well. I don't want a scene any more than you do. May I ask the nature of your interest in her?"

Sterling shook his head a fraction. McKnight said nothing.

In the change room behind the stage, the women were giggling and chattering as they pulled off costumes and dance dresses and put on their street clothes. The room was a flurry of tossing tights, sequins, rhinestones and colourful feather boas. All of the tumult overlaid by a layer of sweat, cheap scent and the residue of their dance partners' cigars.

"Then what did he do but pull out a whole twenty dollars," one of the younger girls was squealing in delight as I walked in. 'My dearie,' he called me. 'One minute, my dearie, and a little kiss, and I'll give you this'."

"Twenty dollars for a minute's dance. Not bad, eh, Mrs. MacGillivray," Ruby shouted above the cacophony of women's voices.

"Not bad at all," I said. "Irene, I need to talk to you."

Irene was almost dressed. She had only to button her scuffed black boots. She looked up at me, her face dark and clouded.

"Can you come with me, please."

One by one, the girls stopped chattering and giggling. They looked around, from Irene to me and back again. To each other. "Irene?" I said, trying to keep my voice level. "Please come with me."

"I didn't kill him, Mrs. MacGillivray," she whispered. The girls closest to her sucked in their breath. The rest strained to hear.

"What'd she say, what'd she say?" Betsy shouted.

"I have an alibi," Irene said.

"That's good. It can all be cleared up quickly then, so I needn't assign anyone to take your parts on Monday."

Irene got to her feet.

"Ladies." I addressed the wide-eyed, gaping, half-dressed audience. "I trust not one of you will mention what you heard here tonight. More than the reputation of your friend, Irene, depends on that. If I hear that one word has been spoken outside of this room, I'll fire every last one of you, without even bothering to find the culprit." I looked at them all. One by one they blushed or studied the floor. "If you don't think I'll do it, think about this: What will the men of Dawson have to say about the Savoy if we turn our backs on their favourite? Good night, ladies. I'll see you all on Monday. I suggest you return to your lodgings without further delay."

I pivoted on my toes and swirled my skirts in a dramatic rustle of fabric of which I am particularly fond. Irene scurried ahead of me, her head down and shoulders hunched.

"Wait," I said in a low voice. I spun around and swept my eyes across the room. Every one of the women averted her gaze. Goodness, but I should have been a dramatic actress. I turned with another lovely flick of my skirts. to address Irene.

"Hold your head up," I snapped. "And straighten your back. Did you kill Jack Ireland?"

"No."

"Try not to look as if you did. Pull your shoulders back, lift your chin, push out your chest. That's better. Pretend you're amused although mildly annoyed at this bit of police foolishness. I expect to see you on stage at eight o'clock on Monday evening. No excuses. Are you ready?"

"Yes, Mrs. MacGillivray."

"Follow me."

The saloon was almost empty when we entered. Ray stood behind the bar, wiping glasses. Sam Collins wasn't even pretending to be busy. Murray and Not-Murray huddled together, and the Sunday watchman stood in the middle of the room wondering what was going on. The two Mounties stood by the door as stiff as guards at Buckingham Palace.

"Look, Inspector," Ray shouted, throwing glass and rag to one side. The glass shattered on the side of the long mahogany bar. "I killed him. He was a swine and a coward. I killed Ireland."

"Oh, shut up, Ray," I said. "You're not helping in the least. Murray, clean that up."

I addressed Inspector McKnight. "I will, of course, accompany you. I cannot allow Miss Davidson to leave my establishment without a chaperone."

"Mrs. MacGillivray, I don't think..."

"That's settled then. Off we go. Close up, Ray, please."

I gripped Irene's arm and gave it a firm squeeze. She tossed me a weak smile, but she held her back straight and her head high as we left the Savoy. McKnight and Sterling followed. I didn't dare look at Ray.

Chapter Forty-Four

The remainder of that dreadful night, I will scarcely mention. Save that, as should go without mentioning, they were perilously short of jail space in which to accommodate a respectable lady. In Dawson a dance hall girl was ranked, just barely, within the boundaries of "respectable". They escorted Irene to a tiny room in the main building and insisted I remain outside. McKnight suggested, somewhat rudely, that I might want to go home and rest.

I informed them that I would remain, and after Richard shut the door in my face, I lowered my bottom to the wooden planks outside the main buildings, there being no seating for visitors. It was most uncomfortable, and I wondered if the dirt and the splinters would wash out of my skirt. I was wearing the pale green satin, formerly my second best. If things continued at this rate, soon I would have nothing decent to wear. I wished I'd had the foresight to bring my book. But even I don't plan my day expecting to accompany a murder suspect to prison.

They kept Irene for a very long time. I might have dozed for a while, and it occurred to me that I should send word to Angus so as not to cause him worry, but I didn't dare move in case something happened in my absence. Both McKnight and Sterling left the room at intervals, McKnight glaring at me and Richard trying to avoid my questioning eyes.

Men crossed the courtyard occasionally, every one of them watching me surreptitiously from beneath the brim of his hat, while pretending not to. I considered growling at a particularly skittish young constable, but thought better of it. I thought I saw the bulk of Sergeant Lancaster scurrying off into the shadows, but I might have been mistaken. At one point someone inside the jail began screaming at the top of his lungs, calling for help. Officers came running, and the dogs set up a chorus of barks and howls. The screamer stopped as quickly as he had begun, but it took a good deal longer for the dogs to settle back down.

The sun returned, after a very brief absence, and at last the two Mounties escorted Irene out. Her dress was rumpled, hair escaping its pins, hands shaking, face almost as white as that of Jack Ireland when I'd seen him last.

"You can take Miss Davidson home, madam," McKnight said. "We have no reason to hold her further."

He looked at Irene. "You are not to leave Dawson until we tell you you can."

I took Irene's arm and half-dragged her across the large square. It isn't normally my habit to waste my time looking out for anyone else. I'd learned the hard way what happens to those who don't watch out for themselves first, but it was in my interest to take care of Irene. What might happen if I lost the most-popular dancer in Dawson was one thing. What might happen if I lost my business partner was a far more pressing concern.

"So," I said, once we'd crossed the parade ground and were back on the street, "what happened in there?"

"I didn't kill Jack Ireland."

"Stop saying that. I wouldn't be here if I thought you had, you fool. Why does McKnight think you did?"

She shrugged. "I don't know." She read disbelief in my eyes. "I don't, Mrs. MacGillivray, I truly don't. Maybe they were fishing. Maybe they'll call in all the girls."

I snorted, considering that it was acceptable to snort in the early hours on a deserted street in the presence of one's own employee.

"I'll admit some folks might think I'd good reason to kill him. But so did a lot of people. Have you ever met anyone who angered so many people so fast?"

I laughed, although it wasn't much of a laugh. More like another snort. "No, I don't think I ever have. And that's certainly saying something."

I'd never seen Dawson so peaceful. The streets were deserted at this hour on a Sunday morning. A drunk lay in the dirt against the wall of a closed cigar store, loudly snoring off his night's misadventures. A priest, recognizable by his white dog collar, came bustling down the appropriately named Church Street. He looked at us warily—two gaily-dressed women unescorted on the streets on Sunday morning—but still managed to nod politely.

We reached Fourth Street. "I go this way," I said. "Do you want me to walk you to your lodgings?"

"You've done enough, Mrs. MacGillivray. I can find my own way home. I want to, I mean..." She struggled to get the words out.

I cocked my head to one side and looked at her with a waiting expression. I'd make her say it. No matter how long it took.

"That is...how can I thank you for helping me?" she mumbled.

"The next time we present scenes from Shakespearean tragedies, by acting Lady MacBeth's handwashing scene with a touch more feeling. I don't think I've ever seen such a pitiful display in all my life as I saw tonight. She might have been distressed at finding a dab of schoolroom chalk on her gloves."

"I was distracted."

I didn't ask what had made her suspect that the police were about to make her their prime suspect. A young constable hoping for the honour of a smile from his favourite in return for issuing the warning, perhaps? Unethical, certainly, but none of my business.

"Oh, one more thing, Irene, dear. Stop playing Ray Walker for a fool. If you enjoy teasing him, you may quit the Savoy, find employment elsewhere, and continue to entertain his apparently hopeless courtship. If you want to pledge some sort of attachment to him, with the full knowledge of us all, then you can remain in my employ. But if you intend to continue toying with his affections and also to work at the Savoy, where you are, undoubtedly, the most popular dancer we have, that will not be possible. You'll have to choose one option or the other. Good night, Irene. Go home and get some sleep."

"Doesn't Mr. Walker have anything to say about this?"

"Most certainly not." I walked away.

"Mrs. MacGillivray?"

The strain in her voice stopped me in my tracks, and I turned back. "Yes, Irene."

She studied the patterns of dust before her feet. "The police suspected me, they said, 'cause I didn't go back to my room the night Ireland was killed."

"And…"

"I've got no interest in Mr. Walker, although he's real nice. My…romantic attentions…are elsewhere."

"I'd suggest you let Mr. Walker know that, before his behaviour embarrasses us all. Bring your young man around one evening. Introduce him to us."

Irene blushed. Will wonders never cease? A Dawson dance hall girl who knows how to blush.

"I don't think so, Mrs. MacGillivray." She reverted to form and lifted her proud head.

"Very well. I'll see you on Monday, Irene. Tomorrow, I suppose, it's already today."

Irene walked down the street, leaving me standing in the dirt.

So Irene had a secret relationship. A married man, almost certainly. I only hoped I, and the Savoy, would survive the inevitable fallout.

Chapter Forty-Five

I walked the length of Fourth Street deep in thought. The summer morning caressed my arms and face, and the air smelled fresh and clean. A rabbit, a tiny, furry, brown thing, all floppy ears and large feet, scurried across my path. I was thinking how rare it was to experience a moment of peace and quiet in Dawson, when a mangy dog, nothing more than skin and bones and huge brown eyes, darted out from behind a shack, setting up quite the racket as it attempted to squeeze under the floorboards of someone's house in pursuit of the rabbit.

When I got home, everyone was still in bed. I stoked the stove and put the kettle on the hob. There would be no sleep for me for a while yet.

"Ma, you're back." Angus stumbled into the kitchen. His blond hair stood on end, and he rubbed sleep out of his eyes. He looked five years old, except that the hem of his nightshirt almost reached his knees, and the sleeves had crawled up towards his bony elbows. I made a mental note to purchase some flannel and ask Mrs. Mann to sew him a new garment.

"Do you want tea?" I asked.

"No." He pulled up a chair and fell into it. "Where have you been? Mr. Walker came by after closing to say you'd be late. He looked real worried, but he wouldn't say what was going on."

"He looked very worried," I corrected my son's grammar automatically.

"That's what I said."

"Never mind. Do you want something to eat?"

His eyes narrowed in suspicion. "Are you going to cook breakfast?"

"I can toss a bit of bacon into the pan without burning it too dreadfully."

"Yes, please. What happened?"

"The police arrested Miss Davidson for the murder of Jack Ireland."

Angus nodded and said nothing. The significance of which didn't go unnoticed.

"You don't seem too surprised, dear."

"Miss Davidson had reason to do it." Angus pulled a loose thread from his sleeve.

"What do you mean she had reason to do it? What do you know about all of this?"

Guilt descended on my son's head like a swarm of what the Canadians call no-see-ums: horrid little bugs that are invisible unless they gather in a multitude. "Nothing." His voice squeaked.

"Angus." I abandoned the bacon. "What do you know about this business?"

He looked me straight in the eye, not even blinking. Now I knew he was lying.

"I know nothing more than everyone in town, Mother. Everyone's saying the police have to make an arrest soon. Of anybody. Otherwise it will look bad on their record. There hasn't been a murder in Dawson this year—until Ireland. So they have to find someone to blame. Uh, the kettle's boiling, Mother."

"Bugger the kettle."

Angus's eyes opened wide at my choice of words.

"They have no reason to blame Irene; there are more than enough other suspects. Half the town, in fact. If you know something about Ireland's murder, you have to tell me."

"No, I don't." He stood up so fast, he knocked his chair over. "I don't want any bacon, you can have it. You'll probably burn it anyway."

"Angus, wait. Irene didn't kill Jack Ireland. The police have let her go."

He stopped with his hand on the door knob. "They did?"

"They said they had no reason to hold her. Which I believe is fair enough, as she didn't do it. If they'd let women into the police force, they would have had someone on hand to tell them that a woman doesn't kill a man because he hits her once. Unless it's at the time, of course, which would be in self-defence. Although the men rarely see it that way. Angus, have you done something you don't want me to know about?"

"No, Mother."

"Very well, have it your way. Pick up that chair and sit down and eat your breakfast. I promise I will not take my eyes away from this frying pan until the bacon is perfectly cooked. In order that I may do so, you can slice the bread. Do you want toast, or shall I fry the bread in the dripping?"

"Dripping, please."

"I might have some toast myself. Get out the marmalade, as I am concentrating single-mindedly on the bacon."

"Yes, Mother."

"You may think you don't have to tell me everything, and I suppose that at your age you don't." I looked at my son, who was holding the pot of marmalade as if it might break if he loosened his grip. It was good marmalade—literally worth its weight in gold. "But if you know something about the Ireland, murder you're legally and morally required to inform the police."

My comment had an unexpected effect. Instead of looking guilty, and hanging his head in shame, my son stared straight at me. He smiled and his chest puffed out—not too much, but enough to strain the too-small nightdress.

"Certainly, Mother. I'm aware of my duty, thank you for reminding me. I'm glad to hear Miss Davidson's been released. Really, I am. I didn't like to think—never mind. You're not watching the bacon, and it needs turning."

I returned the focus of my attention to the pan. The bacon was not in need of turning. The fat was pure white, the meat pink, and the whole thing as soft as a baby's dinner. And my son was lying to me. A serious matter, but of no relevance to Irene and the murder. Whatever secret he was trying to conceal was probably something he'd heard hanging out with boys of whom he knew I wouldn't approve. He was afraid of telling me he'd been listening to wharf-rat gossip.

I poked the flabby bacon; it spat grease into my face.

* * *

I had nothing planned for the day and since it was Sunday, I intended to sleep as long as I liked. A note propped up against the tea canister asked Mrs. Mann to leave me alone.

As so often happens, my optimistic intentions came to naught. At first I simply lay awake, watching the rising sun dance through the thick layers of sawdust on my window, remembering how unpleasant it had been sitting on the wooden bench at Fort Herchmer while splinters found their way into one of my best skirts and men pretended not to see me.

Mrs. Mann stumbled out of her room, coughing heavily. She tried her best to be quiet, but she dropped a log on the kitchen floor while ferrying it to the stove, knocked a pan off the table, and shouted at Mr. Mann to shush.

This Ireland business was threatening my peace of mind. The fellow seemed to be some sort of malicious ghost, even more annoying dead than he'd been alive. Asleep or awake, he never completely left me. Not that I cared one whit who'd killed him, but whoever that fool was he'd killed Ireland in *my* establishment. And thus left the problem on my doorstep. Surely, the Mounties would soon give it up? Forget about Ireland and get back to the more important business of shutting the saloons down at two minutes to midnight on Saturday and arresting anyone who dared to use vile language.

I wondered if Constable Sterling would have taken me into custody for telling a child to "bugger the kettle". I wondered what it would be like to be taken into custody by

Constable Sterling. Would he use force, nothing excessive of course, just enough to subdue me? Would he tie me up? Lean into my face and ask me to confess all, his voice perilously short of breath?

Stop right there! No more of that line of thought, thank you very much.

Now I was wide awake.

But I was so tired that eventually sleep forced itself upon me, despite Mrs. Mann's attempts to be quiet, Mr. Mann's language when he hit his finger with the hammer while trying to secure a loose cupboard, Angus's big feet hitting the floorboards, the mental haunting of the vile Jack Ireland, and my licentious thoughts about Constable Richard Sterling. The latter of which I had absolutely no intention of ever experiencing again, as they were clearly the effects of fatigue, brought on by overwork and worry.

I slept for several hours. When I awoke, not to the sounds of Mr. Mann repairing the window frame of the room next to mine, but of Mrs. Mann berating him to be quiet and show some consideration for the "poor tired dear", I would have said that I'd slept well, without a dream or a stray thought.

Only later did I realize that while I'd slept, my mind had been very busy indeed. Sorting, sifting, and finally understanding.

Chapter Forty-Six

Sundays I wash my hair. It's quite the chore: fetch water from the spring, warm it over the stove, stand in the middle of the kitchen floor in my shift while Mrs. Mann pours the water over my head into a bucket, whilst rubbing in the soap. Mr. Mann and Angus ordered out of the house.

Finally the deed was done. It being a hot and sunny day, I sat outside, hiding in the patch of weeds behind the house that passed as the Mann's garden, combing out my thick, wet tresses and letting the sun do the work of drying it, reading *Wuthering Heights*.

It was late afternoon before my hair had dried enough to gather up at the back of my head, and I was restless from spending the morning in bed and the afternoon on my hair and book. Angus was off with his friends, so I put on my best day ensemble, a dark blue skirt and a blouse that had once been pristine white, with the intention of taking a stroll into town.

Mrs. Mann was in the kitchen, her hands floury with the mixings of scones for supper.

I stuck my head in the kitchen to tell her I'd be out for a while.

The early evening was warm and sunny. The endless sound of wood being sawn and shop clerks shouting the value of their irreplaceable wares had fallen silent, and everyone I passed was relaxed and smiling. If one came to Dawson, say on the back of a giant bird, stayed for a Sunday afternoon, and then returned on any Friday night, they would find it impossible to believe they were in the same place, occupied by the same people.

I walked out of town, heading east, away from the Yukon River towards the hills, greeting acquaintances on the way. I passed beyond the wooden storefronts and semi-permanent buildings and came to where a handful of white canvas tents, interspersed with wooden shacks, clung precariously to the foot of the mountain.

A cheap, cracked mixing bowl, overflowing with tall blue larkspur and tiny yellow buttercups plucked from the hillside, sat outside one of the hastily-erected homes.

Sam and Margaret Collins sat by the open doorway, finishing their dinner by the light of the evening sun, tin plates balanced on their laps. He leapt to his feet as he saw me approach.

"Please, Sam, finish your dinner. I'm out for a stroll and found myself walking this way. Hasn't it been a lovely day? Makes the long winter seem almost worthwhile, doesn't it?" I slapped a mosquito that was hovering above my hand, looking for a safe place to land.

What could he do but offer me his chair? And what could I do but accept? Proper manners do have a way of allowing one to manipulate others. I dread to imagine what civilization would be without them.

Margaret put her unfinished supper on the ground. Their meal looked most unappetizing—a bit of fatty beef, a few leaves of boiled cabbage, some wrinkled potatoes. The ubiquitous beans.

"Can I offer you some tea, Mrs. MacGillivray?" Margaret said.

"That would be lovely. But only once you've finished your meal."

"I have." Her words were friendly, as one would expect when a working-class woman found herself confronted by the unexpected, and most unwelcome, intrusion of her husband's employer. But her eyes were as hard as stone and her face not a whit friendlier.

She stood up and snatched her husband's unfinished plate out of his hands. He opened his mouth to protest, but she didn't give him a chance to speak.

"Didn't you tell me you're planning to join Robbie for a smoke and a walk after supper? It's time you were on your way. Robbie doesn't like to be left waiting."

Sam looked at his wife. He looked at me. He looked at his unfinished meal clenched in Margaret's hand.

And I knew I was right, which in most circumstances is a sensation I adore. But on this lovely northern evening, the knowledge didn't make me happy in the least.

"Mrs. MacGillivray and I rarely get much of a chance to have a nice visit," Margaret said. "You run along now, Sam."

Her husband shook off his confusion. "Well, I'd say that if Robbie were finished his dinner, he'd be along soon enough to collect me. But I guess you're right, Margaret, as always. He don't much like to be left waiting. Will you excuse me, Mrs. MacGillivray?"

"Of course, Sam. Enjoy your walk."

We watched him lumber off down the muddy path. A toddler, dressed in a clean white nightgown, momentarily escaped her mother's attention and rushed directly into a puddle, where she splashed about with delight, until the shrieking mother descended upon her. Not many people were about on such a pleasant summer's evening. This was a hard-working town; tomorrow was Monday and family people, people with jobs, retired early.

"Do you really want tea?" Margaret said, still balancing two half-finished plates.

"Tea lubricates every social occasion, as I'm sure you know."

"I do. You remind me of my father."

"Thank you."

"Don't take that as a compliment. I hated my father. He was always so sure of himself. Completely convinced that he was right and everyone else was wrong. Whether it was better to prune the roses in the morning or in the evening, whether slavery was the natural order of things or an affront to God, whether his only daughter should marry this man or that one."

"I don't care one whit about your father, Margaret. When I first arrived here, I wasn't at all sure of myself. I had considerable doubts. But no longer. So perhaps your father took his clues from the people around him, and from that he made up his mind. Did your mother cringe when he suggested cutting roses if it were evening?"

"I have no intention of discussing my parents with you. State your business and then be on your way." Margaret stood in the doorway of her home, glaring down at me. Apparently I was not to be served tea.

I got to my feet.

"Jack Ireland told me he'd been a newspaper correspondent during your American Civil War."

Long ago, I'd been to the British Museum, escorted by Lord Alveron, because the exhibit of Egyptian artefacts was considered to be exceptionally fashionable. There I'd seen the most amazing carving of a long-dead queen. She transfixed me, that queen, with her steady gaze, the haughty lift to her chin, her imperial presence so strong it crossed barriers of time and space. So entranced was I that my escort had had to grip my arm with more strength than was seemly to drag me away before his grandmother-in-law, unexpectedly visiting from the country, entered the hall. I had always hoped to return, to see her again. The carving, not the grandmother-in-law. But circumstances forced me into leaving London before I had the opportunity.

Margaret's face reminded me of that stone queen.

"I enjoyed our chat in the Savoy the other morning. The story of your brave Confederate husband captured by the Union solders because he chose to remain behind with a wounded comrade was most entertaining."

"It wasn't a story."

"Perhaps it wasn't. But Sam told my son another story. That you left the Eastern States before the war and travelled throughout the west in order to avoid having to take sides."

"You're an unusual woman, Mrs. MacGillivray, if everything you ever say is the God-promised truth."

"I'll admit I've been known to stretch the facts on occasion. But I'm wondering who stretched the truth here, Margaret. You or Sam? I suspect it was Sam, not wanting anyone to know he'd served in the war, although most men, in my experience, love to talk about their time in the army. So dreadfully tedious. But you had told Helen what really happened, and when Helen pressed you to tell me, you could hardly spin a different story in her presence, now could you? Not, I'm sure, that it even occurred to you that I'd hear both versions of your life story."

"Mrs. MacGillivray, if you have a point to make, please make it, and leave. You are no longer welcome in my home."

"What did Jack Ireland have on Sam?"

Then she sighed. "Is any of this your business?"

"Unfortunately, yes. My best dancer was arrested for the murder."

Her expression didn't change.

"Please, don't allow yourself to get too alarmed. She was released. Some silly British legal point about no proof. I would like nothing more than to ignore this whole ridiculous business, Margaret. No one liked Jack Ireland less than I. Well, one person clearly did. But he or she left the body on my property, and thus he or she involved me."

"It's a nice evening, but there's a touch of chill in the air. Let me get my shawl, and we can go for a walk." Margaret carried her plates into the depths of her shoddy home.

Chapter Forty-Seven

Did Margaret Collins regret how far she'd fallen in the world—their shack was so badly lit that even with the sun still lighting the western sky, I could scarcely see a foot inside—or was she happy with her choice? To have turned her back on her rich, but unloving family, and marry Sam, whom to all appearances she still adored?

A pack of screeching children, every one of them dressed in hand-me-downs, their clothes and hair so tangled and filthy, it was hard to distinguish boy from girl, ran up the road in hysterical pursuit of a drooling dog. A stern-faced man with the best muttonchop whiskers I'd seen outside of a Regimental Mess grabbed the children's leader in one meaty fist. The others pulled to a sudden stop, and the dog disappeared into the warren of shacks and tents.

Margaret came out of the house, a tattered shawl tossed over her shoulders. Her eyes were dark in her pale face. "Let's walk this way. I'd like to pick some fresh flowers. Those ones will be dead soon."

We walked up the street, towards the foot of the mountain they call Midnight Dome. Margaret talked about inconsequentials, flowers mostly, gardens her mother had tended back in her childhood, cacti she'd seen in the southern deserts. I let her prattle on, sensing she would shortly run out of chatter and tell me all I needed (but did not particularly want) to know.

"Don't you find the wildflowers here to be incredible, Mrs. MacGillivray? I suppose because the growing season's so short, nature must do all she has to accomplish in one wild burst of colour."

"They are lovely," I said.

The cluster of tents and wooden shacks thinned and soon fell behind us. The roadway ended, but a rough track climbed into the foothills. There were no trees left, only bare stumps, thin bushes—no good for building—and naked soil. The hillsides higher up were ablaze with wildflowers in all possible shades of yellow, purple and blue, dotted with the purest white to be found outside of fresh Yukon snow.

"I would love to have seen this country as it was two years ago," Margaret said, puffing with the exertion of the climb. "Imagine what this wood must have been like as planted by God."

"Perfectly wonderful, I'm sure. Margaret, we've gone far enough. I can scarcely hear the people below. My shoes are not suited to this path."

"Just around this bend there's a delightful patch of larkspur. I haven't told a soul about it, so as not to have all sorts of people climbing up here with their ill-trained dogs and snotty-nosed children to trample all over my flowers."

The path, rough as it was, came to an abrupt end at a large boulder. Margaret gathered her skirts in one hand and climbed over the rock.

Why I followed her, to this day I don't know. Perhaps because I believed that a woman chatting about wildflowers and the harmful effects of dogs and children upon them could do me no harm? Perhaps because my comfortable life here in Dawson, where I was earning a legal, if only vaguely respectable, living had softened my instincts?

I clambered over the boulder, my delicate calfskin boots protesting. When I got to the other side, I couldn't see Margaret. I held onto my hat, jumped carefully off the rock and stumbled to regain my footing.

A cold piece of steel pressed against my throat.

"You are as much a fool as all the rest of them, Mrs. MacGillivray." Her breath was hot in my ear. "Although I doubt you're legally entitled to that title."

"Mrs.? That's no badge of honour to me, but it serves its purpose, on occasion. Isn't this a touch melodramatic, Margaret?"

She moved the knife a few inches away from my throat and stepped to one side so I could see her. Her bushy grey eyebrows were drawn together in determination. With every hair on her head scraped back, forced into a severe bun, and the front of her calico dress ironed flat, devoid of a single wrinkle, Margaret reminded me of my childhood governess, who had tolerated me at best and hated me at worst. But at least she'd never drawn a knife on me.

"Sit down, over here." Margaret gestured to a small, but sturdy, bush, hiding under a rocky overhang. "And don't believe I won't slit your aristocratic throat if I have to."

"I believe you, Margaret. But this is all a bit theatrical, wouldn't you agree? I'm assuming you killed Jack Ireland. So? I most certainly don't care. I should thank you for seeing the bastard dispatched to his reward."

"Shut up and sit down."

I kept talking. At times it is what I do best. "Margaret, I don't see why you've involved me in this sordid mess." I started to walk backwards, one tiny inch at a time. The boulder lay behind me. The crowded safety of town beyond that. I might be able to scale the rock in one magnificent leap. But then again, Her Majesty Queen Victoria might swoop down from the heavens and carry me to safety.

"If you put that silly knife away," I said, "we can both go home."

It was, sadly, not a silly knife, but a good kitchen knife, sharpened to a fine point; no doubt used to slice up sides of raw meat.

As well as the late, unmourned, Mr. Jack Ireland.

"Don't you ever listen to yourself, you arrogant woman? You as much as told me that you wouldn't let it rest as long as your precious dance hall is threatened. I made a mistake; I'll admit it. Please stop moving." She grabbed the front of my dress and almost jerked me off my feet. The knife touched the bottom of my chin, gentle as a lover. And as dangerous as some lovers I have known. "I intended to drag his body out into the back alley, but it was too heavy. I should've thought of that earlier."

"Never mind all that. We can come to some sort of arrangement, I'm sure." I stepped backwards. The knife sliced down my chest, through the bodice of my best day dress. Thick red blood, glistening in the light of the setting sun, blossomed from the wound like one of Margaret's beautiful mountain wildflowers.

The white blouse fell open and pain shot through my chest.

"Sit down, Mrs. MacGillivray. I do not want to kill you, but don't doubt that I will if I have to."

The sight of the ripped blouse spilling lace and my life's blood in a gentle trickle, shocked me as much, if not more, than the pain.

While I stared stupidly at my chest, Margaret whipped out one foot, wrapped it around my ankle and twisted.

I collapsed.

Like me, Margaret spoke well. But she had some history behind her. Also like me.

A rock jabbed into my side, delivering a lightning bolt of pain. I ignored it, curled forward, and tensed to launch myself back upright.

Margaret's foot caught me under the chin with enough force to snap my head back. Before I could recover my senses, she reached out with the knife and sliced it across my cheek.

"The next cut will be to your throat. Move back. There."

She gestured, and I wiggled backwards until my back touched the single tree still clinging to this patch of hillside. It wasn't a tree, really, more of a sapling. Strange that it had been overlooked in the mad lust for lumber.

I touched my face; the spot burned like fire. I looked at my fingers—wet, red and sticky. Blood from the cut in my chest soaked the front of my dress.

Another dress ruined. My hat, the one that I worried

made me look old, lay in the mud, the once jaunty feather squashed flat.

"Hold your hands out." Margaret pulled a length of rope from the depths of her dress. She truly had played me for a fool. While I had stood outside her front door, admiring the summer evening and watching a pack of children tormenting a dog, she had gathered everything she needed.

How had I become so soft?

I eyed the knife and the cold eyes behind it and held out my hands, my fingers streaked with my own blood. She looped the rope around my wrists then wrapped it around the tree, and me, several times. It was a long, thick rope. She yanked on the end, and I gasped as it bit into my chest.

"The high-and-mighty Mrs. MacGillivray brought low."

"You needn't insult me, Margaret. You might think I'm of no importance, but you can be sure that the officers of the law, as well as the prominent citizens of this town, will be looking for me before the sun sets."

"Probably," she said, pulling a large, well-mended, but clean handkerchief from her skirt pocket. A bit of blood, my blood, had splashed onto the front of her dress and the cuffs of her right sleeve. Not enough blood, unfortunately, that anyone would have reason to think she'd been doing anything more dangerous than preparing meat for her husband's evening meal.

"Tell me the story, Margaret." I tested my bonds. Tight, very tight. But if she would forget about that handkerchief, my healthy voice would have help arriving the moment she disappeared. "What was Jack Ireland to you?"

"My Sam was a hero in the War Between the States." She touched the edge of her knife. A spot of blood blossomed on the pad of her index finger. She licked it, her eyes still fixed on mine. And I knew she was mad.

"Jack Ireland, he was a bastard, he was. Made his name supposedly as a war correspondent. Liar and storyteller more likely. He was there when Sam saved that soldier, the way I told you. But Sam was captured by the Yankees, damn them all to hell."

I briefly enjoyed the image of Constable Sterling taking Margaret into custody for swearing.

"After the war, not long after Sam had returned home, returned to me, it happened that Ireland was in town one day when Sam came in with one of his cousins. He was broken, Sam was, a proud, strong, kind man broken in that camp. Damaged, torn up by what the war and the Yankees had done to him. But Ireland had heard that Sam's family had money. Had. That's the word. Before the war, the North Carolina branch of the Collins family had land and wealth, plenty of slaves, and good fortune. After the long years of the war and then the Union soldiers passing through, they were left with nothing but a patch of dirt on which to grow cabbage and turnips. But Ireland wanted money. Pay him off, he told Sam, or he'd tell his newspaper that he'd been there, at Gettysburg, and saw Sam throw the other soldier into harm's way and then try to run away."

"How awful for you! You fought him, of course."

"Are you really that stupid, Mrs. MacGillivray? Or do you just pretend to be? I suppose some men like it when women act the simpering idiot. There is only one way to fight a man like Ireland. But Sam said he'd seen too much killing, and he wouldn't do what had to be done. So we left North Carolina and went to California. Life was good there, for a few years, but the economy collapsed, and Sam could only get rough work. Then he found himself out of work altogether, so we decided to come to the Klondike. Only to find Jack Ireland, the source of all of our troubles, waiting for us. I'd never met the fellow, until the day he died, but Sam told me he'd come into the Savoy and wanted to take pictures of Sam and write about him for his paper. I knew it wouldn't be long before Ireland remembered Gettysburg, if he hadn't already, and North Carolina, and tried to blackmail us again. I did what should have been done thirty years ago."

Sam must have recognized Ireland as soon as the newspaperman first walked up to the bar of the Savoy, which would explain why he'd been on edge whenever

Ireland was around. But Ireland hadn't given Sam a flicker of recognition. Jack Ireland had moved on, and the long years had passed. But Margaret, poor tormented Margaret, hadn't been able to forget. It must have eaten at her soul, all these long years, and finally, seeing Ireland, even unwittingly, bothering Sam, had driven her over the edge of sanity.

"The Mounties will take your story into account," I said. "Now if you'll untie me, we can go back to town and..."

Margaret stuffed her white cotton handkerchief into my open mouth. "You talk too much. There's a boat leaving just after midnight. Sam and I'll be on it. If you free yourself by then, you can come after us. If you free yourself later, we'll be safely on our way. And if you never manage to free yourself, well, that's the way the game is played, isn't it, Mrs. MacGillivray? I hear there are bears and wolves in these woods, and plenty of smaller animals. But you have friends in Dawson, don't you? Powerful friends, I believe you said. They'll find you before morning, I'm sure. I'll leave your legs free, so you can kick if a bear approaches."

Margaret Collins tucked her knife into the waistband of her skirt and folded her cardigan neatly over it. Ireland's blood had soaked the stage—a good deal must have splashed onto her dress. And yet she faced me in the street, Jack Ireland's blood concealed by her heavy coat, and made polite conversation while I thought she must be very hot.

"Uuummmmppppggggg," I said.

"Go to hell, Fiona." Margaret marched down the path and scrambled over the boulder without a backward glance.

Despite it all, I expected to see her grey head pop up and hear her give a hearty laugh at the joke she'd played on me.

I struggled against my bonds and tried to spit out the handkerchief. Nothing moved.

I was furious with myself at how completely she'd trapped me. Knowing she'd killed Jack Ireland, I had nevertheless walked into her home then joined her in a pleasant little nature walk. Me! Survivor of Whitechapel, Seven Dials, Belgravia, country estates in Surrey and Yorkshire, and even the Prince of Wales.

Wouldn't the lads in Seven Dials love to see this: Fee MacGillivray trussed up like a goose intended for Christmas lunch.

If I survived the night, I might kill myself out of shame.

* * *

An animal howled in the bush, sounding close. It might have been a wolf or perhaps an escaped dog. No matter. Either one would be more than happy to come across their supper subdued and ready to be served up.

It wasn't important, I decided, to free my arms and body. If I could yell and scream and raise holy hell, then I might not only be able to keep the ravenous creatures of the night away, but summon help. Trying to spit out the handkerchief Margaret had stuffed into my mouth, I managed only to suck more of the cloth down my throat.

The bushes quivered. The mosquitoes descended.

I gave up struggling, closed my eyes, and wondered what would get me first.

Chapter Forty-Eight

"Dinner'll be cold if we wait any longer, young Angus."

"My ma's always here for Sunday dinner. Let's give her a few more minutes, please."

"I'll keep her serving warm over the stove," Mrs. Mann said, glancing anxiously at the table to where Mr. Mann sat, clutching his knife and fork, his habitual heavy frown firmly in place. "When I was boy," he grunted, "yous late for dinner, yous not eat."

Mrs. Mann served up the boiled beef and cabbage. The meal was made appetizing only by the platter of freshly baked biscuits.

Angus sat at the table and grabbed a biscuit. "It's not like Ma to be late for Sunday dinner."

"I know, dear. But it's not as if we have the telephone, like they do in the big cities. She can't telephone us if she's going to be late."

"We had a telephone in our house in Toronto," Angus said, accepting the bowl of potatoes from Mr. Mann. "Sometimes on the holidays, Ma would let me call my friends from school who were also on the telephone. It was great fun. They say that someday every home in Canada will have a telephone."

"Never," Mr. Mann rumbled. "Plaything for rich people. Not for the like of us."

"But just imagine. Ma could go into the post office and telephone here to tell us she's going to be late. We'd only have to go as far as that wall to talk to her. Wouldn't that be great?"

Mr. Mann spoke around a mouth full of beef and cabbage. “Then my neighbour to mein store, he use telephone and complain for me not switch off light. The butcher he call me to tells mein frau should pay them bill. And you Angus, your friend call to disturb our evening eats... nothing but more bad.”

Mrs. Mann smiled at Angus. “Many wonderful changes you’ll see in your lifetime, dear. Eat your supper. Your mother’ll be along shortly. I’m sure she simply lost track of the time. Perhaps her watch stopped. And you know she doesn’t like to be called ma.”

“Sorry, Mrs. Mann.” Angus ate his dinner.

He’d arranged to meet his two closest friends down by the waterfront once the boys could escape after supper, and he arrived to find them waiting. It was late, but the yellow sun still shone in the northern sky, and boats of all sizes travelled up and down the Yukon River. They stalked frogs, dug in the mud and listened to a wolf howling in the mountains behind town. Finally, the youngest boy said, “I’d best be getting home. Ma told me not to be late. See, Pa even give me his watch so’s I could tell the time.”

Angus leaned over to have a look. It was a nice watch: shiny silver on a long chain that his friend, or most likely his father, had fastened to the inside of the boy’s pocket with a big pin.

Well past midnight, the silver pocket-watch announced.

A steamboat pulled out into the river. It was the tiny *Mae West*. Lights shone from the decks, and men and women, laughing and chattering, watched Dawson slide by. The boys waved and cheered and once the boat passed beyond sight and hearing they walked back into town where they separated to make their way home.

Angus tried not to make a sound as he tip-toed down the hall to Mrs. Mann’s kitchen in search of a bedtime snack. His mother appreciated a good sleep on a Sunday night—the only time she could get in an entire night’s rest at one stretch.

An upside-down plate sat on the counter top. Angus lifted it. Underneath sat a single serving of potatoes, boiled beef and cabbage and two biscuits. The potatoes were dry, the beef curling around the edges.

His ma's dinner. She never missed her meals. Was she sick?

He tapped lightly on her door. There was no answer, so he opened the door a crack. "Mother?" The bed was empty, the blanket tucked under undented pillows. "Mother?"

His mother hadn't come home for supper, and she wasn't in her bed.

Angus stood in the doorway. He could think of no reason why she wouldn't be home at this hour on a Sunday night...Monday morning.

He knocked on the Manns' bedroom door. "Mrs. Mann," he whispered. "Please, Mrs. Mann. She's not here."

The door opened, and Mrs. Mann slid out into the hallway, grey hair tied in a braid, hanging down her back. Her brown nightdress was thick and plain.

"Angus, what's the matter?"

"My mother. She hasn't come home."

"What do you mean?"

"She didn't eat the food you left her, and her bed hasn't been slept in."

Mrs. Mann's face twisted in something almost like embarrassment. "Angus, dear. Perhaps your mother had ...uh...business matters to attend to."

"At this time of night? On a Sunday?"

"In Dawson, anything is possible." The German accent thickened as she spoke. "Come. We talk in the kitchen. Not wake Mr. Mann."

She stoked the stove and filled the kettle.

Women always made tea when they were upset and trying to hide it. Angus's London nanny, Francine, had constantly been putting the kettle on.

"Do you know where my mother is, Mrs. Mann?"

"No, dear, I don't. Would you like a slice of cake? There might be some left." She pulled the tin down from the shelf.

"I'll go looking for her," Angus said, watching Mrs. Mann cut him a slice. The cake was sprinkled with currants which he particularly liked.

Mrs. Mann coughed as she handed him a plate. "Perhaps your mother has found a...friend... with who to...spend...the evening."

"With whom," Angus said, struggling to get the words out around a mouthful of cake. "She'd be home by now."

Mrs. Mann busied herself with kettle and teapot. Her face and neck were turning a bright red.

"It is possible, Angus, that she has...well...I mean your mother...decided that...I mean...she might... Your mother is a widowed lady. Sometimes...I have heard...that... women...ladies..." She took a deep breath and spat out the words as if they were wrapped in vinegar "...miss the company of a gentleman."

"Huh?"

"Go to bed, Angus. Your mother will be home when you get up in the morning. Perhaps she found a supper more to her liking than beef and cabbage." Mrs. Mann pulled the unboiled kettle off the hob. "Go to bed, dear."

"You're sure she's all right, Mrs. Mann?"

"Yes, dear, I'm sure."

"Good night then. That was good cake. Can I have some in my lunch packet tomorrow?"

"Of course you can, dear boy. That's what I made it for."

Chapter Forty-Nine

Monday morning, Angus woke to a light tap on the door of his room. *Ma,* he thought, struggling out of a dream full of large trees and green forest, *you're back.*

"Breakfast, Angus," Mrs. Mann shouted. "Hurry up now."

Angus pulled on his trousers and shirt, splashed his face with cold water from the bowl on the dresser, and checked (as he did every morning) in the mirror for the first whiskers. Nothing yet. Despairing that the signs of manhood would ever come, he stumbled down the hall and outside to the privy.

Mrs. Mann was ladling lumpy porridge into his bowl as he came inside.

"Is my ma...mother up yet?"

"Haven't heard her."

"I'll get her." Angus left the kitchen and rapped on his mother's door. There was no answer. He knocked again and called through the thin wood.

Mrs. Mann came into the hall, wiping her hands on her apron. "Mrs. MacGillivray, breakfast is ready."

She looked at Angus's face and raised her voice. "Mrs. MacGillivray, are you all right?"

Mr. Mann emerged from their bedroom, slipping his suspenders over his shoulders. His wife spoke to him in German, and he leaned up against the door.

Angus's heart pounded and suddenly he felt fear. Cold fear, deep in his heart. Like when he was a baby and had a bad dream, and his mother would be at the nursery door, pushing the nanny aside to get to him, to make the demons go away and to make everything all right once again. When he had left home to go to boarding school, he knew she still watched over him. Hadn't she arrived, full of sweeping silk, bobbing feathers, and sheer indignation the morning after he'd sprained his ankle climbing down (in the middle of the night, mind you, and on a dare at that), the vines outside the younger boys' dorm? She had been so terribly beautiful and so commanding that the weak-kneed, trembling headmaster decided that the boy was obviously sleepwalking. No punishment would be required.

Fiona had tossed the headmaster a smile. She had taken her son by the arm, and they'd walked outside into the sun-dappled quadrangle. "I don't want to come here again, dearest," she said. "It was most inconvenient."

"Mother…"

"No excuses." She'd waved to her carriage. "Do what you must, but never let them catch you." The carriage had pulled up; she kissed him on the cheek and accepted the driver's hand to help her inside.

Angus's thoughts returned to Dawson and the year 1898, as Mr. Mann exchanged another look with his wife, worry etched in their lined faces.

Mr. Mann called to the door. "Mrs. MacGillivray, me coming in. Yous tells me if not okay."

He looked at his wife again; she nodded slightly, and he opened the door.

Angus ran into the room, hoping against hope to find his mother sitting up in bed, wild-eyed, clutching her nightgown to her chest and yelling at them for their impertinence.

But the bed was undisturbed, and the room was empty.

Angus stared at the neatly made bed. "Where's my mother?"

Mrs. Mann wrapped her arms around Angus's shoulders, although he was taller than she. "Let's have a cup of tea, dear."

"I go," Mr. Mann said. "Fetch help."

Angus pulled away from his landlady's loving embrace. "I'll come with you. They know me at the fort."

"Make zee morning eats, Helga," Mr. Mann said. "We be back soon. And be hungry." He said something in German.

Angus looked at Mrs. Mann. "If...when...my mother gets back, you'll come and tell us, right?"

"Of course, dear boy. Immediately."

Angus and Mr. Mann ran into the street. When they reached King Street, Angus continued on, Mr. Mann turned right.

They stopped, turning to face each other. "We have to get the police," Angus said. "Constable Sterling, he'll know what to do."

"Yous go to police. I goes to wheres ze boats tied up. Boatmens, theys knows much."

"Okay."

"Thees Dawson, is ze good towns, Angus. Yours mama ze good woman. She be safe."

Angus looked at the face of his mother's landlord. His own employer. For the first time, Angus saw empathy there, the memory of pain long past, and hope for the future, reflected in the flat cheekbones and heavy mouth.

He managed a weak smile. "Sure, Mr. Mann. We'll have Mother home before opening time at the Savoy. She loves Mrs. Mann's biscuits. She won't stay away for long."

Angus stood in the road, watching Mr. Mann's broad back heading down to the waterfront. Which way to go? Fort Herchmer for Constable Sterling, as had been his first thought? But would it be better to head into town for Ray Walker? Or even Paradise Alley, looking for Graham Donohue? Angus would go there if he had to. And knock on the door of every crib on the street.

Indecision was costing him precious seconds. If his mother was hurt somewhere, maybe lying in the dark, unconscious, unable to call for help....

The Savoy. She might have gone to the Savoy to do an urgent bit of business and fallen down those rickety stairs. He should have thought of that first.

Chapter Fifty

My hair had fallen out of its pins, and at first I was able to whip the worst of the mosquitoes away by throwing my head back and forth to lash loose tendrils across my face. But it wasn't long before my neck began to ache, and the mosquitoes grew emboldened. They ducked in around my flying hair, searching out juicy bits of flesh, and I could hear the disgusting bugs buzzing around the back of my neck.

My skirt was bunched up almost to my knees, but fortunately my stockings presented an impregnable barrier to the horrid insects. I hadn't been wearing gloves, and my arms were bound so tightly in front of me that I could only watch as an army of the monsters settled in to feast on my hands and wrists.

I had heard of a child killed by a hive of angry bees.

Could a person die of mosquito bites?

I eyed the hairpins that had come loose and fallen to the ground. Even if I could reach them, they'd be of no use in cutting the ropes that tied me to this ghastly tree. Now, if I'd been dealing with a nice thick lock, the pins would come in handy as lockpicks. That's a skill I haven't entirely forgotten.

I pulled and squirmed and battled against the ropes holding me to the tree. But my hands were bound in front of me, and as much as I stretched my fingers, they couldn't reach the knots.

There had to be a way out of this. Surely Margaret wouldn't leave me here to die? What had I ever done to her? Other than expose her for the mad, cold-blooded killer she was?

I tore at the ropes holding my hands until the blood ran (how pleasant for the mosquitoes—all the feasting and none of the work). I spat and coughed at the handkerchief in my mouth to no avail.

The sun had almost disappeared below the small rise to the right of me, and the brief Yukon night had descended, when I finally gave up the struggle.

Chapter Fifty-One

Helen Saunderson was behind the bar, wiping dust off the nude hanging to the right of Her Majesty. She took one look at his face. "Angus, what's the matter?"

"Is my ma here?"

"No. It's early for her to come in yet."

"Have you been upstairs?"

"No. Angus, what is it?"

He sprinted for the stairs. "Check the back rooms. Check everywhere. I'll look upstairs."

Mrs. Saunderson dropped her dust rag. She ran as fast as her arthritic knees could carry her into the gambling hall, while Angus's high-pitched, fear-filled voice rang in her ears. "Mother, Mother. I'm here. Say something, Mother."

They met in the dance hall a few minutes later as Mrs. Saunderson came out of the ladies' dressing room, her face red with fear and unexpected exertion.

"Angus, tell me what's going on." She held her hand to her chest to catch her breath.

"My mother didn't come home."

"Since when?"

"I haven't seen her since yesterday around lunchtime. She sent me away while she washed her hair."

Like Mrs. Mann, Mrs. Saunderson was about to tell the boy that his mother might have reasons for spending the night away from her own bed, but then she remembered what had been found last Sunday, in the dance hall of the Savoy. And that Mrs. Mac loved Angus above all else. She would never willingly cause the boy worry.

"Where else have you looked?"

"I came straight here. Mr. Mann's gone down to the docks to question the men there."

"I'll go for the police. You fetch Mr. Walker."

"I can get the police."

"I don't know where Mr. Walker lives. Don't argue, Angus. Hurry. Send Mr. Walker here and then fetch Mr. Mann and come back. We can't be running off every which way. That's no way to conduct a search. Hurry, now."

They dashed towards the door. Angus, with his long legs and young body, was far ahead when Mrs. Saunderson called out to him.

"Don't worry, Angus," she puffed. "I'm sure she's perfectly fine."

He didn't bother to look back. He didn't believe it, and judging by the tone in Mrs. Saunderson's voice, neither did she.

Angus ran through the streets, which were slowly coming back to life on a Monday morning. He took the steps of Ray's boarding house three at a time.

He hammered on the door. An icy finger crawled up his spine as he remembered why he'd been here the last time.

"Mr. Walker, open up!"

"Shut up, kid." A man stuck his head out of the door across the hall, stuffing his tattered, sweat-stained shirt into his pants. "There's men still sleeping here."

Angus ignored him. Ray Walker threw his door open so fast, Angus almost hit him with the fist he'd raised to knock again.

"What the hell's the matter, Angus?"

"Ma, Mr. Walker. My ma. She's gone."

"What d'ye mean gone?"

"I haven't seen her since yesterday morning. Mrs. Saunderson's gone for the police, and Mr. Mann's asking the men down at the docks."

"What!" Ray's neighbour crossed the hall. "You must be Mrs. MacGillivray's son. Spitting image of her you are. You say she's missing?"

"Hurry," Angus said to Ray, "we have to find her."

"Angus, it's only been one night. No need to get too worked up yet."

"Are you crazy, man?" the neighbour shouted. "Didn't you hear him? Mrs. MacGillivray's in trouble. Is there a search party, boy?"

"Meeting at the Savoy."

"Good." The man dashed off, pulling his suspenders over his shoulders as he ran.

"Ray, please, I…"

The neighbour came back, looking sheepish. "Forgot my shoes."

Angus looked down at two feet as furry as a bear's and ten huge, naked pink toes.

"I'm coming, Angus," Ray said. "Seeing as to how you've got half the town in an uproar." He opened the door fully. "Come in and wait while I get dressed."

Angus let out a long breath, relieved that Ray was alone and he wouldn't have to confront the half-naked Betsy. "No time. I'm off to get Mr. Mann. Everyone's meeting up at the Savoy."

Ray's neighbour, struggling to tie his boots as he alternately skipped and hopped and ran, followed Angus as far as the street.

Angus headed west, towards the waterfront. As he crossed Front Street, he ran into Mr. Mann coming back into town, his head down and his face grim. A small group of men marched behind him.

"They not see Mrs. MacGillivray. Theys been working since midnight, when one steamboat leave. All people looking for she now."

"We'll find your ma, boy, don't you worry," a deep voice shouted. The men growled in agreement.

Angus swallowed. "The search party's meeting at the Savoy. I was coming to get you. It's after eight, Mr. Mann. Shouldn't you be opening the store?"

"The hell with ze stores. We find Mrs. MacGillivray. Then ze stores open." Mr. Mann placed a hand on Angus's shoulder, and they hurried the short distance back to the Savoy.

They arrived at the same time as Constable Sterling.

Angus's heart lifted when he saw that Sterling had brought Mrs. Miller. The white dog's bushy tail wagged in recognition, and she strained at her leash. Sterling gave Angus a long look but said nothing. The constable wasn't his normal stiffly-dressed self: his hat was askew, his shirttail hung out, and two of the buttons on his jacket weren't fastened. Inspector McKnight followed, and in the far distance, the sturdy frame of Helen Saunderson struggled to catch up.

Quickly, but not quick enough for Angus, the search party gathered in the saloon. The dockworkers, Ray Walker and his across-the-hall neighbour, Constable Sterling and Inspector McKnight, Mr. Mann and Mrs. Saunderson.

Also present were the Vanderhaege sisters, one of them with bandages still covering her burns. They'd asked passers-by what was going on and insisted on helping. A handful of men from the streets had gathered, either concerned at the rising sense of panic generated as Angus and the others ran through town, or looking for some excitement. A few permanent drunks openly eyed the bottles behind the bar. Ray told them that the Savoy was closed for the remainder of the morning and escorted them to the door.

Inspector McKnight stood on a chair and shouted for quiet. "It's early yet to start a search for a missing person," he said. "But in light of what transpired here only last week—I'm referring, of course, to the death of Jack Ireland—we can assume that the disappearance of Mrs. MacGillivray, as reported by her son, is a matter of some urgency. Angus, what was your mother wearing when you last saw her?"

Angus flushed as everyone turned to look at him. "I don't remember, sir. A dress, I guess."

Two of the dockworkers tittered. Sterling threw them a glance that had them lowering their eyes and shifting their feet like schoolboys caught spitting in the cemetery.

"A blue dress, I think, sir. With a pretty blue hat."

"Thank you, Angus." McKnight took off his eyeglasses and rubbed at the lenses with the corner of his handkerchief. "Perhaps you could ask one of your mother's friends to describe her outfit. It would help us a great deal."

"I don't see why, sir. Everyone in Dawson knows my mother. They don't have to be told what she's wearing."

McKnight rubbed harder at his spectacles. "It would be helpful, in case..."

"She's lost her hat," Sterling shouted. "Or perhaps she removed her coat 'cause of the afternoon heat and left it where we can find it."

McKnight gave Sterling a grateful look.

"Meine Frau will know," Mr. Mann said. "Angus, yous gos to ask her."

"I'm not leaving!"

"I'll go." Ellie, the oldest of the dancers, stood in the doorway. She wore a plain brown woollen skirt and white blouse with a stiff collar. Like Sterling, she'd dressed without care—her blouse was buttoned incorrectly, and the top button was left without a matching buttonhole to lace through. Her face was scrubbed clean of paint and her hair scraped back into a tight bun. "I'll get a better description than Angus will."

"Thank you," McKnight said.

"Bring an item of Mrs. MacGillivray's clothing back," Sterling said. "Something to show the dog."

McKnight and Sterling assigned various sections of town to the searchers, and the men and women headed out, McKnight leading. Sterling, Millie and Angus waited for Ellie to return. Ray waited for Rupert Malloy, one of the regulars. Lured out of the Monte Carlo by the fast-spreading excitement, Malloy had been sent to get Sam, so they'd have someone to guard the booze.

"Millie's not much of a search dog," Sterling said, patting the big animal on her head. "But she'll try her best to do her bit."

"Where do you think my mother is, sir?"

"I don't know, Angus. Most missing persons show up within a day or so. Statistically speaking. There isn't far for anyone to go in the Yukon."

"Not far. That's what worries me."

"Me too, Angus."

Chapter Fifty-Two

"What's this I hear? The town is in an uproar." Sergeant Lancaster burst through the doors of the Savoy. "They say Mrs. MacGillivray is missing. No one thought to alert me!"

Richard Sterling and Ray Walker exchanged a questioning glance.

"Now why would we do that?" Ray asked. "Inspector McKnight's organizing the search, and Sterling's waiting for some o' Fee's clothes to get here to show the dog."

"Mrs. MacGillivray and I have come to an understanding. I see she hasn't told you, son. But in light of the circumstances, I'd better let you know: Your dear mother and I have reached an agreement."

"An agreement, sir?" Angus said. "About what?"

"Why, about marriage, young man."

Angus gaped.

Ray laughed.

Sterling coughed. "That's neither here nor there right now, sir. Inspector McKnight's gone down to the waterfront to start a search of the boats. He might need assistance."

"Assistance. Right. Don't worry, young Angus. I'll find your mother. And Constable, tuck in that shirt and fasten your uniform before the inspector sees you."

Once the Sergeant left, immersed in a bustling wave of self-importance, Angus turned to Sterling. "Do you know anything about this?"

"I suspect, Angus, that this *understanding* exists more in Sergeant Lancaster's head than in reality." Sterling stuffed his shirt into his pants and refastened his jacket, leaving only one button undone. His hat remained tilted to the side. "But you'll respect the fact that he's chosen your mother as the object of his honourable attentions."

"I guess."

Ellie ran in, her face flushed from exertion and her chest heaving. She waved the red dressing gown, Angus's mother's favourite, the one with the rampant gold dragon streaming across the back.

"Got something. Mrs. Mann says Mrs. MacGillivray wears this when she relaxes in her sitting room. When she left home yesterday, she was wearing a dark blue skirt with a white blouse with lace at the collar and overlarge sleeves and a blue bow and a black belt. With a straw-coloured spring hat with a large blue feather and a piece of fruit. She can't remember what. What fruit, that is."

Sterling took the dressing gown out of Ellie's hands and held it to Millie's nose.

The dog sniffed and looked at the circle of people, all of them staring intently at her. They wanted something from her; she wasn't entirely sure what, but by the eagerness with which her favourite human held out the scrap of cloth, she knew she would make him happy if she sniffed at it a bit more.

So she sniffed.

The room was full of that smell. Every chair, every floorboard. Even the human who had gone with them on the journey into the wilderness smelled of it. The dog looked at the man. Now what?

"Mrs. Miller isn't a bloodhound," Sterling said, "and I'm not a trained handler. I guess I hoped it might help."

"Where the hell is Fiona?" Graham Donohue burst into the Savoy. "My landlady woke me with some cockamamie story about Ellie running through town waving a red flag and shouting that Fiona has been kidnapped by pirates. Pirates? In the Yukon?"

"I never shouted anything," Ellie said. "I asked a few people to be on the look out for Mrs. MacGillivray, that's all."

"Sterling, what's going on here?"

"Ma's missing, Mr. Donohue," Angus said. "People are looking everywhere for her."

"Missing, how can she be missing?"

"Never mind that," Sterling said. "You can help with the search."

"Glad to. Where do you want me to start?"

"Paradise Alley," Angus shouted. "No one's gone to look there."

"I canna imagine your mother would be found there," Ray said as a touch of colour crept into his sunken cheeks.

"And I can't imagine that my mother would just disappear. But she has. There are some people in this town who don't mean her any good. You know who I mean. Someone should talk to Mrs. LeGrand. I thought that as you know your way around the cribs, Mr. Donohue..."

"Angus," Ray gasped, "mind your tongue."

"If Mr. Donohue won't go, then I will," Angus said.

"That's a good idea," Ellie said. "But not you, Angus. I'll go with Mr. Donohue. This time of morning, the ladies'll be in bed. They'll talk easier if I'm there."

Donohue tossed a pained look at Angus, but he followed Ellie.

"What was that about?" Ray asked no one in particular.

"I'll take Millie." Sterling waved the dressing gown in front of the dog's nose once again. "Maybe if we start at the house, she can catch some sort of scent."

"I'll come with you." Angus said.

"We need a signal, Walker, if...when...she's found. Get one of the steamships to blow the whistle five times. That can be the sign that the search is over."

"Right."

"Let's go, Angus. And try not to worry. We can be thankful it isn't winter."

They started to leave, Sterling clutching the dressing gown and leading the big dog. But before they got off the step, the regular Rupert Malloy ran past them and into the Savoy.

"Sam's gone, Ray."

"Ask his wife where he is."

"She's gone too."

"What?" Sterling dragged Millie back inside. "Gone where?"

Malloy scratched at an angry patch of blistered skin streaking across his cheek. "They've cleared out their house and taken their things. Left the furniture behind, but clothes and personal type stuff's gone."

"When did this happen?"

"Don't know."

"Did anyone see them leave?"

"Didn't ask."

"Mr. and Mrs. Collins are missing too!" Angus yelled. "What's happening?"

"Inspector McKnight's gone down to the waterfront with a search party. Malloy, tell him to meet me at the Collins place. You'll have to take him there; he won't know where it is. Hurry."

Malloy looked at the constable. "I ain't going anywhere no more. I did what I was asked and went up to Sam's place as a favour for Ray. I ain't even had my breakfast yet."

"You get McKnight to Collins's house inside half an hour, Rupert Malloy, and ye can drink here for free every night this week."

Malloy stared at Ray, his mouth hanging open. Ray checked his watch. "It's eight thirty-five now. Be there by nine-o-five. Ye'll have to hurry."

Malloy ran.

"If McKnight isn't there, bring Sergeant Lancaster," Sterling called after him. "But make sure you can't find McKnight first."

"Tell me what time he gets there, Sterling," Ray said.

"I will. Where's Collins live?"

Ray gave directions.

"Let's go, Angus."

This time they almost collided with Murray as they tried to leave. "What's this about pirates?" the bartender shouted, falling though the doorway. His hair was standing on end, his shirt unbuttoned, his eyes wide.

"Guard the Savoy," Ray told him. "The bar and the tables is closed till I get back. But you have to let anyone in who's with the search party."

"Search party? I heard the police are handing out rifles so we can defend the town."

No one bothered to explain.

"Maybe someone's kidnapped them. For ransom. My ma and Mr. and Mrs. Collins." Angus leapt over a banner advertising G. Barnes, Dentist, which had torn free from its pole to come to a sad end in a pile of fresh horse dung.

Sterling tossed the dressing gown over his shoulder and didn't stop to think that he might look somewhat odd running through the morning streets with a large dog, a gangly boy and a skinny Scotsman, a golden dragon streaming behind him.

The wind had come up, and the dressing gown snapped in the breeze, the rays of the sun catching the gold threads and reflecting the brilliance of the red fabric. Monday morning, and the town rang with the sound of hammer and saw, everyone back to work after the forced day of rest.

"This is it." Ray slowed as they arrived at a neat but rough wooden house. Two small chairs and a pot of colourful wildflowers sat outside.

The neighbours, heading off to work or running errands, stopped whatever they were doing to stare at the strange group.

Sterling knocked once, with almost as much force as required to rip the thin door off its cheap hinges. But that wasn't necessary; the door, left off the latch, swung open.

Sterling handed the dog's lead to Angus. "Wait here with Millie." He went in, moving cautiously.

Ray Walker followed.

Uninvited, Angus ducked through the low doorway, although Millie seemed more interested in sniffing at something outside. He gave the lead a good tug and the dog followed. It was a very small house, but in a town in which many families lived in tents, it was almost luxurious. The rudimentary kitchen was pushed up against the back wall. The single cooking pot still held the scrapings of a stew, more potato and onion than meat.

Sterling held his hand over the stove. "Stone cold."

Plates, encrusted with the remains of the meal, had been tossed on the table.

"Looks as if they left in a hurry."

"Aye. Margaret's a good housekeeper. Kept this wee place neat as a pin." Ray checked through the slim contents of the pantry.

Only one door led off the main room.

Sterling kicked it open, and Angus peered in over his shoulder. A bedroom. Two drawers of the handmade wooden dresser hung open, the third lay on the floor. Clothes were tossed around the room, as if someone had packed in a great hurry.

Sterling crouched down and sifted through the debris. "Winter clothes, mostly. Stuff folks won't need for a couple of months. Did Mrs. Collins have any jewellery? Any valuables?"

"Not that I ever saw," Ray said from the doorway.

At a shout from the street, they went back outside.

Malloy and McKnight ran up, both of them breathing heavily.

"What have you got, Sterling?" McKnight asked.

"Made it," Malloy chortled, "in plenty of time."

Millie walked in circles around the two chairs, her nose to the ground. Angus unwound her leash from the chair legs.

"Sam and Margaret Collins. Americans. He tends bar at the Savoy."

"Head bartender," Ray said.

"Looks like they up and left in a rush. I just got here, don't know more."

"Were they taken? By the kidnappers?" Angus asked.

A crowd had begun to gather. A woman cried out at the word "kidnappers," and whispers spread rapidly.

McKnight turned to the crowd. "Did any of you folks see what happened here? When do you suppose they left, Constable?"

"Looks like last night's supper was abandoned, sir. The

bits of potato are hard around the edges."

The townspeople looked at each other and shook their heads. One woman stepped reluctantly forward. She was thin and weatherbeaten, and her dress had been mended many times. She spoke in a voice that was pure London.

"I saw Margaret an' Sam yesterday. They sat there, in them chairs, 'aving their tea. They liked ta sit out on a nice night, to 'ave their tea. Wot's happened to 'em then?"

"Did you see them leave, Madam?"

"No. I walked by, said 'ello ta Margaret and went ta make me own tea."

"Did you see them after teatime, say closer to supper?" McKnight asked.

"Sir," Angus said, "when she says tea she means supper, right, ma'am?"

The woman nodded.

"Oh. Any one else see Mr. or Mrs. Collins last night? After they ate their evening meal?"

People glanced at one another. Heads were shaken, and no one spoke.

Giving up on the neighbours, McKnight ducked through the doorway into the house. Sterling and Walker followed. Angus dragged Millie away from the path she was intent on taking, up towards the hills.

"What do you think, Sterling?" McKnight asked.

"Walker, did Sam have any dealings with Jack Ireland?"

"What does this have to do with Ireland?" Angus said.

"Angus, why don't you go outside," McKnight said. "That dog looks as if she needs to do her business."

"She's just excited, sir. Please, we're talking about my mother."

"Then be quiet."

"Yes, sir."

"Nothing I know of other than that fuss about the fire," Ray answered the question. "When Sam saved the bakery woman and all. He dinna care for Ireland trying to make a story of it, Sam didn't."

"That's it?"

"Far as I know."

"Sir?"

"Yes, Angus?"

"Mr. Collins was real angry at Mr. Ireland. For taking his picture and writing about him for his newspaper. My ma said it was strange—most people would want everyone to know they were a hero."

The three men looked at each other.

"Constable, get down to the docks, fast. Find out if anyone's seen the Collinses. I'll ask around here. Someone must have been up late last night."

"Me, sir," Angus said, "what can I do?"

The men exchanged glances once again. Ray swatted a mosquito on his cheek. He looked at the crushed little body.

"You mind that dog," McKnight said. "Go with Constable Sterling. While he asks questions, maybe she can pick up a scent down at the docks."

"I'll head back to the Savoy," Ray offered. "Perhaps someone's got news."

"One thing before you go, Constable."

"Sir?"

"Is that extravagant cloth a new addition to the standard uniform?"

Sterling whipped the dragon off his shoulders. "Mrs. MacGillivray's dressing gown. For Millie to catch the scent."

"I understand, but you look a mite—unconventional."

Sterling rolled the garment into a ball, stuffed it under his arm and, without another word, took off down the street towards the riverfront.

Millie dragged at her lead as Angus tried to keep up with Sterling. The stupid dog was intent on heading out of town into the woods, wanting to chase rabbits most likely. At last, he managed to persuade her to give the rabbits up, and Millie sprinted off in pursuit Sterling. Angus's long legs covered the distance that had opened between them.

Chapter Fifty-Three

I dozed fitfully, dreaming that Angus called out for me while a golden dragon hovered over his head. Richard Sterling watched something at his feet and looked terribly sad. And Angus's father—curse him—called out for me to come back.

A branch broke, and an animal snorted, and I snapped back to consciousness.

Even in the Yukon, there are not many people who can truthfully say they have stood (or sat) mere feet away from a grizzly bear. And lived to tell the tale. From my perspective, he was about twenty feet tall. Twenty feet of bristling fur and teeth and claws. His beady brown eyes stared into mine, and he let out a roar they would have heard in town. And yes, those were impressive teeth.

I closed my eyes, saw my son's lovely blue eyes, which always remind me of my father, and wondered what sort of a man Angus would grow up to be. I comforted myself with the thought that Ray would take care of him, while Richard looked over his shoulder to make sure Angus kept to the straight and narrow. My parents stood in front of me, smiling, holding out their hands, waiting for me to join them.

Twigs broke under the massive feet, and branches snapped as the bear lumbered back into the woods. I opened one eye. My parents were gone, and where they had stood there was nothing but the Yukon bush.

Chapter Fifty-Four

"You don't think Mr. and Mrs. Collins were kidnapped along with my ma, do you, sir?"

"No, I don't."

"You think Sam killed Ireland."

"I don't know what I think, Angus. And that's the truth." Sterling didn't relax his pace. "Let's just concentrate on finding your mother. We can sort out the details later."

The waterfront swarmed like a hornet's nest. Men, and a handful of women, were shouting "Fiona" and "Mrs. MacGillivray" and crawling all over the layers of boats nestled out into the river. Several men were dripping wet—presumably they'd fallen in while leaping from one boat to another. Boat captains were either trying to fend off the waves of intruders or encouraging everyone to search harder.

"Will you look at that," Sterling said, with something approaching surprise in his deep voice. "People in this town do care about each other, and about your mother. You should be very proud, Angus."

"Right now, sir, I'd settle for just having her back."

They waded into the crowd.

Anna Marie Vanderhaege watched them approach and nudged the man standing beside her. The two of them walked towards Sterling and Angus.

"My sister tells me you're looking for Sam and Margaret Collins also," she said with a shy smile. "But about that you need not worry. They left on the *Mae West,* shortly after midnight, the men say. I'm glad Sam is safe, he is a brave man."

"Can you point out the man who told you this?"

"I saw them, Constable," her companion said,

scratching his beard with hard-working, callused hands. "I was getting the steamboat ready to shove off when they arrived all in a fluster. Didn't have no tickets, but that don't matter much. Captain said he had room, told 'em the price, and they boarded."

"You know Mr. and Mrs. Collins?"

"Know Sam from over to the Savoy, been there once or twice, I have." He winked. "Don't you worry, son. We'll find your ma. Safe as Sam, she'll be. I guessed that the woman with him was his wife. It weren't Mrs. MacGillivray, that's for sure."

"Did they have luggage?"

"Couple o' small cases, not much."

"Angus, why don't you let Millie sniff around." Sterling handed over the dressing gown. "See if she can pick up a scent."

"Sure." Angus led the dog away, waving his mother's garment in front of her face.

"How small? Large enough to hold a body?"

Anna Marie gasped; her eyes flew to Angus, who was bending over and letting the dog have a good sniff of the robe.

"Nothing near that big. Couple of packs like they woulda come over the Chilkoot with. No trunks."

"Thanks. You've been a help."

"Lots of the men who mighta seen Mrs. MacGillivray yesterday will still be off. I'll spread the word when they get here."

"Angus might like something to eat. For sure he has not had his breakfast, and now it is near lunchtime. I will take him back to the bakery for a waffle. Would you care to join us, Constable?"

"No, thank you, Miss Vanderhaege. I'll stay here."

"Then I will bring you a waffle. Make it special."

"Thank you," he said absentmindedly. "That would be kind."

Sterling looked into the dark brown water swirling around the hulls of the boats. So thick and dirty was the river he couldn't see more than an inch into its depths.

The waters of the Yukon and Klondike Rivers were cold, even in summer. It didn't get warm enough, for long enough, to heat them so that anyone other than the most adventurous boy might want to go for a swim. White gulls flew overhead in lazy circles, cawing loudly and occasionally taking a dive at the scraps of garbage floating in the water. It was a warm day, and the sun shone in a cloudless blue sky.

His skin pricked under his heavy uniform coat. Richard Sterling felt very, very weary.

Sam Collins had packed up his wife and a handful of their belongings and left Dawson without a word in the middle of the night, apparently without even bothering to inform his employer or collect wages owed. And Fiona MacGillivray had disappeared that same evening. Sam had killed Ireland, for reasons unknown. Fiona had found out what had happened and—all on her own—had confronted him. No doubt she expected him to confess, beg forgiveness, and meekly accompany her to Fort Herchmer in order to turn himself in. She was a genuine lady, Fiona, obviously raised with a great deal of care, left to make her own way in the world on the death of her husband, Angus's father. She might be a dance hall queen in Dawson, Yukon Territory, but what, really, would a well-brought-up lady such as Fiona MacGillivray know about men and the depths to which they could fall?

A dead fish bumped up against the shore, its exposed eye glassy and unfocused. A wooden box, marked as property of the Eastern Canning Company of Cleveland Ohio, floated past, bobbing on the tiny waves.

"I found a girl who was up in the night, with an earache." McKnight arrived on silent feet—or perhaps Sterling had simply been too lost in thought to hear him. The inspector stood beside the constable and gazed into the dark water, stroking his moustache rhythmically.

"She was sitting outside while her mother heated some tinned milk, and she saw Mr. and Mrs. Collins pass, carrying packs. In a right hurry they were, the girl said.

Mrs. Collins was yelling at Mr. Collins to keep up or they would 'miss it'. She—the girl—didn't know what "it" was."

"The *Mae West*, apparently. There was no one with them?"

"Not that the child saw."

An eddy caught the dead fish and dragged it around the bow of a small boat. A few yards off shore, two gulls flew after a can that had once contained condensed milk. They squawked at each other, and the smaller pulled up and flew away, complaining all the while.

"It doesn't look hopeful," McKnight said. "They've torn this town apart. I hear Joey LeGrand is screaming up a storm about people disturbing her girls when they should be resting and is threatening to complain to Inspector Starnes."

"She won't. The Inspector doesn't give LeGrand the time of day, and she knows it. He tolerates her and her ilk because the miners won't have it any other way."

"We may never find her, you know." McKnight touched Sterling lightly on the shoulder in a surprisingly familiar gesture. "These rivers are treacherous, and there's a lot of wilderness between here and the sea."

"I'll find her," Sterling said.

"Constable Sterling. Constable Sterling." Angus ran across the flat expanse of mud that led from the steamboat dock. Mr. Mann lumbered behind as well as Anna Marie, holding her skirts above her ankles. "Millie, we have to follow Millie."

"Why don't you go home, son," McKnight said. "Get some rest. We'll fetch you if anything turns up."

"No! Listen to me. I've been so stupid. Ma hated every step on the Trail, and never, ever left Dawson, not even to go hunting for frogs."

All around the waterfront, attention was drawn by the excitement in Angus's voice. Heads popped up and people drifted towards them.

"Now, Angus, I don't see what frogs have to do with this. Miss, would you see that the boy gets home."

"You must hear what Angus has to say," Anna Marie almost shouted.

"No one would think to look for Ma in the wilderness. But Millie did. Millie doesn't know Ma hates the bush. She picked up a scent at the Collins's house. Those two chairs outside. Millie wouldn't leave them alone. Then she wanted to go up the road, into the hills. Into the wilderness. I had to drag her back to town. But there's nothing here, and she's getting confused about why I keep stuffing this robe into her face."

"Angus, I...."

"It's better than anything else we have, Inspector," Sterling said. "Lead the way, Angus, Millie."

The big white dog ran. Away from the water and back towards town. Her pace was slowed by the rope pulling against her throat, and she tried to encourage the boy behind her to run faster. Millie didn't look back, but she knew that a stream of people followed her. As they ran through town, more and more people fell into place in the pack.

Millie ran so hard, the leash jerked out of Angus's grasp. Free, she sprinted back to where she'd picked up the scent, and from there to the wildflower-covered hills.

Chapter Fifty-Five

I watched the morning sun crossing the southern sky from east to west. I'd spent the night alternately dozing and shaking bugs away with my hair. Painful cramps shot up my arms. At least my legs were free, so I could wiggle them to keep the circulation going.

It was early afternoon of the second day when I realized I'd lost contact with my hands. I tried to move my fingers, but there didn't seem to be anything happening beyond my wrists. I was thirsty. Hungry to be sure, but thirst dominated everything. Any moisture that might be in my throat was instantly soaked up by this damned handkerchief.

Pictures swam behind my eyelids. For a while I believed that I was back in London, dangling from a rope tossed out of the second-story bedroom of a Belgravia townhouse on a rainy February night. As usual, I was dressed in men's clothes, all in black. I had a pocket full of rings and necklaces and a sack containing the family's good silver tossed across my back, and I was trying not to breathe too loudly while a constable, tardy on his rounds for one cursed night, stood below, sneaking a quick smoke. My arms ached under the strain and, momentarily trapped between memory and reality, I opened my eyes.

If I fell asleep, would I wake up in my mother's arms? I decided to give up, to let the wondrous sleep at the end of it all claim me.

Then I remembered Angus, who needed me more than I needed my mother.

Whatever would become of the Savoy with Ray left to manage it on his own?

I struggled back to consciousness. Margaret may not have planned to kill me, here on the mountainside, but she was a poor judge of the amount of restraint required to hold one woman. If someone didn't find me soon, she might just as well have stuck her knife into my heart.

It was Monday afternoon. Ray would have noticed by now that I wasn't in my office, but I came and left the Savoy as I pleased, so he wouldn't question my absence at least until the dance hall opened at eight. Angus would leave for work, not wanting to wake me. Sunday evening, he would have gone off with his friends as soon as supper was finished—hunting for frogs and spying on girls and whatever sort of boy-foolishness they got up to. When Mrs. Mann came in to clean my room in the morning, she'd see that my bed hadn't been slept in. She would assume I was with a gentleman friend, and not breathe a word to Angus or to her husband.

So it would be seven o'clock, eight at the latest, before anyone began to wonder where I might be. By the time they thought to do something about it…it might be days before they found me—or whatever remained of my decaying corpse.

I wiggled and jerked and tugged at my bonds. Nothing moved. I kicked my legs in a wild tattoo on the ground and screamed as loudly as I could. Only the mosquito settling on my cheek heard.

But all that effort had some effect: the handkerchief in my mouth shifted. I used my tongue to attempt to ease it out, one fraction of an inch at a time. Fresh air slipped in through the corner of my lips, and I allowed myself to feel a touch of hope.

All hope faded as a great white wolf leapt over the rocks. Its teeth were filed to sharp points; its claws dug deep into the hard earth. It looked directly into my eyes for a slice of time, threw back its massive head and howled in triumph to the northern sky.

"Take care of Angus," I whispered as I closed my eyes and waited to feel teeth dig into my unresisting neck.

* * *

"Ma. Ma. Oh, thank God. You're safe."

I opened my eyes to see half the population of Dawson crawling through the bush. There was Constable Sterling, and Inspector McKnight. Ray Walker and Not-Murray and Jake. Several of the dancers from the Savoy, including Ruby and Ellie, and even a percentage girl or two. One of the Vanderhaege sisters. Sergeant Lancaster and Mr. Mann, who appeared to be weeping—that was surely an illusion. Graham Donohue, who tried to shove everyone aside to reach me but was discouraged by Angus's sharp elbow in his stomach. Mouse O'Brien was there and Belinda Mulroney. The Indian Fighter and regular Rupert Malloy. Joe Hamilton, who copied reporter's dispatches before they left for the Outside. A pack of dockworkers and some of the regular barflies, including Barney, who dropped to his knees and seemed to be offering prayers to the sky.

And a gigantic, slobbering, hairy white dog who, if someone didn't get it off me, was as likely to kill me by licks and kisses as by eating me.

Angus pushed the overly-affectionate animal away, crouched down, and looked into my face. "You'll be free in a minute, Mother."

For the first and, I hope, the last time in my life, I fainted.

Chapter Fifty-Six

By all accounts, my return to town was a grand celebration. Some say it was almost as impressive as the Fourth of July celebrations which followed a week or so after. But those are probably Englishmen or Canadians, trying to downplay the numbers of our friends from the south who are pouring into the Yukon Territory every day.

I have only second-hand knowledge of the event. If I wished, I could dine out on the story for the rest of my life, but I'm reluctant to talk about it. Perhaps because I realized that people did care about me. People other than my son, of course, and my business partner, and those men who are interested in what type of undergarments I favour.

They covered me with a soft mantle of red silk and a gold dragon and I was carried home, so they tell me, on a stretcher hastily constructed of weak green wood and half of someone's canvas tent, which had been collapsing anyway. They laid me in my bed while Mrs. Mann fussed and fluttered about and tried to make me comfortable, and Mr. Mann stood guard at the entrance to his home and threatened to bash out the brains of anyone attempting to cross the threshold.

Fortunately for me, someone managed to locate a respectable doctor to tend to my injuries.

I remember telling him that the big wolf was coming and I remember his kind smile as he checked the abrasions on my wrists, and that was about all I remembered for a long time.

"I'm dreadfully thirsty."

"You're awake, Mrs. MacGillivray. Praise God."

Gentle hands lifted my head and a glass of fresh, clear water touched my lips. I drank every drop, terrified that there would be no more.

"I have to get to the Savoy," I said, struggling to sit up. "Something's wrong."

"You rest. I'll be right back." Firm hands pushed me back into the soft bed.

"Angus, come. She's awake."

My son came into the room. It was late afternoon. The summer sun spilled through the tiny window and lit up Angus's blond head in a halo of golden light.

"The dance hall," I said, scratching at my right hand. "It will fall to rack and ruin without me there to supervise. They'll cheat us blind. Help me up."

"Ray's managing perfectly well, Mother. Miss Ellie's supervising the dancers till you get back, and everyone's been so worried about you, they haven't dared misbehave. Not that Constable Sterling would let them."

"I don't believe a word of it, Angus. Help me up."

"Here's a mirror, Mother. Perhaps you should have a look."

He held it up to my face, and I screamed so loudly, Mrs. Mann hurried back into the room.

"Oh, spare me nothing," I cried. "Is it the smallpox?"

Angus laughed and fluffed my pillow. Mrs. Mann poured more water.

"No, Mother. Only the Yukon mosquito. The doctor said the bites'll be gone in a day or two, and as long as you don't scratch at them, they won't leave a mark."

I was a very grumpy patient for the next two days as, regardless of how I well I felt, there was simply no way I would leave my sick bed until that hideous mass of mosquito bites disappeared. Angus dug my heavy winter mittens out of the storage boxes, and I sat in bed for two days and nights with my hands confined in the mittens so I wouldn't scratch at the bites.

I allowed only Ray Walker to visit me to report on the

day's takings, which were greater than ever.

He brought my big ledger and carried a bag of gold and money over twice a day. I sat in bed instructing Angus on how to do the accounts. I could hardly write in the books with my hands in Yukon-strength winter mittens, now could I? If I took the gloves off, even for a second, my nails would have been tearing at my throat and face.

When Angus finished, Mrs. Mann took the money to the bank, escorted by Constable Sterling, and everyone politely stepped aside to allow her to go to the front of the line.

On his daily visits, the doctor tut-tutted a good deal about the cut to my face, while looking quite worried and telling me that there was absolutely nothing to worry about.

As soon as he left, Mrs. Mann slipped in with her green paste. And before I was ready to get up and face the streets, the mark of the knife slice across my cheek was fading, save for a tiny nick beneath the cheekbone that Angus assured me gave me quite a fetching and mysterious air.

The scar running from the base of my throat down to the swell of my breasts, I still carry today. I am told that men find it fascinating.

Chapter Fifty-Seven

"Heading back to work, Mrs. MacGillivray?" Richard Sterling fell into step beside me as I left Mrs. Mann's boarding house, for my first visit to the Savoy after what would forever be known as "The Collins Incident".

I would have thought his arrival a coincidence had I not glimpsed Angus disappearing around the corner of the house as I nibbled on a slice of breakfast toast.

"It's time," I said.

"May I walk with you?"

"Of course."

Mr. Mann had insisted he would escort me to the Savoy. I insisted, with equal passion, that I did not need assistance. We had glared at each other across the kitchen table, each one of us more stubborn, I suspect, than the other. He hadn't liked me very much, Mr. Mann, when Angus and I had first come to live at his wife's boarding house. Now I feared that he liked me too much—as if he were my father or elder brother. Mrs. Mann quietly intervened and passed me a warm package containing freshly baked scones for my midmorning snack, and more of the magic green poultice. I might walk to work by myself, she told me, offering a compromise, but I was to be ready precisely at noon, when Mr. Mann would be at the door of the Savoy to escort me home for lunch. Angus, she said, would mind the store in her husband's absence. We all meekly agreed.

I was still shaky, and although I would never admit to weakness, I was pleased to take Constable Sterling's arm.

We walked down York Street towards the river then turned onto Front.

"No news of Mr. and Mrs. Collins," he said. "Without telegraph or telephone, we've no way of alerting the stops up the river to hold the *Mae West*."

"Will you think less of me, Richard, if I say that deep in my heart I hope they get away?"

He lifted one eyebrow.

"Sam would have let it all go a long time past, but Margaret couldn't. If Ireland had recognized Sam, and gone on to write his most-certainly dreadfully biased account of what happened in some long-forgotten battle in that long ago war, who in Dawson, who in the United States come to that, would care, after all these years? I suspect Sam knew that, and as much as he might not have been happy to see Ireland in his town, he knew he had no need to run. But not poor Margaret. She gave up everything for Sam—wealth, family, position—only to be tormented for thirty years by some insignificant incident in some silly little war.

"I believe Margaret was driven by fear of what her disapproving family would think if ever they got wind of Sam's supposed disgrace. Although they probably wouldn't even recognize his name, all these years later, if they came across an account of it in the *San Francisco Standard*. Assuming any of them are still alive."

It was going to be another beautiful day, a long, soft, precious summer's day such that you only get in the North. A day of gentle sunshine, warm winds and circling birds. A day worth savouring and remembering well into old age and long winter nights.

A raft, so loaded with boxes and barrels of supplies, it was a Yukon wonder that it had made it this far, drifted down the river. They'd gone too far; helmsman asleep probably. Hopefully someone would wake him up before they drifted another few miles up river and back into the unrecognizable wilderness. At the sight of the passing of their hard-sought destination, the cluster of men crammed in amongst the supplies yelled and leapt into the air, waving hats and arms.

"Will they ever stop coming?" Sterling said.

"Perhaps not." I lifted my face to the sun and let my heart warm. "Before much longer, I believe every person in the world will drift up the Yukon River. Why, if we stand here long enough we may see Her Majesty, and the President of the United States, and the King of the Zulus pass by on a raft just like that one."

"If we apprehend Mr. and Mrs. Collins, you'll be expected to testify, Mrs. MacGillivray."

"I understand. I haven't forgotten that she left me out there, not much caring whether I lived or died." Or if I was scarred for life by bears and wolves and ravenous insects. "It's sad that some people live lives tormented by their past. The past is over. It should be forgotten."

Sterling watched the river. "Have you forgotten your own past, Fiona?"

I threw back my head and laughed. Fresh air, tinged with sawdust, filled my lungs.

"The past is past, Richard. Another time, another country. But perhaps I should ask you about your own history. I suspect that there's a story to be told in that.

"Oh for heaven's sake: are those the Gearing twins on the Savoy doorstep? They've been banned. Ray will be in a rage. He hates to be disobeyed."

I ran across the road. A horse and wagon pulled up sharply to avoid hitting me. I tossed the driver a poisonous look. I was crossing the street—couldn't the man keep his animal under control?

* * *

Richard Sterling, Constable of the North-West Mounted Police, watched Fiona MacGillivray stare down a bad-tempered packhorse and nasty-faced driver.

The past was past. Indeed it was.

But the future was looking to be very interesting indeed.

Vicki Delany was fortunate enough to be able to take early retirement from her job as a systems analyst in Toronto, and is now enjoying the rural life in Prince Edward County, Ontario, where she rarely wears a watch. She is the author of several standalone novels of psychological suspense as well as the Constable Molly Smith series (*In the Shadow of the Glacier*) published by Poisoned Pen Press. She can be visited online at www.vickidelany.com

Acknowledgements

Early reading and excellent advice was provided by Gail Cargo, Carol Lem, Julia Vryheid, Jan Toms, Karen Wold, Joan O'Callahan and Karen Mitchell. Jerry Sussenguth provided advice on the German accent. My sincere thanks to you all. Thanks also to Sylvia and Rendezvous for taking a chance on Fiona and Angus, and to Rick Blechta for the introduction.

I have attempted wherever possible to keep the historical details of the Klondike Gold Rush, and the town of Dawson, Yukon Territory, accurate. Occasionally, however, it is necessary to stretch the truth in the interests of a good story. As Fiona remarks, there wasn't a single murder in Dawson in the year of the town's heyday, 1898, therefore I have taken the liberty of inventing one. A few historical personages make cameos in the book: Big Alex McDonald, Belinda Mulroney, Inspector Cortlandt Starnes, but all dramatic characters and incidents are the product of my imagination.

The reader who is interested in learning more about the Klondike Gold Rush is advised to begin with the definitive book on the subject *Klondike: The Last Great Gold Rush 1896-1899* by Pierre Berton. Also by Berton, *The Klondike Quest: A Photographic Essay 1897-1899.*

Other reading:

- *The Klondike Gold Rush: Photographs from 1896- 1899* by Graham Wilson
- *Good Time Girls of the Alaska-Yukon Gold Rush* by Lael Morgan
- *The Last Great Gold Rush: A Klondike Reader*, edited by Graham Wilson
- *Women of the Klondike* by Francis Blackhoue
- *The Real Klondike Kate* by T. Ann Brennan
- *Gamblers and Dreamers: Women, Men and Community in the Klondike* by Charlene Porsild
- *The Klondike Stampede* by Tappan Adney

For information about the NWMP:

• *They Got their Man: On Patrol with the North West Mounted* by P.H. Godsell

• *The NWMP and Law Enforcement 1873-1905* by R.C. Macleod

• *Showing the Flag: The Mounted Police and Canadian Sovereignty in the North, 1894-1925* by W.R. Morrison

• *Sam Steele: Lion of the Frontier* by R. Stewart